come home to my heart

come home to my heart

Riley Redgate

UNION
SQUARE
& CO.

NEW YORK

UNION SQUARE & CO.
NEW YORK

UNION SQUARE & CO. and the distinctive Union Square & Co. logo are trademarks of Sterling Publishing Co., Inc.

Union Square & Co., LLC, is a subsidiary of Sterling Publishing Co., Inc.

Text © 2025 Riley Redgate
Cover © 2025 Union Square & Co. LLC

All rights reserved. No part of this publication may be reproduced, stored in a retrieval system, or transmitted in any form or by any means (including electronic, mechanical, photocopying, recording, or otherwise) without prior written permission from the publisher.

ISBN 978-1-4549-5711-9 (hardcover)
ISBN 978-1-4549-5712-6 (ebook)
ISBN 978-1-4549-5713-3 (paperback)

Library of Congress Control Number: 2024041771

For information about custom editions, special sales, and premium purchases, please contact specialsales@unionsquareandco.com.

Printed in the United States of America

2 4 6 8 10 9 7 5 3 1

unionsquareandco.com

Cover art by Tillie Walden
Cover and interior design by Julie Robine

For you,
if you're keeping quiet
or feeling invisible.

Part One
Autumn

Gloria Forman

In the moment of darkness before the page loaded, I saw myself in the computer screen, my face tensed like I was bracing for a slap. I wondered if I looked that way all the time, or only here, in this room, in late afternoon.

A patch of clouds shifted outside, and sunlight flooded the office. This was the smallest and most colorless room in a house of small, colorless rooms. The desk was a gray plastic castoff from a local store closure, the floorboards' varnish had faded down to nothing, and I guess you could've called the wallpaper ivory if you were feeling charitable. Three pale frames hung by the window. Two held pages from Ecclesiastes, the third a crucifix.

With my eyes lingering on the cross, I thought, *I can still stop myself.* I could delete the blog once and for all, stop doing this every day. Half a dozen clicks and it would be gone.

Then the page loaded, a blaze of color in the corner of my eye, and my resolve collapsed.

I angled the monitor away from the door and leaned forward. *Five minutes*, I told myself. I never went a second over. That was the first part of my justification.

Riley Redgate

The second part was the privacy of the blog, which I'd set up on a remote little site called Collekt. No one at school used the site, and I didn't follow anyone. I didn't even write posts about what I was feeling. The point was to silo those feelings off into this nowhere corner of the internet, where they wouldn't infect any other part of my life.

That was the idea, anyway, but as I scrolled through the blog, I could hear my parents talking down the hall in the kitchen, and there went my heart, accelerating. There went my breaths, too deep. My whole body was my guilty conscience.

The blog was filled with photos of girls. They were sitting in fields with soft things woven into their hair, or tugging at the waists of their jeans, or intimidating the camera with wild makeup smeared across their eyelids, or licking their lips in a way that did something to my lungs. Some of them looked sweet and tender. Others were taking selfies at the gym with uneven grins and hair shorn short. The photos zeroed in on the backs of their necks or the curves of their shoulders or the taut lines of their Achilles tendons emerging from ratty sneakers. On days I'd felt especially out of control, I'd added pictures of girls in bathing suits or underwear ads, whose eyes glittered like they knew everything, whose fingertips hovered in dangerous places.

I pressed "Search this blog." *When she*, I typed, not looking at my fingers.

The contents filtered. To the top rose a link that read, "When She Loved Me."

I clicked. The story opened in a new tab, posted to someone else's dark gray blog in small white text. I scrolled down to the spot I'd left off yesterday and began to read.

Come Home to My Heart

Why hadn't Anastasia brought up our kiss? Hadn't she liked it? Sometimes during cheer practice I got distracted from the routine because I was looking over at her, wishing she would look at me, too...

I didn't allow myself to sink too deeply into the story. I tracked the seconds ticking away. As the five minutes began to run out, I clicked back to my own blog and scrolled downward, hunting for the photo I'd found last week, which looked exactly like my mental image of the story's characters.

There. I stopped on a picture of a tall, dark-haired girl leaning against a tree, kissing a redheaded girl who was pressed up against her. The taller girl had her hands twisted into the back of the redhead's shirt.

As I looked at her stranglehold, my heartbeat slowed. I imagined being held that way. A heavy, squeezed feeling took me over, like the sensation of compression you feel behind your eyes before the headache hits. I didn't know what the feeling was, longing or fear or some blend of the two. All I knew was that it drew me back into itself again and again, the way the ocean reclaims its waves.

My eyes strayed to the clock. Time was up.

Part of me wanted to keep reading, but I thought of Romans 8:6: *The mind governed by the flesh is death, but the mind governed by the Spirit is life and peace.* I would never let any of this govern me.

With a few methodical clicks, I logged out, closed the tabs, and deleted the URLs out of my history. When I restarted the browser to double-check the address list, no evidence remained.

I imagined somebody sweeping dirt out of the corners of a small room, polishing a mirrored surface. Then I stood, straightened my blouse, and headed down the narrow hall to the kitchen.

"Right on time," said my mother with a smile. She was bent over our rickety table and ladling chicken soup into porcelain bowls, wisps of light brown hair stuck to her brow. My dad, tall and balding and barrel-chested, was already seated, filling our glasses from the water jug with one hand while tilting back a ginger beer with the other.

"It smells amazing, Mom," I said, hurrying to fetch the silverware.

"Well, it better." She set the pot back on the stove. "You've been working so hard this week, you deserve something nice."

"She's not the only one," my dad boomed, tugging out the chair to his left. "Here, Gloria, come relax with your dad. Time for a breather."

I tried to ignore the curl of guilt in my stomach as I settled beside him. He clinked his ginger beer against my water glass. "How'd that test go, Glor? Your big Chemistry one?"

"I got a ninety-six."

He reached out and mussed up my hair. "'Course you did."

"Well done, honey bear." Smiling, Mom took her seat opposite Dad. "Gloria, would you say grace for us?"

"Of course." We bowed our heads, clasping each other's hands, and a contented silence settled over the kitchen. What I'd done a few minutes ago dimmed, outshone by this moment of togetherness: the familiar warmth of my parents' palms, the rich steam rising from the broth, the sounds of crickets that crept in through the cracked windows. This was my real life. The rest was imaginary.

"Lord," I said quietly, "thank You so much for this amazing food in front of us and the roof over our heads. We're so grateful for the blessings You've given us today and every day, so please keep on guiding us so we can share Your light as best we can. Amen."

"Amen," said my parents together, giving a respectful glance to the crucifix on the wall. They squeezed my hands before they let go.

Come Home to My Heart

"Did you have a good day, Mom?" I asked. "Did y'all get that stuff cleared out of the church basement?"

My mother laughed. "Oh, it'll take a lot more than a day to get that place clean. That could be halfway through November, the rate we're going. I'm trying to get everybody organized, but it's like herding cats."

"If you want me to help out on weekends—"

"No, honey bear, no need for that. You focus on school."

I nodded, spoon in my mouth. Dad and I usually offered to join in with church activities, but we never pushed. The church community was Mom's world, the way I had school and Dad had his job. Our lives were neatly compartmentalized like that.

"How was work, Freddie?" Mom asked. "Any jerks at the car wash today?"

Now it was Dad's turn to laugh, a deep-from-the-belly sound. "We've got nothing *but* jerks at the car wash. This guy today, big guy, comes in. Car stuffed full of papers and takeout tubs and cardboard boxes, like he hasn't cleaned the thing since 2010. After we wash the thing off, do his mats and all, he's trying to bully me, tell me we didn't do our jobs 'cause the car's still full of his trash. I say, 'Man, we're a car wash, not a disposal service,' and he goes off all sour, ranting on about leaving bad reviews online. Like I care." Dad chortled, took a sip of his soup, and let out a sharp whistle. "That is *hot*. We got any more cream, Ashley?"

As my mom fetched the cream from the fridge, my dad's round face slackened. He always tried to joke about how much he hated his job, but it never quite worked.

A few years back, Dad had worked at a paper mill on the Fisherton outskirts, but the place had shuttered one winter, leaving more than a hundred people jobless. The closure hit the town hard. A dozen kids transferred out of our school in the months after, their parents relocating for work, and those were the better scenarios. Back then you'd hear a lot of crappy jokes about the Caldwell kids and the Williamson brothers, whose families had moved to the trailer park out east.

As for our family, I'd overheard my mom on the phone with my grandpa that spring, thanking him in a low voice for helping us out with bills—reassuring him that things were just about to turn around.

I'd prayed that she was right. I'd seen Mom eyeing people's benefits cards in the grocery checkout line, her expression caught between distaste and dread. My parents never even let friends treat them to dinner. They'd hate the idea of being one of those families, taking tax dollars out of people's pockets.

But our prayers, and Dad's hard work submitting applications, came through. Early summer, the car wash hired him, and Mom stopped cooking the same simple staples every night. Still, the new job wasn't good enough for my dad, and all three of us knew it. At the mill, he'd been a shift supervisor, in charge of streamlining processes and keeping things efficient. He was ordered, exact, like me. It worried me that he'd stayed with the car wash so long out of seemingly nothing more than inertia.

My mother shut the fridge and bustled back to the table with a carton of cream in hand. As she tipped it into Dad's soup, she said, "The Richmonds asked us over for the game on Sunday. That okay with everybody?"

I nodded. Dad said, "Works for me." A pause. "That older daughter of theirs isn't going to be there, is she?"

"No." Mom's smile faded as she settled back into her seat. "No, thank goodness, she's staying at school for fall break. You would not recognize that girl from the way she was in middle school. Used to be such a sweet little thing."

Come Home to My Heart

Dad shook his head, looking glummer than ever. "It's hard to watch the way things are going these days."

Mom squeezed his hand. "I know, sweetheart."

An unhappy silence spread through the kitchen. I glanced around, trying to think of something to lighten the mood, but instead my eyes found the leak that had pooled under the refrigerator again, and the ancient little TV at the edge of the counter, which was saying something doom and gloom about inflation. Meanwhile, my dad's eyes had strayed to the cabinet under the sink, where he kept a whiskey bottle behind the cleaning supplies. I knew he was thinking of Ephesians—*Do not get drunk on wine, which leads to debauchery*—and trying to hold to his resolve.

Then it came to me. "Oh, I have good news! Mrs. Molina said she's making me Math Team captain this year."

The stress lines in my parents' foreheads eased. Their smiles returned in full force. "That's my girl!" my dad hollered.

"Sweetheart. That's amazing," my mom said, pressing her hand flat to her chest and blinking hard.

Dad grinned and nudged her. "I'd bet Gloria's the only one in this town who ever got both Math Team captain and Homecoming Court."

I returned an embarrassed smile. "I really thought it was going to be Justin . . ." We passed ten easy minutes talking about my life at school, which they drank in, glowing. I already knew that, come this weekend, they'd mention my news to half the congregation.

The sun was just kissing the horizon line when my dad straightened, seeming to remember something. "You done with the computer, Glor?"

"Oh—" The curling thing in my stomach stirred. "Yes, sir."

He stood and hustled down the hall, calling, "Sorry, Ashley, I'll be right back."

Once he'd gone, Mom folded her arms over the tablecloth, leaning closer. "You are so sweet, always finding ways to cheer your dad up like that."

I made myself smile. "Least I can do. I just hope he gets a different job soon."

"I know." She swept my hair back from my forehead with the tip of her thumb. "But the Lord's going to guide us through."

I nodded. "I'm praying on it."

We ate in silence awhile, but I barely tasted the salt and herbs. A part of me had followed my father down the hall, hovering behind him small and silent like a firefly. I knew he was entering the office. He was hunching over the desk, humming to himself, his mind probably half on the Carolina Panthers' game last weekend. He was opening the browser and scrolling through the site history, clicking any unfamiliar links.

When I was little, my parents had been more relaxed about the computer. Until I was twelve, I hadn't even known that Dad was checking my history. But then, late in seventh grade, he'd spotted something off. He'd seen that I'd gone through dozens of screenshots and clips from a movie called *Second Chance Girls*—a movie about two girls who end up together.

I remembered that conversation so clearly: my parents rigid on the sofa; their horrified tone as they asked what I'd been thinking, looking at something like that. I'd told them I hadn't meant anything by it, that the kids at school hadn't mentioned what the movie was about. They questioned me until I was teetering on the brink of tears, until I felt appalled by what I'd done, and that night, I'd fallen back into a recurring nightmare I'd used to have when I was little, back when I'd first grasped what hell was. It always started the same way: with me pushing open the door to our bathroom and finding that a

Come Home to My Heart

darkened stairwell had replaced the white tiles beyond. I walked down into pitch darkness, and an open mouth full of red-and-orange flame grew before me.

In the aftermath of the incident, my parents grounded me from the computer for a month. During that month, we set aside hours for prayer every night. We went to church three times a week instead of our usual two—twice on Sundays, once on Wednesdays—and on Saturdays attended counseling sessions with Pastor Collins, who also asked me about my thoughts.

I hated myself for lying to a pastor. But I also knew that if my parents were this shocked by an apparent mistake, my actual thoughts would cut them a thousand times deeper. All I could do was try to change.

Eventually the counseling and extra prayers tapered off. My parents seemed to chalk it up to childish curiosity, but they no longer made a secret of checking the computer history.

That was okay. I didn't make mistakes these days. And when Dad went through the computer, he would never find anything that could hurt this family.

Right on time, I heard footfalls in the hall. Dad jogged back into the kitchen. "So, what are we bringing to the Richmonds' on Sunday, Ash?"

"I was thinking coleslaw. When Laura makes it . . . well, bless her heart, you'd need a baster to move that stuff around." A secretive chortle went around the table, and then Mom and Dad were into Panthers talk. Dad loved talking through plays and strategies, but Mom was the real football geek of the family. She could rattle off season stats like a commentator. Dad said I got my mathematical knack from her.

Spoons clinked on ceramic. The cool water had warmed in my glass. I breathed evenly. We didn't talk about what my dad had been doing in the office; we never did. It was just part of the routine, but my systems always took some time to settle afterward.

I told myself I was doing what was best, keeping that blog. I would never act on any of those feelings. I just needed somewhere to store them.

Together, we talked the sun down. Outside, twilight settled over the mixed grasses in our yard and over Fisherton, making all the neighborhood's ranch houses look the same vague shade of beige. As the light withdrew, sliding up the wide, cracked street as if it were skipping town, my heart slowed, and I felt safe again.

Xia Harper

You had to hand it to Mrs. Molina: The woman didn't quit. She'd taught my math classes three years in a row, and she was still doing this shit to me.

"Ms. Harper, come up and write the derivative of the function, please."

"It's three t minus nine," I said without looking up from my book.

Her tone sharpened. "As I said, Xia, I want you to come up to the board and show us how you got there. Don't make me ask again."

I sighed, flipped *Eileen* spine-up onto my desk, and trudged to the front of the classroom. Titters rose from the desks around me. The other kids at school found it hilarious when I did anything, even something as mundane as walking up to a whiteboard.

Mrs. Molina proffered the marker, her face pinched with dislike. I kept my expression indifferent as I began to write.

Every teacher in Fisherton Senior High School loathed my schtick. Per my report card comments, I was not a pleasure to have in class. I had attitude issues. I needed to learn how the real world would respond to my problematic personality. None of this was news to my parents, so I couldn't have given a particular fuck what my teachers wrote. But I preferred the ones who left me alone to the ones like Mrs. Molina, who dragged me into participating, seemingly hoping I'd do something outright insubordinate so they could send me to the office to reap my just rewards.

I finished the proof and circled $3t - 9$.

"Thank you *so* much for your valuable time, Xia," said Mrs. Molina.

I slouched back down the aisle with my jaw tight. Not that I had any illusions about life being fair, but if I'd said something like that to her, I probably would have gotten suspended.

I was nearly back to my seat when something moved, fast, at the bottom of my vision, giving me barely a split second to register it. Some guy had stuck his foot across the aisle.

I had just enough time to reorient my foot so I didn't trip—and the toe of my boot collided hard with the guy's ankle.

"Ow!" he burst out, his leg jerking back under his desk. "What the *hell*?"

Steadying myself, I gave him a disbelieving look. Did he seriously have the audacity to play the victim when he'd tried to trip me?

But Mrs. Molina didn't know that. We were near the back of the room. I didn't think anybody had seen.

"Oh my goodness! Aiden, are you okay?" his girlfriend was exclaiming, one of those Homecoming Court girls, Ellis or Ellie or something. Clutching his shoulder, she glared at me. "What is your *problem*, you psycho?"

"What's going on?" Mrs. Molina called.

My stomach dropped. I was in for it now. Mrs. Molina was about to get exactly what she wanted: somebody who'd narc on me for violence.

Come Home to My Heart

Real panic sparked in my blood. I couldn't get suspended. The only thing that made my life tolerable in Fisherton was the lifeline of my college applications.

"Mrs. Molina," said Ellie/Ellis, tossing back a foot and a half of immaculately curled hair, "Xia just ki—"

She broke off. The girl behind her, a blond with freckles and ramrod-straight posture, had leaned forward and whispered something in her ear. The blond's hand made a calm, stiff gesture toward Aiden's foot.

Ellie/Ellis glanced back at the blond. One of those best-friend looks passed between them, the nonverbal exchange of half a conversation.

I scrutinized the blond's face. She was unreadable. Face like a mannequin. What had she said?

"Ellis? Gloria?" Mrs. Molina prompted. "What happened?"

Ellis faced forward again, and I held my breath.

"Nothing," said Ellis. "She tripped."

My stomach unclenched. My shoulders loosened.

But my fists were still balled up in my jacket pockets. I stalked back to my desk without another look at any of them.

As I slumped into my seat, all sound dulled in my ears except the buzz of the fluorescents overhead. Picking at the desktop's peeling laminate, I tried to breathe out the claustrophobia I'd felt every day since the beginning of high school, when my family moved to this hellhole of a town.

It was almost funny to remember it now, but when I'd started at Fisherton High, I'd been determined to give the place a chance. Sure, I was the only Chinese kid out of six hundred students—shockingly, Fisherton wasn't the landing pad of choice for the Asian diaspora—and so I sat through a bunch of predictable jokes about my grades and my eyes and, when my algebra seatmate got Covid, about me being patient zero. But I told myself I was being too sensitive. The town was about a quarter Black and Hispanic, and the race jokes went every which way. Channeling my mom's relentless optimism, I told myself it was a regional difference, that this was just something I should get used to if I wanted friends.

But then, a month into freshman year, something happened that changed my trajectory here for good. A senior called Will Chandler got forced out of the closet. Apparently he'd hit on a friend on the football team, but how he'd done this was unclear. According to some people, he'd said it outright, *I like you.* Other people said he'd tried to grab his friend's crotch or flash him, since the two had been alone in the locker room at the time. Will quit the team the next week.

Apparently, a childhood in Atlanta and my preferred gay-friendly corners of the internet had done a number on me, because the way people talked about him completely blindsided me. It seemed so retrograde, borderline unbelievable. If Will wasn't being judged, he was a punch line, and if he wasn't a punch line, he was the focus of crude speculation. He was never allowed to be normal again.

Then and there, freshman Xia said goodbye to her optimism. No, actually, I wasn't going to make friends with these people. I wasn't going to waste four years explaining why race jokes felt like shit to hear. I wasn't going to engage with anyone, even the people who seemed decent, because I wasn't going to be the next gay kid to get outed.

So I tried to act aloof and distant, but in a town that prided itself on its southern hospitality, aloof distance wasn't enough. I really had to be rude to get people to go the fuck away—but eventually, I'd done it. I'd wound up here, alone at the back of every classroom, hearing monthly rumors about the drugs I supposedly sold. Victory.

Come Home to My Heart

    I let out a slow breath. Mrs. Molina had gone back to her lesson now, and nobody was looking at me anymore. In moments like these, I felt invisible, or nonexistent. It felt amazing.

    I sank farther down in my seat,cracked my book open again, and slipped deep into the pages with a sensation of delicious relief.

◊

    After the final bell, as I stalked through the senior lot toward my Pontiac, my phone buzzed. I tugged it out, steeled myself, and answered. "Hey."

    "Hi, sweetie," my mom sang. "You said you'd pick up dinner for yourself after work tonight, didn't you?"

    "Yeah."

    "What time do you think you'll arrive home?"

    I slid into my car. The beating sun had turned my Pontiac into a sauna. Stripping off my jacket, I said, "I don't know. Eight forty-five, maybe."

    "Okay, very good! What will you be eating?"

    "Not sure yet."

    "Well, I'm trying a new recipe for tarragon chicken. You can have the leftovers tomorrow for lunch. Ooh—and I'm using herbs from my garden for the first time! It's amazing how fertile the soil in the backyard is. I also found a jar of honey at a farmers market in Wallerville last Sunday . . ."

    I restrained a sigh. Talking with my mom was like talking to the president of some nonexistent Fisherton Tourism Board. I could have recited her talking points myself by now: No traffic. No noise. Rock-bottom cost of living. Huge plots of land with South Carolina's tiny property tax costs. Forests a stone's throw away, and secluded river trails to stroll on, and—oh, yes, how could I forget?—such a welcoming congregation.

My parents weren't Baptist, like 90 percent of the people here, but they'd found a little Methodist place to go to every Sunday. It was almost impressive how we'd ended up at such opposite ends of the Fisherton enjoyment spectrum.

"Cool," I said, when she'd finished describing the farmers market. "It sounds, uh, cute."

I twisted the Pontiac's key a few times. As the engine sputtered indignantly at me, my mom said, "How was school?"

"Fine." I closed my eyes. "I've got to go, I'm about to start driving."

She didn't say "I love you" before she hung up. She never did anymore. But I could still detect the pause in there, when she considered saying it.

The Pontiac's engine finally turned over. I tossed my phone onto the passenger seat and negotiated my way out into the line, staring through the windshield, not really seeing the cars in front of me.

I didn't blame my parents for our move to Fisherton. We hadn't had much of a choice at the time. Back in Atlanta, my parents had worked for the same construction company—my dad in low-level management, my mom part-time in the office—and when I was thirteen, the place went bankrupt. My parents sent out hundreds of applications all over the Southeast, but only one place made an offer: a Fisherton construction company called Norman & Rowe. Just like that, the life we'd had in Georgia was over.

Even after I realized that Fisherton and I would never get along, I'd told myself, *Just stick it out for a little while.* At my dad's new firm, he was a big fish in a small pond, landing his first promotion six months after we moved. And my mom, who'd used her stint of unemployment to do a computer science boot camp online, had gotten a remote data job that paid five times what she'd made working in the office in Atlanta. Soon, I figured, we'd have enough of a financial

Come Home to My Heart

cushion to go home to the city. A year or so, and everything would be normal again.

But as sophomore year loomed closer, and my parents avoided my increasingly obvious hints about moving back, I'd realized the worst had happened. They'd fallen in love with this place.

When sophomore year ended, I'd brought them to the dining room for a sit-down conversation. Last-ditch, Hail Mary stuff. "I'm just not happy here," I told them. "I'm serious. I'm really—I'm miserable."

"Well . . ." my father said, exchanging a look with my mother. She'd worn an A-line dress that day, and her shining black hair was blown out into full, bouncing waves. My father's button-up matched his eyes, light blue behind his dark-rimmed glasses. Even in Atlanta my parents had been image-conscious, but they'd never been quite this Clark Kent and Lois Lane.

My dad looked back to me. "Well. We hate to hear that, kiddo. What can we do about it? Has something been happening at school?"

And by then, the truthful answer was no. After the first year, most people ignored me. "That's not the . . . I just don't fit in here."

My parents' eyes dipped to the beat-up army jacket I'd started wearing that spring, and the scuffed work boots, and the T-shirt with the demon from *Death Note* on it. They studied my face, probably considering the newly built-in permafrown and the absence of makeup.

"Sweetheart," said my mom, "it seems like you've been trying to stand out. If you want to express your style in such . . . unique ways, then you're going to feel like you don't blend into the crowd."

"I'm not talking about style, Mom." My voice rose. Did she seriously think I was that shallow, that my issue was some aesthetic problem? "I hate that school. I hate how everybody acts."

Another loaded pause. Then my dad asked, "Is this about Navya and Kit?"

Riley Redgate

My hands curled into fists in my lap. "No."

"Because I know it's been hard," he went on, "not having your friends here, but people grow apart sometimes. It's a fact of life. And—"

"I said it's not about them, okay?" I said loudly. "It's not Navya and Kit. It's *this place*. It's Fisherton. Everything about it is like—I feel like I'm suffocating here."

My mom's voice began to betray some strain. "Xia, please trust us when we say we're a lot more comfortable in Fisherton. I'm not going to pull out our financials, but—"

"Financials? Are you seriously saying money matters more than whether I'm happy?"

"No," my dad said firmly. "We're saying we have to think about this family's future. We're bankrolling your college education, Xia. And my parents are getting older. They may have to go into a home soon, or even move from Florida to live with us; none of that is cheap. There's more to consider than just whether Fisherton resembles Atlanta."

"But it doesn't have to be Atlanta." Desperation crept into my voice, making it sound thin and childish. "It could be somewhere else. Like literally anywhere else."

"Your dad's job is here, Xia," said my mom. "And"—they exchanged another glance—"we've been looking at a new house in a better part of town. It's a beautiful place. We never could have afforded it in Atlanta, and there's room on the first floor if your grandparents need it. Why don't you come to see—"

"Wait. Is this a joke?" I stood up with blood pounding in my head. "I'm telling you that living here is sucking the life out of me, and you want to put down roots even harder? You just said we're staying to save money, but you also want to spend more on a fancy house? Like, do you hear yourselves?" I looked between them, my face burning. "Do you even give a shit about me at all?"

"Okay. That's enough." My dad stood, too, his heavy brows set. "Xia, since the beginning, you've seemed determined to hate this place. You never gave Fisherton a real chance. Within months of getting here, you were already insulting everybody at your school in ways that really concerned us. 'All the kids here are so vapid and brainwashed,' 'Nobody in this place thinks about anything except tractors and Jesus.' *I* grew up in a town like Fisherton, Xia. Do you think about me that way? I mean, for goodness' sake—we didn't think we raised you to be such a snob."

My breathing quickened. Defensiveness and shame clashed together in my chest. So, not only had my parents dismissed all my requests to leave; they'd also secretly thought, for two years, that I was a judgmental asshole.

I wondered, for the first time in my life, if my mom and dad even liked me as a person.

"But we made excuses for you!" Dad pushed one hand through the dark waves of his hair, exposing the threads of gray that had appeared over the past couple of years. "We said, 'It was such a sudden transition . . . it's just a phase.' But no. You've dug yourself deeper and deeper. Well, I'm sorry, sweetheart, but we've made a good life with a real future in this town, even if you don't think it's up to your standards. In family matters, there's no place for this selfishness."

Before I could answer, my mother rose, too. "Xia, we want you to make a legitimate effort to be thankful for what you have. There were times in Georgia when we scraped to make ends meet. Now we're telling you about a house that could keep your grandparents comfortable as they get older, your father and I are working hard every day to save for your future—have you become so ungrateful that you can't appreciate any of this?"

My mouth shut. My lips began to wobble, and my eyes burned.

My parents immediately let out twin breaths, like they realized they'd gone too far. "Honey," said my dad, "if you miss Navya and Kit this much, you need to be reaching out into your community, not pulling away from—"

I strode out of the room, then burst into a sprint down the hall. When I got outside, I slammed the door so hard that I wrenched my pinkie finger.

We never talked about leaving Fisherton again, but we fought about everything that summer, like a weekly appointment. I began to feel a searing sense of shame that I'd begged for my parents to notice my issues, that I'd prized myself wide open to them like some naive little kid. I was never going to make that mistake again.

Every fight seemed to damage their opinion of me even more, but eventually I stopped caring. If they wanted to think I was selfish, fine. That meant they wouldn't pry too deeply into why I loathed this place, and thank God, because I had no idea what my parents thought about gay people. They'd never acknowledged that gay people existed, except when my dad loudly cleared his throat after any gay couple kissed on TV. Not promising.

Now, as I sat in the standstill traffic out of the senior lot and thought back to that first fight, it seemed so far away, hazy and blurred like a vintage Polaroid. Strangely, it occurred to me that maybe I'd taken my parents' advice. Maybe I'd grown up. Because these days, just like them, I spent a lot of time thinking about my future. Actually, it was all I thought about. My life right now didn't matter in any material way. It was all just a way station.

Come Home to My Heart

Why linger on that swimmer guy sticking out his foot, or Mrs. Molina's derisive comments, or the people milling around outside my car windows? *Fifteen minutes*, I told myself, *and you'll be far away from them.* I was good at this by now, exiting my current circumstances, stringing myself along with little promises of some easier future. Just wait an hour, a day, a week. Everything that feels so urgent right now will be a shadow to your future self.

And over it all hung the big promise, ticking away. *Just hold on for nine more months.* After that, I'd be out of here, at whatever college took me, and I was never coming back.

Gloria Forman

I was hunched over the computer, finishing chapter 4 of *When She Loved Me*, when my ringtone split the silence.

I startled hard. Fumbling for my phone with one hand, I hurried to shut the browser with the other, misclicking and reclicking until everything was gone.

Finally I yanked my phone out of my pocket. I stared at Ellis's name, my heart pattering. It was like she'd caught me in the act.

If I didn't pick up the first time, though, she'd call back right away. I imagined her lounging by her bedroom window, her eyes fixed on the ceiling fan, her round face stubbornly expectant.

I answered. "Hey, how's it going?" I said, a tiny bit too brightly.

"What's wrong?" she said.

That was Ellis. The girl was halfway to a mind reader. One false note in your voice and she was on you like a bloodhound on a trail. Some people hated her for it—they were always saying things to me like, "How can you be best friends with someone who can't keep her nose in her own business for five seconds?" Out of loyalty, I mostly pretended I didn't know what they were talking about.

In truth, Ellis was good practice. If I could keep a secret from her, I could keep it from anybody.

The first rule for staying under her radar: the answer to "What's wrong?" was never "Nothing." Ellis would've died before buying an excuse that basic.

"Give me a second," I said. "I'm in the middle of a problem set."

"Oh, right. Sorry to tear you from your precious equations."

"You should be. So rude." I spun in the office chair. "Why'd you call?"

"Aiden just tried to break up with me."

"What?" I stopped spinning. "What do you mean, *tried*?"

"I m—had t—we—"

"Wait, wait, bad connection." I dashed down the hall to my room and climbed onto my bed, making the springs squeal. "Okay. Start again."

Ellis sighed. "We got into this stupid argument about that girl kicking him in Calc today. I was like, well, *yeah*, she's a freak, but you shouldn't have tried to trip her, right? And the whole thing got blown out of proportion. He was all, 'Maybe we've been together too long, I want to branch out, see other people,' whatever. So I said, 'Okay, we can take a break, but that means you're not allowed to get jealous if I go on dates with somebody else.' And he went all quiet and was like"—she deepened her voice—"'Oh, uh, I didn't think about that.'"

Ellis made an irritated noise in the back of her throat. "Then I actually *did* get mad, because it was like, okay, Aiden, so you only thought about yourself and whatever girl you want to try dating. You didn't think about me at all."

"You told him that?"

"Obviously."

Come Home to My Heart

I smiled. "Of course. How'd he take it?"

"He didn't answer, which means I was right." I could practically see her shaking back her long auburn hair. She always did that when she scored a point. "Then I asked him why he was doing this, like, which other girl did he want to ask out, and he couldn't even tell me."

"Would you *want* him to tell you?"

"Of course." She sounded offended. "I wouldn't've asked if I didn't want to know."

I sighed. If Aiden had named a name, Ellis would have regretted asking. She would have looked up the girl in question, spent hours combing her posts and profile, and texted me little dissertations about her bitter feelings. Ellis was blunt, but she wasn't hardened. She got insecure like everyone else.

The problem was, she still couldn't keep herself from asking these kinds of questions. She wanted to know people's entire feelings, no matter what ugly or embarrassing realities might be moving around under the surface, no matter what knowing did to her.

I had a feeling that Aiden could have said exactly who his eye was straying for, but he knew Ellis like I did. He loved her. When you loved Ellis, you protected her from the truth when it wasn't good for her. Sometimes people aren't as ready for reality as they think they are.

I lay back on my bed, and we chatted about school while the light faded from my walls. Ellis was organizing the Young Christian Society fundraiser, and I was senior chair for the Winter Dance Committee, and we needed a theme before Thanksgiving. I wanted something that would look neat and elegant, but Ellis was making the case for loud and colorful. We planned our weekend: long afternoons sprawled in the living room of Ellis's old farmhouse, watching episodes from nineties shows whose massive back catalogs had materialized on streaming. We talked until my dad called my name down the hall.

"Dinner's ready," I told Ellis. "I'll see you tomorrow."

I hurried out of my room, but when I saw my parents standing at the end of the hall, I stopped midstep. They looked like they were posing for a photo, side by side and unmoving. My dad, with his burly build, took up most of the light cast out from the office; it gleamed on the skin at his hairline. My mom was all but left in the dark, save for the sliver of lamplight that curved across her freckled face. Her arms were wrapped tightly around herself as if she'd been straitjacketed.

"Is dinner ready?" I asked, feeling uneasy.

They made the same motion at the same time, a half glance into the office.

Time seemed to stop.

I'd closed the tabs, shut down the browser. What I hadn't done was clear the history.

I couldn't believe my lapse. I wasn't allowed a margin of error, I was not allowed mistakes. I was not allowed a single moment of distraction.

"Gloria," my dad said, "come here."

The softness of his voice felt as wrong as every other part of the scene. Usually yelling was his default, but I thought of it as a cheerful sound, because he yelled at football when he was having a good time; he yelled over the hiss of oil when he was cooking; he yelled at slow drivers when he was taking me to get milkshakes in the summer, because he loved the concrete-thick ice cream they used at Stella's, so really, his volume was a measure of excitement more than anger. Every time, his face became pink and animated, his eyes big white hoops, like a cheerful cartoon's. He was over-the-top and energetic, but never scary—never until now.

I didn't move.

Come Home to My Heart

"Gloria Lee Forman," said my mom, "you get over here right now." Her voice jittered as though she were taking a motorcycle over gravel.

My feet moved me down the hallway. The walk seemed to take a lifetime. When, finally, I reached my parents and looked into the office, a photo of two girls wound up in each other was glowing on the screen.

"You made this site?" my dad asked hoarsely.

It occurred to me to lie, but I couldn't think of a story that made sense. We could all see the menu at the top of the page: "Log out," "Settings," "See my profile."

"Yes, sir," I whispered.

The words seemed to hit him physically. He rocked back like a javelin had sunk into his chest.

Nobody spoke for a long time. I stood stock-still and watched my parents' faces transform. The color leached out of my dad's cheeks until his face was a grayish slab. My mom cried at everything, and cried like a movie star, so I wasn't surprised when tears began to leak from her eyes and cling to her painted lashes in a picturesque way, but then she mashed her fist weirdly into her mouth, knuckles first, like she was trying to chew her fingers off, and little screaming gasps came out from behind her hand, and the violence and disorder of the image transfixed me. For their expressions to bypass anger or disappointment and plummet all the way into horror—I felt as if I were physically mutating in front of them.

"I don't understand," my mother moaned, her knuckles mangling the words. Her lipstick smeared onto her chin. "Oh, Lord. How could you do this to us? What did we do wrong, for this to happen?"

My dad said tunelessly, "No. Uh-uh." Then he heaved himself away from the wall, lurched past me down the hall, and disappeared into my room.

Riley Redgate

Something slammed inside. My mother flinched and rushed after him. I found myself gliding that way, too, drawn inexorably to the open door like a magnet attracted to its opposing pole.

I stopped at the threshold of an unrecognizable room. Drawers dangled out of my dresser, half emptied. My father was on his knees, socks bursting out of both hands, forcing the fistfuls of cloth into the yellow suitcase that lay open on the floor.

I watched, unspeaking, as he yanked the underwear drawer clean out of the dresser and upturned it over the suitcase, pads and deodorant showering down after a mix of elastic and cotton. Next he threw open the closet door, tore a few dresses off hangers at random, and stuffed them in. He pulled my rolled-up sleeping bag out of the closet and flung it onto my bed. Not even five minutes ago, I'd been sitting there, tracing the tessellated triangles on the quilt, talking with Ellis about the dance.

My mom was staring at the suitcase. She'd stopped crying. "Freddie . . . maybe we should talk to Pastor Collins again, or . . ."

"No."

"Sweetie, hold—"

"*I said no.* We tried the rest back then, and she's been lying for— how long?" My dad zipped the suitcase and stood. His eyes bored into mine, the whites gone pink. His chest heaved, releasing his voice in harsh, whispery snippets. "Ev-everything we've done for you, and you choose this? You sleep under this roof and the, the clothes on your back—for years, sitting in church like—acting like—"

The sentences couldn't come together. He shoved the suitcase toward me, the thin rug bunched beneath its wheels. "Get out."

I looked around at the empty drawers, the discarded hangers, the pile of papers that had cascaded off the top of the dresser. It took such careful, constant maintenance to keep something in order and not even sixty seconds to upend it all.

Come Home to My Heart

"Where am I supposed to go?" I said quietly.

My father's voice rose to a tremulous shout. "Out that door, that's where! You've turned your back on this family, everything we stand for. Now you see what happens." He thundered past me into the living room and yanked the front door open so hard that the screen door whined in the frame.

The square of dusk beyond the screen stared through, into our house, into me.

I said, "Mom?"

Because she was tottering my way. She was taking my winter coat from the hook on my door and carrying it into the living room, one hand twitching in my direction, beckoning. She was saying something over and over under her breath. *We love you so much* or *We loved you so much*—I couldn't tell which.

When she reached my father and the open door, she let my coat fall onto the sideboard. Then, fingers shuttered over her eyes, she began to cry again, so hard that there was no sound, just the rhythmic rocking of her shoulders, just streams of water coming out from under the heels of her hands.

Until that point, my brain had felt foggy and slow, but now a sliver of my mind became as clear and hard as glass. As I looked down at my suitcase, that sliver took over from the rest. The instincts to collapse, to weep, to beg—*Please, I didn't know what else to do, I don't know how to stop*—all that went silent, as though I'd cut the power to some turbulent radio feed in my mind.

I wasn't like Ellis. I was ready for reality. I had to be.

I curled my fingers around the suitcase's handle and extended it with a mechanical *click*. The motion felt easy, like muscle memory, as if I'd practiced for this, and maybe I had, in a way. Every time I'd loaded that page, this possibility had played like background music in my mind. I'd acted knowing the consequences, and now I had to face them. This was simple action and reaction, a formula like any other.

So I tugged my phone charger from the wall and pocketed it. I lifted the sleeping bag from the bed and secured its elastic over the suitcase's handle. Then I stepped up to the door, donned my winter coat and backpack, and wheeled my life out into the dark, cool evening.

Xia Harper

By the time I got off work, night had settled over Fisherton. My Pontiac glided from little ponds of streetlight into the dark, over and over; it felt like drifting in and out of existence. Meanwhile Patsy Cline's voice wavered gently over me, and trios of backing vocalists *ooh*ed and *aah*ed. Brushes shushed over the surfaces of snare drums. I'd been on a real Patsy kick lately, though sometimes she got so romantic that I had to chase her with the vaguely menacing pulse of German EDM.

I lit a cigarette and rolled the windows down. With the Midlands caught in an October heat wave, it was a relief to feel the wind rolling over my skin, nicotine sharpening the world.

I knew I would quit smoking at some point. I'd started last year because I was bored, and only kept going because I continued to be bored, but I wasn't going to be bored forever. Smoking and drinking were just tools. They allowed me to access different modes of being myself, which felt useful for now, while I starred as the only major character in my life. It was almost like interacting with somebody else, and I needed the variety.

On the outskirts, the streetlamps got patchy, then petered out altogether. Across from Fisherton's last shitty single-pump gas station,

Riley Redgate

I turned into a vacant lot and killed my engine. The music died, the only remaining sounds the scrape of the wind and the distant hush of trees.

Carter was late, as usual, and I'd finished reading *Eileen* at work, so I tugged out my phone and tapped into the Discord app.

Over the past year, I'd joined a few literature servers, but most of the users were in their twenties and thirties, so I hardly ever joined in with chat. I didn't want to make an idiot out of myself in a server full of people with English PhDs.

That was what I wanted someday. A literature doctorate. I wanted to find books that broke down the doors into my heart, gut, or mind, then take them apart piece by piece until I could see the clockwork that powered them. When the world felt flat and ugly, I wanted to drown in gorgeous language; when the world felt numb and anesthetic, I wanted to be lacerated by insight; when the world seemed determined to squeeze all emotion out of me, I wanted to be startled and frustrated and understood. I wanted to bury myself so deep in fiction that I could stay there forever.

For four years, I'd been trapped in English classes whose teachers were still trying to teach us what a theme was, but everything would be different at college. Some people in this particular Discord server had gone to a few of the schools I was considering: Smith, Wesleyan, and Berkeley. Yet another reason to be intimidated.

When I opened the *#currently-reading* channel, though, I brightened. Two forum regulars were having a conversation about *Giovanni's Room*.

BookishBirder: Loved the writing, loved the confessional feeling, lots of psychological movement in there

Come Home to My Heart

ukeface: Yes. Interesting ideas about misogyny too. No easy answers

The sight of BookishBirder's username gave me a tingle of excitement. She was only a year older than me, which I knew because I followed her on Instagram, where she posted beautifully written book reviews. Her name was Annie, and she was a tall Vietnamese girl with a seemingly infinite supply of vintage dresses and dark lipsticks. In her nonbook photos, she lounged on the steps of various Brooklyn brownstones, stylishly disinterested. She'd gotten a haircut this week, which looked unbelievable. She looked like the photo you show to the hairdresser in hopes that a new haircut will transform your whole face and also possibly your personality.

Also, her Discord profile had the same emojis of rainbow flags and girls holding hands that mine did. And no, emojis weren't an invitation, but they *were* proof that this wasn't more pointless interest in a straight girl, so that was a step up from all the previous years of my life.

I couldn't help myself. I jumped in.

xiaxiagabor: i love giovanni's room, it's one of my favorite books ever written!
xiaxiagabor: the first time i read it, i remember thinking, i didn't know books could do this! James Baldwin was a genius.

A pause. I scrutinized my messages. They were pretty basic, but I didn't want to come across as pretentious.

I wondered if *Giovanni's Room* was a favorite of Annie's, too. Maybe we'd start chatting and be unable to stop. Maybe we'd take it to DMs and talk about a dozen other gay classics and she'd be floored by my insights. Maybe she'd follow me back on Instagram, thereby wordlessly inducting me into a secret circle of cool literary lesbians with amazing book opinions.

Then:

BookishBirder: **@ukeface** Did you think the misogyny thread sold Hella short?
ukeface: **@BookishBirder** No, I think it served the narrative. Not pleasant reading obviously but it felt more true to life than apportioning her more space and distracting from Gio & D

Something shrank in my chest. I wondered if either of them would come back and reply to me, but my messages slid higher and higher up the screen, then vanished. What I'd written began to seem juvenile verging on idiotic.

I sighed, thinking, *God.* Why had I even said anything? Hadn't I learned by now that this stuff wasn't worth the emotional disturbance?

Out of nowhere, I caught myself envisioning those two girls in Calculus this afternoon. Their moment of eye contact. The way they so clearly and deeply knew each other.

Staring out the windshield at the stars, I felt the nape of my neck itch. I needed another cigarette.

As if on cue, headlights swept through the lot, and Carter Larson's Camry crunched into the space beside mine. *Finally,* I thought, slipping out into the night.

Carter was a tall, lanky guy whose baseball cap might have been surgically affixed to his skull, for the number of times I'd seen him without it. Other permanent fixtures: the hemp necklace, the powerful whiff of weed, and the wide-eyed "Who, me?" expression on his face, like he was a seven-year-old naïf trapped in a twenty-year-old stoner's body.

"You're late," I told him as he shut his driver's side door.

Carter gave me his injured-puppy-dog look. "No one else complains when I'm, like, thirty seconds late."

"Fifteen minutes."

"Fifteen minutes? I thought we said eight thir—"

"Whatever, I don't care." I slid my wallet from my pocket. "How much?"

"Eighty bucks."

I handed the money over. "I hope you got the Camels this time. That menthol shit was awful."

"Yeah, I know, I read your text." He turned the carton of cigarettes over in his hands. "So . . . what do you think? Interested in anything else tonight?"

Discomfort gnawed at my gut. Back in sophomore year, I'd started getting nervous about certain jokes people were tossing my way, the ones about my combat boots and general lack of femininity. I'd felt like I was one haircut away from getting outed by aesthetic alone.

Carter, a senior then, had slept with anything that breathed, so I'd gritted my teeth and gone to second base with him a few times, until people very obligingly started calling me a whore instead. He'd never stopped bringing up this delightful month between us.

I stuck my hand out. "Cigarettes."

Irritation displaced his innocent expression. "Jesus, fine. You don't have to be such a bitch all the time." He shoved the carton into my hand. "No wonder no one can stand you." Then he pouted his way back into his car and revved out of the lot.

Riley Redgate

Watching his taillights shrink down Ninth, I leaned against my Pontiac and lit a fresh cigarette. Tried to ignore the oddly jagged edges of my feelings.

Who cares? I told myself. Yeah, obviously, nobody could stand me—because I'd carefully constructed a persona with all the social appeal of a rabid jackal. It wasn't because of anything true.

A lump rose in my throat.

I ground out my cigarette stub with my heel and lowered myself back into the Pontiac. I hesitated, then picked up my phone.

Don't do it, I thought. But my thumbs were already tapping into my texts, scrolling down into the past, through dozens of unimportant threads. Confirmation codes from websites flew by, interspersed with texts from unsaved numbers about school projects. March. February. January. I scrolled further, flying past spammers and robots—all the way back into sophomore year.

I saw their names and stopped. Navya Ahuja and Kit McCallister.

My hair tangled against my headrest as I sank farther down in the driver's seat. That jagged edge in me seemed to nestle against my solar plexus.

Why are you doing this, I thought. *Why are you doing this to yourself again.*

I tapped Kit's thread.

The last three messages were all from me. In October of my sophomore year, I'd said: **Lol I watched Jupiter Ascending. You weren't wrong, it is ridiculous. I can't believe people think this is good**

Two weeks after that: **What did y'all get up to for Halloween?**

A month after that: **Hi want to do a Facetime or something soon?**

He'd never answered. I'd spent a lot of time that winter drafting texts and deleting them, wondering whether to bring up *Jupiter*

Come Home to My Heart

Ascending again. Maybe Kit had secretly liked the movie and I shouldn't have insulted it. Also, even if I'd hated it, why did I have to be so negative about everything?

I hit the Back button. As I opened my messages with Navya, that sharp-edged feeling dug more deeply into me.

Kit and I had met in seventh grade, but Navya and I had been friends since we were eight. We'd coordinated our outfits on the first day of middle school. For years, she'd borrowed my favorite books, and I'd come over to her place to play her favorite fantasy video games. I'd been there for her when she'd gotten her period in seventh grade, had shoved my hoodie into her hands and stood behind her until she'd tied it around her waist. And she'd been there for me at the end of middle school, when my parents had broken the news that we were leaving Atlanta.

But at the end, this was what our relationship had looked like: a line of blue bubbles on my side of the screen.

> God I miss Atlanta so much. I keep imagining you and me going to the Silver Diner. Or doing stupid school shit like dances or football games or all the things I hate here and wouldn't touch if they literally paid me, but I wouldn't hate it if it was us.

> Not to be clingy and weird lol.

> sorry I'm dumping on you again I feel like all I do these days is vent

Her last text to me had arrived four days after this self-centered ramble:

> Hi X, I'm so sorry, school is crazy right now! Miss you too, I promise I'll respond as soon as I get time to breathe

She never had.

I knew she hadn't lied about being busy. When Navya had started at Lincoln Academy, soccer and track had vacuumed up all her time. Besides, she'd always been the kind of sunny optimist who was liked by everybody. To me, our friendship had been rare. Probably to her, it had only ever been a minor item on a long docket.

Part of me wondered if she'd also started to suspect certain things about me freshman year, during the late nights that I'd texted her. Maybe she'd started, in a small, nagging way, to feel uncomfortable about our closeness.

I could be wrong, though. Maybe time had just gotten away from her.

Maybe even now, she missed me.

Slowly, laboriously, I typed: **Hi Navya, I know it's been a long time, but I was wondering how you've been.**

I hesitated, finger hovering over the Send button, my heart suddenly pounding. Was I seriously considering doing this? I had a car now. If Navya answered, I could actually drive to Atlanta. See her.

But then she'd see me, too. She'd see this: a burnout, a friendless loser.

She hadn't wanted to talk to me sophomore year. Why would she want to now, when the only thing left of our friendship was the memory of what we'd been to each other?

My grip tightened on my phone. Why should *I* want to talk to *her* when she'd clearly never cared about me like I'd cared about her?

Come Home to My Heart

I hit Delete and shoved my phone deep into my jacket pocket. Forget this. I wasn't going to spend my time trailing after anyone, pathetically asking them to give a shit about me. Not my parents, not Navya—not anybody.

I restarted the Pontiac with a hard twist of the key and drowned out Patsy Cline with the irritated roar of the engine.

Fifteen minutes later, I was pulling into Fisherton Oaks. Our neighborhood was a newish development whose houses remained 70 percent empty, half a dozen years after construction. I drove by vacant driveway after vacant driveway, untouched yards, windows that looked deep gray. In the high windows above glossy front doors, you could see the shadows of unlit chandeliers. FOR SALE signs stood in some of the yards, but only some. Too many, and the existing residents would feel like we were living in a ghost town. Too many, basically, and we'd be forced to acknowledge the truth.

Our house, at the end of a cul-de-sac, stuck out. My mother had entered a horticultural phase of her life, and our front garden teemed with perfectly pruned plants and flowers. In the moonlight the place looked like a dollhouse.

I parked on the concrete driveway and sprayed Febreze onto my clothes, masking the scent of smoke. My dad was on-site for the next few weeks—these days he was a senior construction manager who traveled on the company's dime, staying in fancy hotels, overseeing their most important projects. But there was no escaping my mom, who'd pepper me with questions about school and work, making monologues out of my monosyllables.

Before high school I'd loved her so much. I'd been one of those kids who described my mom as my best friend. Rebecca Gou, the energetic extrovert who thought everything in front of her was *the best thing!* Rebecca Gou, chameleonic, who could assimilate effortlessly into any place: any city, any town, any social scenario. She'd come to the US from Hong Kong at age eighteen, and at UGA she'd reshaped herself to fit seamlessly into a whole new country. Whereas I couldn't even blend in someplace a three-hour drive from Atlanta.

But maybe I didn't want to blend in. Maybe I wanted to draw a sharp, unbroken line between me and the world around me. Maybe I felt like if I let everything into myself, some part of me would be obliterated.

Bracing myself, I opened the door, but the house was quiet. I frowned, kicked off my boots, and padded down the unlit hall. In the kitchen, I set my backpack on the marble island and flicked on the lights, but the cool white glow only made the place feel emptier.

I spotted a note on the island in my mom's loopy handwriting. *Migraine—went to bed early! Leftovers in the fridge!*

My eyes lingered on the smiley face she'd drawn under the words. She'd given it dimples.

So I didn't have to interact with her, didn't have to watch her relentlessly spinning every negative into a positive. Even as the dread faded from my chest, I wondered why, somehow, I felt disappointed.

Gloria Forman

I awoke to birdsong and a murky twilight, gray mixed into deep blue.

For an instant I was disoriented. My body tilted up into a seated position, and strands of my hair fluttered across my vision, breeze-touched. I brought my hand absentmindedly to one stiff shoulder as last night sharpened in my memory.

After leaving home, I'd floated through town in the dusk with the fight replaying senselessly in my head, a slideshow of weird images. My mother's fingers twisted up in her mouth. The colorful window of the girls glowing on the screen. As I walked, the thought of hunkering down in Dad's old paper mill occurred to me—thrill-seeking kids sometimes sneaked in through a shattered window around the back. But then I remembered the news stories about the cops clearing out squatters from the factory in winters. My parents would have died of shame if that were me.

So instead my feet had brought me to school, to the dugouts at the baseball field, where I'd unrolled my sleeping bag onto one of the benches. It couldn't have been later than 8:00 p.m., but after I'd wriggled inside and nestled my head onto my hoodie, I'd fallen asleep immediately, as if my body had been waiting to shut down.

Now I navigated my feet back into my tennis shoes, sending a cigarette butt skittering across the dugout floor. I watched my cold fingers work like hinges in need of oil, resisting every motion, as I tied my shoes, then rolled my sleeping bag up tight. I had no time to sit, to think, to feel. Already the hard, tiny voice of survival was pushing me back into action. I needed somewhere to hide my suitcase from everyone at school. That was the problem I had to solve.

I hurried across the field to the main building, thinking up excuses about the suitcase as I went. Even this early, a staff member might spot me lugging this around.

Sure enough, when I reached the front steps, I found a custodian unlocking the doors, a lean, sun-weathered man in dark coveralls. "You sure got here early," he said, giving my suitcase a questioning look. "What's that for?"

I fashioned a smile. "Prop for theater class."

"Oh, right. Here, let me take you round the side. You could put that thing backstage." As we headed toward the auditorium entrance, his eyes lingered on my face. "Got to get you a comb or something."

I made myself laugh, tugging my fingers through my tangles. "I know. It—it serves me right for sleeping on wet hair." I gestured at my face. "Ruined my night's sleep, too . . ."

Thankfully, he accepted all this without much apparent interest. Once he'd left me in the auditorium, I carried the suitcase downstairs to the greenroom beneath the stage. But when I tried the door to the prop shop, it was locked. I hauled the suitcase back up the steps, wondering if I really *could* just leave it backstage—hidden in the set for the play, maybe?

Halfway up the steps, I stopped. To my right, a narrow passageway sloped up to the orchestra pit, a small chamber under the front of

Come Home to My Heart

the stage. Fisherton High hadn't put on a musical since 2005, and the pit had been covered over some years after that.

I hustled up the hall and tried the door to the pit. Locked. It probably had been for years.

But as I retreated, a dark shape caught my eye overhead. Set into the low ceiling was a black opening, a chute leading up to the stage. A school play in the nineties had called for a trapdoor, a death scene in which someone fell through and disappeared.

I clambered up onto my suitcase and hoisted myself into the dark, narrow chute. Two of its sides were covered over with plywood, but the crisscrossed beams of the others allowed me to slip into the space beneath the stage. In thick, unyielding darkness, I ducked between wooden supports, bent double. Finally, I reached forward and felt empty space.

I pulled out my phone for light, but it had died in the night. As I groped through the dark, something cold slithered against my face. I flinched, then seized the chain of metal beads and tugged.

The orchestra pit appeared before me. It was filthy, and the light bulb made a sound like a radiator, but I knew immediately that this room was what I needed. Psalms came to mind as I unlocked the door and wheeled my suitcase into the corner: *Under His wings you will find refuge.* I could all but feel God's guiding hand, leading me here.

At long last, I lowered myself into an ancient wooden chair. Only there, hidden under the stage, did I feel myself coming back into my body. Pins and needles pricked my freezing, whitish fingers, and I realized how much my shoulder was throbbing from the dugout's hard bench.

But I was safe. There were no more immediate threats.

Measuring out a long, slow breath, I felt my numb composure crack. I looked down and found my hands trembling. This was all really happening to me. It wasn't just some nightmare, and I couldn't pinch myself awake.

I wondered if my parents felt this way, too—half fearful, half disbelieving. How had they spent last night? I imagined Mom praying in bed, crying herself into hiccups. I imagined Dad swaying at the kitchen table, that forbidden bottle of whiskey at his elbow.

I picked at my nail beds, guilt frothing up in me like a chemical reaction.

For a moment I wondered if I should tell someone what had happened, but I shut that instinct down. If I ran my mouth, there was no chance my parents could take this back.

I stopped picking at my nails and folded my hands tight. *Of course they'll take it back*, I told myself. They'd been in shock last night, but after school today, we'd hash this out.

This family matters to them, I thought defiantly. By this evening I'd be rolling up the sleeping bag. I'd take everything home and sleep in my bed again, burying my face in my pillow and breathing in the scent of fabric softener. My dad would have made his point. I'd get out of the shower with clean hair, I'd wash my face in our sink and look down at the soapy water draining over the coral porcelain, and I'd never take any of it for granted again. In a few years we'd talk about tonight with disbelieving voices, and it would seem like something that had happened to some other family.

Or maybe we'd never talk about it. If they didn't want me to mention it, I would keep it a secret forever, lined up on the shelf next to the other things I kept inside. I would do whatever they wanted without anger or resentment. This time I'd be better: no secret blogs, no

Come Home to My Heart

slipups, nothing. I'd be the perfect daughter in every way that it was possible for me to be.

All I had to do was get through the day.

◊

For the first time since I'd started at Fisherton High, I ate breakfast in the cafeteria. Washed in the harsh light of sunrise, the lunch ladies looked as tired as I felt. But Dawn, a counter worker in her fifties whose steel-gray hair curled beneath its net, found a smile for me anyway. She wasn't naturally the friendliest person, but she'd warmed to me in sophomore year after I'd started greeting her by name.

"If it isn't Granny Smith Gloria." Dawn leaned one gloved hand on the steel counter. "Never seen you here for breakfast before."

"No, ma'am. I never get up this early if I can help it." I made myself smile back at her, but I couldn't help feeling self-conscious. I'd been on free lunch ever since Dad lost his old job, but we'd never resorted to taking the breakfasts, too.

I set my tray at a booth in a corner and, gnawing through a biscuit, watched other students trickle in. The athletes moved in rowdy packs, unloading bagel sandwiches and bottled smoothies from their backpacks, but then there were the Caldwell kids in their threadbare T-shirts, moving through the line, too, settling at a nearby table with their own biscuits and trays of watery scrambled eggs.

I dropped my eyes to my own food and bolted the rest. As the unfamiliar tight feeling in my stomach eased, I started to plan a strategy.

The biggest issue was Ellis. People called her a gossip, but that was a distortion of the facts, and the facts were: Someday Ellis Marsden was going to be the kind of detective that made criminals shake in their boots. When we were little, seven or eight, she and I had watched whodunits during every sleepover. She'd always been the one to guess who the bad guy was. Now, ten years later, I was going to have to bend myself into knots to get away from her keenly placed magnifying glass.

The first class we had together was Chemistry. "Hey," she said, sliding into her usual seat in front of me. "Why weren't you on the bus?"

It would have been too much to pretend that everything was fine. I rubbed at my reddened eyes, my lips pursed. "Missed it. Me and my parents got in a fight last night, right after we talked. I slept like crap."

"Oh my goodness. Are you okay? What happened?"

I lowered my voice. "I'll tell you about it on the bus, but basically I've been talking to my aunt Jen, and they found out."

Ellis looked sympathetic. "I'd want to talk to her, too. It's so stupid that y'all have to be cut off."

"They think she's a bad influence."

Ellis shrugged. "I mean, she probably is, but don't they trust you not to get influenced? Like, do they really think you're going to have one conversation with somebody who made some bad choices and turn into a big old slut?"

"Ellis," I muttered, my cheeks coloring. Andy Glover across the aisle was examining a blank sheet of paper with too much interest.

"Sorry." She followed my sightline and lowered her voice. "I'm serious, though. You're eighteen. They have to let you make your own choices at some point."

"That's what I said." I sighed. "Anyway, maybe I can get my dad to start driving me to school in the morning. This is the third time I've missed the bus this year."

Ellis pushed out her lower lip in an exaggerated pout. "You're going to leave me all alone on the bus?"

Come Home to My Heart

"You're never awake," I pointed out.

"Yeah, but you're such a good pillow."

I rolled my eyes, my smile coming easier, as the bell rang. Talking about Aunt Jen had given me fresh reassurance. After her whole scandal, my parents wouldn't want any more of our family's business publicized. They'd want me to come home fast, keep this quiet.

It was disorienting how normal most of the school day felt. I turned in the homework I'd done yesterday, before the fight. I ate lunch with Ben and Deanna from Young Christians, who were, as usual, arguing over which Bible passage we'd study this week. I raised my hand in Calculus, and Mrs. Molina beamed at me.

By the end of the day, I felt more like myself. I'd planned out the perfect apology to my parents. I just needed to ensure I could get back into the orchestra pit tonight, so that after we talked it out, I could retrieve my suitcase.

So, when the bell rang, I headed back down to the auditorium's greenroom. The room was mostly underground, but a few dusty windows sat high on the wall. I climbed onto the sofa and rotated the corner window's lock out of its catches, then dashed to the bus lot with a minute to spare.

On bus 798, Ellis was curled in our usual seat, head pillowed against her backpack. "You look comfortable," I said, sitting beside her.

"Just settlin' in for the long haul," she said, exaggerating her drawl so the words stretched like taffy. For her it was a long haul. Our route passed through downtown, then my neighborhood, then fifteen miles of country roads, before finally stopping outside her family's ancient farmhouse, close to 5:00 p.m.

"You'll ruin your hair, lying on it like that," I said.

"Please. I couldn't ruin this hair if I tried."

Still, she straightened. Ellis was famous in school for that waterfall of loose auburn curls, which shone like she waxed them every morning. As the bus trundled out of the lot, she let the locks slide through her fingers, and I smelled coconut. I held my breath. Touched my own hair, making sure it was still tied up tight.

"So," she said. "Details."

And, having spent all day preparing, I gave them to her.

Ellis knew all about Aunt Jen already, having watched our family go through that mess in eighth grade. Back when we'd first found out Jen was pregnant, my parents had given her as much money as we could spare and urged her to get the father—whoever he was—to propose, to make a real, loving family from a bad situation. But the whispers around town built and built, and finally, Jen confessed that we already knew the father: Jesse Wilcox, a married father of four, and my parents' closest friend in our congregation.

My parents were cheerful people, but when they got angry, you didn't want to be within a mile. That night, they'd been furious in a way I'd never seen before. They had a screaming fight with Jen, and the next day, she left Fisherton forever, leaving my family humiliated in her wake.

"I guess I've been feeling bad about how we left things," I told Ellis. "So a few weeks ago, I started texting her, and last night, my mom went through my phone and saw the thread."

As we discussed my made-up conversations with Jen, the bus trundled into Fisherton's downtown. We passed the public library, three blocks of struggling shops, and one glass office building of medium height. Soon Ellis got indignant on my behalf, like she always did. "I can't believe your mom went through your phone."

"Really? You can't believe it?"

We shared a knowing look. She sighed.

Come Home to My Heart

"Let's talk about something else," I said.

I'd given her enough to satisfy. "Fine," she said, squeezing my knee in reassurance.

I forced myself not to tug away. Ellis had always been affectionate like this, hugging people she barely knew. Her little touches hadn't felt weird until sometime last year.

These days, I never touched her if I could help it. Sometimes I even had trouble talking about her. At parties, our friends would look her up and down and declare, "Ellis, you look *hot*," like it meant nothing, but the idea of me saying something like that made my gut clench. No. Ellis was pretty, like sunlight off a river. She was elegant, like a marble sculpture. She was everything to me, like a sister. Even the idea of thinking about her in another way panicked me—the knowledge of what it could do to our friendship.

I tilted my head until it barely tapped her shoulder, said, "Thanks, girl," and she let go of my knee. Then the conversation turned to Aiden's attempted dumping, and as we fondly trash-talked him, I relaxed into the seat, my guilt mingled with relief.

When the driver let me off at my house, I waited for the bus to round the corner. Then I hurried up our concrete steps and hit the bell.

A cheerful *ding!* echoed inside. A scuffling noise sounded beyond the door, but the curtains were pulled so I couldn't see through the front window. When I leaned close, I could hear the TV on inside, recorded laughter.

I tried the knob. It was locked.

My breathing began to quicken. I rang the bell again and said—loudly enough to penetrate, but not so loudly that some neighbor might overhear—"Mama? Dad?"

The television noise loudened.

Riley Redgate

A dull ringing filled my head. I backed down the stairs, each step beating an impact up through my heel. The heat of the afternoon pushed down on my skin like a duvet.

Breath by breath, though, my mind cleared. So my parents didn't want to talk yet? That was okay. The orchestra pit was secluded. I could sleep there for a night, or two, or three, until this shook out.

I sat on the steps, opened my English notebook, and jotted down a note.

Hi Mom and Dad. I'm so sorry for last night. I understand if you're not ready to talk to me just yet, but I want you to know I have a private place to sleep and I'm not going to tell anybody what happened. I know we can fix this together. I'll keep taking the bus home, so I hope you'll meet me at the stop soon so we can talk.

If we don't see each other before Sunday, I can go to a different church. And if anybody at First Baptist asks why I'm not with y'all, maybe you could tell them I'm trying out another pastor, just to see how the sermons can vary around town? I love you so much and I'm sorry again. I'm praying hard for forgiveness and guidance.

I severed the note on the dotted line and slipped it into our mailbox, whose small red flag quavered in the wind.

Then I headed up the sidewalk toward downtown, not looking back at our house. The image hung in my mind, the gray clapboard siding, the neatly trimmed yard, the nicked screen door. But each

Come Home to My Heart

step reinforced the slender barrier between me and last night, and I wouldn't shatter it by glancing over my shoulder.

I'd done what I could. Now I had work to do.

I walked forty minutes to the public library in eighty-degree heat. By the time I passed between the scanners at the circulation desk, my socks had soaked through with sweat, and in the building's sudden coolness, I felt that the back of my neck and calves had burned. They were sticky to the touch, like old flypaper.

But the library had what I needed: computer access. I hurried to the desktops at the back, where I flipped open my planner and scanned my assignments. Worksheets or problem sets, anything I could do offline, I'd save for the orchestra pit.

Still, time management could only get me so far. The library closed at 6:00 p.m., and by the time I'd posted a reading response in the Psychology class forums and taken notes on an eighteen-minute video describing the fall of Rome, it was 5:55. I still had to write a three-page paper on *Jane Eyre*.

I'd just have to check out a library copy—mine was sitting on my dresser at home—and handwrite the essay. Mr. Barnes might give me a confused look, but he wouldn't say anything. There were enough kids at our school whose families didn't have computers or printers; our teachers couldn't afford to be snobby.

When I hurried into the stacks, though, I came into more bad luck. *Jane Eyre* wasn't shelved, only peeling copies of *Wuthering Heights* and *Agnes Grey*.

Outside on the steps, I watched the librarians lock up, the itch of panic starting to set in.

Just get back to school, I told myself. With my charger in the orchestra pit, I'd get some juice in my dead phone and find *Jane Eyre* online. It'd be slow and irritating, navigating the book on my phone, but it was better than nothing.

Then I stopped at the foot of the library steps. Across the street, in a narrow gap between two buildings, hung a sign that read, THE BOOK ALLEY.

I'd lived in Fisherton my whole life, had passed the sign a thousand times, but I'd never gone into that store. I wasn't a big reader.

Worth a try, I thought, jogging across the street. A dozen paces down the alley, set into the brick wall, was a faded red door with a brass knob. The yellowing card in the window read that the shop wouldn't close until 8:00 p.m.

When I stepped inside, I felt momentarily blind. Outside, the day was all sunshine, but in the Book Alley it could have been midnight. The single smudged window hardly let in a candle's worth of light, and the yellowy lamps between the shelves didn't help much, either. All the way at the back, though, was a reading light on the cashier's desk, and behind it, her face illuminated in curves like the subject of an old painting, sat Xia Harper.

At first I thought it was a trick of the light. The idea of Xia Harper having a job was ridiculous. I blinked hard, but the sight didn't change. It really was her.

If that girl *was* going to have a job, I supposed it made sense that it was here, in this deserted store, where no one would see her following directions.

A tarnished little bell had rung when I'd walked inside, but Xia hadn't looked up. She had her combat boots propped on the desk, and a book mostly covered her face, *My Brilliant Friend*. I might not have recognized her without the boots or the weird book, which were her defining characteristics at school, as well as being hated by everyone.

Come Home to My Heart

Xia shifted in her seat. Two fingertips flicked a lock of dark hair behind her ear, then pushed her thick-rimmed glasses up her nose.

I hurried into the nearest aisle before she could see me.

The splintery bookcases were a labyrinth, but eventually I traced my way to the Brontës. The most battered paperback of *Jane Eyre* cost eight dollars.

I chewed my lip. I'd spent last summer lifeguarding in a Columbia suburb. My paychecks had gone toward family expenses, but the day after I'd given my parents my final check, they'd handed me an envelope with a hundred dollars inside. I still had eighty-odd dollars of that in my wallet, but spending a tenth of it in one go didn't seem smart, not with the prospect of paying for my own food for a little while.

Maybe I could write the essay here in the shop.

I peered around a shelf. Xia sat at the desk ten feet away, still reading. Signs hung at intervals on the walls: SUPPORT YOUR LOCAL BUSINESS—DO NOT READ BOOKS IN STORE! And then, in a smaller font: (THE PUBLIC LIBRARY IS RIGHT ACROSS THE STREET!)

I'd just have to finish the essay before Xia realized what I was doing, then.

I settled on a velveteen armchair crammed between two bookcases and set to work. A shiny streak of graphite accumulated on the side of my right hand as I went, and the words blurred. Without my phone, a watch, or a clock in sight, I couldn't tell how long it had been. I hardly even felt like I was in Fisherton anymore. The silence was absolute, except for the occasional shush of a page turning at the register.

I knew it was getting late when my stomach started to growl at me. I gripped my pencil tighter and tried to zero back in on the essay, but the thoughts of dinner only got louder, rattling my train of thought. What, exactly, was I going to eat? And where?

Focus, I told myself irritably. One problem at a time.

Riley Redgate

I'd nearly filled three pages when I heard footsteps and a squeak. Xia was wheeling a cart through the store, reshelving. Before I could move, she stopped by the biographies and looked over at me.

I froze cross-legged in the armchair, my pencil hovering over my conclusion. I forced my eyes not to stray toward the DO NOT READ BOOKS IN STORE! signs.

Xia had on black jeans and a ripped sweater printed with a faded Polaroid. It was a miracle she hadn't died of heat stroke. She was always dressed like this, even in August, when most days it was a hundred degrees.

Her eyes slid from my face to *Jane Eyre* in my hand. I held my breath and waited for the axe to fall. Any second now she'd snarl me out of the store, or ask me in tones of pure acid whether I could read, or cuss at me in a way that would have shocked a sailor. No one cussed like Xia. She drove a junky old muscle car that people called the Zombie Pontiac, and when it had broken down in the lot last spring, I'd passed her fiddling around under the hood, wreathed in steam, calling the car some truly vile words I'd never heard anywhere else in town.

Her face turned away. The lenses in her glasses flashed as the light glided against them. Without a word, she pushed her cart down the biography aisle.

I looked back down at my essay, relief rolling through me. Of course Xia Harper wasn't going to tell me to behave. This, after all, was the girl who scowled and yawned through every class, alternately responding to teachers with sarcastic nonanswers and getting their questions right with an expression of deep boredom. This was the girl who walked to the baseball field every lunch period and came back reeking of cigarette smoke—the girl who'd spat on Jason Knox's windshield when he'd told her she might be pretty if she just put some effort in.

Come Home to My Heart

I finished my essay fifteen minutes later. By then, my stomach was pulsing with hunger. When I stepped out from the aisle, Xia was back at the register, boots up on the desk, book in front of her face again.

She didn't say anything as I left.

◊

While I walked back to school, the buildings cast huge polygons of darkness that stretched across the wide intersections, and the town seemed to strain, glued together weakly with shadow and unmarked space. The whole sky shook with thunder, dim threads of lightning crawling over the clouds. I held tight to my backpack straps as I walked, trying to feel more secure.

It was finally time to fill the hollow pit in my stomach, and I'd decided where best to do it. After half an hour's walk, I reached the gas station across from school, where everybody bought chewing tobacco and candy and cigarettes. The same man worked the counter every day, wearing a rotating lineup of plaid shirts. He had a deeply pockmarked, expressionless face and didn't look up as I beelined for the microwaved foods at the back.

As I passed the toiletries, though, my steps caught. My teeth felt fuzzy, and I knew my breath was foul. I picked a toothbrush and toothpaste from the shelf, then rushed on to the food.

The cheapest meal was a pair of instant mac and cheese tubs, $1.07 for them both. I paid, pocketed the toothbrush and toothpaste, then bolted down both tubs of mac and cheese in the corner, beside a prehistoric microwave and a pot of coffee that looked like its first ingredient was asphalt.

After gorging myself in two minutes flat, I stood there, staring into the gummy residue left in the tubs. How had they emptied so fast? They'd barely taken the edge off the hunger.

Riley Redgate

When I looked around the convenience store at all the brightly colored cellophane, my mouth filled with saliva. Three feet away, in a plastic case, sat a fat, glazed doughnut. Its price tag read $1.99.

I waffled. That doughnut was almost two nights' mac and cheese, and I didn't know how long it might be before my parents and I had our sit-down.

But I imagined tearing into the doughnut, the softness of it, the way it would wipe out that dark, lingering spot of hunger. *If I buy it, I'll still have seventy-five dollars*, I thought. At $1.07 a day, that was two and a half months of dinner. I couldn't imagine this whole situation lasting longer than a week, two at the outside.

Feeding myself on weekends would raise that daily spend, of course, without free school breakfasts and lunches. But maybe I could save pieces of cafeteria food from the week to help with money. Maybe I could even sneak extras, another waxy apple from the basket here, another cellophane-wrapped muffin there.

I finished the doughnut before I'd walked the block back to school. It did satisfy me, but I had to push back a fluttery, nervous instinct, the feeling that I'd been irresponsible and this would be one more thing I regretted.

Two cars sat in the school lot, far apart, gleaming under the greenish lamps. I slid into the shadow of the building, not wanting to run into the drivers. Security guards? Custodians? Nobody who'd be thrilled about me breaking in, that was for sure.

I crouched behind the school building and pushed open the greenroom window. Trying not to touch the mildewed frame, I wriggled inside, closed the window behind me, and dropped to the sofa.

The skin on the back of my neck tingled as I straightened. The school after hours looked unfamiliar, darkness repainting every surface, shadows spiderwebbing every corner. Not wanting to draw

Come Home to My Heart

attention to an illuminated window, I left the greenroom lights off and groped my way upstairs in the dark.

When I tugged the light bulb's chain in the orchestra pit, flooding it with harsh light, my heart sped. I half expected a custodian to burst out of nowhere and ask me what I thought I was doing. But nobody appeared, and after several nervous minutes, I breathed more easily.

The first thing I had to do was make this room something near livable. Words cycled through my mind for an hour as I cleaned the place: *Thank you, Lord Jesus.* He was good; He was taking care of me. I swept the floor with a broom from backstage, creating tumbleweeds of dust and dirt, then flushed the tumbleweeds down the greenroom toilet. When the floor looked something like clean, I rolled out my sleeping bag, a zigzag of pink and green.

Next I unzipped my suitcase, whose sunny yellow was scuffed gray around the edges now. I folded my clothes, tallying up outfits. One dress I liked had made it, but all my other favorites were still at home. Until I got back, I'd be wearing the same few pairs of fraying jeans, a lineup of neutral T-shirts, and two dresses I hadn't worn since freshman year. I'd just have to hope Ellis wouldn't notice.

This place was unnervingly quiet. No Dad cheering USC, or flipping on the fan when he got too worked up, or popping open a soda can with a pressurized *crack-hiss.* No deliberate clicking of my mom at the computer in the next room over. Here, there was only the relentless buzz of the light bulb, and then a skittering noise that made me go still and scan the room. A mouse?

Nothing came out of the shadows beneath the stage, but I zipped my suitcase shut anyway.

At last, after this long, harsh whirlwind of a day, it was time to clean myself up.

Riley Redgate

The bathroom off the greenroom always smelled like pee, but it was secluded and windowless. I stripped naked and washed my back, armpits, and scalp with hand soap, then ran my razor over my shins.

I kept glimpsing myself in the mirror, and every time it happened, I looked away with a hot, nauseating surge in my stomach. I watched the razor gliding over my skin instead. Held my hand steady.

Only when I was rinsed and dried did I grasp the edges of the sink and stare into my face, trying to figure out what I was feeling.

Last night, when my mother had said, *How could you do this to us*, when my father had faced the whole truth of me and said, simply, *No*, I'd had this weird feeling of reflection—like I was standing at the end of the hall beside them and seeing myself for the first time. My whole life, I'd tried to arrange myself properly, to fit correctly into every space I was placed. But in that moment, I'd seen that I really was the way I'd always secretly suspected myself to be: wrong and unfixable.

Now, as I looked into the mirror, their feelings were beating through me, their disappointment, their repulsion.

I wished I could show them, somehow, how hard I'd tried to stop this.

During most of elementary school, I'd thought I'd never had a crush, but around the end of fifth grade, I started realizing that I *was* having the feelings other girls were describing, just not about boys. So I picked the boys that every other girl had a crush on and tried to make it work for me, too. I stared at Noah Allman in class, memorized his face. When Ellis gushed about how cute Jordan Lynn was in sixth grade, I agreed vigorously. I made up stories about how I'd had a secret crush on him for months. I even told my mom I liked him, even though I wasn't allowed to go on a date until I was seventeen. I'd waited for the other feelings to fade.

Come Home to My Heart

They didn't. They ran under everything like radio static. As everyone else started whispering about kissing and the different bases, I tried to picture myself doing any of it with boys, any kind of boy. The image only ever felt wrong.

The picture around me, though, was growing clearer. By late elementary school, boys were getting teased for supposedly being gay. Other things that qualified as "gay" included bad movies, mean teachers, and anything else that people hated for any reason. And when I was eleven, my parents sat me down and taught me how important it was to respect myself and wait for marriage. During that conversation, they also explained how men and women—men and women *only*—supported each other through matrimony.

"A marriage is going to be the most important part of your life, sweetie," my mom said, squeezing my dad's hand. "It's a sacred bond. It's about walking through life together in the way that God intended."

Dad nodded. "These days, a whole lot of delusional garbage out there makes it seem like these things aren't important anymore, but that just means they're more important than ever. We want to make sure you're getting healthy messages."

For this reason, Dad went on, they would pre-watch any PG-13 movies I wanted to see until I was fifteen. It wasn't that they didn't trust me. It was that adolescence was a time of trials, and they wanted to give me the tools to rise above the Devil's influence. In a society full of worldly distractions, where you could get blasted with sin and idolatry just by turning on the TV, my parents cared about my soul, my values, my relationship with our Savior. That was always what they'd cared about.

Now I stepped back from the mirror, feeling sick. My parents must think this was for the best, that a sharp shock could help save me from myself. And it made sense. I was already reassessing the mistake

I'd made with that blog. Why *hadn't* I just deleted it? Would it have been that hard?

Compared to all this, hitting Delete would have been the easiest thing in the world.

As I soaped the seams of my shorts and T-shirt, I refused to let myself sink into self-pity. This was my own doing, after all. Instead, I focused on my stomach's fullness from the doughnut, and the clean water in front of me, and the roof over my head. These were blessings, I reminded myself as I crept back upstairs. So many people had things a hundred times worse.

In the orchestra pit, I plugged in my phone and found that it was already 10:00 p.m. No wonder my eyelids were starting to droop—I'd been awake since six thirty or so.

As I crawled into my sleeping bag, my gaze fell on my backpack. *I'll finish my homework tomorrow morning*, I told myself. This would have to be my new schedule.

So I set my alarm for six o'clock and nestled my head against my rolled-up hoodie. *Thank You, Lord*, I prayed, *for this place to sleep, for helping me find my way to safety, no matter my mistakes. Thank You for guiding me through these trials, and please help me figure out how to make things right with my parents.*

I'm learning my lesson. I'm going to show them that.

But I'm scared.

I curled up, trying not to dwell on the skittering sound I'd heard out in the pit. When I closed my eyes, I could still see the light bulb hanging, red, outside my eyelids, a shapeless and infernal glow. I'd made it through the first day. Now the task was not to dream about tomorrow.

Xia Harper

The girl came back to the Book Alley the next day. I should have kicked her out the first time.

When I was nine, my dad taught me the same basic lesson about stray cats: If you fed them, they'd learn you were an easy target and trail back, and that went double if you did stupid sentimental shit like pet them or name them. Whereas if you shooed them away the first time, they'd scurry off to harass someone else and you wouldn't have to deal with ongoing feelings of guilt and responsibility.

With all that explained, my dad had aimed a kick at the stray cat rubbing her knobby spine against my ankles. She'd hissed at him and bolted.

The cat didn't come back. My dad always kept his promises, which was a shame, because an Eric Harper promise was generally a pretty depressing thing. Dad was the pessimist to my mother's optimist, although he'd have referred to it as pragmatism.

Later, realizing I was sad about the cat, he'd tried to reassure me: "Oh, Xia, come on. You realize you mean nothing to her emotionally? You're just a food source. You're a human-shaped food dispenser."

My dad was great with small children.

Now, thanks to my lack of intervention, the girl was back and moving toward the fiction section again. I watched her over the top of my book. She was anemically pale, with freckles massed across her features like a storm mapped over a weather radar. A silver crucifix hung from a chain around her long neck. Her eyebrows curved slightly over her wide eyes, giving her a look of permanent fear, but the effect was offset by the rigid way she moved. When she looked into the aisle, her head turned like a periscope; when she tightened the strap of her backpack, her arm worked like an automaton's. Watching her made me want to let out a long breath.

I should have known her name. We had classes together: English, I knew, because she'd been reading *Jane Eyre* yesterday. There were probably others, too, but alas, everyone at our hell school blended together. If I'd been held at gunpoint and ordered to differentiate between any of the people in my grade, I'd have pulled the trigger myself just to spend less time with them.

Still, I knew her from somewhere specific.

She disappeared into the aisle with the chair, and I shook my head. She'd get a nasty surprise if she tried this when the owner was working. Mr. Avery was dead serious about those BUY BEFORE READING OR YOU'RE PERSONALLY RESPONSIBLE FOR THE DOWNFALL OF THE ECONOMY signs.

I didn't blame him, honestly. It was a great day over here at the Book Alley if we made twenty bucks. God knew how he paid his mortgage, let alone me.

Suddenly I remembered where I'd seen the girl. She was Ellis Whatever's friend, Ellis with the hair. She was the one who'd whispered in Ellis's ear a couple of days ago.

Mystery solved. I went back to my book.

Come Home to My Heart

◊

"Xia?"

I looked up. My mother's face was expectant across the dinner table. I had a fork in one hand and my phone in the other, open to Discord, where I was reading old chats about *My Brilliant Friend*.

"I said, I'm planning to leave for your dad's site after work tomorrow," my mom said. "So I probably won't see you before I go."

"Oh. Right."

"Would you like to join us? Myrtle Beach is beautiful this time of year."

I pretended to consider. "No, um, I want to make a dent in my college apps this weekend."

"Ooh. Of course! How are they going?"

I shrugged and mumbled out, "Fine."

"I think you have a good chance at most of these schools, Xia. I really do. Isn't it exciting? I was researching Berkeley yesterday, and *what* a beautiful campus! Of course, the schools in New England have those wonderful autumn colors . . ."

I hesitated, feeling something dangerously close to interest in what she was saying. Admissions departments had been sending me recruiting emails for ages now, full of gorgeous photo spreads, like tourism ads. They'd worked on me. I thought about colleges like a lot of people thought about crushes: breathless, rolling their names through my minds while I invented our futures together.

"Yeah," I said, "Berkeley's pretty. Barnard would be cool, too."

I caught surprise in my mother's expression. Her whitened smile shone brilliantly. "Another excellent option! Have you decided who to ask for your recommendations?"

"Um," I muttered. "Don't worry, I'll deal with that."

"Your grades holding strong, I assume?"

"Yep."

"Very good. Now we'll see if all this outweighs the extracurricular problem."

"Yep," I said again, more irritably.

"But I think your father was right about having work experience. They'll see initiative in that . . . especially work that relates so strongly to your interests."

"Mm," I said. As far as parental suggestions went, "get a part-time job" had been cake. I'd walked into an interview at the bookstore, Mr. Avery's eyes had fallen on Toni Morrison's *Sula* in my hand, and I'd thought the guy was going to cry. He hired me after fifteen minutes' conversation.

My mom took a bite of risotto. I took the opportunity to go back to my phone.

She let out a sigh, but she eventually opened something on her phone, too, and the rest of dinner was considerably less work.

I liked to think that screaming fights and dramatic blowups were behind us. These days our relationship was comfortably transactional. As long as I kept my grades up and stuck to my work schedule, my parents no longer badgered me about making friends, going to dances, attending tailgates, or any of the other things that passed for entertainment in Fisherton. They didn't pressure me to come to church with them. They'd even bought me the Pontiac last December, for my seventeenth birthday, and given me astonishingly few rules for its use. I was free.

People at school probably thought I was full of furious hatred, fires of rebellion, etc., but it wasn't like that at all. Without any expectation of socializing, any interest from teachers, or any direction from

Come Home to My Heart

my parents, I existed totally unpressured in the world, like a subject hovering in a sensory deprivation tank. Nothing required any investment from me. I was driving on a highway past the scenic backdrop of my own life. It was pleasing and distant. It was peace and fucking quiet.

◊

So when Freckle Crucifix Girl continued to come into the store, it got under my skin. I'd taken this job for the isolation, and she was ruining it.

I started having defensive feelings, something I hadn't experienced for years. Defensive feelings! Like I had anything left to defend! I found myself nursing suspicions that this girl was coming in to spy on me so that she could giggle about me later with her friends, which didn't make any sense, anyway, because this girl obviously wasn't the giggling type.

Gloria. Her name was Gloria, which I knew now, because I'd started noticing when she said "Present" in roll call, her arm rising in that perfectly controlled way, like her hand was affixed to a pulley and being smoothly counterweighted toward the ceiling. Terrifying.

Android Gloria and I had AP English, Honors Chemistry, and seventh-period Calculus together. I'd also started seeing her in the hallways, her thin hair scraped back into that excruciatingly tight-looking bun, her expression smooth and blank like a makeup model's. Vague memories of her had returned to me, mostly of Mrs. Molina beaming at her and congratulating her on test results.

In Chemistry, Gloria sat with Ellis Whatever, who whispered in her ear the whole time. Gloria rarely responded, but she did smile sometimes, the corners of her mouth drawing outward by a matter of millimeters. The smile came nowhere near the fearful eyes. There was something uncoordinated about it, like her body was running on two separate operating systems.

This was Gloria's routine at the store: She came in every weekday just after 6:00 p.m., did a circuit through the shelves, and then, books in hand, glided down the aisle with the velvet chair. I didn't appreciate the weird satisfaction I felt when she entered on schedule.

The fifth time she came in, the pattern broke. After she walked in, she glanced toward me. I couldn't look back down at my book quickly enough. Our eyes met. She stopped dead in front of the door.

Years at Fisherton High had taught me to hold my ground. I glared mulishly back at her.

There was something uncanny about the way she was looking at me. After several interminable seconds, I realized what it was. She had on one of those scoop-neck T-shirts that all the girls at school wore, and thanks to the tissue-thin material, I could see how still her torso was, so motionless that I realized she wasn't breathing. She was standing there, holding her breath, like she expected me to shoot her.

I blinked first. Immediately, she turned and strode down the history aisle. The back of her neck was red with sunburn, and the silver necklace drew a thin line across it. Even as I watched, she adjusted it a millimeter, so that its clasp was precisely centered on the nub of her vertebra.

She crossed my sightline one more time, carrying two battered textbooks, and vanished back into the fiction aisle.

I stared down at *Outline* and couldn't find my way into the next sentence. Another irritating thing about Gloria: She distracted me from my reading.

Usually I tore through three or four books a week. When I read fast enough, the momentum made me weirdly hypersensitive to words.

Come Home to My Heart

The world inside each book became so vivid that every drab element of my life evaporated, like a shadow under bright light. The magic worked on Fisherton, too. When I read the way I wanted to, the town existed only in rare moments of interruption, startling me out of the pages once or twice a day to remind me that I was trapped inside a body and pinned to a map.

I pushed my glasses up, held *Outline* in front of my face, and pushed onward until I found a rhythm.

The bell rang fifty minutes later. I glanced up and felt my stomach drop.

Mr. Avery was bouncing through the door, always shockingly spry for someone in his seventies. He was big and round-faced and dark-skinned, with white clouds of beard and hair, like a Black Karl Marx in faded denim. I'd forgotten that it was Wednesday, and he was due to stop in at seven.

"Ah!" he declared, blinking rapidly as if it were a shock to see me. He made a little wave-salute in my direction. "Xia."

I lowered *Outline*. "Hey, Mr. Avery."

He chuckled. Tufts of his beard shivered. "How many times? Lawrence, call me Lawrence."

I sighed as he approached. He must have known by this point that I was never going to call him Lawrence. Before I could answer, though, he glanced down the fiction aisle and halted, his friendly expression collapsing into suspicion.

"Young lady," he called. "What are those?"

Paper rustled down the aisle. "Chemistry textbooks, sir," said Gloria, out of sight, soft and cautious.

Mr. Avery's eyes narrowed into slits. "And have—"

I spoke before I knew what I was doing. "She's fine. She bought those earlier."

"Oh!" Mr. Avery's smile flooded back, making his wrinkles bunch up. "Sorry to interrupt, then. And thank you very much for your patronage!" He sidled up to the desk. As always, he smelled strongly of wood varnish. I prayed he wouldn't ask me to open the register, which had precisely no dollars inside.

He looked fondly around at the store and said, "Everything good here?"

I shrugged.

"School going all right?"

"It's okay."

Mr. Avery drummed his fingers on the desk. "This place is going to miss you next year. Sally Hopewell always asks after you when I see her. Always wants to know how you're doing."

I shifted in my seat. "Um, right." Mrs. Hopewell was an older woman who came in every week and bought everything I recommended, which was weirdly flattering. Still, I had no idea why she cared about how I was doing.

"How about you skip college and stay here?" My horror must have shown on my face, because Mr. Avery laughed. "Only joking! I'm joking. But when you're back for the summer, you've got my number."

I did, in fact, have his number. Mr. Avery texted me my schedule on the first Monday of the month. For the remainder of the month, he sent me enormous quantities of book-related memes. I never answered, but I did occasionally hit thumbs-up on some of the better ones.

"What schools are you considering?" he asked.

On another day, I might have answered that question, but Gloria was still sitting in the fiction aisle, and I didn't want the fact that I was applying to several women's colleges circulating at school. "I'm still making my list," I mumbled.

Come Home to My Heart

"Good, good. It's a big decision, take your time. Let me know if you want me to read your essays. I used to work in college admissions, you know."

"Really?"

"Sure did! Up in North Carolina. That was before admissions turned into this bloodbath, but I could still be some help. Say the word."

I bit my cheek, suddenly wondering. What if I asked Mr. Avery to write one of my recommendations?

"What's that look?" he asked.

I looked away. "Sorry. Nothing." Better to stick with my original plan—to ask Mr. Gillen, my English teacher last year, and Ms. Barringer, who'd taught me Physics. Neither of them had shown any indication of liking me as a person, but who cared? I'd had spotless grades in their classes. That was more reliable than trying to guess whether somebody really liked me or was just being polite.

Mr. Avery cleared his throat with a little rumble. "All right, well, let's talk inventory. Did you see the Willow Books catalog? The new Brant Bonner's out in March."

"Yeah, I ordered eight or nine of those, and a couple of his backlist..."

While we talked, part of me remained aware of Gloria sitting around the corner. She could have heard every word if she wanted.

I didn't like the feeling. Usually I could relax when I was talking to Mr. Avery. I wasn't going to call him *Lawrence*, but I didn't filter myself around him, either.

Now I caught sentences transforming on their way out of my mouth. I dodged questions about school and my family even more vigorously than usual, but weirdly, when he asked what I'd thought of *My Brilliant Friend*, I found myself giving a long, detailed response. Halfway through a sentence about the relationship between autofiction and imagination, I thought, *Why am I saying this?* Yet I kept talking, unable to stop. As Mr. Avery nodded at me in that fond way he sometimes did, I found myself wondering whether Gloria was listening, and whether she would think I was smart or just hideously pretentious.

"So," Mr. Avery said, "you think telling a story about yourself is always reinventing yourself, then?"

"I mean, it kind of has to be, right? No one remembers things perfectly. Lots of people have totally misleading memories. And if you're writing about somebody else, it's twice as imaginary, since interpreting other people is just like a wild stab in the dark. You're making everything up."

"That's a big claim. Don't you think you could describe your reality?"

I hesitated. "This feels like a trap."

Mr. Avery laughed, and made some comparisons to the Impressionists, and I was just realizing I was actually halfway enjoying the conversation when he checked his watch and made his goodbyes.

The store was quiet. Frowning, abruptly self-conscious, I flipped *Outline* open again and tried to focus on the next paragraph.

I'd only read the first few words when footsteps made me look up.

Gloria stopped in front of the desk holding the chemistry textbooks. She'd never come so close to the desk before. She had on frayed cutoffs and flip-flops, and random bruises patched her shins and thighs, like the ones I always found on my legs without knowing where they'd come from. I spared a glance at her face. At this distance I could see how her freckles bled into the edges of her pale lips.

"Thanks for doing that," she said. Every word was clipped, precise, radio-ready. But there was a muted quality to her voice, too, as if she were keeping it captive in the back of her throat.

I looked down and watched my hands close my book. "Yeah. Sure."

She slid the textbooks onto the desk. "Can you tell him I returned these, or will he get mad at you?"

"Those are used. We don't do returns on used books."

Gloria's eyes fixed on the price stickers. Her body took on that complete motionlessness again, unblinking, unbreathing. Watching her, I felt like someone had hit pause on the world.

Then she drew her wallet from a pocket in her backpack and looked down into it like someone gauging the jump off a cliff. And I found myself muttering, "Don't worry about it."

"What?"

"Put it away. You don't have to drop like twenty dollars on those because I couldn't think up a better lie."

When she didn't react, I sighed, fished my billfold out of my jacket, and stuck two tens in the register. Then I shoved the books toward her. "There."

She picked them up. She was regarding me curiously now. "Thank you."

"Yeah, whatever," I mumbled, aware that I was being an idiot. *Don't feed the cat*, said my dad's voice in the back of my head, but all I could see was the look on her face as she'd stared into her wallet.

"How's your book?" she asked.

"What?"

"That book." Her eyes fell to *Outline*. "Is it good?"

"Oh. Yeah."

"What's it about?"

I shrugged. "A woman. A writer. She's traveling. It's . . ." I trailed off. I could see what I was about to say as if it were written down. *It's mostly people talking to the narrator, or at her, so that she's almost excluded from the conversations she's having, she's kind of perceived as other people's blank page.* But this girl was probably just asking to be polite. "Yeah, it's good," I muttered.

Gloria waited, expectant, as if she could tell I'd mentally deleted everything I was about to say. Eventually, she said, "I don't know how you have time to read on top of all the work we have."

Even though the words sounded like small talk, there was something alien in the way she casually said "we," *the work we have—* as if she and I occupied the same universe. She, this girl who glided through the halls with crowds of friends and made announcements for club meetings after school. And then me.

"I work fast," I said.

"I know. You always finish first in class." She knelt and zipped the books into her backpack. Her fingers were long, her nails neat ovals.

This is my chance, I thought. She owed me for the books. I could say that I wouldn't risk my job for her again, and if she expected to keep doing this, forget it, she shouldn't bother coming back.

More than that, I somehow knew that it would work. One sentence from me and I'd never see her here again. She'd evaporate as quickly as she'd appeared, and I could return to flying through books undistracted, and she could return to being a normal girl who didn't just fit in at Fisherton High School but matched the monolith of that place down to the eyelash, blond and pretty and visibly Christian. She'd lose her reading spot, but so what? Didn't she have the rest of the world?

Didn't she?

As she rose to her feet, I wondered for the first time why she was here every night.

"I'm Gloria," she said. "I'll see you at school."

I watched her go for the door. A wisp of hair hung beside the curve of her cheek. When her hand was on the knob, I said, "He comes in every Wednesday at seven. And he works all day on Saturdays."

She turned back with that mechanical smoothness. One side of her mouth moved. It wasn't even half of the tyrannically repressed smile she sometimes gave to her friend. There was no change in her eyes, which were gray, irises like full moons.

"I'll remember," she said.

When she was gone, I put my head down on the desk. I was going to regret this.

Gloria Forman

The day was almost over, and the sick feeling was coming back into me like a bad memory.

It was something between nausea and nerves, and it always set in near the end of seventh period, when everyone began to sneak their notebooks into their backpacks. But Mrs. Molina was strict. She heard the buzz of a zipper and whipped away from the whiteboard. "Did you hear the bell?" she demanded, looking from face to guilty face. "No? Then why are you packing up?"

The classroom went motionless again. My stomach settled with the others' bodies.

"Thank you," said Mrs. Molina. "Now. T equals . . ." Her eyes fell on me. "Gloria?"

"Eighteen," I said, and she smiled. For that instant, the churning in my gut stopped. I wasn't looking at the clock. I was fully in the moment, like there was no future, let alone one I was responsible for. I could have sat in that room and answered questions forever.

Thank you, Lord, I thought, *for this much to hold on to.*

Riley Redgate

At the nine-day mark, I wrote my parents another letter. It shouldn't have taken me almost a week and a half to realize it, but my first note had been too short. I obviously hadn't explained myself properly.

This letter would be more comprehensive. I turned on my sleeping bag so that the light landed square on the paper and made the gray lines of writing gleam.

I'd chosen not to tell them where I was staying. Written down, the situation sounded worse than it really was, and seeming as if I was begging for help wouldn't ingratiate me to them.

So I also didn't mention that my cash had already dwindled down to fifty-four dollars, courtesy of my period hitting this week and my needing more pads. I didn't say how humiliating it had felt, hiking my leg over the bathroom sink to get myself clean. I didn't mention that my deodorant stick was running down to its plastic frame, or that the orchestra pit was getting colder by the night.

Instead, what I had written was this:

Dear Mom and Dad,

I hope you've been doing okay this past week and a half. I keep thinking about how upset and worried you were the night I left home, and I want to say I understand that. I understand why you've needed this time to process. And I hope you haven't been worrying about me. I still have my safe place to sleep, my grades are the same as usual, and I'm almost done with my college essays. These past two Sundays I went to Fisherton Faith Church, just around the corner from school. The services are sweet, but a little lukewarm. I prefer Pastor Collins and First Baptist, of course.

Come Home to My Heart

I know you still might not trust me, but I'm ready to come home and do everything I can to fix this together. This experience hasn't been easy, but it's given me the perspective you were trying to show me. Thinking back on what I threw away has taught me so many valuable lessons, and having Christ to turn to has reminded me of everything that's really important.

The paragraph after that, though, was tripping me up. I'd known this would be the hard part, so I was writing it out on a separate sheet. The sheet was covered in first sentences.

I'm so sorry about what you saw, but I want you to know I'm still the same person, even if I have thoughts about

I'm sorry about what you saw, but you should know I've never acted on any thoughts that

I'm sorry that I've thought about

None of it was right. Saying sorry didn't feel good enough. Aunt Jen had begged for my parents' forgiveness during their fight, apologizing for lying and sinning and all the rest. But at the end of the day, she'd still been pregnant. Nothing had changed.

Maybe that was the key. I had to convince them that I could still change, still turn into the person they'd always thought I was.

I put my pencil back to the paper.

I'm sorry about what I did, and I want you to know that mistake doesn't represent the person I'm growing up to be. I'm praying for guidance night and day, I still have the good values you taught me, and I'll never follow that lifestyle. Like I said, I'm still going to church every Sunday and it's still the most important thing in the world to me. All I want to do is grow with you as a member of this family and a child of God.

I sat back. That was it. I knew my parents, and that was what they'd want to read.

They'd also taught me to be honest, though, and what I'd written wasn't the entire truth. The truth was, if I hadn't managed it after this long, I was pretty sure I'd never be able to stop having these feelings. The truth was, when I'd watched all those PG-13 movies they'd approved, starring good girls in safe situations with good, safe boys, I'd only ever imagined myself standing across from those girls as they looked into my eyes. The truth was how I felt when I imagined those things, the plunge inside me, the wash of cold and brilliant heat, like a whole day of high fever compressed into a single violent pulse.

The truth was, I didn't want to be wanted if it didn't feel like that.

◊

When I got off the bus the next day, Friday, I opened our mailbox with trembling fingers. Letter in hand, I looked up at the sky, thinking, *God forgive me.*

Was this dishonest? Trying to convince them I could change, when I wasn't even sure of that myself?

I stood there until I felt time pressing down on me. The library was closed most of the weekend; I needed this hour for my World History essay. I slid the note into the mailbox and walked up the street, moving quickly so I couldn't change my mind.

Come Home to My Heart

Everything I wrote is true, I told myself. My faith *was* still the most important thing to me. When I prayed, I didn't just feel comforted and protected, but strong, too, and capable. Mom always described her faith as a North Star in the night, something she could follow back to the right path when she strayed, but I felt like mine was a compass deep inside my chest. Sometimes that needle wobbled, but if I just prayed hard enough, I could steady it onto the right path. In that way, believing in something bigger than myself was an act of self-determination.

Thunder chased me into downtown. Heavy clouds hung overhead, and by the time I left the library for the Book Alley, a fine haze of mist had lowered over the rooftops.

Set in my usual velvet chair, I worked sluggishly, unable to focus. My stomach began to rumble, and I set the heel of my hand to my abdomen, tried to massage the discomfort away. A week and a half of this, and I still wasn't used to working through dinnertime.

My mind drifted to the letter in its metal can, waiting for my parents. Sometimes our mail got damp—would the drizzle make the words run? Maybe I should reconstruct a second copy tonight from my drafts and deliver it tomorrow, just to be safe . . .

"Hey," said a voice.

I looked up. Xia Harper stood at the end of the aisle, tall and surly, black jacket slung over her shoulder. She stood with a pronounced slump in her shoulders, head cocked to the side.

I no longer spent every evening expecting her to kick me out, but it was still impossible to look at her without feeling intimidated. Cold disdain was fixed into her facial features. Her dark eyes were diamond hard and always a bit narrowed, and they roved over me as if she were mentally ripping me apart.

"Hi," I said.

"It's eight ten. We're closed."

"Oh, gosh." I stood quickly. "I'm sorry, I didn't realize." I flitted around the shop, sliding books back into their gaps, as Xia fished through a key ring.

My heart sank as I approached the exit. I could hear the rain before I'd even opened the door. As it swung wide, the sound of the storm roared into the shop. Outside, puddles like lakes rode up over the edges of the sidewalk, their surfaces pockmarked by thousands of simultaneous droplets. I could make out streetlamps only faintly through the water, struggling ovals of light.

I wandered out into the alley, where runoff poured in a near-solid sheet from the overhang. *No*, I thought uselessly. I'd have to wait here until the storm ended—my backpack wasn't waterproof—and there was no ignoring the jabs of hunger now, like someone was sending the point of their elbow into my gut. I hadn't had a bite since noon. How long would I have to stand here before I could get to the convenience store and eat something?

Something brushed my arm. I jerked back and got a faceful of rain. Xia's backpack had touched my bicep, but luckily she hadn't noticed my reaction. She was still working on the door's three ancient locks, muttering something at one of them. I stood at the edge of the overhang, hugging my bag, wet gusts blowing droplets onto my cheek.

Xia shoved the keys into her pocket. She moved like a butcher, rough and efficient. I expected her to disappear into the rain without a word, but she turned to me and said, "Where's your ride?"

"I usually walk home."

"Well. Might want to call your parents."

I opened my mouth to lie that my phone was broken, but I caught myself. If she offered me hers, I'd have no excuse not to make a call.

Come Home to My Heart

Before I could think up something else, she let out a short breath. "Whatever, I can drive you." She pointed to a dim shape hovering at the edge of the street. "That's me. Ready?"

"I—what?"

"Go." She ran for it.

I hunched over my backpack and threw myself into the downpour, too, splashing over the sidewalk. Xia was barely visible ahead. The Zombie Pontiac slowly emerged before us, the storm waterfalling off its hood. I plunged ankle-deep into a puddle to reach the passenger side, and by the time we got in, I felt as if I'd just stepped out of a bath.

I palmed water off my face, glancing around. I'd expected the car to be trashed, but it was meticulously clean, although the stale musk of cigarettes clung to the old leather.

Xia tossed her bag into the back seat and shook her hood down. Dots of rain were caught in her dark hair, like beads of water on a raven's wing. She twisted the key in the ignition once, twice. "Come on," she muttered.

The engine turned over with an exhausted roar. Looking satisfied, Xia yanked the stick and plowed us out onto the street. I squinted through the windshield, which was permanently fogged at the edges, and felt as if we were driving through a river.

"Where am I going?" she asked.

"You can drop me near the school. I live right by there."

Xia didn't bother to make conversation as she drove. I faced stiffly forward, sneaking occasional looks at her out of the corner of my eye. She kept a one-handed grip on the wheel and her eyes on the road. Rain still rolled down the leather of her jacket.

I didn't understand why she was doing this. At school, everyone knew that the best you could hope for with Xia Harper was to be coldly ignored during group projects. Back in freshman year, when she'd first moved to Fisherton, some kids had gotten it in their heads that she was just sad and troubled, and they'd approached her, meaning to break through her tough exterior. She'd spoken so viciously to some of them that she'd reduced them to tears.

So why offer me a ride? Why lie to her boss to get me out of trouble? When we'd spoken afterward, she'd stared at her novel as if wishing I'd evaporate, but I'd hardly finished calculating what those textbooks would cost me in food when she'd paid for them. It was like I'd escaped the blanket hatred she seemed to feel for everyone at school, but I didn't know how.

Maybe I'd earned respect in her eyes by spending so much time in a bookshop. I decided never to tell her that I hadn't read for fun since I was eight years old.

When Mr. Avery had come in on Wednesday, I hadn't been able to keep from eavesdropping. Mostly Xia had been as curt and reluctant as she was in school. But then they'd started on about that book she'd been reading, and it was like someone else had started speaking in her voice. She talked like the articles we read for English sometimes, the ones by critics who referenced so many other books and ideas that I felt like I'd need another ten years' school to fully understand their points. She sounded so grown-up that it embarrassed me; it made me feel embarrassed for our whole class. That girl was sitting in the back of our classrooms, watching us gossip and joke, while that kind of analysis was happening inside her head.

Yesterday, when I'd seen her slumped over in the Chemistry classroom, ignored by everyone as usual, I'd felt weirdly envious. Maybe I did understand something about her: that she could do whatever she wanted. I understood that nothing worse could happen to her than what she'd already invited.

Come Home to My Heart

We stopped at a red light. The storm hammered on the roof, but it didn't fill the silence. I snuck another look at Xia. In the rain, the red glow flickered over her face like firelight. I felt a sharp discomfort like another hunger pang.

There was no reason to feel uncomfortable, though. She couldn't figure out I was sleeping at school just from dropping me off nearby. In fact, I should be grateful for this stroke of luck.

"Thank you for this," I said.

"You've got to stop thanking me for stuff."

"Then maybe you should stop doing nice things."

"Yeah, probably," she said, like this was not a new thought to her. "Fuck, I'm hungry. I'm going to drive in here, one second."

I flinched at the cussword. "What?"

She pointed through her window. Up the block, the McDonald's sign glowed. It was pretty when you couldn't really see it, turning columns of rain into gold.

"It'll be five minutes," she said.

"Right. Okay."

We pulled into the drive-through. "What do you want?" she asked.

"I'm fine."

She looked up at the ceiling of the car. "Just tell me. I got it."

I clasped my hands tight in my lap and felt ashamed. As we'd pulled up, I'd remembered Wednesday, and the books, and part of me had secretly hoped this would happen. With the hot-oil smell wafting through the window, my hunger had grown so intense that I felt like part of me had been scooped out in surgery.

After our order came through the window, I said, "We should park here."

"Why?"

"It's not safe to drive and eat in this."

"Oh. Sure." She looked amused. "Safety first."

Xia sat the Pontiac in the lot. I had an enormous, grease-slick Quarter Pounder in my lap and fries bursting out of their carton. At first I tried to make myself eat one fry at a time, not wanting her to see how hungry I was, but then I saw that Xia was cramming six in her mouth at one go. She took new bites before she'd swallowed the first. My mom would have said she ate like a pig, but occasionally she stopped and licked the salt off her mouth and made a little sound like *mm*, looking happier than I'd ever seen her. There was something nice about the way she let herself enjoy it.

I let myself speed up too, first two fries, then three. They tasted impossibly good, so decadent it almost felt wrong. I was licking the grease off my fingers when I felt Xia's eyes on me. I put my hand down quickly, a lump forming high and hard in my throat.

"So," she said. "What's your deal?"

"My deal?"

"Why are you always in the store."

"I come there after the library closes."

"Right." She downed another couple of fries. I waited for her to tell me I hadn't really answered her question, but she didn't push.

I hesitated, then asked, "Do you like working there?"

"Yeah."

"Oh," I said. "Hm."

"What, should I not like my job?"

"You don't seem to like many things."

At that, Xia cracked a smile. It was lopsided, mostly showing teeth on the right side of her mouth. "True," she said, "but, you know, what's to like?"

"There's plenty to like here."

Come Home to My Heart

She barked out a laugh. "Yeah, I'm sure, when you're the Homecoming Court type."

My cheeks grew warm. I lifted my chin. "So, what you're saying is, you kept track of who made Homecoming Court."

She chortled again. "Yep, wrote all the names in my diary in glitter gel pen."

I looked at her in disbelief. That had been an actual joke. And she was laughing at jokes I was making, even if her laughs did sound dismissive.

I felt like I was having a bizarre dream. Was I really sitting in the Zombie Pontiac, having a back-and-forth with Xia Harper? And it was a normal conversation. She hadn't offered me drugs, like half a dozen people at school claimed she'd done to them. She hadn't even said anything insulting yet. Derisive tone or not, reminding me that I'd been on Homecoming Court definitely didn't count as an insult.

"Maybe," I said, "you'd like school better if you joined a club or something."

"Doubt it. Me joining a club isn't going to change the general school atmosphere of, you know, dead-eyed conformity enforced by recreational totalitarians."

I frowned. "Oh, right, and completely disengaging from the school *is* going to change the atmosphere of dead-eyed conformity."

Xia's gaze played curiously over my face. "No, obviously not. But it will make my life a lot easier."

I didn't understand how anyone could think it was *easier* to go through life without any friends, but clearly there was a lot I didn't understand about this girl. For one thing, I'd expected someone with her reputation to act mutinous and angry. Ellis had been paired up with her in Biology last year, and she'd told me Xia communicated mostly by grunting. So far this didn't match at all. Her husky voice was low, but it was confident and expressive, too.

Also, people had teased Jason Knox for weeks after he'd suggested she was pretty, but I didn't think he was wrong, exactly. Once you got over the shock of that critical stare, magnified through her glasses, there was something about her that made it hard to look away.

I closed my empty burger carton. I hadn't been so comfortably full in a week and a half, and my thoughts felt clearer. "Okay. So you hate our school. Was your old one really that much better?"

Xia shrugged. "I mean, it was middle school, but yeah."

"Where'd you move from?"

"Atlanta."

I blinked. "That's not even that far."

"Have you ever been?"

"I've never been out of South Carolina."

Her eyebrows rose, and I steeled myself for a snide jab. But she just said, "Atlanta could basically be a million light-years away."

"It's that different?"

Xia fixed her mouth around her straw, took a long pull of her milkshake, and nodded.

"Like how?" I asked.

She kept drinking from her milkshake. I could see the chocolate ice cream inside the straw sliding up at an excruciatingly slow pace. Finally, she said, "Everyone in this town cares so much what everyone else is like."

The statement sounded sophisticated somehow, mature and objective. Again, I felt embarrassed, like she knew more about everything than me, to a degree that maybe I couldn't even conceive of, never having been farther from home than Columbia.

"You don't think people should care about each other?" I asked.

"That's not what I meant." She set down the milkshake and examined me. I touched my bun and my hairline. For an instant, her eyes followed my fingers. Then she said, "You're kind of difficult, aren't you?"

"Maybe you just say a lot of things that need clearing up."

"Maybe." Her eyes glinted with amusement. "Well, I'm saying, people here care a lot about whether you play soccer versus football, or where you have a piercing, like any of that makes you a better or worse person. It'd be great if they cared more about if other people were happy."

"And what if it makes you happy to be a terrible person?" I said without thinking.

Even as the question came out, I realized that it sounded like I was talking about her.

My face heated right up. I knew I'd gone bright red, which was even worse, because it would seem to confirm it.

This was Xia Harper, though. She wouldn't care. I waited for her to shrug or sneer or put me in my place.

Instead, her lips contracted, and something happened in her eyelids that made her look confused. She crumpled the napkin in her lap and held on to it for a second. Then she said, "I'll, um, drive you back. The rain's a bit better."

My heart beat hard as we drove. I finished eating the fries, which were going cold. I felt worse with each one.

She stopped around the block from the school. As the car sat back, I said in one breath, "I didn't mean you. I wasn't talking about you. I don't think you're a terrible person."

Xia turned off the engine. Maybe it was the darkness, but she didn't look so cold or disdainful then. "Sweet. That makes one person."

She said it like a joke, but I thought I heard bitterness in her voice.

I lifted my backpack into my lap but didn't reach for the door. I felt like I understood her even less now than when I'd gotten into her car. How could Xia feel bitter about everyone thinking she was a terrible person when she'd spent so much time and effort making it happen? And even if I *had* thought she was terrible, why should my opinion hurt her? People said outright mean things to her at school and she never let on like she cared. Sometimes she even seemed to relish it, snarling back with vicious satisfaction like a mountain lion about to end a fight.

Xia broke the silence. "I swear, if you're about to thank me for the ride and the food . . ."

I smiled, surprising myself. "You'll do what?"

Her mouth twitched. Several tiny granules of salt were clinging to her lower lip. "I'll think of something," she said.

After a second, I realized I was still looking at her mouth.

A cold feeling shot down through me, and at once I tore my eyes from her.

My questions shriveled, my curiosity evaporating, as the whole car ride thudded horribly into perspective. I'd had dinner with a girl alone on a Friday night. For the past twenty minutes I'd done nothing but think about where she was looking, and when I could look at her so she wouldn't notice, and what she thought of me, and the way she ate and the sounds she made, and the shape of her smile, and the darkness of her eyes behind her glasses.

My discomfort hadn't been fear that she'd figure out where I was sleeping. It had been the sensation of something tightening in my chest, like a pulled muscle, when she looked at me the way she was now: that keen, narrowed look.

I felt a rush of shame and anger. *Just look back at her*, I told myself—*just look back at her like anyone else would*—but I couldn't do it.

Come Home to My Heart

In that moment I felt more alone than I had for ten days, maybe more alone than I ever had in my life. As much of an outcast as Xia was, she could still fit in with the rest of the world in a way I never could. Other girls could have conversations over dinner like this and feel nothing but friendly interest. Other girls fantasized about how guys might ask them to prom, or agonized over kissing the wrong boys at parties; even Xia had spent a good while in sophomore year hooking up with some senior guy. Other girls at school played with each other's hair and kissed each other's cheeks, and at sleepovers undressed around each other, without the feeling of standing frozen in headlights. Ten years and I hadn't even been able to train myself into the smallest thing on the list.

I knew then that I was going to tiptoe through my entire life with my breath held, locking doors left and right, trying to keep myself at bay.

The storm slammed down on the car roof. Not even five hours ago, I'd put that letter in my parents' mailbox promising I'd do better. It was probably soaked through now, and unreadable.

Tonight I'd rewrite that letter, and with every word, I'd rededicate myself to its contents. I *would* do better. I *was* learning my lesson. When I felt hungry this weekend, scraping the bottom of those mac and cheese tubs, and when my body ached in the night from the concrete floor, I'd remember why all this was happening: because of my own bad choices.

On Monday at 6:00 p.m., I'd go straight back to school from the library. This would never happen again.

"Good night," I said. My voice sounded cold. I shut the door too hard and walked fast into the rain.

Xia Harper

The Saturday after the storm was long, lazy, and deeply unproductive.

In late afternoon, I made a sound of disgust and tossed yet another book aside. I'd read the same paragraph seven times in a row, and still, the only words I'd processed were *the* and *have*. Not useful.

The stack of discarded books ran the gamut from teen rom-coms to Ocean Vuong. Apparently, I couldn't read *anything* right now, which felt similar to not being able to breathe or blink.

Reclining in the window seat, I closed my eyes. The sunlight settled on my forehead and began to tickle. Last night's storm had rolled out this morning, leaving steam to rise from the asphalt all through town. When I'd gone out to smoke at dawn, it had been like walking through a battalion of ghosts.

For a while I listened to the hum of faraway appliances. Nobody was home; my mom had gone to Myrtle Beach again.

Usually I relished these weekends alone. Mom always left money on the counter for me to order pizza, and she didn't roll back in until late on Sunday afternoons. Over dinner I'd ask how Dad was, and she'd tell me he was fine, and the silence hanging over the table would feel almost companionable. Maybe, I thought on those nights, we were actually a normal family, and I'd tricked myself into thinking we were uniquely dysfunctional when in fact we were totally banal.

So weekends were heaven, usually. But today had been a wash. I kept getting caught on the memory of last night, replaying how Gloria had said "good night" before slamming the door and disappearing out of my headlights.

I thought I was pretty good at reading people. I was alone all the time, yeah, but I wasn't clueless. I knew that in order to get people to like you, you were supposed to cater to them in some way, and the method of catering varied from person to person. Sometimes, if the person was really awful, they wouldn't warm up to you until you acted deferent in some way, fawning over some aspect or talent of theirs and subjugating yourself in comparison, so they could be "friends" with you in a way that allowed them to maintain the upper hand at all times.

Other people just wanted to be acknowledged. You didn't have to share their opinions on music or sports or politics; you just had to show that you accepted what mattered to them. People didn't want to be picked apart or diminished, didn't want to feel like they were living the wrong way. Knowing these basic facts had made it very easy to estrange everyone at school.

I hadn't been trying to estrange Gloria, though. Actually, I had no idea what I'd done wrong, which was annoying. Usually I did all my wrong things on purpose.

I went back over what I'd said: *I swear, if you're about to thank me for the ride and the food . . .* I knew that hadn't been the thing that spooked her, because the corners of her mouth had drawn out into her freckled cheeks in the closest thing to a real smile I'd seen, and she'd said, *You'll do what?*

Come Home to My Heart

I'll think of something, I'd told her.

Why had that made her smile disappear? What had it set loose inside her head?

"Jesus Christ," I muttered, standing up from the window seat. This was ridiculous. I needed to distract myself with food.

But as I chopped onions and listened to Europop and simmered chicken in tomato sauce, I started to feel paranoid. What if she'd somehow figured out I was lesbian from those four words?

I'll think of something . . . It could have sounded flirtatious. I'd even felt a bit daring at the time to say it.

Still, it wasn't like I'd twirled my hair around my finger and batted my eyelashes, and the sentence wasn't more inherently flirtatious than what she'd said to prompt it.

You'll do what?

When she'd said that, I'd felt an unfamiliar, pleasurable tingling in my face and hands. It was almost funny. A real girl had said those words to me. Cluelessly, sure, but she'd said them. Someday, when I was out of this place forever, I would meet a girl who would say something like that and she would actually be flirting with me. And then maybe I *would* twirl my hair or bat my eyelashes, and I'd say, *I'll think of something,* and she would know what I meant.

◊

On Monday, I figured I'd be able to gauge within thirty seconds whether Gloria had figured out I was lesbian, because she would tell Ellis, who would proceed to tell everyone else in the known universe. So when I made it through first period with everyone as uninterested in me as they had been last week, I knew I was safe.

Halfway through second period, though, I caught myself checking the clock every few minutes. Gloria was in my next class.

I didn't know what I expected—some explanation of the way she'd left my car? Obviously not. We'd never acknowledged each other in school. No reason she would start now.

Still, I felt tense as I slouched into my desk at the back of the Chemistry classroom. I folded my arms, rested my chin in the crook of my elbow, and glanced toward the door at the exact moment that Gloria materialized at the threshold.

Her full-moon eyes fixed on mine.

Her face turned red. The blush spread fast, like signal smoke fanned by a strong wind. It flooded across her cheeks. For a long moment we just stared at each other.

Then I looked down at the desk, at the stubble of pencil marks across the wood. A heated weight bore down on my stomach. I felt conscious of my appearance with an impossible intensity, aware of how my legs stretched out across the aisle, and where my fingertips dug into my biceps, and where my jacket left pressure lines against my skin. It felt like the day I'd found a spectacular zit on my chin and walked into school feeling painfully conspicuous, as if my entire face were emitting light and nobody would have any choice but to stare at me.

But no one was looking at me. To everyone else, nothing had happened at all.

Gloria glided into her seat two aisles over. She didn't look at me again for the rest of the period, but I kept glancing at her. It took ten full minutes for the pink color to fade from her face, her ears, the sides of her neck.

At lunch I chain-smoked without really wanting to. Something in me had gone hyperactive, and I needed to feel like my brain could catch up. Lying on the bench in the dugout, knocking one foot hard against the wall, I saw the curve of her cheek, the warm redness behind her freckles.

Come Home to My Heart

So she *did* know I was lesbian. The full-face blush had to mean she knew.

I hadn't considered this possibility: being out to someone in Fisherton who wouldn't tell the whole town like it was their God-given command. And speaking of God, I was surprised Gloria didn't think it was her religious imperative to let everyone know that I followed the homosexual lifestyle.

Then I felt bad for thinking that. Gloria had been nice to me, and talking with her in the car had been weirdly fun. She was quick, curious. She'd taken everything I'd said in stride, and her questions had made me think twice about myself, about Fisherton, about her.

She was more interesting than I'd thought she'd be. *And* she was keeping my secret, even from the best friend.

That made her the first real candidate for friendship I'd ever had here.

The idea unnerved me. Gloria had in her back pocket something that, at any time, could drop a bomb on my carefully ordered existence. But then, that was how it worked, wasn't it? Real friendship was always an open contract, and anyone at any time could humiliate the other person, and we all just had to trust each other not to.

Maybe I can trust her, I thought as I headed back across the baseball field.

But in English class and then in Calculus, Gloria didn't look at me once, and I started feeling irritated with myself. The only positive signal she'd given was deciding not to summarily ruin my life. Probably she had no interest in being friends, or thought I was a moral abomination, or was grossed out by the idea of a girl being attracted to her.

I would have liked to argue this last point. Obviously I wasn't attracted to all girls just because they were girls. But Gloria was actually very attractive, so guilty as charged.

Sitting in the back of the Calculus classroom, I let my gaze stray to the back of her neck. The silver chain, the fading pink sunburn, the flex of her muscles as she tilted her face toward the window.

I looked down at my worksheet, my palms suddenly damp, and told myself, *No*. So what if she was nice to look at? That was irrelevant to all this.

Just be patient, I told myself. We'd never talked in school. Maybe I could bring the subject up when she came to the store later.

At the Book Alley, I spent the first two hours of my shift wondering how to phrase things delicately. When six o'clock came, I sat up straighter behind the register and stopped even pretending to read.

I wanted to say something. I could admit that much to myself: I wanted the chance to finally be honest with someone. I could tell her up front that just because I was gay, it didn't mean she had anything to worry about, I would never infringe on her boundaries or do anything to make her uncomfortable. These feelings were ringing through my whole body, so big and earnest that I felt like I needed to siphon them out somehow or else they'd magnify to the point of doing internal damage. I prearranged sentences in my head to make sure I would express myself perfectly, my thoughts accelerating until I felt almost lightheaded. I couldn't believe the feeling, like I'd held my breath too long and my vision was starting to blow.

But then it was 6:05, and then 6:10. By 6:15, I knew she wasn't coming back.

Little by little, my thoughts slowed, finally going motionless, like molecules at absolute zero.

Come Home to My Heart

At 8:00 p.m., I locked the door twice. The first time, I locked the store from the inside, so no one could come in and see me leaning back against a bookshelf, looking up at the ceiling, gulping rapid breaths and blinking so hard that I gave myself a headache deep behind my eyes. I thought of Kit, of Navya, of all the messages I fired into the world, waiting for anything to come back around. The feeling pressed in on me like the slow heat of suffocation. I was so lonely. I was really so lonely in this place.

But after twenty minutes or so, I calmed myself down, let myself out, and locked everything up behind me.

Gloria Forman

"—starting to think the black dress was kind of slutty, so I returned it, even though . . . Gloria? *Gloria.*"

"What?" I said, glancing away from the empty seat at the back of the Chemistry classroom.

Ellis was looking shrewdly at me. "What is up with you today? You look really tired."

"Oh, no, I'm just . . . I got a bad grade on an essay earlier."

Her expression softened. "Was it Mr. Barnes? He sounds like the worst."

"He's okay. It wasn't a good essay. I hate English."

"You're too hard on yourself. I'm sure it was fine." Ellis paused. I knew she was registering the breakout on my forehead, the circles under my eyes. "Hey, I never asked. How have your parents been the past couple of weeks? Is it still bumpy, with the whole Jen thing?"

I hesitated, considering the guilty patter of my heartbeat. Maybe talking to Ellis could help.

"Yeah, it's bumpy," I said quietly. "We're actually not talking right now. I said something awful to them on Friday night."

"No way. What'd you say?"

"I sort of implied my mom was a terrible person."

"What?"

"I—it was a misunderstanding. But I still feel bad." I rubbed my hands over my face, remembering Xia's confused expression. "She didn't even do anything wrong, and I slammed a door on her, and I avoided her all of yesterday evening because . . . because it's uncomfortable. And now"—I didn't let myself look back at Xia's seat—"I mean, this morning, she shut herself in her room. And I'm pretty sure it's because of me."

Ellis frowned. "Well, it could be something else. Maybe she got a bad night's sleep. Or—your mom gets sick all the time. She could be coming down with something."

Could that be it? I thought. Could Xia just be sick, or skipping class?

"I don't know. The timing doesn't seem like a coincidence."

Ellis sighed, her forehead creased sympathetically. "So you were having a bad day and hurt her feelings. You can just apologize, Glor. Is it that big of a deal?"

"It feels like a big deal."

"But why?"

"I guess . . ." My fingers found the crucifix hanging between my collarbones, the metal warm to the touch. Of course I'd had my reasons for rushing out of Xia's car on Friday, but when I subtracted my own feelings from the equation, two facts remained: She'd been nice to me, and I'd slammed a door in her face. I thought of Matthew: *I was a stranger, and you welcomed Me.*

I let go of my crucifix. "I guess the way I acted feels selfish. And I don't want to think I'm a selfish person, but my parents always say, 'Your character is who you choose to be on your worst day.' So who does that make me?"

Come Home to My Heart

Ellis arched one auburn brow. "Gloria, you're not selfish. Trust me, your mom's going to forgive you. You're every parent's dream."

At that, my throat closed completely.

I'd really thought that my parents would respond to my new letter. But four days later, nothing.

It had been two full weeks now. Two weeks of terrible sleep and unhealthy food and sink baths. How else was I supposed to show them how sorry I was?

Ellis nibbled at her lip gloss, looking concerned. Eventually, she declared, "You need to do something fun. What if you came over on Friday? We could go to that party at Anna's. Or just watch a movie or something." She gave me a teasing grin. "We can make sure to pick something parent-approved."

I made myself laugh. Ellis was Baptist, too, but her parents had never checked her browsing history or anything. She'd thought my parents' prescreening policy for movies was hilarious. It had become a running joke, but I was starting to wonder why I'd ever found it funny.

"Friday," I repeated, trying to think of any real risks in going to Ellis's. I couldn't come up with any. In fact, I thought with a sudden jolt of hope, maybe I could even sleep over. Have a normal night in a real bed. Take a real shower.

"That sounds amazing," I said. Ellis squeezed my arm, and I squeezed her wrist back. She finally seemed happy, turning away as the bell rang.

I tried to focus as Mr. Robertson started writing net ionic equations on the whiteboard, but my eyes slid back, yet again, to Xia's empty seat.

I still had this choice to make.

Shutting her out had seemed so clearly the best decision before, the obvious way to stay on the right path. But now, with her empty seat watching me, the right thing seemed hazy and uncertain. Our car ride had probably been Xia's longest conversation with any kid in Fisherton for months, if not years. That thought was sad, but it also made me feel a strange sense of pride. She seemed to think I was different from everyone else.

But I wasn't different. I'd proven that. I was just another person who'd turned my back.

My chest warmed with shame as I looked at the whiteboard, not registering the elements written in Mr. Robertson's scrawl. I wanted everything to be disentangled. I missed when I'd been able to post pictures on my blog and feel that I was really, successfully compartmentalizing how I thought about girls. But I couldn't go through my life being mean to every girl who looked at me in a way that I noticed. I had to be kind, even if I was afraid of doing something wrong.

My mouth felt dry. I closed my eyes and saw, like a photograph projected across the dark screens of my eyelids, Xia as she'd looked yesterday when I'd stopped in the classroom door. I saw her head nestled in the crook of her arm, her mile-long legs extended and crossed at her boots' buckled ankles, her dark hair shading one eye, the other fixed on me. Even the memory made heat resurge in my face.

I wished I didn't have to make this choice. I even wondered why, atop everything I was already struggling with, God had thrown her into my path like this.

Maybe that was the answer, though. We'd met for a reason. Maybe this was a test, my temptation in the desert. If I could figure out how to befriend Xia, how to be normal around her, I could use that knowledge forever. Maybe this fear meant I was about to overcome something.

◊

Come Home to My Heart

I walked into the Book Alley at six o'clock, and Xia looked up from *The Color Purple*. She froze, her long fingers fixed to one corner of her glasses.

"Hi," I said.

"Hey."

"You weren't in class today."

"I . . . yeah. I didn't feel so good." She straightened slowly in her chair and pulled at the neck of her red sweater. The color brought out the warmth in the dark, choppy layers of her hair.

There was an embarrassed silence. She looked like she was trying to decide what to say.

"What'd I miss?" she asked, and with that, she put down her book and closed it.

◊

Xia started giving me lifts back to the neighborhood by the school every night, and soon we'd found an odd sort of rhythm. Talking with her was different from talking with my other friends. In some ways, I could pin down the differences: the way Ellis spoke smoothly and steadily, following organized pathways of thought, while Xia zigzagged off in all directions. In other ways, though, I didn't know why it felt different. Because Xia did, like Ellis, ask about ordinary things like the Winter Dance.

Maybe it was just that when Xia asked about those sorts of things, it was coming from her: the girl with combat boots and a pack of cigarettes in the cup holder, who had disavowed everything in the same universe as dances. So there were layers of irony built into her questions that made me feel like we were sharing a joke. There was also the fun, silly feeling that I was contributing something exotic to her life by explaining that I was on the dance committee.

"Oh, the committee, right," she said. "What's the committee like."

"Very official," I said.

Actually, during those car rides, we talked about a lot of things I wouldn't have thought she'd be interested in. She asked me questions about church, and faith, and not in the mocking way I'd been bracing for. "Wait—so you *do* believe in evolution?" she asked once with genuine curiosity. "I thought Baptists were all creationists."

"Well, most of us are, but there are different camps. In the past few years I've gotten really interested in theistic evolution. Like, the idea that God used evolution as a tool for intelligent design, and the six days in Genesis are long, uneven periods."

"Oh. Huh. Are your parents into that, too? What about the other kids in Young Christians?"

"My parents are very literal six-day creation people. But we've got a lot of different opinions at Young Christians."

That segued into another whole batch of rapid-fire questions, first about Young Christians, then about all the other clubs I was in. Xia seemed especially interested in the social dynamics of Math Team.

"You know," I said, "if you want to join Math Team, you can just show up. We always need new people."

Xia laughed. She laughed at a lot of things I said that weren't jokes, which made me feel like I was reporting my life to an alien who had a soft spot for human beings. Adding to this feeling was the fact that when I told her about Math Team or Ellis's dramas with Aiden, Xia never related the stories back to her own life in any way. She just listened, and joked about minor details, and then suddenly went off on tangents like: "Do you think you'll still be friends with Ellis when you're forty?"

I tried to take it all in stride. "I don't know," I said. "Probably. We've been friends since we were little, and best friends since seventh grade."

Come Home to My Heart

"Why seventh grade? What happened in seventh grade?"

"I'm not sure. Wait, no, I do remember—we did this really hard project together for science class, and it was fun instead of a nightmare."

"Cool. Forged together in the crucible of struggle."

She talked like that sometimes.

"What are you smiling at?" she said, half smiling back as we rolled to a stop at a red light.

"The way you talk, is that because of books? Like, if I read more, would I say stuff like 'crucible of struggle' randomly when talking to people?"

Xia considered for a while. This time I actually had been joking, but sometimes she did this, too, giving serious answers to joke questions. "It's probably because of my mom," she said. "She came here from Hong Kong when she was eighteen, and she still has a bit of an accent, and sometimes I think she feels like she has to overcompensate so people will take her seriously, in terms of English. So sometimes she gets all like, *tendentious* this, *macroscopic* that, whatever." The light turned green, and Xia hit the gas. "But then when people comment on her vocabulary, even if they're complimentary, it gets hard to tell whether that's a loaded thing."

"A loaded thing?"

"You know. 'Oh, you have such good English for an immigrant,' clap clap, little baby.'"

"Do you ever think about that?"

"I'm not an immigrant."

"No, I know. I mean, do you think people judge you for being Chinese?"

Xia shifted her hands on the wheel. "I'm half, so it's kind of weird. You kind of feel like you get judged everywhere." She grimaced, clearly searching for words, but eventually she just shook her head. "Yeah, people say shit sometimes. It's whatever. Mostly I think they're busy judging me for other things."

"Is that why you do it?"

"Do what?"

"You know," I said. "Pretend to be mean."

She laughed as she parked the car. "I'm not pretending. I mean, what's the difference between pretending to be mean and being mean? You're doing the same thing."

I was quiet for a while. I was always hesitating during our conversations, mostly because she said things like that a lot, big, sweeping statements that seemed to demand a whole philosophical worldview from me. But Xia didn't seem to mind. She found things to do when I was quiet. She'd examine her chewed nails and chew them a bit more. Or she'd clip and unclip the leather bracelets around her wrists. Or she'd flick one of the three piercings in her ear. Or she'd move her long, dark hair from one shoulder to the other and rub unconcernedly at the slope of her neck, like she was doing now.

"I think," I said, "the difference is that when you're only pretending to be mean to people, you can stop anytime you want."

As I reached for the door handle, she grinned her lopsided grin. "Nice try. See you tomorrow."

"Oh—actually, I'm hanging out with Ellis after school tomorrow."

"Right, okay." Xia paused. "What are y'all going to do?"

"We might go to . . . you know, Anna May Turner has that birthday thing."

She feigned realization. "Ah, right, Anna's birthday thing. A party that I both knew about and was invited to."

I couldn't help a smile. "Oh, sorry, do you *want* me to invite you? Because from all our conversations, it sort of seems like you'd rather d—"

"Rather die, yeah, I would rather die."

Come Home to My Heart

We both broke into laughter, and suddenly neither of us was looking at the other. I watched my hand on the Pontiac's handle, waiting for myself to open the door. Our laughs faded, leaving a silence that rang strangely.

"Have—have a good weekend." I slipped out without looking at her again. But before I shut the door, I heard her say, a smile in her voice, "You too."

Standing on the side of the road, I watched the Pontiac's taillights go, taking a deep, cool breath. The fresh night air woke me up.

I didn't know what happened to time in that car. Yesterday we'd parked on this corner and talked for what had felt like ten minutes, and then my stomach had made an annoyed sound and Xia had told me I should probably go and take care of that, and when I'd looked at the clock on the Pontiac's dashboard, I'd seen that nearly an hour had gone by.

It wasn't that talking to her was effortless. I'd become twice as familiar with every line on my palms because I'd spent so much time studying my hands the past three days. But Xia never asked questions about my parents or home in general, and I liked that. It almost impressed me. It made me feel like she not only noticed what I wasn't saying, but that she also unquestioningly respected my reasons for keeping some truths quiet.

I was doing okay at this so far, I thought—being friends with her. As long as I didn't look at her except in short glances, and didn't focus on the low rasp in her voice when she was being ironically teasing or very serious, and held my breath when she walked by in the bookstore so I couldn't smell the faint scents of sandalwood shampoo and smoke, I could keep everything locked in a box at the back of my head.

I was figuring out how to do this, and I knew that was important. But as I stood on that curb, I imagined dozens of identical locked boxes that I would have to build over the course of my life, and suddenly I felt exhausted.

After eating at the convenience store, I retreated to the school. I followed the route that had become my usual, picking along one of the mulch dividers with their row of concealing pine trees, then cutting over to the stone steps that led up to the gym doors. Keeping in the shadow of the steps, I crept around the corner of the main building, one eye as always on the parking lot. One copper sedan sat beneath a light. Usually, as long as I got here after 9:00 p.m., the place was all but deserted, the games and activities and cleanup having finished.

But as I crept toward the greenroom windows, I heard the clank of a door opening nearby. I flattened myself against the wall, clutching my backpack straps.

Someone whistled his way down the auditorium steps: a gray-haired custodian sifting through a palmful of keys. He jogged away into the lot as I hunched down into the narrow shadow of a windowsill.

Unmoving, I watched him disappear into the copper sedan and drive off, leaving the lot deserted.

Out of nowhere, frustration and longing barreled through me. I strode to the greenroom window, pushed through, dropped onto the sofa below, and just sat there, curled up in the dark, hugging my knees to my chest. This was my senior year. I was supposed to be focused on college, on Winter Dance planning. After two and a half weeks, surely my parents had had enough time to process, talk to Pastor Collins, and figure out our next steps?

I knew I'd sinned. I knew I'd broken their trust. But we all strayed sometimes—even my parents weren't perfect. One night last March, I'd gotten home to find Dad slurring drunk, crumpled on our sofa.

Come Home to My Heart

He'd looked to me, eyes red and wet, and mumbled, "My sweet girl. Know you'll . . . never . . ."

I'd come over to him. Knelt.

His hand had patted my shoulder, soft and clumsy. "Raised you better . . . got that right."

I'd never said a word about that night, never judged him. All I needed was that same grace from him and Mom.

Didn't they want to help guide me back?

When was this going to end?

◊

I woke up to my usual alarm at six o'clock on Friday and put on my nicest dress for Anna's party, a long linen sheath in dark blue. It was my favorite, but as I slipped it on in the orchestra pit, I felt somehow embarrassed, like a little kid caught playing dress-up. The details didn't gel: ratty sneakers where I should have had my matching flats, and my hair up in this bun when it would have looked better down, and razor burn peeking out from the hem, since I wasn't about to splurge on shaving cream.

I popped open my deodorant and felt my heart sink. For the past few days, I'd been scraping out the chalky white remnants to spread onto my armpits, but the fragments were so small now that they melted against my fingertips. I considered running out to the convenience store before school to buy a new stick—but I didn't want to take a chunk out of the forty-five dollars left in my wallet.

Did I really *need* a new deodorant stick? Washing myself with hand soap had been going okay so far. I usually worked up a sweat walking to the library, but the days were cooler now that we were deep into autumn.

Before heading toward the cafeteria, I stopped by the greenroom bathroom and washed under my arms again. As I dried off with a spare T-shirt, I rubbed my armpit with the tip of my finger. The skin was slick, a little oily, but didn't smell. Satisfied, I crept up the auditorium steps and slipped out into the half-lit hallway.

As the day passed, nobody at school seemed to spot anything out of the ordinary. "Hey, girl, you ready to *par-tay* tonight?" Ellis sang as we collided going down the hall toward Chemistry.

I heard a derisive chuckle, and a second later Xia was slouching past us, her hands deep in the pockets of her canvas army jacket.

"Wow." Ellis scowled at Xia's back and raised her voice. "Sorry *you* didn't get invited. Rude."

Xia aimed a look over her shoulder. "Tragic." For an instant her amused eyes met mine, and warmth prickled over my chest. Then she turned away.

"Some people," huffed Ellis.

"Some people," I agreed, trying not to let my mouth twitch. I already knew somehow that when I walked into the Book Alley next week, Xia would say, *Hey, girl, are you ready to par-tay?*

"Anyway," I said to Ellis, "tonight should be fun."

"Fun? It's going to be the freaking *best*. Apparently Anna May got, like"—she lowered her voice—"a bunch of handles from Jeremy Andrews. Not that that's relevant to you. But *I'm* going to have the ultimate senioritis Friday night."

I smiled. "This time, when I drive us home, I get to pick the music."

"No," Ellis wailed, grabbing my arm, "not fair. It's my car."

"It's *sober* Ellis's car. Drunk Ellis has no rights."

As the day passed, I began to feel genuinely excited. It felt so good to be doing something normal again. In the past few years, I'd gotten used to making social excuses if money got tight, but I'd never

Come Home to My Heart

walled myself off from my friends like I had these past two weeks. I'd missed Deanna's big soccer game, turned down every trip to the smoothie shop downtown, not wanting to risk any deviation that could disrupt my routine or raise some question about money.

But this party wouldn't cost a cent, and it seemed like half the senior class was coming. Best of all, at the end of the night, I'd be falling asleep in Ellis's guest bed.

That afternoon, we rode the bus all the way to her stop, and after reaching the old, familiar farmhouse, we put on some country-pop over the speaker in her bedroom. Ellis threw open her closet door, and we started digging through for options.

After a few fruitless minutes, she tugged at the strap of my dress and said, "What if I just stole this one?" As I swatted her away with an uncomfortable smile, I saw her nose wrinkle.

My stomach dropped. I'd smelled it, too, as I'd lifted my arm: the rich reek of sweat that had wafted from my armpit.

Ellis put on a grin pretty quick and waved her hand in front of her nose. "Girl, P.U. What, did you run a 5K between classes?"

I affected surprise, raising my elbow and taking an exploratory sniff. "Oh my goodness. I must've forgotten to put on deodorant."

"Use mine—it's in the bathroom by the cat statue."

My pulse quickened. "Actually," I said, trying to keep my voice casual, "could I take a shower to freshen up? Apparently I've been marinating in sweat all day, so . . ."

"Gross. Do it," she said without batting an eye.

In her bathroom, suddenly clumsy with anticipation, I fumbled out of my clothes. I twisted the knobs, took a deep breath, and stepped into the tub.

As the hot water tumbled onto the crown of my head—as it poured warm and clean over my body, loosening the oils that had built on my scalp, tingling and rushing down my back—I pressed my hands against the tiled wall and found myself shivering, hard, like something more was sloughing away from me than the accumulated sweat and dust and dead skin of weeks. Looking down at the porcelain, I watched the runoff from my hair come out gray. Were those really my feet wrinkling in the water, my ankles flushing red from the heat?

I suddenly thought of being eight years old, waist-deep in cool water. Pastor Collins's low, reassuring voice saying in my ear, "Have you accepted Christ as your Lord and Savior?" I'd dreamed of that, my profession of faith, three times in the past week. In the dreams, Pastor Collins's hands plunged me under the surface, and in the baptismal bath a silt-like substance swirled away from my skin. I'd woken up more aware than ever of how sticky I felt, how unclean.

Now, for an instant, I felt dangerously exposed, vulnerable, and I forced my eyes closed, breathing the steam into my nose and mouth.

When I'd collected myself, I lathered my scalp twice with shampoo, used three full palmfuls of body wash to scrub every pore on my body, and stepped out feeling brand-new. I even blow-dried my hair and left it falling over my shoulders.

I applied Ellis's deodorant, then hesitated with the stick in my hand. I felt a tug of guilt, but I couldn't help wondering: What if she had an extra, or a travel-sized one? Something she could spare?

Moving quietly, I checked the drawers and cabinets but came up empty. I replaced the deodorant hurriedly on the shelf and straightened the place up, the guilt intensifying. I'd just bite the bullet tomorrow and buy one from the convenience store.

For now, anyway, I was fresh, clean, and shining. I smelled like lilac. Looking at myself in the mirror, I even felt pretty.

"Hair-down Gloria is *back* and ready to have *fun*!" Ellis hollered when she saw me. "Okay, wait, you have to try this." She handed me a

Come Home to My Heart

tube of lip stain. "I just ordered it last week and it's incredible. Even when I put it on, I was like, this is going to look *so* good on Gloria."

The whole afternoon was like that, blessing after blessing. Even the simple act of settling into Ellis's comfy armchair reawakened something in me that I hadn't realized had gone dormant. I hadn't set foot inside a house for over two weeks, and until now, I hadn't realized the ways it had worn on me, only ever being in public spaces. You could be allowed somewhere and still never feel like you belonged. Ellis's place had the comfortable, secluded atmosphere that only homes do, the flow of her family's everyday life visible in scattered dish towels and half-open curtains. I belonged with that rhythm. I belonged here.

By the time her parents came home, all smiles and welcomes, I almost felt like myself again. My real self, the one who didn't spend her life covering her tracks. Ellis's mother whipped up a delicious Bolognese casserole, and Ellis and I drove off to Anna's with full stomachs, laughing ourselves lightheaded about how Mr. Robertson always managed to drag his questionable personal life into chemistry lectures.

Just before we got there, Ellis looked over at me from the driver's seat, shaking back her barrel curls with a flick of her chin. "Having fun yet?" she asked, and I heard the questions beneath: *Is this distracting you from your parents? Am I being a good best friend? Did I find the right answer?*

I smiled. "You know it."

The party was in full swing when we arrived. Dozens of cars were parked on the shoulder of the long, unlit street, pointing uphill toward Anna's house, a three-story yellow confection. Even with the size of the place, the party had spilled into the fields behind the backyard. The noise was incredible, but we were miles and miles out of town. Anna's closest neighbor wouldn't have heard the music even if she'd opened all the windows and blasted the speakers at top volume.

Riley Redgate

I smoothed down my dress in the car, brushed my hair over my shoulder. As I checked my makeup in the passenger mirror, I found myself thinking about the orchestra pit, and the Book Alley, and Xia's car. The time I'd spent in those dimly lit places these past weeks seemed so weird, just then, like something that had happened to another person. This shored me up, the sight of myself looking so much more polished. This was my body properly taken care of, honored as a temple of the Holy Spirit. This was me.

When we got into the house, Anna May looked swamped by her soccer friends in the living room, so we settled for a wave from across the room and headed out back. "Babe," called Aiden's voice from somewhere on the harshly lit sprawl of the patio. We spotted him waving to Ellis, standing in a circle of our people—Ben and Deanna from Young Christians, plus a few other kids on the Winter Dance Committee.

Soon enough we were all seated on the weatherproofed furniture around Anna May's firepit, glutting ourselves on chips and salsa and laughing as Ellis made appalled exclamations over the drink Aiden had concocted for her. Aiden bounced between defending himself and trying to convince Ben to join spring track. "Bro," Aiden said, "if you and Josh aren't on the team, we're gonna lose to *everybody*, even South Central. Do I have to beg?"

"You can try begging," said Ben with an easy grin. He was an easy kind of guy, sandy-haired and loose-limbed, with a tuneful singing voice that he sometimes broke out during Young Christians. "What do we think? Do we want to see Aiden begging?"

"Nothing new for me," said Ellis, and we all laughed.

Ben was sitting to my right, and I felt him watching me a little too long as I smiled into my lemonade. I felt a nervous jitter in my stomach. Ellis had started making noises over the summer about how tall and cute Ben had gotten, and wasn't that interesting, and maybe shouldn't I do something about it. I could only hope *he* didn't want to do something about it.

"Jennie!" Ellis exclaimed, hugging a petite, freckled girl into our circle. "Sit down, there's room! Y'all, this is Jennie—she's a junior on Yearbook."

Another jitter. At first I thought I'd recognized this girl from the school halls, but no. She went to Fisherton Faith, my new church. I'd seen her milling around in the lobby after last weekend's service.

I hurriedly stood and excused myself to the restroom, but when I got back, Jennie was still there. I couldn't do anything but return to my seat, and as I sat down, Ellis said, "Glor, do you know Jennie?"

"It's great to meet you," Jennie said with a bright smile. "I've seen you at church, right?"

"Oh, you go to First Baptist?" Ellis asked her.

I leaped in. "No, we saw each other at Fisherton Faith. I've been trying out some new places. No offense to Pastor Collins, but I kind of want to see what's out there."

"Really?" Ellis looked startled. "Wow, I'm surprised your parents let—" She broke off, her eyes straying to Jennie, and laughed. "Well—I'm glad y'all met, anyway. What's Fisherton Faith like? It's that little place by school, right?"

As Ellis let the conversation flow along, the hot prickle on the back of my neck slowly faded. I tried to relax again, but I felt like something had slipped out of my grip. I asked questions about Aiden's football stories and laughed along with everyone's impressions of our teachers, and that felt normal enough—but it seemed like every two minutes, somebody would say something like, "We should all go see that movie next weekend," or "Gloria, you have to get this moisturizer, it's only like ten dollars on Amazon," or "Do you guys want to go shopping in Wallerville soon?" and I'd try to fix my smile in place, already planning excuses. My eyes began to stray to the bowl of chips on the table, and I found myself wondering if there were plates in the kitchen, and if I could find an excuse to take a snack plate home for this weekend. I didn't want to consider these things, but I couldn't stop.

As the moon rose, distant thoughts began to float through my head, like, *What am I doing here?* and when I looked back at the angled lights painting arcs over the side of Anna's house, I felt as if I was looking at a movie set, or an advertisement. I began to feel like some invisible part of me was walking backward, off the patio and between the groups of laughing kids, into the fields, away from my friends—hunkering down in the dark, just out of sight.

◊

Nestled in Ellis's guest bed, I slept late into the morning the next day. Sometimes I'd drift awake and just relish the cushioning of the mattress, pushing the heel of my hand into it, letting my body turn and sink into the layers of its support.

Around eleven, Ellis finally drummed on the door and called, "Get up, sleepyhead, there's breakfast."

I got dressed and started down the hall to their kitchen, but halfway there, I stopped. To my right was the door to their laundry closet.

After a moment, I quietly opened the door. On a side shelf sat an enormous plastic detergent tub, which boasted *172 PODS!* on the outside.

Before I could think too hard about it, I cracked the tub and slipped a few into my backpack. I felt a little ashamed as I hurried toward the kitchen—but the pods would make a huge difference for me, the Marsdens wouldn't notice the dent, and I'd find a way to repay the favor.

Ellis and I ate quickly—fluffy, syrup-soaked waffles and strawberries and tall glasses of cold milk. I could have eaten another whole

Come Home to My Heart

stack, but Mr. and Mrs. Marsden were clearly trying to get me out the door as politely as they could, since they were meeting family friends in Columbia in early afternoon. They drove me home and dropped me in front of my parents' house, and as I watched them scoot off, I tried to relish the feeling of a full stomach.

Once they'd gone, I turned and looked at my home. The screen door and the familiar welcome mat. The lawn was no longer neatly trimmed. Tufts of grass encroached on the walkway, and weeds thrust their flowered heads up between the paving stones.

What do you want? I thought, staring into the screen door, into the shadowed window behind it. *What do you want me to do?*

Silence. Nearly three weeks of silence.

I walked up the street with a hard lump budding in my throat, confusion roiling in my mind.

◊

The rest of my Saturday passed quietly, a slipstream of homework, reading, and the strange tasks that had become my routine at school. I punctured one of the detergent pods and gave every piece of clothing I had a real wash, then hung them around the orchestra pit to air-dry. I went to the convenience store and spent a nerve-racking $9.50 on supplies: deodorant, packs of mac and cheese, a few greenish bananas, and more college-ruled paper to replenish my empty English binder.

Just over thirty-five dollars left to my name. There was no way around it: I had to start thinking about how to earn more money.

Back in the orchestra pit, I hunched over my phone and pulled up a job site, but as I began to filter, I started to realize exactly how unemployable I was. With my extracurriculars, schoolwork, and college apps, I had only a spare handful of hours on weekends. After

I'd eliminated every job listing for over fifteen hours a week, everything on the Monday-to-Friday day shift, and everything that required degrees or training, the site turned back: *13 results in Fisherton, SC.*

I scrolled through the list of cleaning companies and restaurants. *I only need one yes*, I told myself, tapping through to their applications. But as I answered their questions, my hope wavered. *Do you have a valid driver's license? Do you have a car? Do you have experience in customer service? Do you have a high school diploma?* No, no, and more no. And when I typed Craigslist into my browser, looking for odd jobs, the nearest listing was fifteen miles away.

"Crap," I muttered, checking the time. Somehow I'd spent four hours on these applications. I put my phone away, cracked open my Chemistry textbook, and dove back into homework.

On Sunday morning, I went to church at Fisherton Faith wearing the same dress that I'd worn the past two weekends. It was shapeless and worn at the collar, but neither of my other dresses covered my shoulders. When I got back to school, I hesitated on the sidewalk across from the building. The place had grown busy, the way it sometimes did on weekends. A couple dozen cars were arrayed closer to the baseball fields, where I could see the team doing weekend drills, and a maintenance truck had pulled up near the auditorium.

So I went to a small park nearby, where I sat on a bench in the thin November sun, texting Ellis. It wasn't long before she got around to the topic I knew she'd bring up: **Ben was looking at you allll night on Friday.**

I replied, **Was he? I think he's had a thing for Deanna for a long time.**

No definitely not lol

I mean no offense to Deanna, she added, **but he wasnt staring at Deanna trying to get her attention! All you girlie!**

Come Home to My Heart

I swallowed. Unsure what else to say, I typed, **Haha. I trust your judgment. I'm just oblivious sometimes.**

Yeah obvi!!

And, I added, **I don't know if I like him.**

Oh yeah why would you like him . . . you only have EVERYTHING in common plus he's the second cutest guy in our class (number one is miiineee lol)!!

Ben and I do have a lot in common. I just don't understand how anyone has time for a relationship.

Welllll for me, it sure helps that I'm not spending time auditioning new churches left and right (without even telling my amazing best friend about it lol!)

My chest tightened. **Haha. The church thing just isn't that interesting.**

Sure but what I was going to say the other night was I'm surprised your parents are letting you. Arent they like in love with Pastor Collins lol?

They like him a lot. But they also understand that I want to try and deepen my faith by hearing new perspectives.

Ellis didn't reply to this for a while, and I sat straighter on the bench, beginning to feel nervous. But eventually she said, **As always you make me feel like a super inadequate Christian haha. Like here's me drinking and everything, meanwhile you're going to extra churches to understand the Bible better**

El, don't talk like that. It's not a contest.

Tell that to my parents. Nothing I do is ever good enough.

I sighed, feeling a pang of sympathy for Ellis. Her family went to an Independent Baptist church in Wallerville. It wasn't the type of church where you'd get shunned for showing your ankles or reading anything other than the King James Bible, but the pastor there *did* seem to foster a spirit of competitiveness. Ellis vented to me about it sometimes. Who could raise their hands most often during worship? Who could be the loudest about how often they volunteered, how much money they gave? Ellis herself had been barely six years old when, to a cheering congregation, she'd leaped up and asked to get baptized, not wanting to be late to the game. In my family's opinion, that was too young to profess your faith in any real way. Not that any of us admitted that to the Marsdens.

Soon enough, she and I moved on from the subject of my switching churches, but I had the sense that wasn't the end of it. On Monday, our conversations felt careful. We were both smiling too much and talking too in-depth about Friday, even though the party hadn't been all that discussion-worthy.

And there it was: On the bus home that afternoon, Ellis found a segue into talking about church, then said, "Okay, level with me. There wasn't some juicy secret drama at First Baptist that scared you off, was there?"

She said it like a joke, half looking at her phone, but I wasn't fooled.

My mouth dry, I said, "Not unless you count Pastor Collins having the sweatiest handshakes on the eastern seaboard, but that's not really a secret at this point."

Ellis didn't laugh. She turned off her phone. "Okay. But, like—if there was. Or, like, if something happened. You know I want to be the first one to hear it."

My heart squeezed. "Yeah, I know. You're the best."

And I *was* grateful that she was in my corner, making my life feel normal for a few minutes at a time. But the conversation left me with a strange ache throughout the afternoon. As I walked downtown and worked at the library, I kept thinking about her incomprehension, and the way I'd sat on Anna's patio among all my best friends, feeling so adrift.

When I walked into the Book Alley, that tightness in my chest eased for the first time since those good hours at Ellis's house on Friday afternoon. "Hey," said Xia from the desk, letting her book flip shut. "What's the story, morning glory? How was the *par-tay*?"

I couldn't help a smile. "You're so predictable. I knew you were going to joke about that."

"Well, yeah, it was hilarious. So? Was the party life-altering? World-changing?"

"It was fun," I said. "I can tell you about it later. I have to finish this problem set."

Afternoon faded into evening, and after shutting down the shop, Xia drove me back to the corner beside the school. "So," she said, putting the Pontiac into park, "describe this *'Friday-night party.'*" She drew air quotes around the words. "What happens at these mysterious meetings, exactly? Beer pong? Streaking?"

"Mostly people sitting on sofas."

"Ha. I can do that at home. What was Anna's place like? Fancy?"

"Yeah, actually. Her house is huge. I didn't realize."

"Nice," said Xia. "Is it the kind of big house where it's a hundred years old and there are probably bodies in the basement? Or the new kind where everything smells like plastic?"

I laughed. "The second one."

She looked pleased with herself, her eyes glimmering. She always looked like that when she got a laugh out of me. "Well, glad you had a good time."

And she seemed to mean it. There was no undertone of resentment or wistfulness in her voice.

"I know we were joking about it," I said hesitantly, "but don't you kind of wish you were invited to stuff like that?"

"God, no." When she saw my skeptical expression, she laughed. "Gloria, come on. I wouldn't have any fun. Like, I'd just be sitting around watching other people talk, thinking about how little we have in common. How is that not lonelier than being at home, watching a good movie or hanging out online or something?"

I watched Xia slip off her glasses and clean them with her sweater. Quietly, I said, "Yeah."

What else was there to say, when without even trying, she'd put it into words? Somehow, in the middle of senior year's biggest party, around a dozen people who'd been my friends since we were little, I'd managed to spend the whole night feeling lonely.

But I didn't understand why. Friday night—that was my life. That was the girl I'd been for eighteen years. Why hadn't it felt like coming home?

I said a quick goodbye and got out of the Pontiac. Before I'd taken a step, though, Xia did a fast U-turn in the middle of the street and stopped beside me, rolling down her window. Her face was shadowed as she looked up at me. "Hey, you okay?"

"Yeah, I'm okay."

"Cool." She picked at her shaggy braid. "Uh, I wanted to—what're you doing this weekend? Like, Saturday?"

"I don't have any plans yet. Why?"

"Want to hang out?"

I felt a prickle of heat in my fingers. "Um—okay."

She drove off, waving out of her window.

I watched the Pontiac disappear down the street, my life settling back over my shoulders like a lead blanket. By the time I went into the

Come Home to My Heart

gas station, the last of the strange heat had faded from my fingertips, and the sick feeling had returned to slosh around in my gut.

I tried not to look into my wallet as I paid for my usual mac and cheese, but I could have recited its contents to the cent, and I knew that in the absolute best-case scenario, that amount translated to seventeen more days of steady meals.

What would happen after the money ran out? I was already saving the sides from my cafeteria meals to supplement my thin dinners, usually a biscuit or a yogurt cup from breakfast, then an apple or a roll from lunch. I could start thinking longer-term, divide my stash into perishable and nonperishable. Apples, graham crackers, and oatmeal bars lasted a while. I could redistribute those for my weeknight dinners, after I'd spent the last of my cash.

But if none of those jobs got back to me, how else was I supposed to make money?

As I hurried back across the street toward the school, a vague image drifted into my mind of homeless people panhandling in big cities or bagging up cans to sell as scrap. The image made my steps slow. I stopped on the edge of the parking lot, frowning. I wasn't homeless. It wasn't like I was sleeping in an alleyway or going into a shelter system.

Still, I needed to be prepared when my money ran out, especially with Thanksgiving break coming up.

As I crawled through the greenroom window, I remembered Thanksgiving last year, my mother folding dish towels on the table and resting a steaming platter on each one. This year, Thanksgiving break meant five days straight of not knowing where my next meal would come from.

Real fear reached dark tendrils into my mind.

Riley Redgate

What was I going to do?

More and more, I'd been remembering the moment I'd lifted that doughnut, sticky and sweet, out of its case. In my hands it had felt heavier than it really was, secretly weighted like a millionaire's credit card. Buying it had been shortsighted, and now I was coming up on the consequences, but it had tasted so sweet in the moment—it had made me feel good. Sometimes I thought of that feeling when I came into the bookstore and Xia looked up at the bell, her hair shadowing one side of her face, her long fingers sliding through the pages of something. These mental comparisons felt wrong, but they were so instantaneous and involuntary that stopping them seemed impossible. Apparently all my faults were bleeding together inside my head, my imprudence and my lack of self-control, all the appetites I wished were gone.

Lying awake that night, I ached for a time I didn't remember, before I could think or do anything wrong—when I was four years old and unformed, when I was one year old and completely out of my own hands. I was starting to feel like every memory I had was dangerous, and I would have to cut my entire past out of myself if I wanted to be pure again. I would have to be reborn. I would have to disappear.

◊

The week passed mostly without event—until Friday morning, when I woke up feeling groggy with sleep. I knew instantly that I'd made a mistake.

Footsteps thumped on the stage overhead. I shrank down into my sleeping bag, breathing hard. A theater class was up there. How late had I slept? Why hadn't my alarm gone off?

I clawed my way out of my sleeping bag and grabbed for my phone. Tried to turn it on. I'd plugged it in the whole night, but it didn't respond to my increasingly urgent pushes of the power button.

Come Home to My Heart

I dressed, shouldered my backpack, and crawled through the maze of beams under the stage toward the trapdoor chute. At the mouth of the chute, I hesitated. If somebody saw me lowering myself out of the passage—if some teacher realized I'd been accessing the orchestra pit and unlocked the door—

My heart drummed in my throat. I squatted lower and angled my head, trying to get a good look at the hallway below and ensure it was deserted.

But as I moved, my hand caught on the sharp, splintered edge of something wooden.

Pain seared over my palm. I stifled a noise against my forearm and, with watering eyes, craned my neck to get a look at the hallway. It seemed empty enough.

I braced myself and clambered out of the chute, dropping to the concrete floor. As light flooded over me, I held up my hand, looking at the rough scrape across my palm. Blood beaded to the surface.

No disinfectant, no Band-Aids, no time. I rushed up the hallway and up the stairs. Caught a snatch of Tennessee Williams as I slipped through the dark curtains backstage.

My heart didn't start to slow until I'd snuck out of the auditorium and into the first-floor hall. I detoured into the nearest bathroom. The hand soap burned the scrape so badly my eyes stung, but I told myself, *You're okay*. Nobody had seen me. From the outside, the orchestra pit still looked locked and disused. That was the important thing.

Soon I was moving toward the front office with my hand in my pocket, wrapped roughly in paper towels.

As I walked through the blazing light of the hallways, I felt like I was in a trance. Usually I was the first one into the cafeteria for breakfast, and I saw the school waking up around me, teachers trickling in, classroom doors cracking and lights kindling, and I felt like a conductor coaxing the first measures of music out of a symphony. Now a tiny freshman wandered past me holding a hall pass. Second period was already in full swing, and as I glanced through the glass panes in the doors, I saw kids asking questions, teachers writing formulas on whiteboards. This had been happening all around me while I dreamed of things I couldn't remember now.

I slowly came to a halt in the middle of the empty hallway, holding tight to the straps of my backpack, looking into a senior literature class. Ellis's immaculate curls glimmered there, in the fourth row. My cut hand ached in my pocket.

I drew a shaky breath. In that moment I understood why I'd felt so lonely on Friday. And I understood, too, why I somehow hadn't felt lonely last night, sitting in a darkened car on the edge of a baseball field with Fisherton's most aggressive outcast. For the first time in my life, I really was on the outside of normal, like Xia. We were outside in different ways, maybe, but something about her distance and isolation also belonged to me now.

And as much as I loved Ellis, and as much as she cared about me, she was on the other side of that door. She was still sitting comfortably in the crowd, the way I'd used to.

In that moment I felt a thousand miles away from her, and from everyone in those seats, who had ridden buses from their homes to school, who had brought packed lunches made from ingredients out of their refrigerators, who had slept under sheets in cozy bedrooms filled with decorations.

It was the first time I thought, *I am not one of you.*

Xia Harper

I was acting like a complete, full-blown idiot, and apparently I had no power to stop myself. So much for my illusions of self-control.

I'd had so many opportunities to broach the subject with Gloria, and I'd said exactly nothing. No wonder she'd looked so on edge when I'd asked her to hang out on Saturday. She'd probably been wondering if I meant it like a gay thing.

In fairness to myself, obviously it was hard to bring up being lesbian. It would be the first time I'd ever spoken about it, unless you counted the private ramblings I typed in my journal.

Also, I knew it would be a destabilizing topic, and I liked how things had been this week. I liked *her*. Gloria Forman, member of the Homecoming Court, Winter Dance Committee chair, and secretary for the Young Christians: Against absolutely all the odds, I liked her. In fact, I probably should have been trying to make myself like her less, rather than asking her to hang out on Saturdays. Like a complete, full-blown idiot.

I knew for sure I'd screwed up when I awoke at 7:00 a.m. on Saturday, wide-eyed and wired like I'd just chugged three cups of coffee. Downstairs, everything was gray and humming, a house in sleep mode. My mom had driven back to Myrtle Beach last night, but I actually could have used her morning routine, the yoga videos and the chirpy "good morning" and the whir as she blended chia seeds and blueberries. With nothing to distract me, I paced around the kitchen and adjusted objects with no real goal.

Gloria had said yesterday that I could pick her up at one. We could drive for a while. Then what? The forecast was good, but we couldn't walk by the river or anything. Kids from school always went there and they'd see us, and then Gloria would get asked questions about why she was hanging out with that bitch, and if she cracked under the pressure, all the work I'd done over the past three years would be ruined.

Maybe we could drive an hour and change to Columbia, or see a movie. But I didn't want to spring the cost of a movie on Gloria, since she obviously had a hard time with spending money. I should have thought about that. If I paid for her movie ticket, or dinner, or anything really, it would probably make her uncomfortable. She would think I'd meant the whole thing as a date, when I hadn't. And just because she hadn't outed me, it didn't mean she was *fine* with gay people, or with being implicated in potentially gay activities.

This was exactly why I should have talked to her about boundaries before now.

I hunched over the kitchen counter and looked at the shape of my downturned face hanging in the marble gloss. I had to crack open the conversation today. I'd bring it up at the start of the afternoon before she got any ideas of what I might be trying.

The thought was excruciating. I walked down the street, smoked a cigarette, and walked back home.

The following four hours crawled, then sped to an impossible pace. By noon, I'd entered a state of low-grade hyperventilation. What if I just didn't show up? Then nothing could go horribly wrong.

Come Home to My Heart

I couldn't cancel without being a complete asshole, though. Gloria's phone was broken, so I couldn't text her to say I'd caught tuberculosis and was on my deathbed and therefore unfortunately couldn't make it. I saw now why it had been harder to flake out of social engagements before the advent of the cell phone.

Eventually I did it. I drove across town and there she was, waiting for me at the intersection. She wore a dark blue T-shirt that I'd seen her wear several times and jeans with worn-out knees. Unencumbered by a backpack, her posture was like a dancer's, and her hair was up in its small, hard knot as always.

I rolled to a stop. She got in and said, smiling, "It's so nice outside." She had a dimple in her left cheek that I hadn't noticed before. In the clear blaze of sunlight, her freckles were a hundred shades of gold and tan and brown.

It's time, Xia, I thought. Bring it up. She already knows. There's no harm. You just need to tell her that, by the way, yes, you might be gay but no, you're not interested in her like that, and then she won't freak out if you happen to open a door for her at some point.

Except, I realized, I didn't want to say I wasn't interested in her. I was a lot of bad things at this point, but not an all-out liar. Not yet.

I put the car in drive and said, "Yeah, it's gorgeous."

I was an idiot.

◊

To my knowledge, my car's air-conditioning had never worked. We rolled the windows down as we drove out of town. Every so often we'd pass a farm, and the smell of old mulch would ripple through the car. Then the wind would lift it out again and all I could smell was sun on the hood, metallic heat.

"Why'd you come late to Chemistry yesterday?" I asked.

"It was a whole thing," Gloria said. "I overslept, and my dad was in a rush, so he couldn't drive me. I had to go hash everything out with the office . . . I feel bad about it."

"Don't feel bad. Sleeping was probably a better use of time." I sighed. "God, I can't wait for college."

She smiled. "Do you know where you're applying?"

I shifted my fingers on the hot leather of the steering wheel. "Uh, right now my list is Barnard, Mount Holyoke, UNC, Berkeley, Wellesley, Wesleyan, and Smith. Also, Brown and Columbia, but that's just to keep my parents happy, basically. I have no interest in Ivy League worship."

"I've never heard of some of those. Mount Holyoke, where is that?"

"Massachusetts. It's a women's college."

Gloria didn't say anything. She was looking out at her side of the road, where hundreds of fence posts ticked by. A cow in a pasture eyed us with interest, its wide, friendly face peeking over the enclosure.

"How about you?" I asked, my mouth dry.

"I'm not quite sure yet, but I'm looking at the county college, UNC, USC, Duke, and North Greenville."

"North Greenville?"

"It's a Baptist school."

"Oh." I hesitated. "You don't want to get out of the Carolinas?"

She smoothed both her palms over her head, from her hairline back to her bun. She did this every few minutes without seeming to notice she was doing it. "I'm happy here," she said.

I didn't answer. I knew that if I tried to reply, whatever I said would sound sarcastic, like I was sneering at the fact that she liked Fisherton. In reality, I felt a little envious that she could say something like that and mean it.

Come Home to My Heart

But I also didn't know if I believed that was the whole story: that she was just happy, and she felt nothing else about this place. Maybe I was projecting things onto Gloria, but even though she looked the part, something about her felt out of step with Fisherton. Firstly and most obviously, she didn't look at me like she hated me, or like anything about me appalled her. But she wasn't friendly like people in this town usually were, either. The most you could say about her was that she was polite; there was no warmth in it. She asked me questions with neutrality. She showed that she wanted to be my friend just by continuing to be in proximity to me, not by the usual cues of friendship like laughter or jokes but by simple reliability. That blankness, that restraint, made her slippery.

I wondered if it was sad that I looked at neutrality and felt attracted to it. Probably that said more about me than her. Still, neutrality *was* an impressive trait when you lived here. In Fisherton, everyone was conscious of the correct behaviors and attitudes, even if they didn't conform to them. That went for me, too. I knew that I was embodying a whole list of stereotypes about counterculture, and that in doing so I was actually showing a kind of hypersensitivity to the culture. Sometimes I felt annoyed by this—that there was no way for me to exist in conflict with Fisherton without reacting to it and so acknowledging how much influence it had on me.

Gloria was different, though. The way she interacted with people, and the school, and its groups and events, it was like she'd found some secret to disengaging from all of it even as she floated to the top. Even today, with me: she hadn't asked where we were going, like the events of her life didn't much affect her. Everything glanced off her surface like moonlight. You could see it in her reactions. Her muted little non-smile. The scrubbed-out sound of her voice, smooth and sweet and free of inflection.

That was why she was happy, I thought. She'd already escaped. She was here, but somehow elsewhere, too.

We drove for a while and kept talking about college. The topic was a relief. Ever since Gloria had asked me, *Do you think people judge you for being Chinese?* I'd sort of worried she would come back to my vague answer.

I just didn't want to get into that with her. Yes, people made unfunny jokes in Fisherton, but it wasn't like racial alienation was some new or tragic feeling for me. Back in Atlanta, my mom had brought me to Chinese New Year celebrations—the one time of year I sort of felt like a Chinese person, and also the time of year I'd felt most aware that I spoke no Chinese. During our two visits to Hong Kong, I'd been the American cousin, pure and simple, swimming through a culture that felt rich and overwhelming and not at all like home. Then, after two days of flights, I'd get off the plane in Atlanta and walk back into my country, where people would assume I belonged somewhere else.

Maybe it was less confusing to stay put, to hover close to home. Maybe in that way I could understand why Gloria wanted to stay here for college.

I did press her on the idea of leaving South Carolina, later, and she thought for a while, sliding her fingers up and down her seat belt.

"I don't know," she said at last. "I haven't thought about schools far away. If I went out of state, it should be for a good school, but with a lot of good schools, there's no way we can pay for them."

"There's always financial aid."

She paused. "Well, but my parents don't really like the culture at a lot of colleges, either." She left a bit of distance between each word, picking them carefully.

"The culture," I repeated.

"Yeah. The values."

Come Home to My Heart

"How about you? Do you think the—?"

But she pointed through the windshield, leaning forward. "That's Ellis's house—do you see it?"

"The white one?"

"Yeah," she said.

We passed the farmhouse, and she turned on the radio. I didn't argue. The topic had been dangerous anyway.

After a couple of songs, which she said she liked and I pretended not to dislike, I turned randomly onto a smaller road. It wound along the edge of a field, then cut into a wooded area before eventually forking into two dirt roads. The left fork was barred, but the metal gate in the right fork had been propped open.

"Have you been here before?" Gloria asked.

"Nope."

"Do you think we're allowed through there?"

"We'll see, I guess." I drove through the open gate. We bumped over the path, which snaked back and forth like a dropped ribbon, so you couldn't see more than ten feet ahead. The underbrush was thick and untamed. I heard a creek somewhere close.

Then we broke into a clearing. Before us, in a huge emerald oval of grass, the sun made thousands of dandelions glow like tiny crowns. The dirt path had ended, and when I killed the engine, the burble of the creek rose up out of the silence.

"Wow," Gloria said.

We got out of the Pontiac. I shrugged off my jacket and tied my hair into a ponytail while Gloria came around the car, her footsteps hushing in the long grass. There was no breeze in the clearing; the air hung warm and still. "Beautiful, right?" I said absentmindedly.

She smiled and leaned against the hood a few feet from me. She looked so good, and content to be near me. She looked like someone out of a life that wasn't mine. It was strange to have something like a friend so suddenly.

"I don't agree with my parents about everything," she said. "I mean, they don't want me to. They raised me to think for myself."

"Right." I had to take the claim at least a little seriously, when she was spending time with me.

She started walking, and I fell into step beside her. I watched her feet as she went. She was moving in a particular meandering way, and after a moment I realized she was stepping carefully so that she didn't crush any of the dandelions.

I felt a weird squeeze in my chest. I glanced back at my car so she wouldn't see the way I was smiling.

We walked down a gentle incline and sat in the middle of the clearing.

"But," she said, "I guess I am worried that if I went to somewhere like—like a lot of the schools you're applying to, or—well, if—"

Her voice sounded disturbed in a way I'd never heard before. She made the smoothing motion with her hands over her head again. For a split instant, turmoil showed on her face, angry confusion. Then she blinked a few times and a breath rushed out between her parted lips, and when she'd finished, the expression was gone.

"I just want to be a good person," she said.

I bobbed my shoulders. "Being around a bunch of heathen leftists or whatever isn't going to make you a bad person. I mean, you're hanging out with one now and it isn't ruining your life." I cracked a smile. "So far."

"So far." Her gray eyes glittered. "Do you take anything seriously, ever?"

"Like, besides books?"

"Besides books."

"Then no."

She laughed.

I lay back on the incline and gazed up at a wispy disc of cloud. "No, I don't know, I'm exaggerating. I do care about things, just at a distance, I guess. Like how you care about the weather when you're still inside."

She lay back beside me, and I went on more quietly. "I guess, for the past couple of years, I've felt like I'm on pause. Like this is me in sleep mode or something, and my life is going to start next fall, when I'm . . . wherever I am, for college. That's when I'm going to wake up."

She didn't answer for a while. When she did, her voice was small. "I feel the same way sometimes. But not like I'm going to wake up."

I watched the clouds drift as her words settled onto me. It took me a minute to feel their whole weight. Then I turned my head toward her. "Gloria."

"Yeah?"

"That's kind of a scary thing for you to say."

Her eyes remained fixed on the cloud above us. "Why?" she asked, and there was definitely something cagey about the word. Her lips barely moved.

"I mean, when I say on pause, I'm saying—this isn't a sustainable feeling. If you feel like you're not—" I shook my head, trying to slow down my words so they would make more sense. "I don't know if I'm explaining this right. If things feel like really, fundamentally wrong to you, which is what I'm saying, then you can't actually spend your whole life like that. Because that'd be—it'd just be really messed up."

She didn't answer. Reluctance stiffened her expression. She clearly wished she hadn't said anything.

Maybe I shouldn't have made a big deal out of it. I suddenly worried that I'd ensured she would never say anything that honest again.

"Sorry," I said, looking back at the sky. "I don't mean to sound like a life coach or whatever."

"You don't."

"Good, 'cause that's at the bottom of both the 'jobs I want' list and the 'jobs I'd be good at' list."

She let out a little laugh, and I riffed a bit more about which careers I'd bomb the most spectacularly, and soon enough we worked our way out of the hole, and then we were coasting on conversation about school again. I described all the colleges I was applying to like they were close, intimate friends of mine, like all my gut feelings weren't based on the aesthetics of their admissions emails. We stayed there the entire afternoon. But the whole time, I couldn't stop thinking about her in a cryogenic freezer, never waking up.

When the sky began to darken, we stood. Gloria held her hands out like a tightrope walker and said she was dizzy. It was probably five or so, but I'd left my phone in the car, so I couldn't be sure.

"Do you mind if I smoke?" I said, fishing a lighter and a pack out of my jacket pocket as we walked back uphill to the Pontiac.

"Do you need to?"

"You mean, like, am I addicted?"

She lifted her shoulders.

"I don't think so," I said, "but I haven't made a real try at quitting, and it's been a year now, so maybe."

"Your parents let you smoke?"

I lit the cigarette. "I'm not sure they know. I lock these in my glove compartment when I get home, I buy them with my own paychecks, and I smoke in ventilated places so the smell doesn't stick to my clothes as much." I paused. "Anyway, they mostly don't get close enough to smell it. I do my own laundry, and we aren't big huggers."

"I'm shocked."

Come Home to My Heart

I laughed. Gloria wasn't smiling, though.

"You know cigarettes are really bad for you," she said.

This was funny to me for some reason. "Yes. I do know. In Europe they put pictures of throat cancer on the boxes."

She looked curious, maybe a little confused. "Why wouldn't you at least try to stop when you know it's bad for you? Does it feel that good?"

"I mean, not really." As I drew the smoke into my lungs, I tried to find words for how smoking felt useful more than it felt good, how it made me interesting to myself in new ways I couldn't achieve in Fisherton otherwise. But the circulating sentences didn't feel like the emotions I was trying to express. They didn't seem to embody power or control. I could practically hear them out in the air, and they sounded pathetic and sad, painting a picture of a weird, lonely girl grasping at shreds of self-definition by destroying herself in a way a billion people had destroyed themselves before.

And maybe I *was* lonely, but I didn't want to be a lonely girl to anyone. Lonely girl was an object of pity. Lonely girl had no choice in her fate. Lonely girl sought desperately for a place in the world, and it was everyone else's choice whether or not to accept her. At least if I was angry, that was mine, I'd made the choice myself.

I abandoned the explanations as we stopped beside the car. "So many questions," I said, holding out the lit cigarette. "What, do you want to try it?"

"What do you think?"

I laughed, took a last drag, and stamped out the cigarette. "Let's head back."

When we were nearly to Fisherton, I said, "My parents left me some money for pizza if you want to order something to my house. They're out, so we wouldn't have to deal with them or anything."

Gloria hesitated.

"Or I can drop you home," I added quickly.

She still didn't reply.

I didn't know what else to say. I tried not to ask too much about Gloria's home life. She'd told me her dad worked in a car wash out in Columbia, while her mom was a community leader at their church and wrote on the computer in her spare time, short stories like fables. Her parents sounded decent, but still: Gloria spent every day downtown after school and didn't go home until eight thirty. I didn't know why she'd choose that if she really *liked* being at home. And when I got into questions of why she might not like being at home, I started wondering about things that were none of my business.

Back in Atlanta, there had been a kid in my eighth-grade class, Peter, who was chronically nervous and twitchy. People had liked doing impressions of him, flinching and cringing, speaking in his soft, halting way. Then, over winter break, his dad had landed in jail and his mom in the hospital. People said his dad had been beating Peter, too. As mean as some kids could be, nobody ever made fun of him for being twitchy again.

Even Kit had told me once that he hated being at home when his mom was drinking because she got so depressed she started scaring him. The next day he'd told me he hadn't meant to sound like his mom was a burden; she was actually an amazing mom and I couldn't think anything bad about her. I'd never seen him look so guilty.

Maybe Gloria needed an excuse, something that wouldn't make her feel bad for avoiding home.

"No pressure," I said, "but, um, I kind of fell behind on those Calculus worksheets, and I know Mrs. Molina is obsessed with you, so I do have an ulterior motive."

She raised her eyebrows. "You want my help on math homework?"

I sighed. "Dude, I specifically phrased it in a way that wouldn't hurt my fragile ego."

She let out a silvery little laugh. "Okay. Of course."

"Thanks." I made the turn toward Fisherton Oaks. "Does it get exhausting, being a kind and giving human being?"

"Yes, it's torture."

"You Christians love a martyr, I guess." I shot a grin at her.

She returned her thin, restrained smile. "Apparently."

Gloria Forman

Xia's house was in Fisherton's nicest neighborhood. Sunlight shone through tall banks of windows, dappling room after room full of color-coordinated furniture, so many rooms that most of them didn't seem to have a particular purpose. I liked the front room best. Tufted cushions lay in the window seat, which stretched from one end of the room to the other, and long curtains shaded the corners, tied in bunches with braided ropes. We sat in the window seat and went through derivatives, finding inflection points.

There were only a few wrinkles in Xia's comprehension, such minor things that I secretly thought she could have worked through them herself. Soon she was breezing through the worksheet, and by the time she finished, the sun had set and food had arrived.

"Amazing," she yelled from the hall as she skidded down the hardwood toward the kitchen, pizza box in hand. I watched with a little smile. The prospect of food was a disarmingly simple thing for her to love so much.

I took my eyes from Xia and forced the smile off my lips. *Rule one*, I reminded myself, *don't look too close.*

I'd been good about following the rules all day, but it didn't feel good. Every time I pulled my eyes away from her I felt a sting of disappointment. I'd wanted to watch her driving, her fingers brushing around the steering wheel, clearly loving the old texture of the leather. I'd wanted to watch her walking through that field, the sun making her skin glow like amber, the way her hips and shoulders shifted. I'd happened to glance at her as she shrugged off her jacket, and I'd had to look away from the moment's contortion instantly, my arms hot.

As I followed her down the hall, I wondered for the dozenth time if I should have gone back to the orchestra pit instead of coming here. My internal compass couldn't tell which choice was right or wrong. It was disorienting, like being unable to feel gravity. All I knew was what I wanted, and that was to keep spending time with her. Friends spent long days together all the time, so there was nothing bad about it, I didn't think, but the sheer fact that I wanted it made me suspicious that it was wrong.

Xia poured us big glasses of orange juice, and we sat in front of the TV to eat, which I associated with sleepovers at Ellis's house. It made me feel more at ease. The pizza box lay open on the coffee table, and I let the first bite sit in my mouth for a while, feeling it melt, unknitting, so much sweetness and sodium in the mouthful that my tongue and teeth felt almost pained.

See? I told myself. *It was the right thing, coming here.* My feelings aside, I needed this meal. Earlier today, I'd finished the scattering of granola bars and apples I'd saved from school this week, and the pizza in front of us was enormous. I could probably bring a few slices back with me—a way to stretch the twenty-seven dollars in my wallet a few days further.

I waited to feel truly relaxed. It didn't happen. Somehow, with my belly full and my senses alight with a warm, pleasant buzz, I felt even more like I was making a mistake.

Come Home to My Heart

But why? Why would it have been better to sit in a dusty, darkened room, alone and hungry in a deserted school?

Mom and Dad would rather have you there, said a small voice in my mind.

I felt the usual guilty lurch. It was true. They'd never have let me come here if they'd known the thoughts I'd had about this girl, even if I *was* just trying to learn how to cope with the feelings.

More and more, thinking about my parents at all made me want to punish myself. I knew being kicked out *was* my punishment, but that just made me feel even worse when I didn't think about them for an hour or two—like I wasn't even practicing contrition consciously enough.

But I had to do what I thought was best. That was all I had left now; where my parents' support and advice and conviction had once been, now I had nothing but hazy uncertainty, a fog that thickened every day. I was out in the wilderness.

Xia put some old folk music on the smart TV. With the guitar strumming along in the background, the feeling of being at Ellis's for a sleepover only intensified.

I doubted Xia was a sleepover type of girl, but suddenly a painfully appealing idea crept into my mind: collapsing onto the huge king bed I'd seen in her guest room. I'd have given so much for another real night's sleep, with no creeping thoughts about bugs, no sore muscles, no waking up with dust itching in the back of my throat.

I imagined another hot shower to scrub away days and days of stickiness. A week had gone by since I'd gotten to wash properly at Ellis's.

Guilt nagged at me. I was already eating Xia's food, drinking her parents' expensive organic orange juice. And here I was, trying to figure out what more I could get out of her.

"Hey, do you want a beer?" Xia asked.

I looked up, startled. "What?"

"Beer. My dad has some in the garage."

"No thanks," I said. "I don't drink."

"Really?"

"You sound surprised."

"I am," Xia said. "I thought all the popular kids spent half their time getting wasted in fields."

"I'm not popular," I said, though I'd felt a weird flush of pleasure when she said it.

She laughed. "Okay. Sure. You're not popular." She took another massive bite.

I thought about it for a moment. I didn't dislike anyone, and no one really seemed to dislike me, but I didn't think a lack of enemies translated to popularity. That seemed like a Xia kind of perspective to have, though.

"Be honest," she said with her mouth full. "Have you or have you not been to field parties?"

"Well, yeah," I admitted.

"And were you or were you not on Homecoming Court?"

"Both of those are only because I'm Ellis's best friend."

"So what? It's the same thing."

I sighed. "You say that a lot."

She took off her glasses and unwound her hair where it had caught in the frames. "I say what a lot?"

"'It's the same thing,'" I repeated. "You say that about all kinds of things that aren't really the same."

"I do?" She looked surprised. "Huh." She went back to wolfing down the pizza, but a while later she did go to the garage and return with a couple of silver beer cans, teardrops of condensation trickling down their sides. "Better not to try it," she said, cracking one of them. "It tastes like ass anyway."

"Then why do you drink it?"

"Feels nice."

"I'm seeing a pattern," I said, leaning back into the sofa cushions.

"I hate to break it to you, Gloria, but most people do things because they feel nice. That's not a me thing."

I could tell she was partially joking, but I still disagreed. I felt like everyone at school lived their lives tugged between a thousand influences, fear being high on the list, along with the need to impress people. Xia drinking beer, or scarfing her food the way she did, or reading impossible books, purely because these things made her feel good—it made her seem in touch with herself in a way that the rest of us weren't. She seemed so self-possessed, even self-centered, but not in an arrogant way. I'd just never met anyone who so clearly knew what she was already.

Earlier, she'd told me she felt like she was on pause. If this was Xia when she felt half-asleep, I didn't know if I could handle meeting a version of her that felt wholly awake. It would be too much, like being exposed to radiation. I'd get sunburned off talking with her.

My face grew warm. I wished for the dozenth time today that I hadn't confessed that feeling to her, like I was never going to wake up. Concern had fractured her surface in a way I'd never seen. I hadn't meant to worry her. It was just that I'd never heard somebody else speak that feeling aloud before. I couldn't believe how much I'd understood her in that moment.

The truth was that I did feel awake sometimes. I felt awake right now. I'd felt awake all day, maybe most of all while standing on the curb at twelve fifty-five, waiting for the Pontiac to appear down the road, nervous—for some reason—that she wouldn't show.

"Hey, Gloria?" she said.

She was sitting on the cushion beside me, the sleeves of her sweater pushed up to her elbows. She'd taken her usual boots off by the door, and without them, her feet in their red socks looked small and vulnerable, like soft animals out of their shells.

"Yeah?" I said.

She thumbed her glasses up her nose and placed the beer can on the coffee table. "Um, I'm glad you came back to the store last week."

Something rippled up the surface of my skin like a cold breeze. I'd thought we'd had a silent agreement not to acknowledge the afternoon I'd avoided her, her missed classes the next day.

Suddenly my pulse was quickening. Was she going to ask me why I'd run out on her in the thunderstorm that weekend? I didn't have an answer. I should have designed one beforehand. I was only good at lying when I prepared for it.

"This is really fun," she said. "Like I'm having a really nice time. Just, um. Being friends with you. I just wanted to say."

She sounded stiff and uncomfortable, but I could tell she meant it.

"Me too," I said quietly.

Then we looked at each other. Something squeezed tight in my chest, and I thought, *Rule one.* But I couldn't look away. *Rule one. Don't look. Too close.* The words repeated uselessly in my head to the accelerating thump of my heart. I was looking at Xia like I'd wanted to all day. A fine sheen of oil glimmered on her eyelids, and her heavy brows slanted dramatically above them, the same glossy black as the rims of her glasses. Her lower lip had a thin vertical groove in its center. Her irises were so dark that the web of texture in them was nearly invisible, a soft and inviting play of blackness, like shadows crossing in the night.

Come Home to My Heart

And she was letting me look. Her face angled toward mine felt like something given to me, like she was allowing me what I'd been trying to deny myself.

"Listen, I have a question," she said. Her voice was softer now, and it had taken on that low, raspy edge.

I felt dizzy, had to force myself to breathe. *Rule two*, I thought, *don't listen too hard*—but it did nothing. I wanted to keep hearing her voice like that. I remembered her in the car at night, licking salt off her lips: *I'll think of something.* I saw her in the field, looking out at the grass: *Beautiful, right?* It seemed impossible that she could fail to see these thoughts passing across my face.

"Yeah?" I managed to say.

"You don't talk about us hanging out, do you?"

"No. Why?"

"Okay. I just wanted to make sure you wouldn't tell anyone where I'm applying to college. I feel like it's kind of a giveaway."

"A giveaway?"

She looked at the ceiling and let out a short, preparatory puff of breath, as if blowing out an invisible candle. "Well, you know. I really appreciate you not telling people about me, but people talk a lot of shit, and I feel like if they knew I was applying to a bunch of women's colleges, somebody would figure it out. And I don't trust other people not to say anything."

The dizziness intensified. A dull roar was rising in my ears. "What do you mean?" I said faintly. I heard my own words as if someone else were speaking them in another room, with the door shut.

She didn't need to answer, though. *Somebody would figure it out.* I knew. I understood.

Rule three, I thought. *Don't breathe too deep.*

I couldn't breathe at all.

Shock stretched Xia's features, a look of horrified realization. "Oh," she said. "Oh no."

The silence rose and circulated like heat. I could see her shoulders lifting and falling as her breaths sped. Again, that sensation of zero gravity. I had no idea what I was supposed to do.

"I thought you figured it out before," she said. She looked sick.

Every inch of my skin flooded with heat. I remembered sitting in front of the family computer, looking at a photograph on-screen of two girls, one caressing the other's face. As I'd stared at the image, my own hand had risen up to brush my cheek. I'd tried to pretend that I had no feeling in my fingers, that the two parts of me were disconnected, so that I could imagine what it would be like to feel someone else there with me.

"Gloria," she said, "I need you to tell me you won't say anything at school. Please. I really need—"

She looked down at the place where my hand was touching her wrist.

The quiet intensified until the air felt like cotton, pressing gently in on us from all directions.

I moved my fingers slightly over her wrist, just pushed them forward over the smooth surface of her skin, and I heard an uneven breath come from her mouth, and at the same time, her whole body angled a degree toward me as if I'd magnetized her.

I watched her fingers move haltingly. She shifted her hand so that her palm was beneath mine. Heat accumulated where our skin touched, humid warmth, like the height of August.

Then her fingertips brushed up my forearm. Goose bumps rose on my skin. Lines of cold feeling shot over my back, up and down. Her thumb rested against my hammering pulse point. We were on the edge of the sofa now, facing each other, our knees touching, threads of pale denim from my jeans clinging to the dark fabric of hers.

Come Home to My Heart

I looked up at her. She was already watching me.

Uncertainty flitted across her expression. Her other hand rose haltingly to my face. I wanted to close my eyes, but I couldn't. Her hand touched my cheek, and breath startled into me. I nearly choked.

Her hand faltered. "You okay?" she asked.

I closed my eyes and rose up into what I was feeling, like a charged atom into an electric cloud. "No," I whispered.

I didn't know how long we were there, not speaking, just sitting in what we knew. I let myself breathe, and I smelled her. Sandalwood, cigarette smoke, this home, some dark, rich scent that came out of a glass bottle.

Slowly, gravity turned back on. I remembered what I'd been trying to do here: figure out how to keep these feelings at bay. But this was too dangerous now. I had to tell Xia I needed a ride home and then never speak to her again. I could practically see myself doing it, jerking to my feet, backing away, saying ugly things if I had to. Hurting her so she would stay away.

But she was touching me. Her thumb hovering at the juncture of my neck and shoulder. And I didn't want to go. I'd never wanted anything more than to stay here, in this bewildered silence, in the space between what I'd thought before and whatever might be next.

She was like me. I couldn't really fathom what that meant yet. I had to break it into bits and consider each tiny possibility, feeling the epiphany over and over. For the past three weeks, she might have been thinking about me the way I'd thought about her, feeling weird rushes of heat or cold or fascination, untimely skips of her heartbeat. When I'd felt so abnormal, sitting across from her and fighting the urge to stare, she might have been battling the same instinct. And now she was looking at me in a way nobody had ever looked at me before, as if she was transfixed by the sight of me, as if she could not physically look away. I tried to think of any other time in my life something had felt like this, and all I could think of was the day I'd been brought to tears during church on Easter, the thunderclap feeling that something transcendental had tipped onto the earth and touched my body.

Eventually, she said, "I'm going to clean up."

I nodded, numb. She removed all the disorder to the kitchen, the crumpled napkins with greasy fingerprints folded up in them, her still-mostly-full beer can, the pizza box with its scattered slices, the glasses with shreds of orange pulp clinging to their sides. I watched her do it, stupefied. In the moments she was out of the room, I just faced the empty threshold and waited for her to reappear.

When she'd finished, she came back and stood in the open door.

"Do you want to talk?" she said.

I rose to my feet. I knew what I was doing. I followed her anyway.

◊

I asked if her parents knew.

"No way," Xia said. "I don't know if they'd care, but it seems simpler to wait until I move out to say something."

She was lying on her bed, and I was sitting beside her, hugging a pillow. Xia's room was easily twice the size of mine at home and felt even bigger because of its emptiness. My room had a corkboard filled with pictures of me and Ellis and our parents. I liked the one with all six of us on my thirteenth birthday, when we'd driven to Columbia for dinner at a fancy restaurant. Money hadn't been so tight then.

When I looked at Xia's room, I saw all the things she didn't have. No photos, no mementos. No old stuffed animals or dolls, like the dozen that Ellis kept lined up on a shelf. No art, like the two glossy posters that hung next to my bed, one of my favorite Christian rock band, the other dreamy concept art of a princess twirling alone in a forest glade, wearing a crown of ice. Xia's room had the scattered, impersonal clutter of a hotel room that someone might check out from in an hour. A bottle of cologne and a couple of skin products sat on her dresser. A jacket dangled from an armchair shaped like a cube.

"How about your parents?" she asked. "Have you told them?"

"No."

"They wouldn't take it well, huh?"

I picked at a loose thread on the pillowcase, knowing I couldn't tell her what had happened. She'd been so disturbed this afternoon by the simple idea that I was keeping some part of myself in check; I couldn't imagine what she'd say if I admitted why I'd come into the store in the first place. I couldn't stand the idea of her pity.

"Sorry," I said after a second. "I can't . . . it's hard to talk about this."

"I know what you mean."

Slowly, I lay down next to her, and we turned, lying on our sides, looking into each other's faces. I had to count my breaths so I wouldn't squeeze my eyes shut.

"So," I said, "this is why you don't want to be friends with people at school."

"Basically."

"Why don't you just keep it a secret?"

"I'm not good at secrets," Xia said. "Obviously. You should give me some tips."

I thought about it for a second, but then her hand was brushing my knuckles. She slipped her fingers into mine.

My whole hand tingled as though I'd sunk it into snow. I whispered, "I shouldn't."

"Why not?"

"I'm trying to stop."

"Stop what?"

"Feeling like this. About girls."

Xia hesitated, a line forming between her eyebrows. "Why?"

"Because it's not right."

"You actually think that?"

I looked at our hands. I waited for the touch to feel sinful. I'd read all the reasons that this went against God's designs. When I closed my eyes, I saw the way my parents had stared at me, their disgust frozen in time like a photograph. I could hear the way people talked at school. I could dredge up my own words and the frustration I'd felt as I'd pressed them hard into the page: *I'll never follow that lifestyle.*

But as I looked at my hand in hers, all that felt like it was far away, hammering on a glass case, and I was here, inside, with someone who wanted to be here with me. That was all. I wanted to be here with her, too.

"I don't know," I whispered. "Why would I be scared if it weren't wrong?"

Xia seemed to search helplessly for a second. "Because of how it is here. But this isn't the only way it can be. I'm . . ." The words clearly cost her an immense effort. "I'm scared here, too."

"*You're* scared?"

She let out a disbelieving breath. "Gloria. Yeah."

"But you're . . ."

"I'm what?"

"You're *you*. You let yourself . . . you do what you want." I wasn't saying it right. I couldn't describe how she looked from where I stood, someone who followed her impulses like they were natural and uncomplicated, who declared her opinions like absolute fact until they became a kind of truth.

Come Home to My Heart

Xia shifted her head on her pillow. Her hair tumbled over her ear, brushing her cheek, a soft, dark wave. "This is what I want, and I've never done it before."

I closed my eyes.

I didn't realize I was tired, or that the spinning in my head was real exhaustion, but when I woke up, it was dawn, and I felt better-rested than I had since Ellis's house last weekend. Nothing ached. The mattress was so soft, so comfortable, the pillow cool and smooth against my cheek.

The sun was coming over my shoulder to touch Xia's face. Her glasses lay folded between us, her dark lashes fanned over her cheek, a delicate detail on her serious features.

She was a light sleeper. When I drew my fingers from hers, she stirred, then opened her eyes.

"Your parents," I said, suddenly nervous.

"It's okay. My mom won't be home until afternoon, and my dad's in Myrtle Beach until Tuesday." She didn't look or sound tired. It was like the night's sleep had hardly lasted a minute. "You hungry?"

I hesitated, then nodded.

"I'll go make something." She cracked her back and rolled out of bed. "Um, if you want to use my toothpaste or take a shower or whatever, the bathroom's down the hall on the left. We've got a couple of spare toothbrushes in the bottom drawer." She glanced down at my clothes. "You can borrow a change of clothes if you want, too. But no pressure."

In the bathroom, I stood beneath the jet of hot water a long time, relishing the pressure. None of it quite felt real, not the woodsy scent of Xia's shampoo or the sweet-smelling steam hanging in the air. I scrubbed every inch of my skin with slow, deep attention, scrubbed away the week. And after I'd dried off on the fluffy bath mat, I flossed and brushed, rinsed and spat, then opened a small first aid kit I'd found in the cabinet.

The scrape on my palm from the orchestra pit had grown puffy, pink, and tender in the past two days. Moving gingerly, I smeared Neosporin onto the cut, then applied a crisp Band-Aid. Letting out a slow, relieved breath, I slipped half a dozen more Band-Aids into my pocket alongside the spare toothbrush I'd used.

When I reentered Xia's room, I opened her top drawer and saw stacks of dark sweatshirts. I reached in and touched the sweater I'd seen her wear the first time I'd gone into the bookstore, the ripped one with the faded Polaroid.

I felt dizzy. I didn't know why. I stood there in front of her dresser for a long second, my eyes closed, just feeling my head spin.

When I came back to myself, I pulled the sweater over my head and examined the photograph as I walked down the carpeted steps. In the image, snow spotted the black trunks of trees in winter, and inside, the sweater's fleecy lining felt soft and worn. Every time it touched my skin it reminded me of how clean and dry and comfortable I was.

When I entered the kitchen to the smells of warm toast and butter, melting cheese and eggs and oil, I looked up and saw Xia in the morning sunlight, drinking coffee from a mug, tangles in her hair. It was the kind of feeling that was larger than my body. It was all around, in the light and the silence. Everything beautiful was here with me. No one would ever know.

Xia Harper

Gloria.

    I had no idea what to do with this. When I saw her in the halls on Monday, my thoughts vaporized. I couldn't keep my eyes off her. In classes I watched the wisps of hair at the base of her skull. Sometimes she bent down to put something into her backpack, and when she did, she always hesitated, then stole a look back at me, like she couldn't resist doing it, and in the moment of eye contact I'd feel the softness of her cheek under my fingertips again and I had to bury my face in my forearms to keep from smiling.

    Obviously I'd never felt anything like this. All my previous crushes had been mingled with irritation that I'd failed to suppress them. This was another feeling entirely. It was the shock of something cold up through the soft palate and right into the brain. It was the charged feeling of rapid acceleration, of suppressed laughter, of secrecy.

    All the things that I'd noticed before—Gloria's controlled movements, the caution in her smile, her rigid posture, the soft way her syllables curled up over her tongue—it was like they'd been put in a photo editor and saturated with meaning. When her hand slid up in class, I thought about how that one movement showed what kind of a person she was, dedicated but disciplined, engaging with the world around us with quiet determination.

No one here deserved her, and I hated that she was scrubbing away part of herself just to keep them all comfortable. Not that I thought I deserved her, either. She was going through the same things I was, but she didn't have enemies everywhere she looked. Instead, she walked through this place with quiet grace, holding so much invisible weight on her shoulders.

It seemed impossible that a month ago she'd sat in that same seat, and yet I hadn't known her name. At the same time, it seemed equally impossible, practically cosmic, that we'd found out about each other at all.

For the first time since freshman year, I caught myself looking at the rest of Fisherton High differently, wondering how many other kids like us were walking the halls, unknown to each other, feeling like we were the only ones.

At lunch I tore the weekend apart like an unsolved mystery. I thought about her fingers on my wrist, and her voice saying, *Why would I be scared if it weren't wrong?* And I felt so frustrated that the sound of wind raking over the baseball field grew hollow in my head. I wanted to take all her fear and guilt away.

But as a profoundly nonreligious person, I also didn't want to seem like I was brushing aside what she was struggling with. So I would stand back and let her steer.

I'd wanted to kiss her so many times, though. When we'd been lying on my bed, hardly a foot apart. When she'd come down the stairs in my favorite sweater, her wet hair falling over one shoulder. When I'd driven her back to her neighborhood in the exposing daylight, and we'd sat there in the car, sneaking nervous glances out the windows, the school looming over us like an expectant teacher, before she'd

Come Home to My Heart

reached over and touched my hand again in goodbye. Then she was gone. I drove back home in a delirious haze, and when I walked into my house, it had this glow, like the place had been baptized by the hours before.

When Gloria came into the Book Alley on Monday evening, I felt a spiraling sensation like vertigo. I think I said something stupid like, oh hey there, or something, but I wasn't fully aware of what any of me was doing. I looked down and *On Earth We're Briefly Gorgeous* had closed itself and marked its own page. I was on my feet with no memory of standing.

Gloria wasn't smiling. "Hi," she said. "No one's here?"

"No."

She took a slow breath. My heart plummeted as I realized how nervous she looked.

She was going to tell me she couldn't talk to me anymore. She was going to choose God over me, because she thought that was a choice she had to make, and there was no way I could debate her out of a lifetime of religious ultimatums in the space of a single conversation.

She stopped in front of the desk. Now in full-on panic, I thought about how to preempt the conversation. If I told her I hadn't stopped thinking about Saturday night for a single second of the last forty-eight hours, would it make her reconsider? Could I say something that would make her feel so good that she'd delay the decision?

I opened my mouth, but nothing came. The person I'd made myself into didn't plead or say soft things. I'd made myself an iron tongue, and now it wouldn't shape the words I needed.

Then she said, "I need to work on that English paper."

"I . . . what?"

"I'll be over there. Okay?"

She touched my hand. My frantic thoughts stilled.

"Yeah," I said, dazed, my heart hammering. "Yeah, I—I'll drive you home?"

She smiled her disconnected smile. Her fearful eyes held mine. Then she was around the corner and I was breathing hard like I'd broken the surface of water.

A week passed in excruciating hesitation. She hadn't been exaggerating. She *was* scared—so obviously scared that I couldn't even tell whether I made her happy. But then we'd sit there in my car in the dark, and I'd trace a pattern on her forearm, and she'd sway in the passenger seat like she was drunk and grip my hand like she couldn't stand it, and I knew if she hadn't wanted me there, she would have let go.

Even better, when I invited her over to my house that Saturday, she said yes immediately. She was strange and quiet when I picked her up, and even quieter as we ate Italian takeout, making occasional eye contact over my dinner table. I hadn't seen her jittery like this before—near the end of dinner, she spilled a full cup of soda all over herself. But after she'd taken a quick shower and tossed her clothes in the washer, she seemed to loosen up.

She was quiet again the next morning, having slept over in one of our guest rooms. I made her an omelette and tried to understand what was going on in her head. I tried to decode the straying of her gray eyes. But for all the purchase I could get on her just then, I might have been trying to climb a wall made of glass. All I could grasp on to was the way our hands moved distractingly close atop the kitchen island, then brushed, then finally intertwined, her fingertips sliding against the sensitive skin of my palm in a way that sent shivers up my neck.

The next day, when Mr. Avery came into the Book Alley for a surprise Monday visit, he recognized her in the chair.

"That's Gloria," I said as I organized a display of crime novels. "She's a friend of mine."

Come Home to My Heart

"Really!" Mr. Avery said. "A friend!"

"You don't have to sound so surprised."

He smiled. "How are you doing, Gloria?"

"I'm well, thank you," she said.

"You a senior, too?"

"Yes, sir."

Mr. Avery raised his eyebrows at me. "Your friend is polite."

"What, like I'm not a paragon of courtesy?"

He laughed, and when I looked over at Gloria, she was smiling, too. I sighed and went back to the display so they wouldn't see that I was restraining a grin.

Mr. Avery pulled up another chair to the display while I worked so we could have our usual inventory talk. We made the obligatory plans to restock a dozen bestsellers. It occurred to me that the dull, unenthusiastic way we were talking about books that had sold millions of copies might have something to do with the bookstore's miserable commercial performance.

But we did a decent trade in general fiction about wacky families, war, and dysfunctional rich people, and Mr. Avery's pet nonfiction subgenres sold pretty well, too. Especially around the holidays, we'd move a fair number of parenting guides, cookbooks, and Christian lifestyle books. And near the front, Mr. Avery kept a table stocked with Black history books, and memoirs and biographies of Black people. Those did sell, though rarely to non-Black customers.

We talked through a list of recent releases. A lot of the buzzy titles online just wouldn't move if we stocked them, so we didn't bother discussing them. "Oh," Mr. Avery said, "have you heard of this one? *The Sound of Falling*? Came out a couple of weeks ago."

He tilted the phone screen toward me, showing a grainy black-and-white cover with a bold orange title font. I hesitated. I'd definitely heard of this book, some big historical debut about a gay couple in the 1970s backdropped by Vietnam. "Um, it sounds vaguely familiar. Have you read anything about it?"

"Yes, the trade reviews are really something," he said in a frustratingly unreadable way.

I made a show of looking up the book on my phone, buying time.

I didn't want to assume anything about Mr. Avery, but he talked about church a fair bit, and the Book Alley closed every Sunday, for God reasons. He was also the kind of older guy who pontificated about These Kids Always Being On Their Phones Now Really How Do They Expect To Create Meaningful Connections In This Life, etc., so, I wouldn't have been shocked if he were "old-fashioned" on certain other topics, too. Whenever I'd ordered queer books in the past, I'd quietly slipped them into long lists of titles for him to check off on.

But now he watched me scrolling through the synopsis of this very gay book, humming something tunelessly to himself. I steeled myself and said, "Sure. I could order a couple of these if you want."

"That sounds fine to me."

Some tension in my shoulders dissipated.

Before I even really knew what I was doing, I was rushing out the words: "Um—Mr. Avery, I wanted to ask. Do you think you'd be able to write me a college recommendation?"

His brows rose. His mouth formed a silent *O*.

"Sorry," I said quickly, "I get it if you don't want to, but—one of the teachers I asked told me that she didn't think it was a great idea, and I thought, maybe, if you—"

"Xia. Please, say no more. I'd be delighted."

His smile was so warm and genuine that, for some reason, I had to look away.

Come Home to My Heart

◊

"Mr. Avery's really nice," Gloria said later in the car.

"He's not bad." I shot her an amused look. "You just like him because he called you polite."

"I am polite. It was accurate."

We were both smiling, looking through the windshield, parked on the corner by the school.

I didn't want to say good night yet, but I didn't know how to keep her from leaving. I always felt strangled when we got here, dreading the moment she'd reach for the door handle. Last Friday she'd left after hardly fifteen minutes, and I felt like I'd done something wrong, like I hadn't been interesting or funny or attractive enough for her to want to stay.

Her self-control made me nervous. I was pretty sure I'd have sat there all night if she'd wanted me to. I wouldn't have been able to stop myself, but she could. We weren't even together in any meaningful sense, and yet I still felt like we were always on the precipice of her deciding this was a mistake; I felt at her mercy, like an animal on its back. She could do anything, and all I could do was wait.

Just as I opened my mouth, she said, "Do you want to go for a drive?"

"Sure. Yeah." As I restarted the car, my blood began to buzz again.

We passed through the outskirts. I could see silhouettes moving in illuminated windows of houses. Soon the old paper mill shuffled past on our right, a bleak gray prism with windows half-shattered and half-boarded, and I thought of her father. "Your parents aren't going to be mad that you're out late, are they?" I asked.

"No." After a while, she said quietly, "I'm starting to think they really don't care anymore."

We drove down a long, gentle slope. I was going twenty over the limit, but cops never cared about these side roads, lost in dark fields.

I felt an instinct to say the easy thing, *They're your parents, they love you.* But Gloria sounded like she meant what she'd said. It sounded like it hurt her to say it.

I knew things had changed in her family. She talked about her childhood happily and easily, but something had gone wrong.

"The problem y'all are having. Does it have something to do with, um, God?" I asked, knowing how clumsy it sounded. Whenever I talked about God with Gloria, I became aware of how often I said *God, this* and *God, that* and generally blasphemed and swore and did things she would never do. I wondered if she wanted me to stop but was too polite to ask.

I wondered even more often if she prayed for me. The idea made me feel defensive, but oddly flattered, too. The idea of someone caring about the state of my immortal soul was sort of sweet. I'd definitely given up on that ages ago.

"Not God, exactly," Gloria said. "I mean, for me, everything has to do with faith in a way, but this isn't really . . . I don't know."

"Are you testing them?" I asked.

"What do you mean?"

"I mean, you're not staying out all the time to try and get a reaction out of your parents, are you?"

She kept quiet for a long moment.

I went on more hesitantly. "Obviously I'm not an expert, but if there's something you want to say to them, seems like it'd be better to just say it."

"No," she said. "I did tell . . . no, that's not what I'm doing."

It was evasive, but I let her evade. She didn't sound entirely sure of herself.

"Do you want to go to the river?" she asked.

My hands warmed. Starting at sunset, that was couples territory. "Sure," I said, trying to sound casual, "yeah."

When we reached the lane that ran parallel to the river, a single car sat near the turnoff. I could see bodies moving inside, and a little pulse of embarrassed excitement went through me. I drove a mile past the car, until it was just a gleaming speck in the rearview and we had the riverbend to ourselves. The water glided smoothly beneath the moon like something automated.

We walked down onto the bank and sat on a long, flat rock, one of its edges lapped by the shallows. The murmur of the river soothed me.

I sat close to Gloria. After a moment, she said, "It's just complicated, with my parents."

"I get it." I let my hand stray over to brush hers.

She twined her fingers with mine. "You said you've never done this before."

"No."

"Didn't anyone know about you in Atlanta?"

"I probably would've told my friends there if I'd stayed, but we lost touch." I trailed one finger through the river water, feeling the soft resistance of the current. "It happened fast, too. Way faster than I thought it would. We'd stopped texting or anything by spring break my sophomore year." I bobbed my shoulders. "I was probably pretty depressing to talk to."

"You're not depressing," Gloria said.

"Yeah, but that was two years ago, before I developed my thick layer of protective irony."

Gloria laughed, but her eyes lingered on me. I had the sense she was waiting for something real.

My skin prickled. God, I wasn't used to this anymore. Wasn't used to anyone caring what I had to say, let alone wanting to hear the self-indulgent angst I'd been stewing in for years.

I suddenly felt the urge to smoke a cigarette, but I breathed through the impulse. Sometimes Gloria looked upset when I smoked, like she was really concerned what it would do to me—as though my well-being was more than just some abstract concept to her.

I forced the words out. "I was just . . . yeah, holding on to Atlanta pretty hard back then. I kept imagining this life I should've been living in Georgia, with all my favorite restaurants and bookstores and theaters and stuff. And my friends. Even after we stopped talking, I was like, maybe if we just moved back, things would snap back to how they used to be."

Gloria's thumb moved over my hand, but she didn't speak.

I drew a slow breath. "And . . . um, after I let go of Atlanta as a real possibility, I guess I switched over to imagining the moment I could get out of here." My throat grew tight. "So maybe my parents were right, and I never gave this place a chance."

"That's what they said?"

I hunched, tugging my army jacket tighter, feeling as exposed as though I were sitting naked in front of her. In my head, my fights with my parents were simultaneously my most painful memories and totally unoriginal teenage bullshit. I didn't want Gloria to know that I was actually a hopeless cliché, but it was too late to back off now.

"Yeah," I mumbled. "Between sophomore and junior year, we fought nonstop. I wanted to go back to Atlanta, but I obviously couldn't tell them the big reason why I'm so—why Fisherton is so hard for me. So they think I'm this self-obsessed, elitist asshole now." I tilted my head backward, watched the stars wink. "And looking at it now, I *was* really immature about some stuff. My dad is doing great at his job here and, like, money-wise, we're doing way better. I know they were right about a lot of things." I made myself laugh. "Also, I mean, I kind of *am* a self-obsessed, elitist asshole."

"No," she said quietly. "You're not."

I sat very still.

"That's not what you're like at all. Your parents are just confused because they don't know the truth like you do." Gloria looked away from me, down at the water. "Like I do."

My eyes prickled. I held her hand a little tighter. Felt such a powerful rush of feeling toward her that I might have taken a palmful of drugs.

For a full minute, we didn't speak. We just traced the contours of each other's fingers, the dips between our knuckles. We let the conversation settle and breathe, like a lumbering animal that needed rest.

When I spoke again, my voice was hoarse. "Are you still scared? About . . . all this?"

"Yeah."

"And there's nothing I can do."

"No." Her fingers tightened on mine like she was trying to reassure me, but I couldn't feel reassured.

In that moment of self-consciousness, I suddenly found it: the specific worry I hadn't realized I was feeling. I located it like the epicenter of a bruise. "Is it me you're scared of?" I asked.

She was quiet for a long moment. Then: "Yeah."

"Why?"

As she met my eyes, I realized how close we'd become.

"Because," she said, her lips barely moving, "I think about you like this."

Everything I'd wanted to say over the past week and a half, everything I'd wondered, and all I could do was rasp out the words, "I do, too."

She lifted her chin, a matter of a centimeter, maybe less, but in the moonlight everything seemed exaggerated. I was hardly breathing. My focus moved to the infinitesimal parting of her lips, the flicker of her colorless eyelashes, the way her brows had drawn together like she was in pain. Her fingers were cold.

"Can I k—" I started.

She leaned forward until her lips touched mine.

My eyes fell shut, my mind resoundingly empty. The kiss was long and still and fragile, and I wanted to burn it into my memory forever.

My first thought was about the way we must look under the moon, by the river, alone in the crisp, gorgeous cold—the way this was more romantic than I'd ever thought I deserved.

Gloria pulled away, flushed red and breathing slowly, deeply. An alertness in her eyes made her look like a different person. Her guard had fallen away for the first time, and I knew then, I could see in her face, that she cared about this. And that was enough. I didn't need her fearless, I didn't need her with a label or a promise, I just needed her here. Like this. I had never felt so wide open to someone in my life, had never seen someone so open to me.

I kissed her harder. Her soft, thin mouth was motionless under mine a second, then moving, pressing, closing around my lower lip. My hand found the back of her neck, her skin cool in the dark night air, and I pushed my fingers through the tight strands of her bound hair. She took a shaky breath through her nose and was suddenly closer, clutching onto my shoulder hard through the canvas of my jacket.

Come Home to My Heart

The kiss broke clumsily, and I rested my forehead against hers, unable to reopen my eyes. Not yet. The river mumbled along in the background, unconcerned. I listened to the sound of her breathing and moved my thumb in circles over the back of her neck.

"I think about you all the time," she whispered. "I really like you."

I felt an unfamiliar release in my chest, like a knot untying. For an insane second, I thought I was going to cry.

For three years I'd lived with this low-grade unrest that I was always trying to beat back, the certainty that I would have been happier anywhere else in the world, anywhere at all. In this moment, though, my awareness of any universe outside Fisherton faded. She was the single coordinate of my happiness.

◊

We came back to the river the next night, and the next, staying later each time. My dad had returned from Myrtle Beach, so I sent my parents texts like *wanted to take a walk downtown* and *holed up at the store, just doing some homework*. Gloria and I walked along the riverbank and kissed against trees, kissed lying on that flat stone, even once—for twenty urgent minutes—kissed in the back seat of my car. As my fingertips slid against the small of her back, my mind went everywhere. I wanted to touch her everywhere. I stopped myself by looking at her expression, which was never completely clear. We were already beyond the boundaries I'd expected from her.

At school that week, when I saw her talking to her friends between classes, I filled with envy. For the first time in my life, I wanted to be those people, the royalty of Fisherton High. I wanted to do mundane things like stand at her locker before English and make jokes until she laughed. I wanted to kiss her on the forehead like those boys did with their girlfriends. I wanted to skip class with her so we could go back to the only important thing, which was being alone together again.

Every night, I dropped her back at her house, a tiny white bungalow hardly a minute from the school. She always stood on the curb and watched me go. I guessed she didn't want her parents to see my car or ask questions. She'd said her cover story was giving Ellis tutoring sessions for Chemistry, and I was visibly not Ellis, so it was probably a good idea.

On Friday morning, my mom finally confronted me about my late nights. I'd been waiting for it to happen, and last night I'd probably pushed too far. By the time I got home, it was ten thirty and my parents had finished watching a movie after dinner.

"Xia," my mom said now, looking up from her laptop. She was perched at the kitchen island, fresh-faced and alert. Eyeliner drawn at the corners of her eyes. "You've been staying out so late these days. What's going on?"

"Nothing's going on." I shrugged. "I just do homework faster at the store. I think it helps being around all the books."

"If there's something you need to tell us . . ."

"There isn't," I said shortly. "Sorry if I want a little variety in my life. Got to go, I'm going to be late."

Mom was studying me too carefully. I had my suspicions, so that night, I asked Gloria if, instead of going to the river, we could stay in the bookstore after hours.

"Why?" she asked, smiling. "Fulfilling a dream of getting me to read all your favorite books?" But she agreed. It felt peaceful in the Book Alley that night, cozy and warm, the pair of us snuggled in her usual armchair together. We poked through weird old reference books to laugh at the out-of-date maps, eating sandwiches I'd picked up from the restaurant down the block.

Come Home to My Heart

On Saturday night, we did the same. I wasn't working that day, but Mr. Avery greeted Gloria and me warmly when we arrived at the Book Alley around six. He let us hang out in the little back office, watching *Casablanca* on my laptop, and I offered to close up if he wanted to leave early. "I certainly won't complain about that," he said, and headed out around seven thirty. Soon after, my suspicions were confirmed. At nine fifteen, a tap sounded on the Book Alley door.

"Xia?" my mother's voice called. "Are you here? I brought some study snacks."

Gloria shut herself in the back office. I opened the shop door, and when the light fell onto my mother's face, I saw surprise stretch her expression. She hadn't expected me to pass her test.

After a couple more nights with no interruptions, Gloria and I felt safe going back to the river. We didn't stay out too late anymore, to keep under the radar, and it worked. My parents no longer seemed concerned. They were back to their default: my mother full of chipper small talk, my dad reciting rote questions about my grades and my job and my college applications. The surface was freshly veneered and wouldn't crack again.

I felt a weird, spiteful sort of gratitude for my parents, for the blessing of their apathy toward my actual personhood. If they'd cared about me in any deeper way, they could have made everything so difficult. Instead, all I had to deal with was this every morning: "How did you sleep, honey?"

I'd recite, "Fine. See you tonight"—and that was it for my daughterly obligations. In my mind I was totally absent from these non-interactions. I was already speeding down the road, already walking through the school doors, wide awake.

Gloria Forman

I was living three separate lives, and I didn't know how long they could coexist.

The first was my old life, the one I'd had forever, now locked into school hours and shrinking into even smaller windows. That life was lunch with Ellis and the other seniors in Young Christians, and solving equations on a timer for our upcoming Math Team meet, and talk of decorations for the Winter Dance, now three months away. It was Ellis lowering her voice on the bus to say, "So, about my theory . . . I think Ben's going to ask you to the dance. He told Jennie he was planning to ask someone in YCS." It was me whispering back, "You think so?" with a sense of dread.

The second was my new, forbidden life. It was the fall of Xia's dark hair through my fingers, and the way her face animated when I asked her to tell me about what she'd been reading. It was her voice soundtracked by the river, and the rough brush of her lips when she kissed me good night. It was the hours I lay awake, my mind torn between whispered insistences that it was wrong for us to be together and that from God came all things that were good and loving. It was the way Xia lounged in the window seat in that golden hour before sunset on Saturdays, the way her serious eyes burned when she caught me looking at her, the way I could still feel her hands on my waist in classes if I just remembered hard enough. It was the notes she'd started slipping into my locker. I opened them in the bathroom with the stall locked. They'd say, *I can't wait for tonight.* Or *I think about you before I fall asleep.*

The last was my most secret life, my life under the stage, which threatened to ruin the rest. This life was the immovable roadblock of my broken phone, and two more mornings I slept through the first-period bell, and the talking-to I got from Ms. Jensen for my lateness; I could only say, "Yes, ma'am," and stare at my feet. It was the last crumpled ten-dollar bill in my wallet, and the obsessive monitoring of my leftovers stashed from school meals, and the pitifully small pile of aluminum cans I'd accumulated in the corner of the orchestra pit. It was the panic I felt on the Thursday two weeks before Thanksgiving, when my money ran out.

◊

"Hey, are you okay?" Xia said that Friday night.

"Yeah. Why?"

"You seem distracted."

She was right. I'd been thinking about the afternoon, when I'd spent my hour at the library looking up resources for homeless people. It had felt so wrong. I did have a home. It was just across town, just out of reach.

Still, as I'd scrolled past bullet point after bullet point describing every problem I'd had over the past month, I'd felt an uncomfortable shock of recognition, as if I'd seen my own dimly lit face in a candid picture. After a full month of this, *did* my situation count as being homeless?

Come Home to My Heart

I told myself it didn't matter. What mattered was finding practical help, and in that regard, the sites had been a bust. The closest shelters and meal programs were in other towns, Wallerville and Hurston. I'd have to walk for the better part of a day to reach any of them, and even then, how would I get back for school after Thanksgiving break? I would have considered asking Xia for a ride back from a movie theater or a mall, making up some story about my parents being busy, but I had no way to explain my suitcase. As for the idea of hitchhiking, that downright scared me.

It all scared me.

I wished we could park by the river, where the sound of water filled silences, but kids from school always went there on Fridays. We'd tried to go back to the field where we'd spent our first afternoon together, but we couldn't find the turnoff. It was as though the pathway had vanished, sealing that afternoon into the past with the last real warmth of fall. So we were sitting in the Pontiac, on the edge of a fallow field in the middle of nowhere.

"Is it your parents?" Xia said quietly. "Did something happen?"

I squeezed my thighs. My jeans had grown loose around them.

For the first time, I considered telling Xia everything. I knew she would insist on helping in the same stubborn way she'd once shoved a pair of books across a counter at me. She would invite me to stay with her.

The idea gave me a gut-deep ache of longing. Every second I'd been in Xia's house had been a happy one. I knew it would change things between us; there was no way around the awkwardness of it, me needing charity, her having so much at her fingertips. But her house had space—I thought of that guest bedroom where I'd slept so deeply, the Saturday before last—and I'd be able to use the computer for schoolwork, or borrow the books she couldn't stop talking about. I could shower every single day, brush and floss, wake up to the regular tones of an alarm.

But the fantasy stopped dead when I thought of her parents. They would want to know why some stranger needed to stay in their home, and this wasn't something we could lie our way through.

Looking into her face now, I knew that Xia wouldn't care. If she knew what was happening, she would come out for me.

Fear choked me. I wasn't going to break her life the way I'd broken my own. The truth had finally punctured through my hope. If my parents hadn't changed their minds after more than a month, maybe they never would.

In one second's carelessness, I might really have lost them forever.

I moved my palms over my wet cheeks.

"Gloria," said Xia. Her voice was quiet.

"I'm s-sorry. I keep . . . I just r-really miss the way things w-were."

She leaned over, closed me into her arms so tightly that the breath left me. Sobs juddered out from between my clenched teeth, letting me collapse, little by little, into her.

That night, beneath the stage, I ate the yogurt and the hard pear I'd tucked into my backpack from breakfast and lunch. I couldn't stop thinking about my mom humming at the stove, and the balanced meals she'd always pulled out of thin air. Even when my dad got stiffed on shifts, we always ate well. Fresh, crisp, seasoned vegetables. My favorite peanut butter cookies in the cabinets and roasted potatoes at dinner. In all the thousands of times I'd said grace, had I ever really appreciated what I'd had?

Xia's dad had started another business trip halfway through this week, and her mom had driven down for the weekend to join him near Charleston, so I'd been looking forward to Saturday all week. It was going to be our day, but I couldn't enjoy it. When I got into Xia's car

Come Home to My Heart

and she asked what I wanted to do, I said, "Let's go to your house," and I knew in the back of my mind that I was saying it because of everything in her kitchen, the cupboards overflowing with snack foods and chocolate. By the time we pulled into her driveway, I'd already made a plan to ask if we could watch a movie so that snacking would seem normal. When I suggested it, she said, "Sure, what do you want to watch?" like my request had been an innocent one and not a calculation. I felt small and poisonous.

I didn't want to do any of this to her. I hated the feeling of needing her in this way, on top of everything else.

If she ever found out the truth, would she think I'd been using her, manipulating her?

Worse, would she be right?

When I looked back on how things had started between us, all I could see was what I'd taken. From the beginning she'd bent the rules for me, lied for me, bought me things that had—unbeknownst to her—kept me going. Last weekend she'd unquestioningly paid for the footlong sandwiches we'd eaten at the Book Alley on back-to-back nights, which had tided me over through the entire weekend. And what had I ever done for her? I couldn't even be honest with her. I didn't understand how she could look at me the way she did, like I brought something into her life other than need and uncertainty.

As I watched Xia flipping through movies, making excited or derisive comments about each one, laughing when I suggested the obviously terrible ones, I felt a desperate overflow of affection for her. I wished I could tell everyone how wrong they were about her. I wished the kids at school knew how kind she could be, how thoughtful and sensitive she was with me. I wished I could tell everyone how this girl, this brilliant, hard-shelled, skeptical girl, made me feel everything all at once—how I finally understood the giddy whispers about who was dating whom, and who had a crush on whom, because if anything like this had been a possibility to me before, I'd have been just as lightheaded with the world of love as everyone else.

"What?" Xia said, looking over at me.

"Mm?"

"Why are you looking at me like that?" She was smiling.

I took the remote control out of her hand and kissed her. We kissed for a long time before we started watching the movie. My movements were halting and guilty, but her hands felt sure, brushing away some of the fear.

With my head resting on her shoulder, I let myself detach. I wasn't thinking about my parents, or hers. Even when she ordered dinner, the conflicted feelings couldn't get their claws back into me. As the evening darkened, I cuddled into her, turned my face and let the woodsy scent of her hair float over me, wanting to trap this moment in ice and stay in it forever.

"I keep thinking about how much more time we could've had if we'd met sooner," she murmured.

"Don't say that. We have eight months."

"Yeah, but we could've had years."

"I can't even think past tomorrow."

Her hand went still on my shoulder, where she'd been drawing shapes. I hadn't meant to say it, but it was true. Where would I be in another month without my parents? How could I keep things normal for much longer?

"What does that mean?" Xia said.

"I don't know. Nothing."

Xia shifted, forcing me to straighten and look at her. I remembered how I'd once thought she looked icy and disdainful, how I'd suspected that she hated me. And there *was* something unforgiving in the way her face rested, in the blunt lines of her eyebrows and the way her full mouth was always a bit pursed. She was more unreadable right now than she had been in a long time.

When I spoke, my voice was shaky. "Are you mad at me?" I suddenly realized what my life would be right now without her, just a wash of lies and alienation and panic.

"No. I just want to know what you mean when you say things like that. Like you can't think past tomorrow." Xia was looking down at her lap now. "Because I can. I mean, I want this to . . . um, to keep happening." She took a deep breath. "Do you not want that?"

"No, of course I do."

A long pause. She didn't look up.

"Xia. Of course I want to keep . . . Why would you ask that?"

"Because I can't tell."

I didn't understand. All the time we spent together, all the things we'd done. How couldn't she tell what I wanted?

My eyes were burning again. I couldn't even make Xia happy. I was choosing her over everything I'd ever believed, and she couldn't even tell how I felt for her.

"I want this," I said. "I'm sorry if I'm not doing it right. I don't know how to be better."

"No. It's not that." Xia took my hand. "You don't have to be—I just—" She took a shaky breath. "I just don't want you to go." She kissed me. "Because I'm so happy, you know?" she whispered, her eyes shut like the words were humiliating. "You make me so happy."

"Me too," I whispered back, and it was true. The truth felt like a luxury.

◊

That night, under the stage, I startled awake to something bristling against my fingertips.

I let out a little scream and jerked back, flipping my sleeping bag half over. A centipede scuttled away into the dark. Spiders liked this place, too, and one bad evening I'd been treated to a roach barreling up the wall, but they'd never come so close.

With disgust itching up my neck, I curled tighter in my bag, trying to calm my nerves enough to rest. But falling back asleep took what felt like an hour, and on Sunday morning, I slept later than I'd meant to. By the time I brushed my hair into its slick bun, got dressed, and hurried out through the auditorium window, the sun was high, and I only had a few minutes to get to church.

I hustled around the school building and down the small, tree-lined street leading to Fisherton Faith. A few other stragglers were jogging toward the door, and we shared the guilty smiles of everybody who's almost late.

I hurried into the back of the little church house just as Pastor Michael swept up the carpeted steps at the front, settled at the pulpit, and lifted his hands before the congregation. "Romans 12:5 reminds us that we, though many, are one body in Christ! Welcome, everyone, in the name of our Lord and savior."

As I settled into the pew, I exhaled. With my hands folded in my lap, I focused on feeling present with God, chasing away the worldly concerns of the rest of my life. Today's scripture came from John 3, and Pastor Michael selecting such warm, comforting verses felt like a small blessing today. I closed my eyes at the back of the congregation and let the words soothe me. *God did not send His Son into the world to condemn the world, but to save the world through Him.*

After the service, a number of the congregants milled around in the lobby, chatting. I tried to keep my focus on the afterglow of

Come Home to My Heart

worship, but I couldn't push back a sharp squeeze of disappointment when my eyes landed on the empty table to one side of the lobby. Usually a few members of the congregation brought refreshments, a tray of bagels or a box of doughnuts. But today the only things set out on the table were coffee and juice.

I sidled slowly over to the take-and-leave box in the corner, where the congregation made donations of clothes and necessities. Moving quickly, I slipped a new travel-sized toothpaste into my pocket, then went to draw myself some orange juice from the cooler.

"Gloria Forman," exclaimed a woman I knew from the dentist's office downtown. "How have you been?"

I pulled on a smile and greeted her. I tried not to think about how the hunger in my stomach was starting to gnaw.

When I'd returned to school, I partitioned my small pile of leftovers from that week's school meals into two. I ate a fruit cup and a cheese stick for lunch, then a tub of applesauce and a biscuit for dinner. The rest of the hunger I tried to cover with the water fountains beside the auditorium, where I drank until my stomach felt wobbly and the pangs had dulled.

The tactic backfired. I drank so much water that, in the night, I had to leave the orchestra pit for the bathroom three times. Between trips, I couldn't get back to sleep, turning over and over in my sleeping bag. I felt a persistent itch over my fingers, the ghost of the centipede that had woken me.

The later it got, the more I thought about how I wouldn't be able to think straight during my Chemistry quiz, and how I would fall asleep during my classes in early afternoon, when the drone of the heater and the sunlight combined to feel like a cocktail of sleeping pills.

When I woke up on Monday, it was past noon.

"Food poisoning," said Mrs. Henderson, the office attendant, looking down at the note signed *Ashley Forman* in loopy cursive.

I nodded, holding tight to the straps of my backpack. "But I felt better, so my mom decided I should go to my afternoon classes."

"You're already late for fourth period."

"Yes, ma'am. It's my lunch period."

Mrs. Henderson clicked the mouse a few times, scanning the computer's records. "It says here you have three unexcused tardies in the past two weeks. You know that adds up to an unexcused absence?"

"Yes, ma'am. College applications have been keeping me up late. I'm really sorry."

Mrs. Henderson didn't say anything. I was beginning to recognize that flat, unsympathetic expression. I'd seen it on teachers and admins before, directed at kids who messed around in class or made straight D's. Teachers looked at Xia that way—like they expected nothing better.

But it was disorienting to see it on Mrs. Henderson. My parents and I knew her a little bit from First Baptist, and she used to be all sunny smiles for me.

Mrs. Henderson typed for a while, folded my note, and nodded toward the door without looking at me. "Go ahead."

I reused the lie on everyone: on my teachers, during my apology tour to my first three classes, and then later, on the bus, on Ellis.

"Food poisoning?" she said, frowning. "What'd you eat?"

"I'm not sure. Maybe my mom undercooked something."

"That sucks." Her voice was a little too casual. I busied myself with my backpack. "Hey," she added, "you should come over for dinner at mine this weekend or something. How's Friday?"

"Friday works."

"Good. My parents have been like, where did Gloria go? Where is our darling Gloria? They think we're having a massive fight and I'm keeping it secret." She pulled a face. "Which is obviously a tragedy to them, since they like you better than me."

"They do not."

"You wouldn't say that if you heard how they talk about you when you're not there. Saint Gloria, I swear." Ellis's eyes lingered on my bun, and I felt a nervous lurch. Staring into the mirror this morning, I'd worried she might notice how dirty my hair was. The roots were clinging stiffly together, and every so often I felt a crawling sensation, like ants were filing across my scalp.

But she just said, "By the way, this gymnastics look is growing on me. You look older with it up."

Relieved, I managed to smile. "How much older? Like a cool twenty-three-year-old, or like a grandma?"

"I'm gonna say a cool grandma."

"Just what I always wanted."

We grinned at each other, and for a fleeting moment everything felt normal. We talked about Ellis's Labrador, who'd been sick, and our mountain of Chemistry homework. "I can't do all these equations without you," she grumbled. "When are your parents going to buy you a new phone? This is getting stupid."

"I don't know if they will. My dad was so mad when I broke it." Sensing that she was about to say something indignant on my behalf, I added, "Anyway, they probably have to save up."

She shut her mouth. Ellis's family wasn't rich, but unlike me and a good part of our class, she wasn't on the free-lunch plan.

I picked at a frayed patch on my jeans. I knew it was manipulative to lean on her guilt, but she'd dropped the talk about the phone, which was the important thing. Anyway, maybe I was a manipulative person now.

As we turned onto my street, I folded my hands tight in my lap. I leaned into the aisle and snuck a look through the bus's front window.

The corner was deserted. I felt my chest sink as I exhaled. Every day, despite myself, I dared to hope my mother might be waiting at the stop.

I wondered if my parents were happy, if they suspected what I was going through. Could they have guessed that my God-given gifts for clarity and pragmatism, the ones they'd always praised, had been turned to this? Lying to my friends and teachers? Scraping out survival?

I wondered if they still thought this was for the best.

◊

That evening, I told Xia I had to leave the Book Alley early to go home, because I was still feeling queasy from the food poisoning.

"No, stay," she said. "Get massively sick everywhere. Maybe I'll get to leave work early."

"You'd never leave early. This being the only place you actually like."

"Wow, you passed my secret quiz. You know me so well." She checked the door and kissed me. "Feel better."

I left, but I didn't go back to the school. I walked around town in the dusk, slipping into alleys beside the café by the office buildings, the bar at the edge of downtown, and lastly, McDonald's. At each spot, I kept my head ducked and flipped open the lids of their dumpsters, careful to wait until the mouths of the alleyways were clear. McDonald's was the only one that had results. Someone had left a handful of fries in the bottom of a rolled-up bag, and after downing them, I

Come Home to My Heart

crept into the restaurant and sat behind a pillar, out of sight of the girls working the counter. Around eight, someone left their half-eaten tray sitting out on a table. I hurried over to it, salvaging a couple of chicken nuggets and half a cup of Coke.

It was all a blur. I did it without even really thinking. Throughout my life, I'd seen the occasional shadows of people dumpster-diving in the alleys; it felt surreal to be doing the same thing. But I couldn't take another night like last night. I could only fake so many notes to avoid suspension, and assignments were stacking up. I'd have to make up the Chemistry and World History quizzes I'd missed, and Ms. Jensen had looked like she wanted to shout at me when I'd come in to apologize, and when I'd handed Mr. Barnes my sloppily handwritten essay on *The Scarlet Letter*, he'd stared down at the page with something between confusion and irritation. In seventh period, I'd gotten my worst grade on a Calculus quiz all year, riddled with stupid mistakes left and right, distracted by thoughts of what I was going to eat tonight.

"Gloria," Mrs. Molina had said after class, "are you all right? This really wasn't up to your standard."

"Yes," I'd said. "I'm sorry, it was just a lapse. I . . . I came in late today with food poisoning, and I still don't feel great."

She looked unconvinced, but I hurried out of the classroom before she could say anything.

It was weird to think that the school day had once been relaxing, that I'd felt like its structure was supporting me. Now thinking about schoolwork made my pulse speed. It wasn't a stable structure at all. It was quicksand, and I was trying to claw my way out, getting closer and closer to going under.

All week, I scavenged parts of people's dinners from McDonald's trays, but even as I did it, I knew it wasn't a real solution. Eventually the employees would spot me and kick me out, and Thanksgiving break was only seven days away, now six, now five. I tried to find aluminum cans, but, attempting to go unnoticed, I couldn't collect near enough to mean anything. I'd managed to squirrel away forty-five so far—but you needed about a hundred cans to make a dollar, and even then, the scrapyard was seven miles from here. I was running out of time.

I kept thinking about my conversation with Ellis. Her parents *did* like me. We'd been best friends for years, and in all that time, I couldn't remember Ellis ever saying anything outright bad about gay people. She'd joked about Will Chandler our freshman year, but so had everybody. Even I'd laughed along with some of that.

I heard her voice on the bus: *If something happened . . . You know I want to be the first one to hear it.*

What if I told her the truth?

I weighed the idea against the void of Thanksgiving break, against the idea of trying to get to the Wallerville shelter. The idea of staying in that long, bunk-filled room I'd seen online, among dozens of strangers, made me want to hunker down in my space in the auditorium, where at least I had privacy and access to school. Who knew if the shelter would even have space for me when I got there?

But if I stayed put and couldn't find a way to feed myself, I'd have to tell someone about my situation. I *had* found online that one of the churches in town was doing a Thanksgiving meal box giveaway, but that was one meal. I needed to cover fifteen.

If I came clean to Ellis before all this, it would feel less desperate.

I didn't have to tell her about Xia. Maybe she would feel better if she thought I'd never had a real crush on a girl, if it was just a concept we could hold at arm's length. I'd heard of Christians who admitted they had feelings for people of the same sex, but still went into heterosexual marriages. I'd planned on that all my life, hadn't I?

Come Home to My Heart

By the time Friday arrived, my mind was made up. I was going to tell Ellis.

Over the course of the day, the weight of the decision snowballed. I realized exactly how many lies I'd be admitting to. I'd hardly said a true word to my best friend in the past two months. How angry would she be?

Angry enough to tell other people?

That brought up other questions. If Ellis's parents took me in, that was as good as telling everyone I'd been kicked out. Ellis had never been the most dedicated keeper of secrets. Could I really get through this without people finding out the truth?

By the time we boarded the bus that afternoon, I felt nauseated, and by the time we neared the white farmhouse, Ellis was looking at me with alarm. "Are you all right? This isn't food poisoning again, is it? If you throw up my mom's cooking, she *is* going to take that as an insult."

"I'm all right. I just, um, need to talk to you about something kind of important."

"Jeez. Okay, be mysterious."

The bus clanked to a halt. We stood, and I followed her down the aisle, my mind frantically conjuring exit routes. I could still back out. She'd said Ben planned on asking me to the dance. Maybe I could pretend I had a crush on him, and that was my big, important secret.

The bus left us on the roadside, at the end of the long path to her house.

I never realized how loud the buses were until they were gone. The fields around us shook in the light breeze.

"So, what's going on?" said Ellis with a note of sly excitement as we started up to her house. That was the voice she'd always used to coax secrets out of me, like the time I'd drank a beer that my dad had left out on the kitchen table, back when I was thirteen. But her eyes were cautious, and I wondered if she was already piecing together my absences and distractions, realizing this wasn't the kind of secret that made you smile.

"You've probably noticed I've been weird for a while," I said.

"You said it, not me."

"Well, my parents and I . . . that fight we had a couple of months ago . . ."

She stopped with her key in the knob. "Gloria."

"I know."

"You mean the fight about Jen? Why didn't you tell me that's still going on?"

"I'm going to explain. Just . . . just give me a second."

She sighed and unlocked the door, letting us into the warmth. The familiar smells of maple syrup and lavender potpourri tinged the air, and the house was quiet. Her mom and dad wouldn't be home from their jobs in Wallerville for another hour.

We creaked down two skinny hallways to the living room, where a patchwork quilt hung over the back of her long sofa. We'd walked the same path through the farmhouse a hundred times after school, talking about classes, summer plans, Homecoming. Field parties.

I thought of Xia and the warm squeeze of her hand. I pretended she was here, making me feel strong and worthy.

Ellis was looking intently at me, her hazel eyes both critical and concerned. "So? Are y'all still fighting? What's happening?"

"Not really. I mean—" I swallowed. "The fight wasn't actually about Jen. And it was such a big fight that . . ."

I couldn't generate the second half of the sentence. I took a deep breath and tried again.

"It was such a big fight that they made me leave the house."

Come Home to My Heart

Strange things started happening in Ellis's face. She flinched as if someone had flicked her earlobe, blinked hard as if trying to remove a stray eyelash. Her mouth opened and shut. She could have been restarting like a computer, each function being tested.

"What are you saying?" she said. "They—like, they kicked you out?"

"Yeah."

"But where have you been staying?"

"At school."

"At school?" Her eyes were widening. "Gloria, *what*?"

"I left with some things from home. I have a suitcase."

"Yeah, but what have you been eating? Oh my gosh." She looked sick. "That's why you're so skinny. Oh my goodness."

"No, it's okay," I said quickly. "I had some money, so things have only been hard for a few days with food and . . . and stuff. I've been figuring it out."

"The phone," she breathed. "That's why you haven't gotten your phone fixed. And changing churches, and missing class, and everything. And not taking the bus in the mornings . . ."

I felt some relief in watching every little lie of the past two months wash away, and some hope, too, in the shock and dismay on her face. But I knew what came next. I felt a nightmarish sense of not being able to wake up, although I suddenly yearned to.

"I can't believe this," she said. *"Why?* What on earth did y'all fight about?"

And of course there was no lie that could fool Ellis. She knew my family. She even knew the ugly things, that my dad sometimes drank until he passed out with vomit on his chest, that my mom had thrown Aunt Jen against the wall in a rage, that last fight before she'd left town.

Most of all, though, Ellis knew the way my parents loved me. Not much could change that.

"You're not pregnant, are you?" She was looking with a kind of terror at my stomach, and some panicked part of me thought about Xia, and how if it were her, she'd probably say, *Yeah, and it's yours, Ellis*, and for an instant I thought I might dissolve into crazed laughter.

"No. I'm not pregnant. It's . . . I . . ." I swallowed hard. "I like girls."

Ellis stopped looking at my stomach. There was a long silence. She said, "No you don't."

"What?"

"You've been in love with, like, five different guys."

I shook my head. "No, that was, um . . . I tried to . . . I thought if I talked about it like everyone did, I could make myself. But that wasn't really . . . real."

All the concern had gone out of her face. She was staring at me with total bafflement. "But that makes no sense." She shook her head hard, disturbance beginning to show in her eyes. "Wait, are you kidding? Is this some kind of weird joke?"

Something started to collapse in my chest. "No," I said quietly.

"You're serious?" Her voice rose. "Um, and you've slept over at my house how many times?"

Her voice rang with a brassy quality that I'd never heard before. She sounded angry, but there was something hollow about it, too. She almost sounded afraid.

"I never would have—I don't like you like that," I said in a near whisper.

She looked confused, but that faded quickly. "Okay, so, what, you're just gay now? You're going to go around s-*sleeping with* girls?"

"I'm not going to sleep with anyone. I'm waiting for marriage."

"For marriage." Ellis let out a high, unnatural laugh. "I don't . . . You've always been a better Christian than me. How is this happening?"

"I can't help it. It's just always been there. Even when I was a kid, I—"

She stuck up a hand, her face screwed up like she had a toothache. "Stop, ew, I really don't want to hear it, all right?"

I felt like I was being pulled gently into the ground.

"Okay," I said.

A long silence elapsed.

"I'm telling you," I went on, "because Thanksgiving break starts next week, and I don't have anywhere else to go."

"I'm . . ." She unscrewed her face. Tears glazed her eyes. "I'm really sorry. You can't stay here."

She said it like she was talking to a toddler, someone who couldn't understand the words. And it was true: I couldn't fathom this door closing on me. Ellis looked so pretty in that moment, delicate almost, and somehow that didn't seem to make sense, either, that something beautiful and loved to me could cut me to pieces in the space of a second.

My ears rang, a harsh, relentless sound like the buzz of the light bulb in the orchestra pit. The reality began to sink in: I'd solved nothing. I'd done all this, ripped my deepest friendship wide open, for nothing, because Thanksgiving break still crouched ahead like a beast with its mouth open, waiting for me to walk into its jaws.

Didn't Ellis understand what I'd just told her? Couldn't she see what I was up against for the next week?

But she was staring at me with the same incomprehension. "I don't get why you're doing this," she said, and then she was revving up, her voice rising. "Like, you *know* it's wrong. I know you know that, and this isn't even you, Gloria. I don't know where you're getting this, like, online somewhere, or what, but it's not even you."

She waited for an answer. I couldn't speak.

Then hope lit up her face so suddenly that it startled me. "Maybe you just have to find a way to beat this. You just have to grow out of it or something. I mean, you've never even had a boyfriend, you don't know what it's like. What if you just tried dating a guy? Ben really does like you—what if you tried going out with him?"

It was that little thing, her reaching for the rumor she'd told me so excitedly before, that made me feel like something inside me had shattered. Hot tears itched up into my eyes.

I blinked them down and tried to find my voice. Maybe if I agreed, she would let me stay here. Begrudgingly, haltingly, mistrustfully—it didn't matter. I'd take all that, and thank God, if it meant a way through next week.

"Yeah," I managed to say. "Maybe I'll grow out of it."

"Exactly. It'll get easier. I'm sure it will."

"And you're right that I could try, with Ben. I'm just—for this next week, are . . . are you sure you and your folks couldn't . . ."

Ellis took a deep, shaky breath. "Trust me, you don't want my parents knowing about something like this. It's a family issue. As for your parents, and . . . and everything . . . well, like you said, you're figuring it out. I'm sure if you just talk to them with a clear head, y'all can work it out together." She folded her hands tight in her lap. "You just have to tell me when this whole thing settles down, and then we can go back to normal, but for now I think you . . . you need space."

I heard what she was really saying: We couldn't be friends until I renounced this and became my old self again. But this was my old self. This was the person I had always been. I never would have thought I'd see the day when Ellis didn't want to know the truth.

Come Home to My Heart

I sat unable to move, feeling as though a howl were building beneath my collarbones. Every tiny stressor of the past eight weeks seemed to multiply inside my head, turning my thoughts into a dark mass that thrashed against the walls of my skull. My best friend was going to turn her back while I slunk into the orchestra pit tonight. She was going to look the other way while I slipped into my sweaty, dirty sleeping bag and ached through five hungry days, just on the other side of town.

Like my parents, Ellis thought this was what I deserved.

Xia, Xia, Xia, said a voice in my head, growing steadily more insistent. I wanted to disappear from here and reappear wherever she was. I just wanted to be done with this, cut my losses, sink into her arms. I didn't want to think about what I deserved, what I'd done, the lessons I'd learned or failed to learn. I just wanted her to hold me and tell me everything was going to be okay.

"Are you going to tell anyone?" I managed to say. "Because . . . yeah, I need space to work on this. People knowing would make it harder."

Ellis's hopeful look dimmed until she looked as sad and serious as I'd ever seen her. "Gloria, of course I'm not going to tell."

"Do you promise?"

"I promise," she said. "Cross my heart."

Xia Harper

When Gloria got into the car on Saturday, I knew instantly that something was wrong. Her nose was rubbed raw, and her eyes had the rubbery look of recent swelling.

"Hey," I said.

"Hi."

We drove for about a minute before I asked, "What happened?"

She sniffled a bit. "It's that obvious?"

"Yeah." I paused. "You don't have to tell me." I reached out. She took my hand and pressed my knuckles hard to her lips.

"Let's go somewhere else," she said onto my skin, her breath fluttering like fire. "Take me somewhere?"

"Just tell me where to go."

◊

We went to Columbia and became nobodies. No one looked twice at us as we walked through downtown, as we sat in the window of a bakery that served cookies the size of our faces and ate until our lips were smeared with chocolate, as we enjoyed dinner in a tiny booth in the corner of a diner, seated behind a buzzing soft-serve machine. We were near the USC campus, and hordes of college students drifted in and out of the diner. Outside, the November sky was flatly gray, like a sheet of clay ironed out by a rolling pin.

"Is this our first date?" I said as we sipped milkshakes out of tall glasses.

Gloria just watched me with something like gratitude and shifted her foot under the table so that it touched mine.

Looking at her, I felt so happy that it was like a kind of stupidity. Idiotic little fragments of thought kept drifting through my head. *Nobody's ever understood me like this. I feel so here.* And they felt profound. I felt almost hypnotized.

"My mom won't be back until tomorrow," I said as we drove back to Fisherton. "You could come over, if you want."

After a second, she said, "Yeah, okay." I didn't miss the twinge of guilt in her voice.

"Or I can take you home. I mean, I can drive you back anytime. You don't have to stay."

Her voice was even smaller when she said, "I want to. But I have to tell you some things."

"Like what?"

"I told Ellis."

My hands locked on the steering wheel. I felt a sharp pain in my chest and wondered if this was what a heart attack felt like. "You *what?*"

"Not about us. Just about me."

"Gloria." I wanted to pull over, but we were skirting downtown, and I worried that someone would see us in the car together. I kept driving.

"I know," she whispered. "I'm so unbelievably stupid. I just thought . . ."

Come Home to My Heart

"You're not stupid." I couldn't believe she'd kept this in the whole night. I took her hand, and she squeezed so tight that she might've been trying to break my fingers.

"You think she'll keep it a secret?" I asked.

"She will. I trust her."

I don't, I thought, but I didn't say it. "Why did you tell her now?"

"I had a good reason."

I waited for her to elaborate. She didn't.

"What did she say?"

Gloria let out a shaky breath. "A lot of things that I've been dealing with forever."

"Like what?"

"Well. She thinks I'm doing all this on purpose, and ruining our friendship, and she just isn't comfortable with—I mean. She thinks it's wrong."

I tried to focus on the pressure of my foot to pedal, but anger was compressing my vision, dulling colors, making everything sharper and smaller. I rolled down the window an inch, and the cool wind blew through. "She said that to you?" I said, trying to keep my voice even.

"She said we can't be friends."

"Good," I said before I could think.

Gloria's hand went loose in mine. Then she tugged it away. "Don't say that."

"You don't need a friend like that."

"But I do. I need her." Gloria's voice was rising. "She's still my best friend."

"How can she even be *a* friend when she's so wrong about this?" I pulled into my driveway, put the car in park, and looked over at Gloria.

With a shock I saw that her face was streaked with tears. I hadn't heard them in her voice at all. "*You're* not ruining your friendship," I insisted. "She is. You're not choosing anything."

"But I am." She was gazing into my face. "She's right. I'm choosing this right now."

My heart pounded. This felt like a downward slope to an even worse conversation.

Gloria let herself out of the car, and I went after her. She strode up to my porch with her head down and her hands thrust deep into her pockets. I didn't speak until we were inside.

As the door clicked shut beside us, I said, "When you weren't with me, you were still the same person."

"Yeah, but I was fighting it. I was at least trying to be better."

The word felt like a physical blow. "*Better?*" I said, my voice rising. "So because I don't hate myself for being gay, I'm—what, I've just resigned myself to being a bad person? That's how you see it?"

Gloria snapped. Her hands flew up and covered her face, and she yelled through them, "*I don't know!*"

Silence rang through the hall.

"I have no idea what I think," she said, "but my best friend hates me now. I know my—if my parents knew, they'd hate me. How is that not the wrong world to live in?"

I felt a slow pulse of regret and reached out for her. At first she flinched back, but when I touched her arm she let me draw her closer. "I'm sorry," I said. "Gloria. Hey."

She leaned toward me. "No, I'm sorry. Of course I don't think you're a bad . . . I didn't mean—"

"I know." I slipped my arms around her. She was shaking, but no sound came from her. After a while she pulled out of the embrace and kissed me with enough force that I took half a step back, surprised.

Come Home to My Heart

But I leaned back against the door and pulled her against me, suddenly hungry for her touch.

We kissed there awhile, melting into each other. My glasses bumped against her brow. I slipped them off and my nearsightedness brought her into excruciatingly close focus, each hair of her brows, the shape and color of each freckle, the gray tumult of her irises.

"I'm sorry," I said again. "I know you love your friends, and your parents, and this place, but for me it's . . . this is all I care about. Everything else could just disappear."

A ghost of a smile on her thin lips. "You're so dramatic."

"I know," I sighed, "and you're the only one who gets to appreciate it." I tried to smile back, but it couldn't hold. "I'm serious, though. I know how hard it is. I just . . . we think about this so differently, I forget sometimes."

She swallowed. "I don't get how you make jokes about it. It's like it doesn't matter to you."

"Of course it matters. My life would be totally different if I weren't lesbian. I just don't feel guilty about it, because I don't think any of what's happening is my fault, or your fault. I don't think it's *a* fault at all."

"You don't?" she said. "Not even a little?"

"No. Not even a little."

She was looking at me, eyes reddened, like someone clutching to a lifeline.

I needed her to hear this. I needed her to believe me. "Gloria, I spend ninety-eight percent of my life fucking up. I know when I'm doing something wrong. This isn't that." I looked through the frosted glass beside the door at the rippled darkness of the town and took a few deep breaths. "This is actually the one right thing I've got. Being able to do this. To—to love you."

There was a long silence.

"To . . ." she said.

"Yeah."

She searched my face. I didn't know what she was looking for.

"Can I see you on Wednesday?" she said finally.

For a second, I didn't understand. Then I remembered that Thanksgiving break started on Wednesday.

My mom and dad were both coming back home tomorrow, and they'd probably prepare some sort of pageantry around Thanksgiving, but I could sneak a few hours to myself on Wednesday, if I told them I wanted to take a drive. "Yeah," I said. "Of course. Any time you want."

"Noon?"

"Okay."

I saw some kind of decision on her face, and she stepped back from me. "Can you take me home?"

We didn't say a word as I drove. Before she got out of the car, she leaned over and kissed me. Her mouth was soft and sweet on mine. Then she was gone.

Gloria Forman

Please, God, forgive me, I thought, staring at the ceiling of the orchestra pit. The bare bulb was burning a spot low in my vision, so when I closed my eyes, a dark blue-green oval throbbed in the same place. *I'm sorry. I can't do it.*

I didn't know what time it was. Nine in the morning? Ten, eleven? I'd woken up to footsteps on the stage. Dozens of muffled voices. Some rehearsal was playing out on the other side of the dark boards overhead. It was too risky to slip out of a busy auditorium, and I was too exhausted to feign normality at church. Even though I'd gone to sleep with a full stomach, last night hadn't been restful. Nightmares of missing class. Skittering sounds in the dark again.

Pastor Michael was probably greeting everybody in the Fisherton Faith congregation right now. I could practically hear his deep, wobbly voice. "Hello, all, and welcome. Welcome to another celebration of the love of Christ . . ." The blue-green oval on the backs of my eyelids wavered and bloomed into red-orange, burning in the dark.

I must have drifted off again, because when I opened my eyes, it felt like hours had passed. The voices overhead had gone. I took a breath, got a noseful of dust, and sneezed into my arm.

Riley Redgate

I made myself sit up and tugged my backpack to my side. In the side pocket, I found what I was looking for: a single runty orange, tough-skinned, still green at the top.

I dug my thumbnail in. The scent of citrus hit my nose, and saliva flooded my mouth. Something happened to my vision, to the passage of time. *Only a third of it*, I told myself, *only a third*—but before I knew what was happening, I'd bolted the whole thing down.

My stomach felt full of acid, cramps shooting up into my esophagus. I stared at the empty peel.

If the hunger was this bad right now, how bad would it be when break started in a few days?

Don't think about it, I told myself. I'd taken the edge off; one step at a time.

I opened my backpack and did my best on my homework, my brain feeling hot and angry, unable to retain or recall information. I tried to work on my college essays, too, but nothing about growth or passion would come out. I had water for lunch, water for dinner. With every passing hour, I felt angrier at myself for not rationing the orange.

That night I lay there feeling emptier and emptier, cramps scissoring through my abdomen. I needed a distraction. Digging my nails into my palms did nothing. I turned over in my sleeping bag and tugged a folder toward myself. Inside, in the left pocket, I kept all the notes that Xia had tucked into my locker.

I unrolled them one by one.

Been listening to this song a lot lately.
"Run to You"—Roxette

Come Home to My Heart

You mentioned puffins the other night. I was looking them up and apparently they only weigh as much as a can of soda. I agree. Very cute.

you look beautiful today.

Had she really told me she loved me yesterday? The whole day felt like some fantasy, the trip to Columbia, the way she'd grinned all the way through the city, her smile lighting up November.

She wanted the truth. I couldn't put it off much longer. Last night, looking into her eyes, I'd promised myself that I would tell her on Wednesday, but the idea still repulsed me.

I turned over a note and traced the tight cursive.

Pain shot through my stomach again. The notes weren't enough to distract me. There was no way to think about anything else when my stomach was this empty.

The convenience store, I thought. It was right there. I still had about thirty cents. Maybe they had one of those dishes by the register with spare pennies, maybe that could add up to something. Anything—I didn't care what it was.

I climbed out the greenroom window and hurried across the street. The second I walked in, I knew it had been a horrible mistake. There was no penny dish by the register, but my mouth flooded with saliva as I scanned the racks, my eyes raking over packets of nuts and neon-colored chip bags and rolls of powdered doughnuts and gummy sweets and frozen pizzas and even chewing gum. I looked around the store twice, trying to find anything I could buy for thirty cents.

My eyes lit, instead, on a box full of king-sized Hershey bars. Just imagining the way the chocolate would snap and soften in my mouth made my stomach hurt even more.

The expressionless man at the register, as always, was scrolling through his phone without looking up.

My hand moved almost without me, but my body knew what I was doing. My heart beat like a rabbit's, my forehead cold and sweaty, as I slid one of the chocolate bars into the space between my jeans and my hip. The plastic wrapper was cold against my skin, and my jeans were so loose that the bar nearly fell through.

I pulled my shirt over it and slowly moved down the aisle, pretending to look at other items, seeing nothing. Then I meandered toward the door. I would drift through, and then I would gobble the whole thing faster than I'd ever eaten anything before.

My hand was on the door when the cashier said, in a tired voice, "Hey."

An icy feeling washed over my body. I turned toward him.

The cashier didn't look angry, maybe faintly annoyed. "Put it back," he said with a nod toward the aisle.

I couldn't find words. I slunk toward the candy boxes, pulled the chocolate bar from beneath my shirt, and slipped it back into the container.

"Good." He went back to his phone. "Don't try that again. Cops are a phone call away, you hear?"

"Yes, sir," I managed to say. Then I half ran for the door, my head down.

The air outside was cold, the parking lot almost deserted. In the whipping breezes, I felt like I'd just awoken from a nightmare. I blinked back tears all the way to school, trying to control the feeling spinning through me. It was an awful kind of self-recognition, the same thing I'd felt when my parents had discovered my blog. As I pictured the look on the man's face, I saw myself through his eyes, feeling his annoyance twice as strongly as my hunger. He'd looked at me and seen nothing, just some stupid kid turned petty criminal, and he was right. That was what I was now. A liar, and a failed daughter, and now a thief.

As I slipped through the window, I knew I'd been lucky. He could have called the police, and that fast, I would've had a criminal record.

The compass in my chest spun and spun. I heard Ellis's voice in a kind of chorus with my pastor's and my parents': *it's wrong, it's wrong, it's wrong.*

In the greenroom bathroom, I stared into the mirror, facing myself square-on for the first time in a long time. My face was pinched, the bags beneath my eyes deep blue. I thought of Xia, of the glow of her smooth skin, and felt like a phantom in comparison, or else a succubus, feeding on her support and her kindness and her feelings for me, slowly siphoning everything out of her. I thought of disrupting the comforts of her life, of loading my messes onto her back.

I couldn't do it. I couldn't tell her the truth. I wasn't going to drag her down with me.

I trudged back upstairs to the orchestra pit. By the time I lay down, my appetite had died. My torso felt like a solid slab of wood, like there was no room in me for anything, like every open space had collapsed.

I only had one other choice.

My parents had no respect for begging or pleading. Ever since I was little, my mother reacted to me crying with irritation. "Gloria, would you cut that whining out?" she'd say, mouth puckered. It wasn't until I got myself together, showed some backbone, that she'd soften and hug me. But what else could I do? I'd make a scene. I'd bang on the windows and yell and cry until they finally let me back inside. Once I got my foot in the door, I'd convince them, somehow, to let me stay.

I had to try.

I shut my burning eyes, and the light bulb buzzed, and its dull redness yawned in my vision, the open doorway of my childhood nightmares. Even knowing that I was awake, I felt suddenly that I'd arrived there, at the bottom of those steps I'd dreamed, my body licked by crimson flame.

◊

I would do it on Tuesday, the last day of school. I was a coward, I supposed; I had always pushed everything off until I couldn't stand to face it down for another second.

Ellis stayed true to her word that week, the good and the bad. She sat across the room during all our classes, and on the bus home she sat by Lilly Collins. Once I caught Xia glowering at her from across a classroom.

By lunch on Tuesday I'd heard the story Ellis had spread to explain the end of our friendship. Supposedly, I'd snitched to her parents and told them that she drank. I could even appreciate that she'd come up with a good lie. I fielded my half of the story, insisting to the others in Young Christians that I'd let a tiny detail slip to her parents by accident, that they'd mostly figured it out for themselves. In certain strange moments, it almost made me feel close to Ellis, like we were pulling the wool over everyone's eyes together, partners in crime.

Losing her hurt worse than I could have imagined. Whenever I saw her laughing with our friends, I thought of mystery movie nights and dinners we'd made ourselves, conversations where each of us talked the other into and out of tears. I saw us sneaking away from our parents to catch lightning bugs in the evenings. How could I square those memories with this side of Ellis, this girl who was standing silently by while I slept on a hard floor with an aching stomach, who avoided my gaze in the hall as though the very sight of me disturbed her?

Come Home to My Heart

Maybe if I'd just come at the conversation from a different angle it wouldn't have upset her so much. I could have tried to be casual about liking girls, like it was just something I'd thought about a couple of times. Could I go back to her, convince her that was what I'd meant all along?

No. Ellis would never buy a lie like that. And she'd lose respect for me if I tried.

Cheers followed the final bell on Tuesday. I stood up from my desk, feeling shaky, and flowed out into the hall with the spill of students. When I stopped by my locker to collect my books, a note from Xia fluttered out. I caught it in midair and held it tight.

I didn't open it until the bus, where I sat at the very back, alone. It said, *This place is hell, but you feel like home.*

A lump rose in my throat. I rolled the note up into a tiny cylinder hardly larger than a pencil eraser and slid it deep into my backpack, into one of the loops of material meant to hold a pen.

The last of my fear turned to resolve. I was doing this for Xia. She would have done it for me.

The bus lurched to a halt at my stop. I took a deep breath and stood.

Halfway up the aisle, I stopped walking. The bus driver called something, but her words wouldn't penetrate. I couldn't move, couldn't even react to the several people who'd looked up at me with curiosity.

Outside, my mother was standing at the stop, waiting to bring me home.

Part Two
Winter

Gloria Forman

The house had changed since I'd been gone. Ever since I could remember, my parents had kept an array of photos on the mantelpiece like a timeline of my life: left to right, baby photos to junior yearbook, all-gum smiles to braces to lipstick. Now the emptiness of the mantel glared out at me. I tried to draw comfort from it. They hadn't replaced me with anything, not yet.

My mother and I creaked down the hallway. As we passed my room, it took me a moment to realize what was wrong. My bedroom door was missing, taken clean off its hinges. The corkboard hanging on the wall had been emptied, but tiny scraps of color clung to the pushpins as if the photographs had been ripped out. There were other gaps in the familiar landscape, too, but my mom hadn't slowed her pace, and I hurried to keep up.

"In here," she said. Her body was upright, stiff almost, her fine honey-brown hair fastened back into a pearled clasp.

We turned into the kitchen. My father sat at the table, looking out the window. He didn't react to our appearance except that his hand tightened on his beer bottle.

Riley Redgate

My mother pulled out a chair for me. Then she took a seat beside my father, so that they looked at me down the length of the table like a pair of interviewers.

I clung to the fact that, despite my mother's pristine hairstyle and my father's crisp button-up, they looked haggard. Something in the sag of their mouths and the lusterless skin around their eyes. *Regret*, I thought. *Please, let that be regret.*

My thumb passed across a familiar knot in the wooden table, and I found myself pressing down, as though it were a button that could spin time backward, make our home feel the way it used to.

"Well, Gloria," said my mother, an almost imperceptible tremor in her voice. "We've spoken to Pastor Collins, and he gave us some clarity about this situation."

She paused, but I knew better than to speak.

"We showed him your letters, and he agreed that you still seem to have good intentions. We all stray from God's path, of course, but what matters is that we try to find our way back."

My throat prickled. I could have sworn that inside my backpack, hidden inside that elastic loop, Xia's message to me was glowing, throwing off heat like a miniature star.

"But if you're going to stay under this roof, obviously things will have to change. Your father and I can accept some responsibility for giving you so much free rein. We knew the influences that are out there, and we thought—" She faltered. "Well, we thought we'd done enough to keep you away from all that. Clearly we were wrong."

Hearing the pain in her voice, I felt a wrench of guilt. I wanted to reassure her that they'd done everything right, that this was all my fault, but another type of guilt stirred in me at the idea.

Come Home to My Heart

Xia had said she didn't think loving me was a fault. I remembered the conviction that had burned in her eyes when she'd said it.

My mother went on: "It goes without saying, we'll be there in the room with you from now on when you're on the computer. It's been a few years since we watched movies for you, but we think it's a good idea to start that again, too. Right, Freddie?"

My dad made a grunting sound. His face was hard with mistrust, as though he were staring down a rabid animal.

"You'll have noticed," Mom said, "that we made some changes to your room. The door, and all. We hate to do that, but knowing what you were hiding from us for years, we don't think we have another option. We've got to build that trust back up. That makes sense, doesn't it?"

"Yes, ma'am."

My parents studied me. I waited for this to feel right, finally being home together, but all I felt was hunger, a relentless ache in the pit of my torso.

"Phone?" My mother extended her hand.

I extracted my phone from my backpack and handed it over. She pressed the power button a few times and sighed. "You broke this?"

I hesitated—that, at least, hadn't been my fault—but my mother hated excuses, and I was here to show contrition. "Yes, ma'am. I'm sorry."

"Well, when we get it fixed, we'll put on location sharing, get rid of the browser, and set a lock on the app store, just to cover all our bases." The tremor in her voice had gone, replaced by bright determination. And meanwhile, my heart was beating faster and faster. "Then we can go through your contacts, make sure you've only got folks in there who'll be a good influence on you. How's that sound?"

"It's good," said my voice, sounding several miles away. "Really good."

I tried to breathe normally, to hide my rising panic. What had I expected—that if I begged hard enough, my parents would take me back and let things stay exactly the same? Obviously they were always going to do this. Why hadn't I prepared for it?

I thought of Xia's hands coming up to my face in the car, the way she'd tipped her glasses up to kiss me.

Something squirmed desperately in me, trying to find a loophole. Was there some way I could agree to my parents' demands and still keep Xia in my life?

But—no. My nerves quieted, and I faced up to the truth. There was no way to have both. I imagined trying to compress what we had into five stolen minutes during lunch at school and knew it was impossible. Xia deserved someone who could be everything for her, someone who had never once lied to her.

She deserved better than I could ever give her.

As I sat there at the table, my world began to shift back into place, and it felt agonizing, like a dislocated limb being forced back into its socket. I wasn't a nonconformist like Xia. I was this house. Simple bones. Built here. Made to stay and to belong. And she was a car with a snarling engine, made to leave it all behind.

"Thank you," I said in little more than a rasp. "I'm going to be so much better than I was. You'll see."

My mother stood. "Come here, honey bear," she said, the tremor back in her voice, and when she opened her arms, I fled into them. My father stood, too, and enclosed both of us in his arms, and finally, as I sagged against them, the feeling of rightness hit. Relief broke over me, such a forceful wave of it that tears stung my eyes. I had been right all along. My parents did love me. I had proof again.

Come Home to My Heart

△

That night I slept like the dead, dreamlessly, the pillowcase soft and worn against my face. I'd wondered if the mattress would feel uncomfortable after months away, but I shouldn't have worried. I'd hardly closed my eyes before falling asleep.

The next day, before dawn, my dad drove me to school to pick up my suitcase. I climbed down into the greenroom like I had so many dozens of times, headed up to the orchestra pit, and packed my clothes. My suitcase's fabric, once that pale, elegant yellow, had taken on the nondescript color of grime. I rolled up the filthy sleeping bag, snapped the dirt from its surface. I gripped the chain hanging from the light bulb and finally killed its harsh, unending buzz. I shut the door hard behind me without looking back.

Later that morning, I found my mother in the kitchen chopping vegetables, preparing for Thanksgiving dinner. "Wow," I said, "you could feed an army with this."

"Well, I'm not going to let your grandparents go hungry."

"Grandma and Grandpa are coming?"

"Tomorrow morning. And Nana."

I watched her knife glide through the vegetables, dicing them into small, precise cubes. She moved so efficiently, so neatly. Everything in place for her visitors, as always.

That's not why, I told myself. That wasn't why they'd let me come home.

"I can't wait to see them," I said. "Do you think I could take a bath before I come help out?"

Mom didn't look up from her cutting board, but her narrow shoulders had tensed. "Didn't you just shower last night?"

"Yes, ma'am, but my hair still smells funny."

"All right, then. But lunch is at twelve thirty."

I retreated, my mouth dry. I didn't need to do anything to my hair. I just needed somewhere I could shut the door and be alone.

I sat in the steaming bathtub with my knees drawn to my chest, my heart tapping against my thighs. Noon was almost here.

Right now, across town, Xia was driving to our usual spot to pick me up. She'd idle for a while, listening to some playlist of experimental jazz, her new interest. For maybe ten or fifteen minutes, she'd think I'd forgotten our meeting time. She'd probably prepare a quip about how I'd been body-snatched and replaced with an alien consciousness, because the real Gloria would never be late for anything. I could hear the sentence in her voice.

But the more time passed, the more the humor would fade, and she would realize that I wasn't coming.

She'd get that shuttered look on her face. She'd put the Pontiac in gear. She'd drive home.

When I'd left her car on Saturday night, I hadn't realized it was for the last time. I hadn't even known to savor our last kiss.

Pain awoke in my chest. I always used to think that *heartache* was just a metaphor, but this hurt was real, physical, throbbing in me like a nail through the bone. Xia had thought I was uncertain about her. This would seem like evidence. Worse, it was happening right after she'd said she loved me.

For a wild moment, I imagined yanking up the bathroom window, getting dressed, fleeing across town to meet her. Instead, I wrapped my arms tighter around my legs, pressed my forehead into my kneecaps, and listened to the distorted sound of my breathing echoing off the water.

A warm bed, I thought. Food on my plate. This tub of hot water, dull and fragrant with soap. That was what I'd bought, for the price of us.

Come Home to My Heart

Heat and condensation gathered on my face, making me feel feverish. I prayed that somehow she would guess what had happened. Xia was the smartest person I'd ever met. Maybe she would put it all together.

Or maybe she would hate me.

Maybe the person I cared about most in the world would hate me.

I began to cry. Hard, racking sobs that I tried to stifle in my arm. With my other hand, I stirred the water around my body to drown out any sound that might leak out through the door.

Why did You do this to us? I found myself thinking as I imagined Xia's hurt and confusion. Why did it have to be this way?

Why had any of this happened?

The questions came faster and faster, more and more intensely, until they began to burn, feeling disturbingly close to anger. What had I done so wrong that, after this, I had to walk out into the kitchen and pretend my heart wasn't breaking? Why didn't I deserve a life where I could cry on my mom's shoulder about something like this, like any other kid?

I gave my head a hard shake. *Stop it*, I told myself, disgusted by my own self-pity. It wasn't my parents' fault I'd gotten involved with Xia. No, I'd made that choice myself, knowing what the consequences could be.

I breathed slowly, trying to be grateful for what I'd won back. And soon enough, the anger, or self-importance, or whatever it had been, burned itself out. I thought again of Xia driving back home, and this time I felt distant from the image, like I was watching a movie.

I left the bathroom with my face wiped dry. "All right, I'm ready to help," I told Mom in the kitchen, and I was satisfied with the way my voice sounded.

Thanksgiving passed with a sense of routine, like we were moving through the steps of a well-rehearsed dance. My grandparents made a good distraction for Thanksgiving itself, but they only stayed the one night. Once they'd gone back to Georgia and Alabama, they left the house quiet and awkward, too formal.

Of course my mom was right. We needed time for the trust between us to rebuild. So none of us spoke about what had happened the past couple of months. We talked about church and school and too many leftovers; Mom had made five sides to display with the turkey. I upset my stomach the first few days from overeating—I guess my body was shocked by the sudden change—but soon I could eat like I'd used to before, and my pants fit a little better, and I latched onto these comforts, pushing away thoughts of Xia as best I could.

When Monday came, I still felt totally unprepared to see her. How could I look into her face and tell her we had to end this all-consuming thing between us? What was I supposed to say when she asked me why? I could fess up about my parents' new rules, but I couldn't explain why they'd put those guardrails in place—or why I was afraid to break them.

By the time I got off the bus, I'd decided: I wouldn't say anything to Xia at all. If it were me, I wouldn't want to hear excuses. It would only have irritated me to see somebody wringing their hands over why they had to hurt me, as though it wasn't their choice. I was pretty sure the best thing I could do for Xia was to stand back and let her hate me, which would set her free.

Then she could go back to loathing Fisherton completely, and come summer, without our relationship complicating her emotions, she would feel nothing but happiness to get out of here. She would walk into her future, and I would be nothing but a part of the bad dream she'd left behind.

But as third-period Chemistry crept closer, it became harder and harder to fake normalcy to my friends. I had to duck into the bathroom

Come Home to My Heart

between classes to check the mirror. I'd worn my hair down at school today for the first time since October, and the dark blond wisps around my face just made my skin look more ashen.

Jaw clenched, I returned to the hallway. With the sense of walking into a firing range, I entered the Chemistry room.

I didn't look Xia's way, but I could feel her there at the back of the classroom. Everybody else chatted and texted and scrambled to finish their homework; they blurred around me. The only thing I could focus on was the fact that she was watching me, waiting for me to send a secret glance her way like I'd done every school day for a month. Crossing the front of the room, I was so aware of her in my peripheral vision that I banged my shin off Anna May Turner's chair.

"Ow," Anna May said sympathetically, half standing to stabilize me. "You okay?"

"Yeah, I'm sorry," I said with a shaky smile. "Thanks, thank you, I'm fine."

I sat without looking back. I'd done it. I hadn't even begun to turn my head toward her.

I felt sick to my stomach. My whole body was hot, and that pain had reawakened in my chest. I wanted to look over my shoulder so badly. I thought of Lot's wife in Genesis, commanded by the angels not to face back toward her home in a city full of iniquity. But she couldn't help herself and was transformed in that instant into a pillar of salt. I thought of how temptation took her, how with that last glance she condemned herself.

I didn't succumb to temptation. I didn't look. But I couldn't stop myself from imagining. I ached for us to disappear from here and magically reappear in the Book Alley. I wanted to be back in her car by the river at night, feeling her curves against me. The endless fascination of her skin moving under my fingertips.

Riley Redgate

I closed my eyes hard and tried to clear my thoughts.

For the rest of Chemistry, I transcribed notes mindlessly. Our next class together was English, after lunch. I was steadier by then and could laugh with Ben and Deanna about the movie they'd seen over the weekend. But at the end of the day, in seventh-period Calculus, I sat down in my seat a few minutes before the bell, and a shadow fell across my desk. I took a sharp breath and caught the faint, harsh smell of cigarettes.

My skin prickled as every hair on my body rose. Sweat heated my palms.

Longing drove into me, a spit through the center of my heart.

I looked up into Xia's face. Seeing her just then felt like drawing breath after minutes underwater. I drank in the long line of her nose, the point of her stubborn chin, the tangled fall of her hair. Eyes dark and unreadable behind her glasses. She was trying to look collected, but the compression at the corners of her lips and the tiny line between her brows gave her away.

I felt her breath on my cheek when she'd said she loved me.

And in the corner of my eye, I could feel Ellis and Aiden looking over curiously from one aisle away.

"Um, hi," I said, trying to sound politely confused, my stomach a twisting mess. "Xia, right?"

The line between her brows deepened. "Yeah."

"What's up?"

She hesitated, then opened her mouth. Sudden fear bolted through me. She couldn't be about to say something, could she?

Before she could make a sound, I blurted out, loud enough for my friends to hear, "Oh, is this about Math Team? I'm really sorry, we don't have any open spots anymore."

Come Home to My Heart

Xia's mouth closed. Her brows moved farther together, making her glasses slip a millimeter down her nose. I could have reached up and adjusted them, the way I'd done dozens of times.

A disapproving voice behind me made me startle. "Gloria." Mrs. Molina, coming up the aisle, had heard us. "That's not true, Xia. There's still space for new members. But we do require commitment, consistency, and the ability to be a team player."

Mortification flooded me. Half the class was watching now, and I suddenly realized how it looked: like I'd made something up to ensure that Xia couldn't join our club.

I looked back to Xia and saw hurt on her face, raw and exposed. Hurt like she'd never let show in the halls of this school before.

The pain in my chest reawakened. My mortification turned to panic.

I opened my mouth—to say what, I had no idea—but before I could utter a sound, Xia said, "Forget it." Her expression had closed. She turned and stalked back to her desk, where she slumped, her mouth a flat line. A couple of nervous giggles rose in her wake, and Xia shot disgusted looks at the people laughing. But as she turned to face the window, I caught the momentary flutter of her eyelashes, and I realized she was blinking back tears.

My eyes burned, too. I looked down at the blurring blue lines of my notebook paper, self-hatred pulsing through me. Of all the things to say, how could I have chosen that? Something that wouldn't just silence Xia but embarrass her?

But as class began, as my tears receded, I told myself it was for the best—even this. It was done now. She was free. She never had to talk to or think about me again.

A year from now, she would probably have forgotten all about me. She would be at some fancy college up north, taking classes that challenged her and kissing some other girl in her dorm room.

Jealousy flared in my stomach. I didn't want her kissing any other girls. I didn't want her looking at them the way she looked at me, serious and sly at once. *I* wanted her.

I beat back the feeling. *Happiness*, I thought. *Lord, give her happiness.* Even if that didn't include me. And I would go along my own path, safe and clean and well-fed and grateful for it.

I gripped the edge of my desk until my fingers ached. I wondered if, a year from now, my hands would still tingle like this, remembering the way she felt.

four weeks later

Xia Harper

My mom, being a more interested Christian than Dad, always took the lead on Christmas. They never forced me to participate in actual Christmas activities, with Jesus, and all the things that would have made me think of Gloria, such as the hymn that included the word *Gloria* roughly sixty thousand times in three minutes, but I did okay with the commercial version, where the tree signified nothing except a location to place objects purchased at market value. My mom set up the Nativity scene, hung garlands, and displayed gifts on December 25 each year so beautifully that our front room looked like a staging location. For my part, I always bought both of my parents books that they failed to read.

This year, I got an additional, unexpected present. After Christmas dinner, they told me to sit down on the sofa and declared that they were worried about me.

"Worried," I repeated blankly.

"Yes. Worried," said my father.

"Okay."

We all endured an awkward silence.

"So?" my father went on eventually. "What . . . what is this? What's been happening?"

My mother leaned forward in her armchair. Her hair was held back by a glitter-encrusted headband, which sparkled as the light moved over it. "Has something changed at school?" she asked. "Are you being bullied?"

I wanted to say, *Give me a little credit, people gave up on bullying me ages ago.* But with my current levels of exhaustion, I doubted I could strike the tone of charming irony I'd need for that sentence not to sound depressing.

"No. No bullying."

"Well, you look tired," my mother pressed on. "You look like you're sick."

The situation sank in a bit. I began to feel uncomfortable. Why were my parents risking this? We all knew what had happened the past dozen times we'd tried to have a real discussion about anything.

"It's nothing!" I said, trying to sound light and peppy. "Um. I've been stressed about college, I guess! But all my applications are in now!"

Shockingly, they didn't seem to buy this. The silence intensified.

"Honey, we know there's something," said my mom. "Why don't you just tell us?"

"Why don't I tell you?" The pep faded from my voice. "Okay. Well. Again, nothing happened. But if something *did* happen, maybe I wouldn't want to hear that, like, it's not a real problem, and if I just reoriented my perspective, everything would magically fix itself." I closed my eyes, rubbed my forehead. "Sorry. Look, it's Christmas. I really don't want to—"

"We wouldn't say that to you," said my dad.

Come Home to My Heart

Don't take the bait, I told myself. *Just say "okay" and go upstairs. Just say "okay" and go upstairs . . .*

What came out of my mouth was "You said that exact thing to me after sophomore year."

My mother sighed. "That was a year and a half ago."

"Okay, and things have changed . . . how?"

Twin frowns furrowed my parents' brows. "You told us to listen to you, Xia," my dad said, adjusting his glasses. "We've listened, even though you seem to have nothing to say to us most of the time. You told us to leave you alone. You can't say we haven't given you the independence you wanted. And these past few semesters . . . no, you're not going to win any teacher's pet awards, but otherwise you've had a stable school life, a good routine with your job, and lots of interest in reading. All of that looks pretty healthy to me."

Mom's mouth was built to smile, but now its corners gave a rare dip downward. She was watching me closely. "Right, honey?"

I stared back at them. I'd had no idea that any actual thought had gone into their borderline negligence the past year and a half.

Part of me suspected that this was bullshit, that they were trying to retroactively justify not showing any interest in my life since I was sixteen. It was easy to say independence was good for a kid when you loathed interacting with your kid. My dad's words still rang in my head. *We said, "It's just a phase." But no. You've dug yourself deeper and deeper . . . There's no place for this selfishness.* They'd never gone back on that.

Still, I'd take that over the alternative any day. At least with my parents, I knew *why* they didn't like me. They hadn't just disappeared out of nowhere.

My eyes prickled dangerously. *Don't*, I thought.

Riley Redgate

It was too late. I looked at the window seat and remembered her profile catching the sunset. I averted my eyes and stared down at my lap, but she was there, too, her fingers curled on my thigh.

A dull pain throbbed in my chest, as if something inside me had been carelessly reinstalled using blunt equipment.

My mother opened her mouth, but suddenly I couldn't stand this. Hadn't I learned how to pick my battles by now? "You're right," I said. "There's nothing to complain about. I was serious about it just being—being college stuff, though. I'm going to catch up on sleep over break and I'll be back to normal, all right?"

"Xia—"

I was already standing up. *Be the selfless daughter they want*, I thought. *Selfless and grateful.* "I'm actually going to go and sleep now. Um—Merry Christmas. Thank you guys for the books. And thanks for dinner, Mom. It was really good."

I didn't glance back to see their faces as I left.

Upstairs, I shut my bedroom door and lay face down on the bed. My ears felt very hot, my toes very cold. These days I wasn't crying anymore, but I did have to suppress other random fits of rebellion from my body, the sensations of parts of me being detached or unavailable, or other parts going into overdrive.

At first I'd thought Gloria had stood me up over Thanksgiving break by mistake. When she hadn't been on the corner by the school at noon on Wednesday, I drove by her house, instead, but she wasn't there.

So I holed up in the café downtown and read for an hour, wondering if she'd misremembered the time. I did the rounds again at 1:00 p.m., then at 2:00 p.m., and when she didn't show up by then, I told myself she'd forgotten. Thanksgiving was hectic. Maybe she had relatives visiting. Maybe, in preparations with her parents, or in conflict with them, this had slipped her mind.

Come Home to My Heart

But when she'd avoided my eyes on our first day back, I'd started to panic as though I were teetering on the edge of a ten-story drop. I hadn't been able to stop myself from approaching her in Calculus, even knowing the risks.

I could still hear her voice saying, *I'm really sorry, we don't have any open spots anymore.* Polite, smooth as glass, like she was talking to a stranger.

That night I couldn't sleep. I considered putting a note in her locker the next day. *Please, can we talk about this?* or *What happened?*

But I knew what had happened. The chain of events was simple. I'd told her I loved her, and she ran.

Everything I'd said that night before break started to seem almost unbelievable. Gloria had laid her fears bare to me for the first time, told me that her best friend had abandoned her, and all I'd done was talk about myself: how I didn't feel guilty, how I needed her, how I loved her. I hadn't meant to be manipulative, but what else could it be when she'd tried to bring up her reservations and all I'd done was beg her, in a dozen partially visible ways, not to leave me?

I'd stared at the ceiling that night and felt like I hadn't really known myself until then. My parents had been right about me. I *was* selfish. Maybe I couldn't even feel love; maybe I was such a narcissist that this had never been about Gloria at all, it had only been about how she made me see myself. Maybe I'd only wanted her as a passport to that future life I'd spent so long imagining. And maybe I was so deep into my self-centeredness that I couldn't even recognize it until she'd given up on me.

So I didn't leave her a note. I wasn't going to force myself into her life when she wanted me gone. I stared at the floor in our shared classes every day, and even this felt selfish, like a performance of emotional injury that some minuscule, pathetic part of me hoped she would see.

Eventually I managed to act almost normal at school again. Still, I couldn't keep from remembering the way her lips had felt on mine, remembering the quiet instrument of her laugh. She was doing better without me. I could tell. She'd started wearing her hair down, brushed in long, clean waves over her shoulders, and she looked better-rested, and she was raising her hand more often in class. In the halls, I saw her laughing with that tall, floppy-haired guy from Young Christian Society, Ben. He looked at her with an open adoration that made me feel faintly sick.

Sometimes I went into the bathroom between classes and just sat in a locked stall and breathed, looking up at the flickering lights, thinking about the wild, static-shock happiness I'd felt when we walked through Columbia with our hands brushing. I wondered if I could have prevented this. If I'd just shut up and let Gloria talk that night, if I'd been more supportive, if I hadn't told her I loved her, would she still have disappeared on me?

Or was it just that I wasn't good enough? If I'd changed, if I didn't smoke or drink, if I didn't talk so much shit about the hometown she loved, if I dressed like a normal person, if I didn't make so many stupid attempts at humor, if I could be gentle and warm and kind instead of glib and pretentious and everything that I actually was—the spiral went endlessly down into every molecule of myself. If I could just have been a different person, would she still have done this, would she have loved me back instead.

In the few weeks of school between Thanksgiving break and winter break, my feelings for Fisherton had escalated into a kind of manic loathing. I wouldn't have thought I was capable of such an intense, sustained hatred. I hardly scraped a few hours of sleep a night. I snuck out of the house most nights and spent a lot of time driving, and smoking myself into coughing fits, and drinking in a way I never

Come Home to My Heart

had before. I bought a handle of shitty vodka from Jeremy Andrews at school, and it lived in the trunk of my car, and sometimes I went to a vacant lot half an hour out of town and sat there on the cracked asphalt and drank until my head spun, headphones on, destroying my eardrums with violent guitar, effectively trapping myself there until I sobered up. I'd known this was dysfunctional behavior, but it had also made me feel grown-up, which had made me feel that much closer to graduation, and freedom.

Over winter break, though, I stopped all that. My parents were watching me now. Our Christmas conversation, far from reassuring them, had obviously confirmed their suspicions that something had gone seriously wrong with me, so I had no choice but to ditch the vodka and stop sneaking out. Instead, I stayed at home, mostly sleeping. Sometimes I tried to read, but I couldn't get through more than a few pages of my Christmas gifts. My parents, bless their hearts, had given me a couple of cheesy middlebrow novels from the top of the bestseller lists, and Mr. Avery surprised me a couple of days after Christmas with a small and personally curated stack.

"Wait, no," I said with the ribboned hardcovers in my hand. "I didn't get you anything."

"Good," he harrumphed. "I've got too many books to read already."

My throat tightened. I'd used to joke with Gloria about the bookstore going broke, since obviously the place had been operating on a loss for years. But suddenly it felt very unfunny, the idea of Mr. Avery having to shutter the Book Alley. And with the price of books these days, I knew the gift in my hand was worth upward of a hundred dollars. "Mr. Avery, you really shouldn't have . . . I mean, with . . ." I couldn't keep my eyes from straying to the register.

"You shouldn't be thinking about all that," he said with an owlish blink.

"Kind of hard not to. You know what we make."

Mr. Avery's beard twitched in amusement. "Xia, please. I had a past life at a big bank in a big city, all right? And I don't have kids, or nieces, or nephews. I can't take my money with me. If I want to blow it all on this place, then that's my business, not yours." He made a shooing motion with one hand. "Now, you go home, enjoy your break. Enjoy those."

I glanced over the titles, feeling oddly fragile. This man I'd always treated with, at best, begrudging acceptance had taken time to pick out books for me. He'd chosen a pair of absurdist books in translation, an Elena Ferrante stand-alone—and, on the bottom of the stack, one of our copies of *The Sound of Falling*, with its blurry photographic cover and its neon orange title.

I felt an unsettled tug in my stomach. "Did you wind up reading this one?" I said, pointing to the spine.

"I did. I was very moved."

I didn't look up at him, didn't really want to risk eye contact. "Cool," I said to the books. "Thanks."

"Of course. Oh—and I attached that recommendation to your applications."

I went still. Kept my mouth shut. Everything I wanted to say seemed so self-pitying, like, *What could you possibly have said to recommend me to anybody?* But my eyes strayed in his direction.

"I admit, I went on for a good few pages," he said mildly, shuffling papers together at the desk. "Wanted those schools to know they have somebody special on their hands."

Heat flushed up my neck. So he'd also noticed how badly I was doing and was trying to cheer me up.

"Right," I mumbled, sticking my hands in my pockets. "Well, um, thanks again. I'm gonna"—I made a jerky motion with my head to the door—"Merry Christmas. Ex-Christmas. Yeah."

Come Home to My Heart

"And a happy New Year," he said.

Soon New Year's had passed, but the atmosphere at home remained tense like it hadn't been in a long time. At lunch and dinner my parents refused to let me check out from conversations. My dad badgered me about some of the books I'd read this fall, asking for plot points and character descriptions like he actually gave a shit. When I holed up in my room in the evenings, my mom would come up and deliver me cocoa, then hover in the doorway as though waiting for me to crack.

I didn't know how to react. Part of me *liked* it, and that made me feel like such a sucker. Apparently I was so desperate for affection that I'd take even this conditional version of my parents' love, which relied on me visibly hitting rock bottom.

But I knew it wasn't real. Their real feelings were *Have you become so ungrateful*, and a year and a half of bare minimum—just like Navya had said *Miss you too*, while her real feelings had obviously been the opposite.

Just like Gloria. She'd seemed to want me. But I'd known the whole time that she could walk away and be okay, hadn't I? That was why I'd been afraid: because I'd known the truth.

So maybe some animal part of me wanted my parents to be gentle and kind to me, but I was smarter than to trust it when it happened. Overall, their attention just made things worse. I couldn't wait for my dad to start traveling again, but I wished I never had to go back to school. I wished I could fall asleep until my college letters showed up, then fast-forward until all memory of this place became backstory.

On the last night of break, I drove to the river. I parked far from the other cars and looked out at the dark water. The sky was so overcast that I couldn't even see the current. The river looked as black and motionless as asphalt, a road I wished I could take.

I hated feeling this way so much that for the past few days, I'd been trying to convince myself I hated *her*, but it hadn't worked. Now, here, with a sense of miserable relief, I let myself miss Gloria to the very center of my body. I waited to find some comfort in admitting the truth to myself. There was none. I felt so alone that I started considering prayer. I didn't try it—I couldn't get that close to the concept—but I considered how it might have been nice to believe in something like that, to believe in being alone and not alone at the same time.

Gloria Forman

I woke up to the sight of white paint. In the blank space, I could envision what had once hung on the bedroom wall: the poster of the princess revolving in the forest, surrounded by pines and snow. My parents had taken that down, too. Now there was only a finger of light reaching in from the hallway, sliding across emptiness.

I let the phone alarm go on a little while, allowing the ambient music to coax me awake. Late last night I'd jerked up in the dark, disoriented, with the feeling that if I didn't spring out of bed and check the trapdoor, everything would collapse. Then I'd remembered where I was: at home, in bed. This happened a few times a week.

I remembered my dream. Xia had been there with me, both of us on the roof of a house sinking in a flood. I could still see her, lips moving in the dark, the sound of her voice wiped away by the storm. *Well?* she'd said silently. Then she'd dived in. I'd clutched to the weather vane and searched the rising water, frantic. A light shone somewhere down there, but I couldn't let go. I'd screamed her name.

Blinking hard, I got to my feet and tried to let the dream world dissipate. Some hint of Xia always turned up in my dreams these days, even when she didn't make an appearance in person. I'd dream of a field doused in sunlight, or tall curtains bound up in rope, or the color of her sofa cushions. Hands on a steering wheel.

I dressed in the corner beside my vanity, shrinking back against the wall when I heard my mother walking past the doorless threshold. "Gloria?" she called. I saw the tip of her nose in the doorway.

"Morning, Mom. I'm getting dressed."

"All right. Hurry, sweetheart, you'll make us late."

I unplugged my phone and sped into the kitchen. Dad, drinking coffee, didn't look my way. He still didn't much. When he talked to me, he was always talking to his knuckles, though he tried to sound normal. He was, at least, better at pretending than he had been over Thanksgiving.

Mom looked me up and down. Apparently my outfit passed muster, because she didn't comment. A couple of days in December, she'd given me an anxious once-over and made me change, or thrown out shirts or pants she thought were too tight. Sometimes she and Dad did things I didn't really understand, things I couldn't see were related to me liking girls, but I went along with everything. I supposed this was one of Pastor Collins's pieces of advice. Sometimes I wondered if I should thank him for advising our family, though when we went to church these days there seemed something sorrowful in the way he looked at me.

Mom walked me to the bus stop. "Have a good day, hon," she said. I sat on the curb, and a minute later, I watched our gray sedan rumble down the street, Mom in the passenger seat, Dad driving.

A few weeks ago, Mom had picked up a part-time job at a lunch counter in Columbia, not far from Dad's job. They didn't want me in the house alone, since I wasn't allowed on the computer without supervision. So, on the days she worked, I waited here on the curb until the bus showed. It usually took half an hour or so, but I didn't mind. My newly fixed phone had games where I collected sparkling gems or turned the screen to make blocks fall in a correct pattern. Besides, the orchestra pit had been so recent that I felt lucky to sit here in the rising sunlight, rested and shampooed and soaped and brushed, having done my homework last night curled on the sofa.

I didn't take any of this for granted. There were so many things I'd never look at the same way again: deodorant sticks, and cafeteria trays, and recycling bins with crumpled cans inside. Fisherton itself seemed to have changed before my eyes. Last Sunday, when my parents and I had walked through downtown after church, I'd stopped in my tracks when I'd seen a shadow down an alley: a man picking through a dumpster.

Before, my eyes would have glided right over him. I might have thought, *Such a shame*, but nothing else. Now I wondered who the man was. I wondered if he had family in Fisherton, if he'd grown up here, too, if he'd lost his job, when he'd last had a shower or a decent night's sleep. I wondered if he was camping out in the old paper mill, bracing for the police to sweep the place and send him over to a neighboring town.

Then he'd looked up from the dumpster and caught my gaze. I'd looked into his eyes and seen my own exhausted face in the greenroom mirror.

And as I'd hurried forward at my parents' heels, I'd reminded myself, for the thousandth time, how lucky I was.

When the bus came, I headed to my usual seat at the back. After a minute, a figure in jeans and a puffer coat approached. Ellis.

"Hey," I said.

"Hi." She took the seat across the aisle. "How's everything?"

The bus was emptier in the mornings than the afternoons. With only a few kids scattered throughout, I didn't need to speak quietly, but my voice came out soft anyway. "Things are okay."

Her eyes traveled to the phone in my hands. "You started taking the bus after Thanksgiving."

I nodded.

"So things *are* okay."

I nodded again.

Ellis seemed to consider, to steel herself. Her mouth tried a smile, and I knew what she thought. If I was living with my parents, and had been for a while now, something must have changed. I must be trying harder than before. Maybe I was even back to my old self by now.

"Then, um," she said, "would you want to sit together at lunch?"

I looked at the lovely fall of Ellis's hair, at her curious eyes. In the days after we'd talked, I'd thought I would do anything to make her want to be my friend again. Now all my memories of us seemed not to draw me closer to her but to separate us even further, hovering between us like ghosts of a past life that I could never rejoin. My friendship with her belonged to a world before I'd felt real hunger, before I'd met Xia, before I'd known who I was. It had been beautiful in its way, but it was back there, and I was here now.

Ellis's almost-smile was fading, but she still looked hopeful. I could see that she really was determined to do this—to forgive me.

But I wasn't grateful for it. In fact, something was beginning to tighten low in my torso, some hard knot forming in me. I didn't want her forgiveness. I wasn't here to be judged, set aside, and taken back up like a mantle. Who I was had always been between me and God. I could never forget that I'd sat there on the precipice of starvation and she'd told me there was no room at the inn.

I waited a moment, making sure my voice would be steady when I spoke. Then I told her, "I'm sorry. I can't."

"Why not?"

"I just can't."

Come Home to My Heart

We both sat there as the bus trundled into the parking lot. I could see her waiting for me to give her more, but if I said anything true, it'd hurt her, and after everything, I still didn't want that.

Ellis had always been like a magician, making something out of nothing. She took in scraps of information, went away with them, and pulled all kinds of meanings from their insides. I'd loved that about her, before: her theories, the pathways forward she found out of tiny openings. The girl who guessed the endings of movies after fifteen minutes. The girl who saw me blink twice and knew I was upset.

Now that meant I couldn't give her anything of me, because she would take more from it than what I'd given. Silence was better. This way, she could believe whatever she wanted: that my parents wouldn't let me have female friends anymore, maybe, and this was part of some grand strategy. She'd come up with an answer, and I was surprised to realize that I didn't much mind what that answer was. I couldn't control how she felt or what she thought. That much I'd learned already.

◊

That day, I felt more aware of Xia than ever. Six weeks, and I was still imagining her reactions to everything in my life. I knew that if I'd told her about turning down Ellis's offer of friendship, she would have approved—but she wouldn't have wanted to seem like she was cheering on the destruction of my friendship, so she would have said something about how most friendships from high school didn't last anyway, and I should probably read a long article about it.

I controlled myself even more than usual. Every so often I could look at her in English, where we had assigned seats and she sat a few rows up from me, but I didn't let myself that day.

Riley Redgate

In December, I'd tried to think of us completely in the past tense. My time with Xia, I'd told myself, had helped me come to terms with who I was—no, with what I struggled with. And that had been useful.

Wasn't it also useful, now, to feel this mixture of hurt and longing? If I really planned to stay away from girls for the rest of my life, wasn't it good to know what I was avoiding: the pain that came along with losing someone?

I was just teaching myself what it felt like, that was all. That was why I kept her last note to me in my backpack and, on sleepless nights, unrolled it by my window, touching her spiky handwriting, playing her voice in my head until my chest felt so heavy it bore me down to sit on the rug. That was why, when my parents and I walked through downtown after church, I led us down the alley past the bookstore door, glancing left at the darkened window with its handwritten *Closed Sundays* sign. I was learning my lesson.

But sometimes, at school, her physical closeness felt excruciating. I had vivid daydreams about leaving the lunchroom and going to the baseball field, seeing her again, saying I was so sorry for everything I'd done—begging her to take me back. I could stash my phone in my locker so my parents couldn't tell I was a hundred yards away from the school. Just like that, I'd be with her again.

But my willpower had held this long. *This is what you have to do*, I told myself. All my life, I would have crushes on girls, and in weak moments, I would entertain ideas about traveling with them, or going on dates together, or adopting a pet, or kissing them to the point of delirium. I would want to be perilously, disbelievingly happy in the way Xia had made me happy.

I just had to learn how to accept this without ever acting on it.

I just had to stay asleep.

Come Home to My Heart

I felt stifled by the silence, though. My parents never came close to the topic. Ben had asked me to the Winter Dance in December, and although I'd told him I only wanted to go as friends, I'd omitted that part when I relayed the news to my parents, thinking maybe it would elicit some reaction. They'd given each other a quick look, something that might have been relief—but then they'd asked casual questions like it was nothing, like they'd never expected anything else.

I can't do this alone, I thought in Chemistry as Xia stalked out the door and I packed my bag, purposefully not watching her go. I knew that at heart all this was between me and God, but I still needed some kind of earthly road map.

So, during lunch, I told Ben and the others that I needed to work on an essay, and I went to the library to use the computers.

It felt idiotically risky. These computers sat right out in the open, and a stream of people walked by even as I took a chair, but I had no other option. My parents had deleted my phone's browser and changed my settings to prevent new app downloads, all password-protected. At home, my mother sat by me whenever I was on the computer, reading, occasionally glancing at the screen with an encouraging smile when she saw I was still working on homework.

So I turned the brightness on the screen all the way down and zoomed out until I had to lean forward and squint to read anything. *How to be a good Christian when lesbian*, I typed into the search bar. Even to acknowledge that much, to describe myself as lesbian for the first time, set my stomach to tightening.

There were a couple of articles from sites that I knew my parents used, so I clicked those first. They just repeated what I'd been told forever, though: that these feelings were sinful, that they went against the Bible, that I could make the choice to suppress them.

That wasn't helpful. I needed someone like me, who understood what it was like to live this way. Someone who could help me get through every day.

Feeling apprehensive, I clicked on another site.

I didn't find what I was looking for. Not quite. As I read, my apprehension faded into confusion.

This was someone who talked about being gay like Xia always had, without guilt—except that she was Christian:

If you're reading this, if you're feeling scared or ashamed, it's going to be okay. I hope you know that God created you exactly how He wanted you to be. You are held in the light of His love, and no human judgment will ever change that.

As I clicked through the tabs on the site, I found personal essays, interviews, news articles, all by different authors. Some were snidely academic:

... we as Christians are unbound from Old Testament law by Jesus's sacrifice, and we should be grateful, considering some of the other behaviors forbidden by Leviticus: the sowing of mixed seeds, the eating of shellfish, etc. As for the letter from Paul condemning the abandonment of natural sexual relations for "unnatural" ones ... if we accept the definition of something "unnatural" as a choice that transgresses against God-given law, then we should ask ourselves: Why would any thinking person choose to be gay in our current universe, when being heterosexual would mean a life free of people questioning your right to love and be loved? Can we truly say a God-given capacity for selfless, nurturing, faithful love between two people is unnatural?

Other articles were so personal that I couldn't believe they weren't private:

Come Home to My Heart

I just wanted to fall in love. I just wanted to have a family. I felt like an outcast for nearly a decade, and those feelings drove me to three suicide attempts. But at the end of the day, I am still here, and now I refuse to go by my own hand. I refuse unhappiness and I refuse isolation. I cannot and will not believe that the Almighty made me to walk the Earth alone.

What shook me the most, though, was the simple sight of these admissions over and over and over again, in hundreds of voices, out there in public for anyone to see:

I've known I was lesbian since I was twelve.
I started questioning my gender identity in high school.
I only realized I was bisexual after college.
I'm gay.

When I scrolled down to the bottom of each page, I could see the people who had written these articles smiling in photographs next to descriptions of their lives. Here was a woman who owned a bakery in Massachusetts. There, a man who did graphic design in Miami. Many of them were in pictures with their partners. Some of them were younger, some older, but they were all adults, and they looked happy.

I realized I couldn't remember the last time I'd pictured happiness for myself in the future. Somewhere along the way I'd discarded that as a possibility. Even with Xia, I'd never let myself fantasize about more time together than the hours we were stealing. I'd looked down the long road of my life and seen grim determination at best. At worst there was nothing, no future at all.

The five-minute bell rang.

I sat motionless, not wanting to go to English, wanting only to stay and read for hours.

A voice in my mind like my father's was already urgently pushing back on the words I'd read. *They'll say anything to justify their behavior, Gloria, anything to twist the Bible to fit their lifestyle. It's all a circle.*

But then, I thought, so was the way I'd believed all my life: that the Bible could be read only one way, and to do anything else was walking down the Devil's path. That logic reinforced itself, too.

These people cared about scripture and had scriptural reasons for what they were saying. I wanted to believe them so badly that I felt dizzy, but could I trust my own judgment when I so desperately wanted one option to be true over the other? The compass was spinning wildly in me. I wanted to go somewhere and pray. I wanted to stop the world and read a hundred more pages, a thousand more, and figure everything out.

But the bell was about to ring, so I shouldered my things, logged out, and left.

Xia Harper

Halfway through January, two weeks before the Winter Dance, large, handmade posters appeared above banks of lockers, shimmering with glitter that showered down onto people's hair whenever someone reached up and flicked them. Gloria's voice echoed over the speaker that afternoon during the announcements, informing the school that we could buy tickets at the table outside the front doors immediately after the bell.

I considered making a ten-minute detour through the side door and bus lot so that I didn't have to see her selling tickets, but that felt cowardly. It also wasn't much of a defense mechanism, since I already had to sit in classrooms with her for three hours a day.

So I braced myself as I moved with the crowd down the school steps, past the flagpole, toward the colorful advertisements spread over the ticket table.

I thought about the night we'd danced in my living room, swaying to the fuzzy chromatics of old jazz trumpets, laughing when we'd stepped on each other's feet.

"Xia."

Riley Redgate

I startled, looking up from the pavement. I hadn't quite passed the ticket table. A nervous-looking boy with sandy-brown hair was standing in front of me.

"Um," I said. "Hi?"

"Move," said a bored voice from behind us, some guy trying to get in line for tickets. I glanced back, and my eyes went right to Gloria's fingers swiftly thumbing dollar bills into a beat-up metal lockbox. Her nails were painted pale pink.

Fighting the urge to run, I stepped out of the flow of foot traffic. The sandy-haired boy shifted with me, nearly tripping over the base of a streetlight. "I'm Jack," he said, and I remembered where I'd seen him: in sixth period, wearing his soccer uniform.

"Right," I said. "We have World History."

He nodded. "It sucks, right?"

I shrugged.

Jack's hands moved from his hoodie to the pockets of his jeans, then finally curled around the straps of his backpack. He looked so uncomfortable that I said begrudgingly, "You're on the soccer team, right?"

He looked surprised. "Yeah."

"What position?"

"Um, left defense." A weird expression flitted across his face, too quickly for me to read. "Listen," he blurted, "are you going to that?" He pointed at the Winter Dance ticket table.

I probably stared at him for only a few seconds, but it felt like the majority of my life. His cheeks were red in the cold, and his lips were bitten.

"Look," I said, "I don't actually sell drugs, if you're looking for molly or party stuff or whatever."

"I'm not. I'm asking, do you—would you want to go with me? To the dance?"

My mouth opened, but no sound came out. Was this actually happening? I didn't understand how anyone like Very Normal Jack From Soccer could want to ask me to a dance.

But, I thought with a twist in my stomach, Gloria was normal, and she'd told me she wished we could go together. Gloria had kissed me like she'd wanted to do it, she'd adjusted my glasses and told me they made me look sophisticated. It wasn't impossible that this guy might think I was pretty. Or maybe he liked reading and had seen me with books.

I didn't know what to do. I had a persona to keep up, but I didn't want to hurt someone's feelings about something like this. Several people nearby had stopped to watch.

"Um," I said, "sorry, I'm not—I wasn't planning on going."

Jack let out a long breath. "Okay, that's cool."

There was no disappointment in his voice. Actually, he sounded relieved.

Then I saw them. Two other boys standing behind a nearby tree. I'd thought they were just looking at their phones in silence, but one of them snuck a look at me and Jack, and now I saw that both their shoulders were shaking in silent laughter.

The cold sting of the January air disappeared. Heat flooded through me as I realized the whole thing had been a dare.

I understood everything that came along with that, too. I understood that to these guys, I didn't even deserve my own humiliation. I was so low that I was a tool for someone else's embarrassment.

When I spoke, my voice was shaking. "Great joke. Yeah. Really fucking funny, you discount movie jocks."

They stopped disguising their amusement. One of them doubled over. The other looked at me and burst into fresh peals of laughter. They didn't even respond to my insult, which was much worse. My words hung in the air, sounding infantile and pathetically defensive.

Of course, they didn't have to say anything. They'd already won just by getting me to wonder, for a second, if someone really did like me.

Jack wasn't laughing, just grinning nervously, looking at his friends rather than me. The half dozen people gathered around us seemed various shades of mortified. A few hurried away, but others stayed with bright, curious eyes, waiting to see what I'd do.

Pressure built in my head like steam. I didn't know what would come out if I opened my mouth, but I had the feeling that if I kept it shut, I would just fly at Jack and his friends and scratch at them like a rabid animal, until every second of every day I'd spent in Fisherton was mapped out on their skin. My eyes were stinging, the harsh winter sunlight unbearable.

"She's right," said a voice. "It's not funny."

My limbs stiffened. The roar in my ears intensified. Gloria had heard the whole thing.

I genuinely thought about dying, then, about how it would be better if I had a heart attack on the spot, and an ambulance showed up, and these assholes had to live with traumatizing guilt forever, and I never had to see her watching me in a moment of such abject powerlessness.

Jack wasn't smiling anymore, and his friends had stopped laughing. They assumed lazy, unbothered expressions. "I don't know," one of them said. "It's kind of funny."

Gloria stood up from the ticket table. "Maybe if you're six years old."

Come Home to My Heart

I couldn't take this. Not this, too. I rounded on her and words shot out of me. "I don't need your help."

A weird, resounding silence. My eyes were burning hot now. Gloria looked stricken, but she was looking at me, the first time our eyes had met since November. I looked at her shoulders set back and the fall of her hair and the crucifix still sitting there between her collarbones. It felt insane that none of these people would ever know that she had been everything to me.

I backed away from the table, my hands numb. I heard someone say, "Why'd you even bother, Gloria, she's such a bitch."

I just wanted to be in the safety of my car, but when I glanced down the sidewalk, the lot looked several states away, and to get there I'd have to pass through hundreds of kids, and even then, even if I got into my car and locked the doors until the traffic cleared, anyone could look through the windows and see me.

I turned and stormed back into the school, shoving through the crowd. "Fucking move," I snarled at no one in particular. Some freshman dodged out of my way with a terrified bleat that gave me a rush of vindictive pleasure.

There was a girls' bathroom ten seconds down the hallway. I locked myself into the last stall and leaned against the grimy tiled wall, clutching my thighs, feeling like poison. I muffled my sobs in my sleeves, but the hot air rubbed my throat raw. Soon I was overwarm, sweating. I stripped off my hoodie and flung it onto my backpack.

I ached to let this out somehow, but there was nobody to tell. Not Navya, not Kit, not strangers on the internet. Not my parents, with their clueless expressions. I hated the idea of my mom and dad looking at me and seeing some bullied child. I wanted to be so self-reliant that they'd never know I'd needed them the past year and a half.

Half an hour later, the door opened and shut. My gut dropped.

Riley Redgate

I heard stall doors moving gently, stirring the air, hinges whining. Footsteps coming closer.

Her sneakers stopped outside my stall. For a long time, she didn't say anything. Then: "Everyone's gone, if you want to leave."

Of course she would know I'd hidden in here, that I'd waited to ensure my solitude. I hated that she knew. I wanted to take back everything I'd given her. I wanted to be a stranger to her again.

Gloria's feet turned, and I heard the stall door creak as she leaned against it.

"I'm really sorry," she whispered.

"For what?" I said, hard and loud. "For everything going back to normal?"

"It's not normal. You look tired all the time. You're not even reading anymore."

I stared at the graffiti scratched into the plastic door. How did she know that, not having done so much as look at me since Thanksgiving?

My heart drummed, fast and painful. I'd thought Gloria had closed the door and regretted nothing. I'd pictured her life unburdened without me. But here she was, admitting she was still paying attention. Did that mean she wished she hadn't ended things?

Or did it just mean she felt sorry for me?

I squeezed my hands into fists. I wasn't going to guilt-trip her into talking to me. Better not to show the cracks.

"Oh, so you care suddenly?" I sneered. "Thanks for the fake concern. You can go now."

The buzz of the overactive heater took over for a while. The stifling air tickled my sore throat.

"Don't do that," she said quietly.

"Do what?"

"Try to be that person with me."

Come Home to My Heart

I felt a sensation like snowmelt in my chest, something trickling hotly from chamber to chamber. I looked up at the ceiling and blinked hard.

I said, "Tell me it's easier now, at least."

"It's not."

I pictured the way she sometimes folded her arms, her fingers clamped over her upper arms as if she were imprisoning herself in the only cage she could make.

I didn't know why I couldn't think of anything to say. Hadn't I spent six weeks building up a list of what I'd tell her, if she ever gave me the slightest hint that she still cared?

"My parents found out," she said.

My heart stopped.

I slipped the latch on the stall door and pulled it open. Gloria's arms were crossed just the way I'd pictured them. Her skin looked sickly pale in the bathroom light.

"How?" I asked.

"I forgot to clear the browsing history on our computer."

I gave my head a little shake, hearing but not understanding. She'd never said anything to suggest her parents were the kind of strict that picked through their kid's search history.

"So," she went on, "over Thanksgiving, they made a lot of new rules."

"Like what?"

"I can't go out anymore."

"You're eighteen. They're seriously trying to ground you?"

She took out her phone. "They installed this tracking app to make sure I don't go anywhere that isn't school."

I stared at the phone in her hand. I'd heard about parents installing apps to monitor their kids' driving. I'd even read articles about parents keeping tabs on kids at college through their phones, but the idea of my parents ever doing something like that was so ridiculous that I'd never considered what it would be like.

"I'm sorry," she said, her voice strained. "If you hate me, I get it. When they . . . I started trying harder again at Thanksgiving. To stop. I just knew if I talked to you or anything, I wouldn't be able to do it." She shook her head. "I shouldn't even be talking to you now."

"Why are you?"

But she looked at me bright-eyed, like she needed me to understand something she couldn't say, and I felt the tug underneath my stomach, and I knew why. My mind slowly went empty, every thought fading to a blank hush, as she stepped closer, her face tilting up toward mine. I felt the afternoon turning on its head, transforming into something I couldn't believe.

For an instant we were motionless, inches apart. Her breath glided over my cheek, over my mouth. I gazed down at the slope of her forehead and the softness of her hair falling past her brow. The hurt of these past weeks locked hard into a surge of want. I was peripherally aware of her chest and shoulders rising and falling.

Then I took her by the wrist and brought her through the door. It was hardly locked before we were kissing. I pressed her against the wall, and her hands cupped my face, and she was cold from the winter air, but the way she pulled me into her made heat wash up my back, over my shoulders, down into my gut. She tasted like cinnamon gum, and her thin ChapSticked mouth against mine felt just the way I remembered—the way I'd dreamed about since November. But her hands were different. One slid into my hair with a new urgency, her fingers tangling hard at the nape of my neck. Her other hand gripped my waist, then—suddenly—slipped under my T-shirt.

Come Home to My Heart

I broke the kiss just long enough to draw a shaky, disbelieving breath, to look at her with a kind of pathetic desperation that, if I'd seen it in the mirror, would probably have disgusted me. But she was my mirror just then, her brow tight, her eyes urgent. The sight took me outside myself, outside self-consciousness or even self-awareness. All I knew was my heart felt like it could pop. As I closed my eyes, melting back down into her, I felt terrified for a second that I was going to wake up and realize the whole thing had been some elaborate dream.

She didn't disappear.

She tucked her face into my neck and wrapped her arms so tightly around my waist, it hurt. My mind spun upward. "I missed you so much," she said, her breath making shivers shoot down my throat, and I repeated it back to her, whispering it into her hair, feeling icy and alert like she was a nicotine rush. We kissed until my lips were sore, until no part of her felt cold anymore.

"What are we going to do?" I whispered. "How is this going to work?"

"I don't know," she said. But we'd never known.

Gloria Forman

"Here." Mom handed my phone back over the dinner table, having finished scrolling through my calls and texts. She spooned parsnips onto her plate and added, "Ben's been texting you a lot."

"Yeah. We're trying to get a group together for the dance, but it's hard to figure out. It feels like if we add one other person, we have to add all their friends, too."

It felt stupid to say, since Mom had just read everything we'd said, but she nodded like it was new information. "Ellis is going with Aiden, I assume?"

"Yes, ma'am."

"And y'all four aren't just going to be your own group?"

I took my time answering. I hadn't told my parents what had happened between Ellis and me. This being Fisherton, I still knew all about her day-to-day, so whenever they asked about her, I could answer, and had been answering, like we were still friends.

"Me and Ellis kind of drifted apart this year," I said.

My mother inspected me. Her gaze had a steel in it that I didn't think I'd inherited. Dad, on the other hand, was studying his plate, the tips of his ears slowly turning red. His fork had stilled.

"You're not—" he said in a hard voice. "You didn't . . . you and that girl weren't . . ."

"No," I said quickly. "Absolutely not. That's why we're not so close anymore, because I—I mentioned it to her, after I told y'all, and she didn't like it, either."

My father's shoulders loosened, and my mother sighed. "I always liked Ellis," she said, sounding relieved. "I can't blame her, but that's . . . well, that's that, I suppose."

The rest of dinner, we discussed my mom's cousin up in Raleigh, who'd gotten in a car accident, and the revival that First Baptist was planning for early May, and Dad's job. Privately, I didn't think he would last much longer at the car wash, the way he'd been talking. "My ankle's been acting up again," he said. "I'm thinking I should try Walgreens."

"Baby, that place is another half hour in the car," my mom said.

"No, there's another one that's closer. They're hiring now."

"You'd still be able to drive me?"

"Ashley, obviously, why wouldn't I be able to?"

"I'm just asking," said my mom, sounding weary.

"Besides, the Walgreens pays better, and the work's steadier. Maybe you wouldn't need that job anymore."

My mom didn't answer. I found it hard to read their moods these days, but I thought she'd seemed happier since she'd gotten the job at the lunch counter. Dad, though, seemed frosty whenever she talked about it. Sometimes, in response to her anecdotes, he wouldn't say anything, instead sipping from the beer bottles that now sat openly upon our dinner table. I wondered if my parents felt, like I did, the way our family's neat compartments had cracked open.

I broke the silence. "Um, Mom, do you think you could start picking me up on Wednesdays? Math Team is starting practices again."

Come Home to My Heart

"What time?" she asked. "Five?"

"We're going until five thirty through the tournament in April."

She nodded. "As long as you're charging that phone enough to last all day."

◇

Xia had suggested sneaking out to see each other at night. I couldn't do that, of course. For one thing, the house she thought was mine was all the way across town. For another, I knew the risks if I got caught.

Every so often those risks overwhelmed me. I still felt like a part of me dwelled down in the orchestra pit, jittering awake to the buzz of the light bulb. I knew the actual physical danger in what I was choosing. But I couldn't live like this anymore, surrounded by a sea of faces that were either totally unknowing or fraught with disgusted restraint. I couldn't live without a single person in the world understanding me. If I had to choose between my body and my soul, I chose my soul.

I'd started to have dangerous thoughts about what Xia had once said, about leaving Fisherton. I'd started thinking with feverish longing about next autumn, about my college applications, which even now were percolating through admissions systems. Next fall was only eight months away, but those eight months seemed like an unbreakable wall.

We thought of meeting at lunch, but the period only lasted half an hour, and by the time I got through the lunch line and finished eating, I rarely had more than ten minutes left. Now we had a half hour on Wednesday afternoons, and we were lucky to have that much.

Our saving grace was that I had my phone back. We texted from the moment I got on the bus in the morning until the moment I got home in the afternoon. Before getting off at my stop, I deleted our conversation so my mom could check my text history over dinner.

After I returned to my room for the night, I sent Xia the all-clear, and our conversation started up again. Sometimes I called her at midnight, one, two in the morning, and I pulled my sheets up over my head, speaking with a soft lisp so my *S*'s wouldn't slip through my open door and down the hall. When I closed my eyes, I could imagine we were back at the river, or in her house, or in her car, all the places I wished we could return to.

Still, I didn't miss the fall. Yes, we'd had more freedom, but now I could finally be honest with her.

"I've been reading online," I whispered one night.

"Reading what?"

"Blog posts and articles and stuff. At school, during lunch. Anything by other Christians who are, you know." I took a breath. I could say it now, but I still couldn't make it sound natural. "Lesbian, or other, yeah."

"Is it helping?" Xia asked.

"I don't know. Sometimes it makes me feel better, but sometimes it just makes everything feel even more . . ."

"Confusing?" she guessed.

"Big."

"Big like how?"

"Like how am I supposed to figure out what to do, when it's part of the whole history of Christianity, and also the whole history of people being gay?"

I could hear Xia's sheets rustling, her bedframe creaking. "You don't think that's kind of nice?"

"Which part?"

"Belonging to something. Having, like, a cultural legacy."

"I don't feel like I really belong, though."

"You do," she said at once. "Why wouldn't you?"

Come Home to My Heart

I hesitated. "Because people don't know about me. And I guess when I think about LGBT things, I think about flags and coming out and people being, I don't know, open in ways we're not. Parades."

She let out a little laugh.

"I'm serious," I said.

"Sorry. I know you are. It's just—yeah, that's what penetrates through in the news and stuff, but that's not what it means to be queer."

"What does it mean?"

"I don't know." She paused. "I don't want to sound fake deep, but, like, who are you? That's what it means."

"You never sound fake deep."

Xia laughed again. "Okay, well, I know that's not true."

"Not about queer stuff."

"Well, thank God for that." She paused. "What I mean is, there's no rules, you know? Everyone's circumstances are different. Like, basic example, I always used to think lesbians had to be butch. And maybe I'll cut off all my hair when I go to college, but maybe I won't, and whatever choice I make, that's what being gay will look like for me. Whatever I choose to be and do, that's what it means for me."

"But you're already so good at choosing what you want to be."

"What, and you're not?" she said, sounding bemused.

"That's what I'm trying to say, yeah. I feel like everything is out of my hands. I feel like to belong, I have to be . . . like . . . out and proud. Everyone online talks about pride."

"Hey." Her voice was softer now. "You don't have to fit other people's experiences. That isn't how this works. You don't have to learn a new set of rules to replace the old ones."

"I guess I also don't feel like I've done anything to be proud of."

She sighed. "That's not what it means. It's not pride like you'd be proud of winning something. It's pride like—like the opposite of fear."

I snuggled down into my pillow. "I read someone's coming-out story today. This girl up in Boston. She said her parents didn't even blink, and all her friends acted totally normal, like nothing changed. I can't even imagine what that would be like. It just made me want to . . ." I shook my head. It was growing too warm under my bedcovers.

"To what?"

Even as I smiled, my eyes burned. "To go to the dance with you," I whispered.

Xia didn't say anything for a long time, but when she spoke, I heard her smiling, too. "I'll go if you want me to."

"I do want you to." I hesitated. "I'll be there with Ben, though."

"You can escape him for a few minutes, right?"

"Of course." I was smiling like I hardly ever did, already imagining the minutes we'd steal; the way she'd tilt me, kiss me; the way I'd touch her lips with my fingertip and feel like every love song over the speaker was about her.

And for an instant I did feel it. Pride like the opposite of fear. Pride like relief that I was myself, because I was living a life that had her in it.

"Do me a favor?" I asked.

"Anything."

"Wear red."

◊

"What's going on, honey bear?"

I looked up from the stove, where I'd been stirring the gravy and humming to myself. My mother stood in the door to the kitchen, watching curiously. "You seem pretty perky."

"Oh—yeah." I kept stirring. The gravy was beginning to simmer. "I'm excited for this weekend. The dance, I mean."

Come Home to My Heart

An irrepressible smile fought its way onto my lips. I couldn't restrain it to the small, tight-lipped things I'd managed every day since coming home. I imagined my hands entwined in Xia's, envisioned her in a red gown that flowed all the way down her figure, and my cheeks tingled.

Floorboards creaked as my mother approached. I felt a distinct pulse of danger. Her eyes had always reminded me of my own, although hers were blue, as though someone had daubed a layer of watercolor onto my own gray. When I was a little kid, I'd loved looking into those eyes and seeing myself, hoping that when I grew up, I'd be everything my mother was: purposeful and charitable, sharp and analytical.

Now I worried that we mirrored each other too completely—that from this close, my mother might be able to slip inside my head and know the source of my happiness.

"That's great, Glor," my mother said. "What all are you excited for?"

My stomach tightened. I felt the probe in the question, the hint of worry.

I fixed my smile in place, though the happiness had gone from it. "Lots of things. You know how much work I've been doing, organizing and all. Plus, Ben and I have been talking a lot lately. He's just a great guy."

Some rigidity in my mother's face softened. "He is. That boy's always been a real sweetheart. Smart, too."

As she smoothed down the shoulder of my dress, I thought, *But so is she. So is she, and how could they not care?*

It seemed so ludicrous that I couldn't tell my own mother how amazing Xia was—that the woman who raised me could look into the face of my feelings and call them ugly.

I'd never spent a lot of time thinking, *It's not fair*. Maybe I'd been raised in other directions, like *I'll do better* or *I'll work harder*.

But as my mom left the room, I set down the spoon and covered my face with one hand, and I thought, *This isn't fair*.

It wasn't *fair* that I had to slide this bright-burning candle under a bushel. How could it be right that while everybody else got to celebrate their feelings, Xia and I had to agonize over ours in shadowed corners?

I wanted to glow like everybody else. I wanted them to see her light, too.

What we're doing isn't wrong, I thought, testing the idea like somebody putting that first foot out onto a tightrope.

It held.

The way I feel for her was never wrong, I thought again, the words ringing more strongly in my mind. Xia had said as much months ago, but only now could I feel the same.

I wanted to take care of her, to make her happy, to cherish her like she never had been before. And from all I knew of God, that was one hundred percent right.

It's beautiful, I found myself thinking. Maybe it always was.

Maybe I always was.

Xia Harper

I bought my dress in Columbia at a large, blindingly lit department store. No one working there asked if I needed help, which was a relief. I wanted this process to be as anonymous as possible.

The first ten minutes or so made me aware of my body in a way I hated. I liked to think I was above worrying about things like the shape of my shoulders or the proportions of my legs, but trying on roughly three million ill-fitting dresses forces you to consider these things.

Around halfway through, though, I started thinking about what kinds of dresses Gloria might like, and I was surprised to feel the stress abate. After spending three and a half years trying to vanish, finally accepting that someone was going to look at me came as a relief, and the fact that I *wanted* that someone to look at me even made the process sort of enjoyable.

It was Wednesday evening, and I was still basking in the afterglow of her touch. These days I felt like I was living for our half hours in the disused gym, hidden with her in the crisscrossing metal structures under the bleachers. Those minutes were hypersaturated, high-concentration, like an explosion of sugar on my tongue after a week of stale bread.

Riley Redgate

By the time I arrived back in Fisherton, I'd imagined myself all the way into Friday night. I could see Gloria standing with her cluster of friends, wearing something that shone in the threadlike beams of laser lights, her hair falling down her back. The dance venue was the main room of the town hall, a drafty expanse of creaking floorboards with a balcony that ringed the whole place. I'd be standing alone on that balcony, and I'd look down at the spot she revolved on the floor, moving with her stiffened grace, like a flawlessly programmed machine. Her forearms would be draped over Ben's shoulders, but she would look up, past him, toward me. When we saw each other, the pounding pop music I hated would transform into something honeyed and physical, something that shrank the space between us.

I repressed a smile as I unlocked my front door, an excited flutter in my stomach. But when I walked in, a voice startled me out of my thoughts.

"What's that, sweetheart?"

I looked into the front room. My mom sat in one of the armchairs, her work laptop on her lap, pointing at my bag.

"Hi," I said. "It's, um, a dress for the dance."

"Dance?" She looked stunned. "You haven't told us about any dance."

No, I thought, *because I don't want you to ruin it*.

Then I felt almost guilty. Since winter break, my mom and dad had doubled down on their "real parents" act. My dad had been working in Georgia for the past week, but he'd been texting me every single night. **Today was an interesting day at work. Diesel spill left tower crane inoperable. Hopefully will make up time during the rest of the week. Sleep well.**

As for my mother, she'd started waiting to eat dinner until I got home from work every night at eight thirty. As we ate, she'd keep up

Come Home to My Heart

a stream of questions, switching topics until she found one that got an actual answer out of me—usually something about a book or a movie. Then we'd move haltingly through a discussion of said book or movie while, in the back of my head, I thought, *I know you're not interested in my opinions on the* Alien *franchise; you're just trying to pry me open.*

But this felt different. I could believe that my mother was legitimately interested in the subject of a dance.

"Right," I said. "Well. The dance is this Friday and it's at eight, downtown."

"Did someone invite you to go?"

"No. I told the yearbook people I'd take photos."

"Oh. I see. Still, that will be quite exciting, won't it? Your first dance." She folded her laptop shut. "And your dress? May I see it?"

I hesitated, then set the bag on the ground and drew out the folded dress. I'd picked a high-necked number that involved several floaty layers of chiffon. Red, like Gloria had asked. It looked like something an enchantress would wear while casting a spell of eternal darkness.

I handed the dress to my mother. As she let it unfold with a quiet swish, I folded my arms and stared through the window at our neighbor slipping into his Ford.

"This is a good color for you," Mom said. "And the material is high-quality."

"Thanks," I muttered, my face hot, unsure why I felt embarrassed.

She folded the dress back up. "I'll drive you there and pick you up, okay?"

"What? No, you don't have to."

"Oh yes, I do." She waved through the window at my car. "You can't drive a car like that to a dance!"

Riley Redgate

So, two evenings later, I got out of the passenger seat of my parents' massive black SUV in front of the town hall. I had a cheap phone tripod under my arm, which my mom had insisted on buying, just in case I needed it for my yearbook photos. I'd also brought a small, battery-powered light. I'd claimed that was for photography purposes, too.

"Xia," my mom said before I shut the door.

I looked back. "What?"

"I'll be back here at ten thirty precisely."

"Okay."

She paused, then added, "You look very elegant. I hope you have fun."

My mom was smiling, a touch of rosy color in her cheeks. She sounded genuine; she even looked excited for me.

"Thanks," I mumbled. "Bye." I shut the door quickly, wondering what was wrong with me. Compliments were supposed to feel good, weren't they? Why did I suddenly feel upset, seeing that look on my mother's face?

As I watched the SUV drive off, another car pulled up alongside the curb. A girl in an emerald halter dress slipped out with her date, a boy a couple inches shorter than her. They'd hardly closed the door when the girl's beaming mother hurried out of the passenger seat, telling them to pose on the steps. Her father joked that the girl should take off her high heels for the boy's benefit, and although the girl made a show of annoyance, she was clearly used to the affection.

A lump rose in my throat. That was probably what my parents had imagined for me when we'd moved here.

I wondered if it would have made my mom happy to take a photo of me tonight, boy or no boy. She used to light up back in Atlanta when we suggested any little social ritual. Hayrides on Halloween, dinner

Come Home to My Heart

parties with my parents' friends. Taking a ceremonial picture before a dance was exactly the sort of thing she would have loved.

The lump swelled in my throat. No—it was better that I hadn't offered. I didn't think I could stand it if she'd started making hints about dancing with guys or asking why I didn't have a date. Best to keep the interaction as short and safe as possible.

Trying to push the whole idea from my mind, I hurried up the weathered concrete steps. Garlands in our school colors, navy and white, wound up the iron banister to a door that had been propped open. The echoes of music flooded out to greet me, and as I entered, I passed a table for last-minute ticket sales. Ellis sat behind the cash box. I bit my cheek. I knew Gloria didn't wish her any ill will, but sometimes I had vivid revenge fantasies on Gloria's behalf in which I took a pair of scissors and snipped neatly through Ellis's painstakingly curled hair.

The bass thrummed as I entered the town hall's main room. I had to admit the place made a decent ballroom. The uneven floorboards had a kind of farmhouse charm—although some of the girls with higher heels were wobbling off-kilter—and the thirty-foot ceiling made the space echo like a concert hall. A DJ at the front of the room pumped his fist to the collected works of Dua Lipa while lights spun. WELCOME, FISHERTON MARLINS! read a white banner that flowed down from the balcony rails.

I spotted her beside one of the banner's knots, leaning against the rail, looking down at the dance floor.

Her dress glittered just like I'd imagined, such a pale blue that it verged on white. A simple pendant dangled to its sweetheart neckline. Shining thread in her braided hair caught small diamonds of light, and those braids interwove at the back and sides of her head, sleek and tight against her skull. As always, all precision. Queen of ice.

Her eyes tracked to the door and found me.

Riley Redgate

Something pattered in the center of my body, quick rabbit-jump sensation. For the moment, nobody stood beside her, not Ben or any of her other friends. No one was watching me.

Across the crowded room, I mouthed, *Hi.*

Gloria gave me her small, shadowed, public smile. The image of restraint. *Hi,* she mouthed back.

Then the group descended on her. She cast one last look at me over her shoulder before they moved back from the edge of the balcony and vanished.

I spent some time sitting at a high table under the balcony, drinking punch and eating snacks. Not a bad time, honestly. Watching the edge of the dance floor was painful but oddly mesmerizing, those exposed members of the crowd who were all trying to contort their way back toward the center. As the seating filled up, a couple of guys from Academic Bowl approached my mostly empty table and said, with clear anxiety, "Uh—"

"Go ahead." I jerked my head at the empty seats and looked at my phone as though I had important things to do.

The guys looked relieved. They sat down and didn't give me any shit, didn't even seem to see me after a while, and I didn't mind them, either. I looked less conspicuous with company.

About twenty minutes in, I scoped out the other rooms in the town hall building. Most doors were locked, but I discovered a small custodian's closet on the upstairs floor that opened no problem. I texted Gloria: **Meet me upstairs, left side of the hall, second door?**

8:30, she answered.

I sat down right there on a wooden crate and waited.

Ten minutes later she was slipping inside and locking the door behind us. She was flushed, smiling. "You look amazing," she said quietly.

"*I* do? Look at you. Like—wow."

Come Home to My Heart

We both laughed, and her smile changed. It became a big, bright grin, almost uneven. I couldn't look away from her lips, from the dimples pressed into her freckled cheeks—from these small pieces of evidence that I could make her lose control.

There was a pleased silence that made me want to squirm.

Then Gloria asked me, "Do you want to dance?"

"Yeah. I really, really do." I leaned past her—the closet was hardly big enough for us to revolve in place—and killed the light. Then, on a shelf, I set the battery-powered light I'd brought, which melted through neon colors in a slow, dreamy way.

Gloria's smile shone pink, then pale purple in the light as we moved together. I linked my hands around the back of her neck, and hers settled on my waist. The music playing downstairs had a hard electronic pulse, but filtered through a floor's worth of insulation and a wooden door, layered beneath hundreds of whooping voices, it took on a hazy, unreal quality. We swayed back and forth, laughing when I lifted my arm and Gloria revolved under it, no room to spin with any velocity. She made another half turn and leaned back against me, so I smelled something like heather or lavender, something delicately floral. I would never have liked that scent if it hadn't lain upon her hair and skin, making me think about the ways she chose to assemble herself.

I turned her again, and right away we were kissing. She wasn't wearing lipstick, only lip balm, and I'd done the same, not wanting to leave traces. We stopped even the motions of dancing, and I felt the sweet, nerve-prickling rush of holding her. This didn't feel like autumn anymore, when my kisses had been questions and her reactions had been tentative answers. Gloria touched me now like she wanted me, held me like she meant it.

I broke away from her, breathing hard, and pushed a stray lock of her hair back into her updo with my fingertip. "How long did this thing take, anyway?" I said, tracing the braids with curiosity. "How does it stay up?"

Gloria let out a laugh, her eyes traveling steadily over my face from forehead to chin. A tiny shake of her head.

"What? I'm genuinely interested in the physics here."

"Xia . . ."

"Is it like a state secret or something?"

She said, "I think I'm in love with you."

My mouth closed. Something seared across my chest like I'd been sliced by a white-hot knife.

I'd read millions of words in my life, and somehow none of them had equipped me with a single thing to say.

I took her face in my hands and kissed her, let her kiss me, until something at my core unwound and my head felt several pounds too light.

Eventually, she whispered, "I should get back to the others."

"Can you make it back here? Like, later tonight?"

"Of course. Will you be here?"

I almost laughed. "Yeah. I think I can find some time in my unbelievably packed schedule."

In reality, I didn't even leave that closet between her visits, an irony that was not lost on me. I made myself comfortable on my crate and tried, occasionally, to read on my phone, which didn't work; I was too distracted by real life. She loved me. I leaned against the wall and listened to Taylor Swift cut through the door, sly and knowing, and I basked. I loved a girl who loved me.

She came back to me three times that night. The DJ downstairs kept the energy high. Dance music pounded on, and I set my phone on a shelf and killed the neon glow and opened up a strobe light app I'd downloaded. We made ourselves dizzy laughing and jumping in

Come Home to My Heart

tiny, clumsy circles, trying not to hit everything with our elbows. The strobe made Gloria look like a stop-motion film, black and white in the dark, here one moment, there the next, always a little bit ahead of my chasing fingers. But then I'd catch her, kiss her, hold her until I felt her get impatient, grab me by my hips. I could do that to her. It drove me crazy.

Near the end of the night, the music slowed, and I put the neon light back on, and I haloed her in my arms. I felt that delirious, greedy feeling you get after ten hours' sleep, still somehow wanting to glut yourself on the next polychrome dream and the next and the next. I knew the night would be over soon, but I whispered into her hair, "I don't want this to end."

"I know. I could stay here forever," she whispered back, and I thrilled to the word.

"Can we take a photo? To remember?"

She nodded. "I want one, too."

When I picked up my phone, though, my battery had died. "Too much strobing," I said.

"No such thing," she said. "Here, let me."

So we balanced her phone in the windowsill and set the timer. The photos came out washed in green light, then purple, then rosy red. "I love these," I said quietly, flipping through them. Low light, shit quality, the color blotting the air around us—immediately my favorite pictures in the world. I had never seen her so relaxed, her limbs drifting easily into me. I had never seen myself so happy, my eyes squinted into dark curves from the way I was smiling.

"Me too," she murmured. "I wish I could keep them."

I watched her send them to me, then delete them, then remove them from her Recently Deleted folder, silent and systematic. I hesitated, then said, "Maybe someday soon."

Her eyes flicked up from the screen and onto mine, watchful. That faint smile touched her lips. "Someday soon."

"Go on," I told her. "They'll be wondering where you are."

She kissed me one more time. When she left, I held my phone to my chest, reveling in the warmth it still shed gently, like the heat of her hand.

Gloria Forman

Ben had told my parents he'd have me home by 10:30, and true to his word, we pulled up in my driveway at 10:28. He walked around the car to open the passenger door for me. Ben was a safe boy like that, the sort of calm-voiced, well-coiffed almost-man who wouldn't want to look desperate. I knew he wouldn't try to kiss me at the door. He hadn't tried anything all night.

"Thanks for driving," I told him as we approached the front steps. "This was fun."

"I had fun, too. I'll see you at church Sunday?"

I smiled. "Of course."

We hugged goodbye, and as he jogged back to the car I checked myself in my phone screen, making sure my hair and makeup remained undisturbed. Xia had left no trace of herself on me, although I could still feel her, as though she'd daubed paint onto my skin wherever we'd touched.

I double-checked my texts and deleted the only other ones Xia and I had sent today: **Meet me upstairs, left side of the hall, second door? . . . 8:30.**

They disappeared. Safe.

I was one step through the door when my mother's palm cracked across my cheek.

The force of the blow stunned me. It slung my head backward, made me topple against the wall. One of my hands scrabbled against the light switch, my eyes squeezed shut. Beside me, the door slammed hard.

"Give me that—you give me that—" My mother's voice was unrecognizable. She wrested the phone out of my hand and flung it to the ground. I opened my eyes just in time to see smithereens of glass explode across the floorboards.

I clutched my face, gasping. My mother had used her left hand. Her wedding ring, sideways on her finger, had caught my cheek and punctured the skin. The site throbbed. My fingers came away bloody.

"What do you have to say for yourself?" she said through her teeth.

"I—I don't know what you're—"

"Liar!" my mother screamed. "Why are you lying to me? Why did you *do this*?" She grabbed her phone out of her pocket and thrust it toward me.

My gut spiraled. I didn't understand. A copy of the two texts I'd just deleted glowed on my mother's screen, forwarded somehow to her phone. And there, a blur of neon just above, were the photos. Me, pressing my face into the crook of Xia's neck. Her mouth on mine. Us smiling at the camera, my hand in her hair. We looked deliriously happy.

I looked into my mother's livid expression. My happiness had done this to her.

"I changed your settings at dinner!" Her reddened eyes filled with furious tears. "I knew you were acting different the other day. I just *knew* it. And I was right, wasn't I?" She shoved the phone right up into my face. "Who is this?" she hissed. "Who is she? When I find her, when I get a hold of her parents, I'm going to—"

Come Home to My Heart

"No," I burst out. "You can't!"

My mom slammed the phone down on the sideboard. "Don't you tell me what we can or can't do. You hear me?" She pointed her finger between my eyes, and I flattened my back against the wall. My mother was shorter than me and reed-thin, but the sight of her hands just then made me imagine strangulation. And at the sound of scraping in my bedroom, I knew where my father was.

My mother's finger quavered in midair. "Don't you know what you're doing to yourself?" Her shoulders were rising and falling shallowly as she hyperventilated. "I don't know how the Devil got into you like this. Don't know how . . . my little girl . . ." Her voice was hoarse, her blue eyes staring but unseeing. "We gave you chance after chance. We did everything right. You think I've never struggled with anything? I've struggled. But you were too weak to—"

"I am not weak."

The words shot out of me hard and clear.

"Excuse me?"

"I said I am not weak!" I pushed myself away from the wall. My voice rose. Something hot was pumping through my body, something that made me feel like I'd inherited my mother's steel after all. "I'm exactly the way God made me. If anyone's weak, it's you. You couldn't even ask me one question about what I've been thinking or feeling, because—why? It's too hard to be kind, now that it's a tiny little inconvenience? You think Jesus would ever have acted like this? Like either of you?" I turned on my dad, who had stormed into the room with my suitcase packed. "You think He would have judged me or abandoned me, even if He thought I was doing something wrong?"

None of it penetrated. They looked at me with nothing less than revulsion. But somehow their disgust didn't plunge into some vulnerable part of me the way it had in autumn. As I stared back at them, my heart pounding, I realized I didn't see myself through their eyes, not anymore. I didn't see myself as something twisted and wrong, something to discard or disavow. I'd begun to see myself the way Xia Harper did, and the way God did; I could look in the mirror and trust the evidence of my own eyes. In that moment I could see myself whole, and worth loving.

My father set his hand on my mother's shoulder, keeping his eyes on me, like I was a stranger who'd materialized out of the night. She touched his hand with trembling fingers. Her face contorted as silent tears ran over. Then she broke into sobs and fled down the hall.

My fists curled. Hurt and defiance burned in my chest. I kicked back guilt and I slammed the door on shame. The thought burst clear into my mind: I was not something to cry over.

I clung to Xia's words in our secret place in the town hall earlier: *Someday soon.* I didn't know what I was reaching for, but I knew it was coalescing somewhere in front of me—some shining, malleable future that I would form into the shape of happiness if it killed me.

As my father opened the door on the dark night, I held with all my might to that image. I kicked off my high heels, shoved the sneakers by the door onto my bare feet, and strode outside.

I expected him to shove the suitcase out after me and slam the door, but instead he exited, too. He yanked the suitcase toward the driveway, toward our car, unspeaking.

"I can find my own—" I started.

"Get in."

I hesitated. For an instant I wondered if my parents were trying to ship me to a conversion camp or a boarding school, but I was eighteen. They couldn't force me to stay anywhere.

My father had put my suitcase into the back seat of the car and now stood waiting, his bearded face still watchful.

Come Home to My Heart

I moved slowly for the passenger side and got in.

I'd never experienced a silence like the one hanging between my father and me now. Hot, motionless silence, filled with engine roar and pulsing anger from both sides. For fifty minutes we looked directly ahead, barely blinking. I imagined the pair of us driving on divergent roads, in divergent copies of the same car, my father angled several degrees leftward, so that he moved farther and farther from me every second.

The scattered houses began to collate themselves into blocks, and then into proper neighborhoods. We were into the outskirts of Columbia now.

He checked his phone and made another few turns. Then we screeched to a stop in front of a stone building that might have once been a sizable branch of a bank. The sign above the door read NEW DIRECTIONS MINISTRY. He'd taken me to a shelter.

"There," he said shortly. "Nobody can say we didn't try to do right by you."

I stared out at the stone facade for a moment. Then I looked back at my dad, at the quiver of his mouth, the redness in his cheeks. His face was full of pain and anger, like he was walking on a shattered bone.

"Dad," I said, "this isn't what doing right looks like."

Something about my voice must have been too much, because the anger erased his pain. "Get out, now," he half shouted. "Go!"

I got out of the car. My dad's hands returned to the wheel. While I removed the suitcase from the back seat, he sat so still in the driver's seat that he might have been a wax statue.

With the back door still open, I hesitated. I knew the truth in that moment, looking at the back of my father's neck, the rigid posture of his head. I knew this was my last chance to say anything to the man who had raised me.

And with every piece of me, I wished I could change his mind. Some soft thing in me still hadn't hardened—would maybe never harden. I wanted to come out with some perfect argument that would scythe deep into his thoughts, convincing him in one fell swoop that it wasn't wrong for me to be in love. I wanted to show him in a single breath that I could be a good Christian, a good person, exactly the way God made me.

But I knew nothing would work. I drew a deep breath and tried to let go of that need to please him and my mom.

I tried to let go of them.

"This didn't have to happen," I said, my voice breaking. "I hope you know that someday."

Without waiting for an answer, I shut the door.

He was motionless for one more second, both of us still, separated by glass and steel. Then he put the car into gear and drove away without looking out the window.

I shivered. Midwinter, below freezing, and I was still wearing my dress from the dance. I crouched on the sidewalk, fished a sweater out of the suitcase, and pulled it on over the dress. Then I turned toward the shelter and began to climb the steps, hauling my suitcase up after me.

I paused on the top step, looking at the doorbell. It felt strange, standing here on this threshold. Back in fall, everything I'd read about the Wallerville and Hurston shelters, about intake times and screening processes, had made the experience seem so distant, something that was only ever meant to happen to other people. But now I stood here in my sweater bundled over my dress, everything I owned in the suitcase beside me, and watched my own index finger touching the curve of the illuminated buzzer, about to ring like dozens of people had done today, and yesterday, and the day before. Even when I'd been sitting in the school library, waffling about how to

Come Home to My Heart

think about my situation—from this vantage, it seemed so clear that I'd been homeless then, like I was homeless now. I was just another person who had nowhere to go.

I rang the bell. A buzz sounded within the door, the lock clicked open, and I pushed into a lobby. The room reminded me of a hospital waiting area more than anything else. Half a dozen pleather-backed chairs in alternating colors stood along the wall to the left. About half the lights were on, reflecting dully off light tan tiles, the edges of a bulletin board, and a magazine rack.

I approached the desk opposite the door. A wooden sign on its edge read INTAKE, and a woman sitting at a computer was beckoning me forward. She looked in her fifties, with reading glasses balanced on the edge of her nose, and her hair was slicked back so that a bundle of dark curls sat at the crown of her head.

"Hello, ma'am," I said, unable to meet her eyes. "I'm looking for . . ."

"We're all full tonight, hon," said the woman, whose name tag read LYNN. "You come back tomorrow afternoon. We've got a lottery that closes at five."

I managed a small nod, but my hand tightened on the handle of my suitcase.

"There's another shelter east of here," Lynn added. "Holy Way. You might could see if they've got beds open. Here." She tugged open a drawer and plucked out a single-use bus ticket. "The station's about a quarter mile down High Crest, can't miss it. The station's Vance Street. You should make the last bus if you hurry."

I did hurry. I yanked my suitcase up the block at a half run, my suitcase's wheels rumbling and skittering over the pavement. That ruthless drive was taking me over again, the knowledge that I had no choice but to adapt. My fingertips and bare ankles were going numb,

Riley Redgate

but I didn't want to waste time stopping in a gas station bathroom to change. Once I'd reached the bus stop, I parked myself on the bench.

The station was poorly lit, little more than a plastic box on a darkened corner. After checking both ways down the empty road, I extracted a pair of sweatpants from my suitcase and negotiated them on under my dress. I layered on a T-shirt and a thin sweater, then bundled my hoodie over top.

I caught the outline of my reflection in the station's plastic siding. I looked into the shape of that faceless girl, at her meticulously arranged braids, and couldn't believe that an hour and a half ago, I'd been dancing in the town hall, close to carefree, my head full of Xia in a red dress.

The hard feeling cracked. I wanted to show up at her house and tell her everything. I should have let my suitcase go in Fisherton and walked the hour to her door.

I drew a deep breath and unraveled my braids, then tied my hair back into an inconspicuous bun. I didn't want to look dolled up in the middle of the night, didn't want to be noticed.

Fifteen minutes later, the back of my hand glistened from where I'd wiped my dripping nose. I couldn't feel my fingers. But the bus came up over the gentle hill of the road, and its yellowy headlights gave me hope. I hurried to the side of the road and flagged the bus down.

"Hello," I said to the bus driver, my tongue clumsy with cold. He grunted and looked expectantly at my hands. Needles of pain shot through my knuckles as I worked my fingers around the ticket and passed it over the scanner.

The bus jolted into motion. I headed to the very back, passing a few other riders, and sank into the corner seat, my suitcase parked beside me.

If this second shelter was full up, too, where was I going to sleep? The school auditorium hadn't been cozy, but it had been climate-controlled. Tonight was below freezing, and I didn't know Columbia

Come Home to My Heart

from Adam. I had no idea what neighborhood I was headed toward and no way to call a car. And even if I could call a car, how would I pay for it? Where would I even go?

Xia, I thought. She would come pick me up if I could get in touch with her.

I thought of my shattered phone with a pang—I didn't know her number by heart, but I knew her email. Tomorrow I could get to the Columbia library and send her a message.

The pins and needles in my hands had faded to a warm itch, and within another few minutes, they felt nearly normal again. In the quiet, soporific hum of the bus, I set my sleeping bag against the gently vibrating window and nestled my head into the fabric. It had to be past midnight now, and the map overhead showed there were still a dozen stations before Vance Street. The day felt as though it had lasted a week, our pre-dance dinner at Deanna's house a hazy memory. I touched the sticky cut on my cheek where my mother's ring had struck me and winced, my eyes stinging.

Don't think about it, I thought, folding my hands tightly in my lap. Best not to think at all.

I didn't mean to close my eyes, but suddenly I was drifting into the disturbed dark of uncomfortable sleep. My dreams were formless and quiet. A dim stretch of beach that circled back on itself. Walking through mist. The sound of slow creaking.

The next thing I knew, my chin was jerking up to the bus driver calling, "Last stop. Everybody off."

I jolted to my feet, my hands balled at my sides. What had I done? How could I have fallen asleep? So what if I was tired, so what if I felt like my brain had been placed in a clamp and squeezed?

I snatched up my sleeping bag and hurried down toward the front of the bus, intending to ask the conductor if the bus would retrace its route on the way back—if I could get dropped anywhere near Vance Street—but I froze halfway there, realizing what I was missing.

I turned slowly toward the back of the bus. My suitcase wasn't there.

The bus lights began to feel too bright, as though this were a nightmare coming apart at the seams. I forced myself forward, toward the driver. "Excuse me, sir—did you see somebody get off just now with a suitcase? A yellow one?"

He shook his head, his face blank and uninterested.

"Okay." I tried to take a deep breath, but my head was beginning to spin. "The . . . the bus isn't driving back by Vance Street, is it?"

"No, right back to the depot. Time to get off."

I could do nothing else except step out at the deserted station and watch the bus rumble away into the dark, leaving me alone on a quiet, empty street.

I stuck my hands deep into my hoodie pocket, not wanting to lose the warmth I'd accumulated on the bus. *Think*, I told myself, my eyes stinging. *Think* . . .

Shivering, chest heaving, I stared out onto the street. My breaths accelerated, and tears began to prick my eyes. All my clothes. Even the little things like a razor and deodorant. Gone.

Tears spilled over. I reached for that glimmer of the future, but it felt so far away right now, shriveling into nothing, the way a shooting star burns out just as you catch sight of it. At least when I'd been staying at school, I'd had that shred of a hope that my parents would take me back. Now I knew I was on my own.

I reached for thoughts of Xia, of going to the library tomorrow and sending her a message. But the thought suddenly frightened me. What if she looked at me like this—nothing to my name except what I had in my pockets, begging for help—and never saw me the same way

Come Home to My Heart

again? What would happen when I admitted I'd lied to her every single day that I'd known her? What if she hated me for it?

I sat hard on the bench at the stop and hugged my knees to my chest. There were only four months until graduation, and Xia had wanted so badly to come out on her own time. She'd told me that her parents seemed to be making an effort for the first time in a year and a half, and as much as she said she didn't trust them, I'd had hope that this meant better things ahead for her family. And here I was, about to throw the wreck of my personal life into the delicate threads of her relationship with them.

Even worse thoughts started to creep in. My mom had demanded to know who Xia was, had threatened to get in touch with her parents. What if she'd already followed through? She had photos of us together. What if by the time I got to the library tomorrow, Xia's life was already completely upended because of my parents—because of me?

I imagined sending her some desperate email and getting back: *Your mom came to my house and told my parents everything. I can't believe you didn't even tell me the truth.*

Or, *You're not who I thought you were.*

Or, worse, no reply at all.

The idea sobered me out of my tears. I stood and wiped my face. *You're spiraling*, I told myself. When I thought about it, I didn't need to contact Xia right away, when the situation was so fraught. Maybe, if I waited, I could still hang on to my dignity. Short-term, what I needed was a way back to Fisherton. And in this instant, I needed shelter for the night.

My best bet was probably to find an abandoned house and hole up in a pantry or a closet with a door. If I couldn't find a place with heating, I needed a small space to accumulate some warmth.

Riley Redgate

I walked down dozens of poorly lit streets, past neighborhoods of identical, worn-down houses. Tired brick faces and peeling sides. I took my time moving down the roads, checking the look of each house, but most were clearly occupied.

Halfway down the block, I stopped. This place looked promising. No lights on, no decorations, an overgrown lawn.

I hustled up the driveway and tried the door. Locked, but when I squinted through the window, I saw that the place was unfurnished. If I could just get inside, this was my answer.

My legs ached. I'd been walking for what felt like half an hour, and my feet had already been worn out from dancing earlier. My face was so cold that I couldn't feel my lips, but sweat was slicked down my back.

I tried pushing on each window. No luck. Through the weedy strip of side yard, nothing was unlocked.

Please, Lord, I thought before trying the back door. Locked.

But then my eyes lit on a rough little shed halfway down the yard. I hugged my sleeping bag to my chest as I hurried through the grass, hoping beyond hope that whoever owned this house wasn't keeping anything in here. As I approached, I saw no padlock and no keypad.

The door opened at a touch.

Thank You. I exhaled and stepped inside, into the smell of damp, musty wood. The faint glow of moonlight touched empty tool hooks on the wall, a workbench pushed to one side, and a few sheets of siding leaned in a corner.

I closed the door. The shed felt a little warmer than the air outside, maybe by ten or fifteen degrees, but then I slipped into my sleeping bag, and everywhere my body touched ground, the rough lumber floor sapped heat from my body.

Come Home to My Heart

Teeth gritted, I pushed the workbench against one wall, slid my sleeping bag beneath it, and tugged one of the sheets of siding up against the bench. Shut into the small, dark space, I zipped my sleeping bag around myself and waited for some warmth to build.

Finally, when I splayed my icy fingers against my stomach, they started to take some heat. My breaths evened out, and I could think.

As I closed my eyes, I imagined the dark red glow of the light bulb beneath the auditorium stage. I pretended I was there, instead. It seemed like too much to pretend I was home, but I could be in that place I'd lasted two months, safe.

Forty miles back to Fisherton. I still didn't want to risk hitching a ride, but the wallet in my pocket had $9.45 in it, the remnants of last month's allowance. Nobody knew me in Columbia. I could make a sign. I could panhandle. Maybe I could scrape up enough for a cab— or, even better, a cab and somewhere to stay. A tiny motel clung to the westernmost edge of Fisherton, not far from school. If I could get a room there, I could admit to Xia that my parents had kicked me out but make it seem like I'd just gone to the motel to regroup.

Once I was back in town, I could find a part-time job. With my college apps long done and no more Dance Committee on my plate, I had more hours in my week. With a job I could feed myself, buy new clothes, finish out the year.

My plans for the future shrank until I could fit them into my fist. I held on tight.

Xia Harper

Something was wrong. I knew it.

This time, I wasn't just going to accept Gloria's silence as an indictment of our relationship and also my face, sense of humor, and general attitude. I always waited for her to text first—that was one of our rules, in case she was around her parents—but not once since we'd gotten back together had she gone a full day without texting me.

She wouldn't have given me the silent treatment after what she'd said at the dance. Not voluntarily.

When she missed school on Monday after an entire weekend's silence, my worries intensified. Over the weekend I'd thought grounding, but to miss school—had her parents done something to her? Hurt her? Sent her away, even?

I had to do something, but what? Try to talk to her control-freak mom and dad? Break down the door and make sure she was safe?

Every option seemed to lead back to visiting her. So I texted Mr. Avery to call off sick from work, and after the seventh-period bell, instead of heading to the parking lot, I walked south from school, toward Gloria's house. If I could know for sure that both her parents were at work, it would be safe for me to knock.

Maybe I could get away with knocking regardless. I could lie to her parents and say that Gloria and I had a group project to do, so for the sake of both our GPAs, it was vital that I talk to her. A list of other excuses scrolled through my mind—but as I reached Gloria's matchbox house, the thoughts evaporated.

I stopped dead on the sidewalk.

Someone was mowing the lawn. As I stood watching, the woman stopped the mower, returned to the porch, and retrieved a glass of lemonade she'd left for herself. Then she sank into a rocking chair and picked up a magazine. She was an older Black lady, and across from her sat a man who was clearly her husband.

My hands closed viselike around my backpack straps.

This wasn't Gloria's house.

I didn't understand. I took a step in no particular direction. I stopped, had to steady myself before walking up the path. "Excuse me?" I called toward the older couple. "Hey, excuse me, do y'all have a moment?"

"Yes, we do," said the woman between sips of lemonade.

"The Forman family doesn't live here, do they? Or—they didn't move out of here recently?"

"Oh, no. We've been living here eighteen years, sweetheart."

"They're not your neighbors?"

"Formans." The woman glanced at her husband to check. He gave a little shake of his head. "No, we've never heard of them."

I retreated, staring across the street at the cars trickling out of the school lot. I barely saw any of it.

Every night, I had been dropping Gloria off at a house that wasn't hers.

There was no explanation for this, no possible reason, except this: She'd been living somewhere other than home.

Come Home to My Heart

I reached weakly for a nearby fence post and hung on as piece after piece tumbled into place in my mind. So much of what had happened in fall suddenly made sense: her parents' pointed absence from her life, her re-worn outfits, even her broken phone.

Her parents had thrown her out on the street. Maybe even before I'd met her.

And she'd been staying—where? With some friend who'd kept this secret? It couldn't have been Ellis. At her church, or with some member of the congregation?

But that answer came to me, too, as I wandered in a daze across the road.

I stopped in the parking lot, looking up at the brick building of Fisherton High.

The winter sun felt blinding all of a sudden, and I felt tiny and naive and borderline sick. I couldn't believe this was happening. The steel case I'd built around myself began to crack. All my little troubles, all my petty angers, and the girl I loved had been living somewhere in the school building. She'd had no bed, no shower, no really clean clothes. Hadn't I thought every so often, while we were kissing, that a smell had clung to her like raw soap, something almost industrial? And hadn't I noticed her new softness and freshness after our month-long breakup, when she suddenly seemed so much better-rested?

"Oh God," I said. My voice came out small and unsteady, but I needed to hear myself, to convince myself this wasn't some horrible nightmare. "Oh, my God." I felt so far out of my depth that I actually turned around like I might see somebody who could help me. What was I supposed to do?

And the more urgent question: Where was she?

Gloria had been thrown out again. I knew that much suddenly and absolutely. Her parents had discovered something on Friday night and put her back out, and this time, she hadn't been able to get into the school.

What if she'd tried to find somewhere to go and been attacked or abducted? Or worse?

My stomach contracted. I yanked my phone out of my pocket and opened my messages. I jabbed my thumb at my screen, trying to open my chat with my mom, but instead my fingertip hit my conversation with Mr. Avery.

It opened. **Oh no!** he'd said a few hours ago, in response to my claim that I was sick. **Get a lot of rest. Remember to drink fluids. Read Austen. Let me know about tomorrow!**

The whirl of my thoughts slowed. I began to imagine calling my mother, telling her not only that I needed help finding a missing person but also that I'd been secretly dating a girl since October, and had been lying to her face pretty much every waking moment. All this, when we'd barely leveled up our strained dinner conversations to discussing her workdays. All this, knowing she'd immediately tell my dad everything. He'd arrived home from the Augusta worksite yesterday afternoon.

With a rush of abandon, I hit the Call button beside Mr. Avery's picture instead.

It rang only once. "Xia!" he said, surprised but genial as always. "Well, hello there! How are you? Resting well? I assume this call wasn't a misdial?"

"Um—no, it was on purpose. Mr. Avery, I . . ." I licked my lips, tried to steady my words. "I'm sorry. I'm not actually sick. I really need your help with something."

The smile disappeared from his voice. "What's wrong?"

"My friend Gloria, you met her a couple times. The polite one." A half laugh came from my mouth, flat and high. "She's missing. I think I've figured out—I mean—I think her parents threw her out, and she's not answering her phone, and I don't know where she could have gone."

"Where are you?" I'd never heard him so serious. "I'll come pick you up. Have you told your parents about this?"

"No, they . . . it's complicated."

"All right. Tell me where to drive. I'll just close the shop up now, all right?"

"Okay. Thank you so much. I'm right outside the high school."

Barely ten minutes later, Mr. Avery was pulling up in his black sedan, which always shone as though he'd just come from a car wash. I got in on the passenger side. The car smelled like the pages of an old novel, possibly because of the piles of books that swayed in the back seat as we pulled down the road.

"Hey, now, it's going to be all right" was the first thing he said, and to my horror I felt my eyes beginning to burn.

"Yeah," I tried to say. The word was a nasal little squeak. I sniffed and looked out the window. Blinked back the wetness in my eyes. "Thanks."

I told him everything I'd figured out about Gloria's situation, which wasn't much. "I don't even know where her real house is. Let me see if I can find it."

I Googled her parents' names and got a hit: a White Pages entry for an address on the east side of town. Mr. Avery drove us over, blazing through speed limits, and stopped on the curb outside.

The house was a small, pale gray box, clapboard siding, roof shingles missing half their corners. No car in the driveway. When I checked the mailbox, I found a hardware store advertisement addressed to Fred Forman.

I ran up to the door and banged my fist on it. "Gloria?" I yelled, knowing she wouldn't be here, desperate anyway for the sliver of a possibility she'd totter to the door with the flu. "Gloria!"

Nobody answered. Nothing moved inside.

When I returned to Mr. Avery's car, he was tugging anxiously at the puff of his beard. "No one home?"

"No. It's the right house, but there's no point waiting for her parents. They—" Sudden fury flooded me like liquid nitrogen, a freezing burn through every inch of my body. I had to stop and struggle to stem the anger. "They did this to her. They won't help."

Mr. Avery was watching me with obvious concern. I turned my face away instinctively.

"This girl," he said, "she's important to you."

I stole a second's glance back at him. "Yeah," I muttered.

"Do you think she would have contacted the police?"

"Maybe." I tried to envision Gloria standing on the sidewalk right here, beside this battered white mailbox, systematically evaluating her options. "I would have thought . . . I don't know." A leaden weight on my stomach. "I would have thought she'd ask me for help before going to the cops. But she never told me about any of this. So maybe not."

"Xia," said Mr. Avery carefully, but I cut him off.

"Yeah, let's try the police station. We can ask."

He began to drive again, and I sat there with hands folded tight, squeezing until my finger bones ached. I knew he'd been about to say that Gloria might have had any number of reasons for not telling me, but still: How hadn't I figured it out myself? I should have pushed, back in autumn. I should have said, *I know something's wrong at home—tell me what it is, let me help.* But instead I'd let us skate over the issue, and the whole time, she probably hadn't even been eating three meals a day. I thought of the thinness of her wrists in November, and the sick churn in my stomach intensified.

Mr. Avery parked in front of the precinct and undid his seat belt. "I'll speak to the police. They may not take a young person seriously. Do you have a picture of Gloria I can show them?"

"Um, yeah." I tilted my phone away from his view and opened the photo of us at the dance, but I hesitated. When I showed him this, he would know. My face curled into the crook of her neck. Stupid adoration on my face. Gloria midlaugh and a little bit blurred.

But he gave me that book, I told myself. *The Sound of Falling . . . He won't hate me.*

I steeled myself and thrust the phone toward Mr. Avery.

As he took it in hand, he didn't exhibit any signs of judgment or even surprise. He just nodded, exited the car, and disappeared into the anonymous brick face of the precinct.

Not even three minutes later he was emerging, shaking his head. "They haven't seen her."

"Okay, well, she must have gone somewhere that had heat, right? Or at least somewhere with a roof. It was freezing all weekend." Worse possibilities began to lean in on me again, pressing the breath out of me. "I just don't understand what—why wouldn't she come to school? Why, unless she's—or unless someone . . ."

Mr. Avery put a steadying hand on my shoulder. "Easy, okay? She might could've gone to a bigger town. Fisherton is a small place, Xia. There aren't a lot of resources here for folks who are struggling. If Gloria's been going through this for a while, then she already knows that. She's a resourceful young lady, isn't she? Quick thinker?"

I nodded.

"Then she'd know she needed a place that would feed her, keep her warm. Why don't we start with the homeless shelters and soup kitchens closest to here, check if anybody there has seen her?"

"But she doesn't have a car."

"She might have been able to hitch a ride out of town."

I tried to believe that this was the answer, not just a long-shot possibility. Mr. Avery was right. Gloria was resourceful. She had that unbreakable thing inside her; she'd probably handled all this better than I was handling even the news of it. She'd have looked for solutions the second she wound up on that sidewalk.

"Okay," I said. "Let's go."

◊

Within the hour we'd checked the scattering of crisis centers, shelters, and soup kitchens in Wallerville and Hurston. These centers were in old churches and ex-office buildings. Their lights flickered, their floor tiles were slippery underfoot with grease or dirt, and their employees ran the gamut from wan to exhausted to hostile. None of them recognized the picture of Gloria.

We exited the Hurston Community Shelter into an icy afternoon. Sunbeams came sharp through the scattered cloud, and the light had begun to lower, taking a yellow tint like the edges of a vintage photograph. It was 6:00 p.m., night was coming, and we had no leads.

"We should find something to eat," said Mr. Avery. "We can decide what steps to take next. Okay?"

I made an affirmative sound. Mr. Avery drove us to a fraying diner on the edge of Hurston. The checkerboard tiles and red booths were something out of the 1950s, but the huge TVs high on the walls broke the old-timey effect, one blaring basketball and the other a

Come Home to My Heart

closed-captioned Fox talk panel. Mr. Avery and I mowed down a pair of sandwiches and kept our voices low.

"If Gloria came to either of these towns," I said, "she could've caught a bus to Atlanta."

We'd both known it, but the words landed heavily anyway. How were we supposed to pluck one girl out of the six million people in Atlanta?

Mr. Avery took his time with that one, dabbing a worn cloth napkin against his beard. "Let's not put Atlanta on the table just yet. Columbia's closest. I think our next stop should be over there, doing the same we've done here."

I looked down at my useless phone. Gloria and I had never emailed before—too risky with her parents looking over her shoulder—but we knew each other's email addresses, and I'd sent her a few messages over the past hour while Mr. Avery drove:

Hey—where are you?
I'm with Mr. Avery, we can come pick you up
In case you don't have it written anywhere, my number is 4705551309.
Call or text me please. I'm worried about you. I love you so much.

I refreshed. Nothing.

"Yeah," I said, "Columbia."

When we stepped out of the restaurant, the sun had set and a deep blue dusk hovered over the horizon. We drove into the city outskirts in silence, and I watched the plots of land shrink from farms to yards. Houses began to organize themselves into lines, some chipped brick and some peeling wood, some flat-topped and some gabled, with small driveways or chain-link fences. Little decorations hung on front doors.

Riley Redgate

I found myself looking at these houses in a way I never had before. Every time a window turned gold with sudden light, I imagined the people inside: kids complaining that it was cold, maybe, and fiddling with the thermostat while their parents said, *Just throw on a sweater.* Couples absorbed in an episode of TV, snacking on fresh food out of their fridges. A man getting home from work and slipping into a chipped bathtub with a contented sigh.

I thought of my own parents, and the way I'd trailed resentfully at their ankles when they'd taken me to look at the house in Fisherton Oaks. I thought of the warmth of my bed and the way I stayed too long in the shower when I had a stressful day. My favorite sun-dappled spot in the window seat. My eyes were prickling again.

We were deep into the city now and the houses were coming steadily, one after another, hundreds upon hundreds. I looked at the walls protecting these thousands of people from the elements and imagined Gloria outside, disappearing into the dark winter.

It wasn't until I looked down at my hands curled into fists that I realized I was livid. Not at her, of course. She'd probably hidden the truth because she'd thought I wouldn't understand, and wasn't she right, in a way? How could I understand a world where half the houses in my neighborhood stood empty, while the Wallerville shelter only had enough beds for half the people who showed up every night? How could I understand a world where those people got turned into punch lines in comedy sets? How could I understand a world where those shelters were falling apart, where the staffers were discussing the wait time to get an exterminator for the lice problem, and meanwhile some billionaire's superyacht was gliding over the Mediterranean Sea? How could I understand Gloria's love for her God, if that God would make a world like this, and how could

Come Home to My Heart

I understand her love for me, when I hadn't been able to look at her and see the truth?

As I stared out Mr. Avery's windshield onto the dark rush of the road, my entire body pulsed with rage and incomprehension. I'd read so many books that showed the world as a cruel and absurd place, but this was the first time I'd seen that cruelty and absurdity in this kind of high-resolution way, slammed up against my viewfinder, touching my very skin, urgent and material. It wasn't fucking *fair*. Obviously the world wasn't fair, and I'd raged about my ideas of unfairness for years now—Fisherton's small-mindedness, its prejudices—but that anger had been marinated in self-pity. This anger took me outside myself instead, as though some essence of me were hurtling into the atmosphere and staring down at the whole Earth, wishing so, so hard I could hit some button and make things right.

"Shall we?" said Mr. Avery.

I looked up. We'd reached the closest shelter to Fisherton, a gray concrete facility with a set of long, concrete steps. The name emblazoned above its lintel was NEW DIRECTIONS MINISTRY.

I nodded, wordless. We parked and headed up to the door.

The shelter's reception had a fraying welcome mat and several bulletin boards with flyers pushpinned onto them: volunteer opportunities, upcoming food drives, donation cards. Two people were gathered at a bulletin board, pointing to one of the flyers. Down a hall, I could see end tables stationed at intervals, each one topped with a drab little cloth-shaded lamp. An attempt at a homey touch. I could hear showers hissing somewhere down near the end.

At the intake desk, sorting through a stack of paperwork, sat a tall, dark-skinned woman who looked in her early fifties. Her name tag read SUZE. She wore a shoulder-padded black blazer over a crimson collared shirt, her hair was thunderstorm gray and shaved down to a couple of millimeters, and her eyes had the same penetrating force that the shelter workers in Hurston had.

"Hello, ma'am," I said.

Suze's eyes flicked up to us. "Lottery closed at five."

"We're just looking for somebody. We wanted to see if she's staying here." I held out my phone. "Her name's Gloria Forman," I added. "She's my friend from school. We live out in Fisherton."

As Suze peered through her glasses at the screen, the papery skin around her eyes twitched. My grip tightened on the phone. I could have sworn that was recognition.

"Anything would help," I said too fast, leaning too far over the desk. "Anything."

Suze lifted her hands to her reading glasses, took them off, pinched the indentations next to her eyes. "We don't give out that information about our clients."

"But—"

Suze folded her arms on the desk and looked up at me with a no-bullshit stare. "It's for safety reasons, honey. Think about it."

I closed my eyes, imagining situations where somebody had escaped a violent partner or even a sex trafficker. "Right. Yeah." But I was so sure I'd seen recognition on her face.

She didn't answer, already back into her stack of papers. There was nothing else to say.

As Mr. Avery and I turned away from the intake desk, a voice rang across the reception room. "Dad!" I glanced toward the people who'd been standing at the bulletin board. One was an unshaven man, darkly tanned, who wore a fraying knit cap low over his brows. A girl dashed up to him, her long braid swinging. She looked around twelve,

Come Home to My Heart

with a pink backpack hanging off one shoulder. "They have a library shelf back there! Look—"

"They do, huh?" said the man. "Shh, come on, let's let the lady work in peace . . ." As his daughter brandished a book at him, he ushered her toward the door.

The other person standing at the bulletin board was a stout older woman with creased slacks and loose, shiny curls. She moved toward the exit along with the father and daughter, and Mr. Avery and I followed.

As the door shut behind all five of us, the woman turned to me and said, "Show me the picture."

"What?" I said.

"The picture," she repeated. "Couldn't help overhearing you in there. Me and Earl were both here this weekend. Maybe we could help with your friend. I'm Maryann," she added.

"Earl," said the man in the knit cap, giving us a hurried smile as his daughter stuck a dark-covered hardback into his face. "Easy, Emmy, easy . . ."

Emmy kept gushing. "And they have this spaceship that gets sucked into, like, this interdimensional wormhole thing, but—"

"Hold your horses, all right?" Earl said. "Just one second, got to talk to these folks."

Emmy gave an impatient sigh, took the book back, and stuck her nose between its pages. My eyes lingered on her, escaping, and I felt a pull of recognition.

"How about that picture?" said Maryann.

"Right." I hurried to tug out my phone again, then showed Maryann the screen.

She frowned. "Yeah, I think I saw somebody like that. Yesterday, lunch. They've got a service here, then a meal."

I whipped around to Mr. Avery. "That has to be her. She'd want to go to church, too."

Earl craned his neck to see. "Yep, she was here, all right, last two nights. Put her name on the lottery list, but they had to turn her away."

"Turn her away?" I repeated in disbelief.

Maryann shook her head. "Sweetheart, there's seventy beds here, and a hundred and fifty people show up when it's this cold. There were two dozen people sleeping on the floor last night."

"Right." I swallowed. "Sorry. So—she didn't come today?"

The two exchanged glances. "I didn't see her," said Maryann, while Earl shook his head.

I told myself that didn't necessarily mean Gloria had gotten in trouble. She'd been turned away from New Directions two nights in a row. Maybe she didn't want to go through the hassle just to get told no again.

I asked, "Does this place serve dinner?"

"Only if you're staying here," said Maryann. "People can drop in for breakfast or lunch, grab a bag. But dinner they serve in the meeting room."

Then Gloria might not come back until tomorrow, if ever, and she was staring down the barrel of another night of below-freezing temperatures. And we had no way of knowing where to find her. I tried to think of other questions to ask, tried to suppress the desperate feeling of scraping the bottom of the barrel with my fingernails.

Earl made a sympathetic, rumbling exhalation. "There's a soup kitchen called the Hearth a couple miles down High Crest Boulevard. They get good donations. Make some good meals. People here all know."

Maryann snapped her fingers, making a number of wooden bracelets clack together on her wrist. "That's a good thought. If your

Come Home to My Heart

friend talked to anybody, asked for advice, they might've told her to go down that way. And," she added with a wink, "the food down there's better than it is here anyway. At this place, you better like a sad-looking rotini, 'cause that's what you're getting."

A weak laugh startled out of me. I looked from Maryann back to Earl. "Thank you, guys, so much. Thank you." I fumbled for my wallet, my face burning, feeling somehow embarrassed. "Can I—?"

I pulled out all the cash I had and proffered it to them. They accepted it, Earl nodding a few times, Maryann saying, "Thanks, sweetheart. Y'all take care."

"Dad, I'm cold," Emmy said, and Earl turned to guide her back through the ministry door. Maryann followed, leaving Mr. Avery and me on the front steps.

As we stood there in the chill, Mr. Avery said quietly, "I know you may not want to hear this, Xia, but we should think about what to do if we don't find her. I'm perfectly happy to park outside this building tomorrow and wait for her to arrive, but if she didn't come to the lottery today, that may not change. She may have moved on to another place."

We descended the steps, the wind biting through my jacket. I tried to think of another option. Could we report her missing to the police? Would they even take us seriously? We weren't Gloria's relatives, and she was eighteen, and if she wasn't showing up to the homeless shelter, maybe the cops would tell us she didn't want to be found.

We got into Mr. Avery's car. The doors shut, killing the noise of the street. No more of the surge and subside of cars approaching, passing, rolling into the distance. Silence rang off his dustless dashboard and the polished glass.

"I don't know what to do," I said. My voice was very small. "Maybe if she's not . . . maybe I'll call my parents and see what they think."

"If you feel that's best." Mr. Avery was tugging at his beard again. "I understand wanting to keep these kinds of things from your parents. I know."

Slight emphasis on *know*. I looked over at him with a pulse of surprise.

"I mean," I said, "it's not like my parents have ever said anything bad. I don't know. Maybe they'd be fine with me and Gloria, but . . ."

He bobbed his head. "But things will be different."

"Yeah."

Mr. Avery started the car. "First things first, let's check the Hearth."

We started down High Crest Boulevard, a wide, four-lane street divided by a crumbling concrete strip. I looked down at the map on my phone and watched our dot approach the marker of the Hearth, intersection by intersection. My foot jogged against Mr. Avery's meticulously vacuumed rubber mat.

I flipped the phone over in my lap and looked out the window. We glided under a highway overpass where fluorescence cast a sickly glow. Beneath the greenish light, a hooded person sat hunched over on a concrete wedge, breathing into cupped hands.

As we passed, one in a steady stream of cars, the hands dipped lower and revealed a sliver of a face I would have known anywhere.

The sound I let out nearly made Mr. Avery swerve off the road. "She's there," I gasped out. "That was her, she's back there."

As he changed lanes and prepared to make a U-turn, my breath caught, and for the first time in years, I began to cry openly. Through a distorting veil of tears, I watched the way the cars passed by. I watched her, unnoticed by person after person, all but invisible.

Gloria Forman

A car was slowing. I lifted my head, feeling a dull pinprick of worry. My fingers had numbed from cold a while ago.

I stood from the concrete block where I'd perched, readying myself to hurry down the sidewalk if they rolled the window down or shouted something. But the sedan came to a full stop, hazards on. I hesitated.

The door swung open. Xia stepped out onto the concrete.

The sight of her hit like a rush of cold water. She looked the way she always did at school. Dark jeans, dark boots, black jacket over an acid-washed sweater. Her hair was tumbling over her shoulders, and her face—her face was streaked with tears.

"Gloria?" she said.

I wanted to back away. To crumple myself into a minuscule ball and hide myself in the shadows of the overpass.

She closed the distance between us in three steps and enfolded me in her arms. She smelled like always. Sandalwood shampoo. Hint of cigarette smoke and detergent. She was shaking, and the frame of her glasses dug into the side of my skull. A hoarse little sob sounded in my ear, and she immediately shifted; she had swiped at her face with the arm of her jacket.

My body came back to life. I closed my eyes and slid my arms around her, and an enormous, selfish relief enveloped me. She knew, and she was still here.

"I'm so sorry," I said in a parched whisper.

"Come on in the car, get out of the cold," said a deep voice. I thought it was Xia's father, and I braced myself as I broke away from her, but Mr. Avery was the one by the car, shutting the trunk on a load of books he appeared to have tossed in from the back seat.

We both slid into the back. Xia was holding my hand so tightly that it hurt. The car's warmth chafed against my hands, my cheeks, my neck; I couldn't feel the heat in my torso or legs yet, swaddled as they were by chilled-through layers of clothes. But the sudden admittance into this clean, dark place felt dreamlike. I looked at the side of Xia's face—she was wiping tears with the heel of her hand, turning away to hide them—and expected to wake up.

"I'm sorry," I whispered again.

"You don't have anything to be sorry about. I should have guessed."

"I didn't want you to guess."

"Yeah, but it's . . ." She wiped her eyes again, hard, with both palms. "You're okay? Nobody, like, hurt you or anything?"

"No." I drew my hoodie over my head, then my thin sweater. As the layers of cloth peeled away, the feeling of constriction in my chest lessened. "No one hurt me. Somebody took my suitcase, but I'm all right."

"You're not all right. It's not—your parents—"

"I *am* all right," I said, quietly but firmly. It was strange to sit beside Xia and feel, for once in my life, that I knew more than her. I loved her so much in that moment, for the outrage shining on her face

Come Home to My Heart

and the impossible fact that she was here, but there was no space in my mind for outrage just now, between the yawning holes of exhaustion and hunger.

Mr. Avery swung the car into a Wendy's drive-through. I ate until my mouth felt puckered from the salt. Maybe I swayed, because Xia reached up and stroked my hair, applied the lightest pressure to the side of my head, and I found myself tilting down, down, until my head was in her lap. I kicked off my shoes, the first time I'd done so in three days, and let my damp socks fall onto my sneakers, and my feet pulsed and tingled as they grew warm and dry.

The highway rushed by. I curled up in the back seat and focused on the motion of Xia's fingers over my scalp, watching images tumble over my vision. Car after car under the overpass. Averted or apologetic eyes, like people couldn't bear to look at me anymore. The way my stomach had plunged when my name hadn't been called in the Sunday lottery. The inside of the shed in the morning, frost spiraled out over the single windowpane. My parents, and a locked door.

"Where are we going?" I said quietly.

"I thought we should go back to my house first," said Mr. Avery. "Get you washed up and fed, Gloria."

We both murmured our okays and thanks. I closed my eyes. The highway felt smooth and endless.

Thirty minutes of quiet classical radio later, we were turning at a mailbox with a house number stickered onto its side, then bumping down an uneven driveway.

We parked. Everything went quiet. Mr. Avery's house was small and modest, painted a nondescript blue gone colorless in the night. An old-fashioned weather vane turned atop a crooked chimney, and a light glowed by the front door, and a wicker porch swing swayed in the chill breeze. The place had an air of secrecy set far back on its long gravel drive, a line of pine trees planted between the house and the road like sentries shoulder to shoulder. You could barely hear the cars passing.

The three of us crunched up to the side door in silence and entered into a cramped kitchen with a chipped porcelain sink. The place was messy. Lived-in, more like, with a cutting board in the sink and onion skins scattered across the counter. Mr. Avery lit a lamp on an end table with a stained glass shade; the orangey bulb illuminated a stack of magazines and mail. I stood silent, my mind processing slowly, image by image, like an out-of-date computer.

Mr. Avery was first to move. He creaked into the hallway, opened a linen closet door, and removed a towel, a pair of sweatpants, and an enormous T-shirt. "Here," he said, handing me the stack. "The bathroom is down at the end, all right?"

A light was on behind a closed door halfway down the hall, but I didn't ask who was home. I didn't even really feel curious. I just shut myself into the bathroom and stripped off my filthy clothes.

The shower was scalding hot and the pressure powerful, and as water thudded into my back and shoulders, I exhaled. Eyes shut, I turned toward the stream. It struck my scalp with a huge, dull, hollow sound, trickled down over my face. The bar soap filled the air with lavender and made my skin tight and squeaky. Hot mist tickled the inside of my nose.

I was so tired.

The clothes hung off me, but their cleanness and dryness were a blessing. All this was a blessing. The walls' painted tiles, the flickering bulb set in above the sink. The fluffy towel that I pressed against my cheeks. The little bottle of mouthwash, and the way it burned and cleaned the deepest pockets of my mouth until my whole head felt cold.

When I left the bathroom, Xia and Mr. Avery had moved into his living room. He'd turned on a few lamps and drawn the heavy

Come Home to My Heart

curtains, and he now sat in a red cloth armchair near the hearth. A young fire flickered uncertainly in the grate, combed leftward and rightward by the air moving in the chimney. On the coffee table lay a half-finished puzzle of a steam train. Xia was looking up at me with a piece in her hand.

"Please," said Mr. Avery, gesturing to the sofa beside Xia. There was a bowl on the coffee table full of macaroni and cheese.

I sat, a lump in my throat, and took the bowl into my hands. I ate a few mouthfuls before Xia spoke.

"You can stay at mine," she said. "I'll call my parents."

"No." I lowered my spoon. "I don't want you telling them anything before you're ready."

"That doesn't matter anymore. I . . . I want you to stay there."

Shame smoldered in my stomach. I kept eating, but the rich cream of the sauce had become tasteless. I didn't know how to tell her that I never wanted to take from her again, that I wanted to give, and give, although I had nothing to give.

As I ate, Xia went back to the puzzle, clearly biting her tongue, and Mr. Avery to the book in his lap. I knew they were waiting on me to finish.

When my spoon scraped the bottom of the bowl, Mr. Avery's low, gentle voice said, "Gloria."

I looked up.

"If you'd like, you are more than welcome to stay here with my partner and me until you leave for college. We spoke while you were freshening up, and he'd be delighted to host you. We both would be."

The words took a while to sink in. *He'd be delighted.*

I realized part of me was hunting for a reason to say no—for a deep crack riven into the heart of a good thing, some awful consequence that might ripple out from this moment. But as I looked around at this small, comfortable room, sequestered from the outside world, I thought, *Yes*. Months ago, that compass in my chest had guided me to Xia. It was pointing me toward this, too. Maybe what I wanted could be right.

"Thank you, Mr. Avery," I said hoarsely.

"Please, call me Lawrence."

"All right. Lawrence."

Xia let out a sigh. "Gloria, come on. Now I have to do it, too."

I couldn't laugh, but I managed a real smile.

"Here," said Mr. Avery, standing. "Let me show you your room. You must be tired."

Xia and I followed him to the end of the hall. He opened a door with a *creak*, revealing a room with a twin bed and a narrow window overlooking the dark yard. The ceiling was sloped in one corner, and the bedside lamp cast a dim light up onto that slanted plane.

"I'll go tell Paul," said Mr. Avery. "Y'all take a moment. But I'll need to drive you home soon, Xia. It's getting late."

He shut the door behind him.

The small room rang with quiet. When Xia and I sat down on the mattress, the bedsprings squeaked. I remembered the first time I ever touched her. I put my fingers there again, on the back of her wrist, and felt the same dizzying rush of awareness, although I had touched her so many times now. I eased her hand up toward my mouth and kissed her fingers, tasted their salt.

She closed her eyes. "I wish I'd known."

I was too tired for anything but honesty. I told her, "I wish you'd never found out."

"Never?"

I considered. "Maybe in a decade or something. I wish I could've told you then. Like it was just something that happened to me once."

Come Home to My Heart

I tried to steady my voice; it caught instead. "It doesn't feel good. Showing the soft parts. I know you know what I mean."

"Yeah," she said. "Of course I know."

When she looked at me, her eyes were still vividly reddened from her tears earlier. That was Xia, I thought. When she opened up once, it left tracks through her life, the way folded paper never lies smooth again. She couldn't give anything away for free; it always cost her something. I understood that in her. She understood it in me.

I leaned forward. Kissed her until she tilted back onto the bed. We shifted so she was curled around me, lips laid against the nape of my neck. She pressed her palm against my stomach, which burned to her touch.

"I love you so much," I whispered, "it hurts."

She whispered back, "I don't want it to hurt anymore. I want it to feel good."

"It does." I let my eyes drift shut. "It feels better than anything."

Xia played some jazz music over her phone, and her fingers glided through my hair again. Lying there, I felt safer than I had in days—safer, maybe, than I ever had, because I finally knew who I was, and where I was going, and who would walk there by my side.

Xia Harper

I arrived home near the usual time that night. It was eight forty-five when Mr. Avery dropped me off, and the normalcy of that felt strange. I stood on our porch in the cold, unmoving, long after he'd driven away. Our driveway was empty, my car still across town in the school lot.

I hadn't even told my parents I'd called off work. These past five hours, they'd been here at home, thinking I was sitting behind the register at the store and reading about fictional characters with fictional problems.

I opened the door. Warm, sweet-smelling air flowed over me. The hall was quiet, even quieter when I eased the front door shut behind me. I slipped my shoes off and stood, stocking-footed, on the hardwood, looking blankly at the furniture in the front room that my mom had selected over the course of many hours. Early in junior year, she'd shown me photo after photo of sofas that she thought I might like. I remembered my resentment as I'd stared at her phone screen, thinking, *Why does this matter?*

My parents were talking in the kitchen. I moved down the hall and stopped at the threshold. My mother, aproned, was plating dinner at the island: fish in white sauce. My father was setting cutlery on the table, and when he caught sight of me, he startled.

"Xia. How long have you been standing there?" He put a hand to his chest, laughed. "Good grief."

"Not that long," I said.

"Sit down, honey," my mom said. "Do you want—" She broke off. I'd taken a few steps toward the table, close enough for her to see my reddened eyes. "Xia. What's wrong? What's happened?"

My mouth began to tremble. I tried to turn my face away from my parents, even as I forced myself to walk to the table and sit down. "Um," I said. I took a napkin from the wooden dispenser and pressed it hard against my left eye. It drank up the wetness. "Everything's okay. I just made this friend at s-school and she's going through a really hard time right now, so I'm upset about th-that."

My mother abandoned dinner and came to the table. She sat beside my father, across from me. The arrangement of our bodies felt so similar to the fight still burned indelibly into my mind. *No place for this selfishness . . . Have you become so ungrateful that you can't appreciate any of this?*

Something throbbed in me like a cracked rib. I wanted to believe what Gloria had said in autumn, that I wasn't either of those things. But suddenly I felt terrified that she was wrong.

I lifted my head and looked my parents in the eyes. "Do you guys s-still think that I'm an un-ungrateful person?" I asked, voice shaking hard. "Like, a selfish person?"

My mom's lips parted. My dad looked like he didn't understand what I'd said.

I wiped my eye with the heel of my hand. "I just feel like m-maybe you were right about everything you said that summer."

Come Home to My Heart

"Xia," said my dad, his voice hoarse. "Sweetheart, that's not . . . we never thought you were selfish in any deep way. You were just making choices that . . . we couldn't grasp what was going on in your head." He and my mother traded a glance. "And that was disturbing to us when it started happening. You were our little girl, and then suddenly you were a person we didn't understand. To be honest, we still don't know what's happening in your head, most of the time."

"I know. I h-haven't wanted you to."

"Why not?" my mother asked.

"B-because. If you see all of me. You can think it's wrong."

My mother's eyes grew bright. My father removed his glasses, placed his hands over his face, and rubbed. I could hear his breathing, flat and uneven against his palms.

My shoulders were shuddering now. I crushed the napkin to my eyes again. "I d-don't know how things got so messed up," I cried. "I don't want them to be messed up anymore."

"Neither do we, sweetheart," my father said in a defeated voice. "I'm sorry we were so hard on you. We felt so lucky squeaking out of the city, finding this job. But we should have tried to . . . well, we shouldn't have thought it was all about Kit and Navya."

My face trembled. I took three sharp, uneven breaths. "But it was about them. You were right. If I'd had them, I wouldn't have felt like . . . but I didn't. I just didn't have anything anymore."

I knew they wanted to say, *You had us. You had this place. You had the car we bought for you and the efforts we made to reach you.* But they stayed silent. I thought maybe they understood now what I'd felt: that even the happiest family in the world didn't make a whole life. My life was accumulating out there, away from their choices and influences. That, for me, was growing up. That, for them, was losing me.

But I could finally understand how they'd felt, too. My parents didn't come from money; they knew precarity. They'd looked at this town and seen a place to set a foundation, whereas in Atlanta the ground had wobbled under our feet. They wanted to protect me from all the risks I hadn't understood. They *had* protected me, even in the worst of the silent months. Buying my school supplies. Making me healthy lunches and dinners. Saving for my future like they'd always said they would. As steadfastly here as the bones of this house.

"We love you," said my mother. She reached across the table, palm up. "We're going to work on this, okay? We love you, so much. Do you know that?"

I was still crying. Couldn't make myself stop.

"Yeah," I said, and I put my hand into hers.

Gloria Forman

three months later

"Gloria," Lawrence called from down the hall. "You ready?"

"Yes, sir," I called back. "Be right there."

I finished affixing my earrings, gave my hair a quick brush, and hurried down the hallway, smoothing my dress. It was Easter Sunday, and when I got to the kitchen, Lawrence was wearing one of his best suits, a dark blue that made him look snappier than the pastor.

His partner, Paul, a small, lean man in his sixties, was buttering toast at the counter in a worn T-shirt and pajama pants. "Morning, sunshine," he sang. Paul was always singing perfectly normal sentences. "Breakfast?"

"Thank you," I said, accepting the toast.

"Y'all have fun," he said. "Go on, you'll be late."

Lawrence kissed Paul on the cheek before we jogged out the door. According to Lawrence, Paul only joined for church once a year, on Christmas Eve, and Lawrence was pretty sure that had to do with the carols more than anything.

Riley Redgate

I liked Lawrence's church pretty well. It was a fair bit smaller than First Baptist or Fisherton Faith, neither of which were the biggest churches in the world to start with. This place was named Celebration of Christ Church. My dad would've called that a hippie name.

These days, when thoughts of my parents drifted in, I didn't feel the confused muddle of emotions that had made every day tumultuous back in January. For a while it had been pain and longing and anger, then mostly just pain. I'd think about the way they'd loved me and cry; I'd feel a sense of loss like a person had died.

But now a kind of curtain had fallen between me and those feelings. When I considered what my parents might be doing, it felt like remembering something distant from preschool, one of those too-bright, half-blurred memories.

I was coming to the understanding that the love I remembered had always had an expiration date. I'd known that. So we'd played pretend together for eighteen years, and we'd had real fun, real joy, maybe even real love in that time—the way that kids have those feelings in the thick of their imaginary places. But that was always going to end. I was always going to grow up. I was always going to be me.

Xia didn't elaborate on her feelings toward my parents, but I could see her anger in the way her neck and shoulders stiffened whenever they came up. I supposed she hated them. But I had the feeling that if I indulged in hatred, that feeling would agitate some wound that had closed, jitter the whole thing back open. I was still finding stable ground, after one misstep had sent me tumbling through the trapdoor. I would take the muted separation and the feeling of steadiness.

Lawrence and I arrived at the church just in time. Outside the wooden doors, a sunny sign read, HE IS RISEN! and as we hurried over the threshold, I glanced at the bulletin, which boasted egg hunts for kids of all ages. The church felt especially small today, like an old-fashioned

Come Home to My Heart

schoolhouse, packed to the walls with a congregation in their springtime best. A kaleidoscope of florals. Someone had set every high window open so that a sweet-smelling breeze tumbled overhead. Lawrence and I squeezed into the back pew, exchanging a secretive smile.

As the service started, serenity moved through me, gliding like a balm over the surface of a sweet and quiet pain. It still hurt to remember what my parents and Ellis had said and done in the name of God. I prayed for them every Sunday, and I guessed that they prayed for me, too. So maybe we were all praying for each other to change. But in the end, I wondered if that was really the way God moved on Earth, prodding our thoughts left and right at request. As I sat here, looking up into the golden rafters, this place shot through with beatific light, that kind of intervention seemed too small, too mortal, nowhere near the spirit or the soul.

I gazed up at the crucifix that hung at the front of the church, the image of pain that foretold rebirth. I felt like I had never understood any of it before, at least not this intimately. I saw, in my mind, the stone rolled away from the door of the tomb—the empty sepulchre—the message that He was gone, but still alive; the same, but divinely changed; lost forever in some men's eyes, found in God's.

◊

The last day of school was a scorching day in early June. Xia slouched into our final Calculus class five minutes late, wearing a cutoff T-shirt and frayed black jeans.

Mrs. Molina sighed. "Finishing the year like we started it, Xia?"

"Yep," Xia drawled as she slumped into her desk. Her eyes strayed to mine. I barely managed to restrain a smile.

I never took our secrecy for granted. When I'd first returned to school in January, Lawrence had accompanied me to the principal's

Riley Redgate

office to explain my unexcused absence and my new living situation, and since I was eighteen, nobody asked any questions. Principal Reynolds had assigned me a new bus stop without even a small push for details, but I'd expected word to get out at school—if not because of Ellis, then because my parents would say something to the congregation at First Baptist, and word would trickle down, and rumor would become gossip would become scandal.

I waited the whole week for my life to fall apart. It didn't happen.

Nothing happened until the following Monday, when Ben nudged me after our Young Christians meeting and said, "So, what went down with your parents?"

My mouth went bone-dry. "What did they say?" I asked too quickly as we walked out to the parking lot.

Ben traded a look with Deanna, and they broke into smiles. "Sorry," said Deanna, struggling to stay straight-faced. "It's not really funny. But my parents asked them why you weren't at church, and your parents said—they did this pious face—they were like, 'She's having a crisis of faith and is no longer walking in Jesus's light.' Which obviously I knew was bullcrap."

"Also," said Ben, "no offense, but your parents talk like a Christian Instagram caption."

Deanna laughed, and I tried to join in, but at that point it was still too painful.

Ben and Deanna must have noticed, because their smiles faded. "Is something actually going on?" said Deanna.

I thought about telling them then. Just pulling off the Band-Aid and telling the whole school. Nobody had to know about Xia.

But I was still shaky from the previous weekend. I didn't want that kind of instability. All I wanted was to keep my head down and wait for my college responses and have normal day after normal day.

Come Home to My Heart

I didn't want to lose the friends I'd made in high school, even if those friendships wound up being provisional. I didn't want to walk the halls with my head held high, pretending not to care that mean words were being thrown around behind my back.

I said, "Well . . . back in October I told them I'd been talking to my aunt Jen. We fought about it for months, and last week they told me that if I cared so little about following God's path, then I could follow my own path out of our house."

Ben and Deanna both stopped walking in the middle of the hall. "Wait. Seriously?" Ben said, staring. "Are you okay? That's crazy."

I managed a small smile. "I'm okay. I'm staying with this guy called Mr. Avery—he owns the bookstore downtown, and he's really nice. He took me to Celebration of Christ this past weekend, and I like it a lot."

"Well, I think that's awful of your parents," Deanna huffed. "They should be ashamed of themselves."

"Yeah," said Ben. "Gloria, you don't need, like, clothes, or—?" He cleared his throat, his cheeks reddening. I knew he didn't want to make me feel like I was begging for help.

Deanna quickly jumped in. "Yeah, if I can lend you anything to make the new place feel more like home, just let me know."

"Exactly," said Ben.

"Thanks, y'all," I said with a small smile. "But I think I've got everything I need."

And that, astonishingly, was that. As the word spread, people were careful in conversations with me, but that barely lasted a week. By the end of the next weekend, bigger stories were already circulating, like how Shawn Hirsch had gotten too drunk at Ben's birthday party and thrown up in Emily Shannon's lap. Sometimes I understood what Xia meant about Fisherton being a bit on the small side.

So we'd had five months of blissful privacy. Xia would drive the Zombie Pontiac out to Lawrence's and park behind the house, and we'd go slopping through the creek barefoot; we'd have picnics; we'd watch stupid videos on her phone and laugh so hard that she'd start snorting. Paul cooked for us, big, extravagant dinners during which Lawrence and Xia talked about obscure books while Paul and I talked about real life. Sometimes, when Lawrence and Paul went out on date nights in Columbia, Xia and I would shut ourselves in my room, and she'd put on music while we kissed—weird European trance music that seemed to buzz right through the surface of my skin.

Some days, some nights, it unnerved me how much I wanted her, and in what ways. The heat and the doubt I'd feel mixed together. The idea of waiting for marriage had to be different now, and I was still trying to work out what that meant for us—what a sin of the body meant for me. I thought a lot about Thessalonians, the passage saying that to abstain was to control our bodies in holiness and honor.

That still rang deep in me. I wasn't quite sure how it looked anymore to honor my body, to honor God in the vessel of myself. But I knew I still valued control, that spark of self-determination, the feeling that I could rise above impulse and desire.

Xia never pushed me, never made me feel wrong for wanting to go slow. "I like slow," she whispered once into my hair when we were cuddling together. "It makes the little things more intense."

As she traced her fingertips lazily over my hips and waist and rib cage, leaving fire everywhere she touched me, I whispered, "You're right."

In March, we received our college letters, and she took the merit scholarship at UNC, and I confirmed at Duke, who'd offered me more in financial aid than I'd dared to hope. I was still working through the details, but the road in front of me was growing clearer, and now here we were, on the threshold of summer.

When the final bell rang that day, signaling the end of four years at Fisherton High School, I lingered in the Calculus room, alone among stripped-down bulletin boards and half-packed boxes. The sharp scent of cleaning solution hung in the air; whoops and distant yells circulated down the hall. It seemed important for some reason, I wasn't sure why, that I hold this moment in my mind and remember it forever, every conflicting impulse of loss and excitement, affection and sadness. I was going to miss this place so much, and I was so glad to be free of it.

On my way to the buses, I passed the auditorium. My eyes caught on the low window to the greenroom.

I stopped and looked into that dark rectangle for a while. I felt as though some version of me were hovering behind the glass, watching back, seeing me in the clothes Xia and I had bought from thrift stores in Columbia. My past self, I thought, wouldn't have understood the person I was now, but even she would have been able to tell I was happy.

◊

At 7:00 p.m., I borrowed Lawrence's car and drove to Xia's little hamlet of houses in Fisherton Oaks. Empty driveway after empty driveway, unsold home after unsold home. I parked in her driveway beside the Pontiac and rang the doorbell.

The door swung open to reveal a smiling Mrs. Harper in slacks and a fluttery woven top. She was taller than Xia, and her dark hair was loosely braided, wisps escaping at her forehead and the sides of her face in a wind-tossed way. "Gloria, hello!" she said, each syllable precisely formed. "Come in, come in, please."

"Hi, Mrs. Harper. Thanks so much for having me." I placed my shoes on the rack by the door.

"Of course. It's always wonderful to see you. You must be delighted that it's the end of school. Xia!" She aimed this up the carpeted stairs. "Xia, she's here."

Something muffled from Xia's room. Mrs. Harper raised her hands. "Well, the queen will arrive when she arrives! Here, this way."

When we entered the kitchen, Xia's father, tall and wiry with flyaway dark hair, craned his neck to give a subdued smile over his shoulder. His arms were extended over the stove, stirring a fragrant red sauce. "Gloria. Great to see you. How was that last day, huh?"

"Hi, Mr. Harper. It was definitely bittersweet. You know Xia and I have different opinions about school."

"Yeah, in that Gloria has the objectively wrong opinion," said a voice from behind me. I glanced back and found Xia sliding down the hall in her socks, nudging her glasses up with a knuckle. "Hey," she added.

"Hi," I said, trying to tamp my smile down. Sometimes when I lost control of my smile around her, I began to blush. "It must be hard to have the right opinion all the time."

"Just the burden some of us have to bear." Xia heaved an exaggerated sigh. "Can I help, Dad? Mom?"

I tried not to watch too openly as they clattered around the kitchen, but something in me warmed to see them like this, batting questions back and forth. Little things. Xia asking if she could taste the sauce, jumping away with a laugh when her dad brandished the spoon at her. Her mom saying she'd researched some programs at UNC today and had some thoughts, and Xia asking what those thoughts were.

"I've been trying to get Gloria to join in with my summer reading list," Xia said as she placed plates and cutlery on the table. "Like a book club. Do you two want in?"

"How many books?" asked her father, looking dubious.

Come Home to My Heart

"Not that many. Like, ten or something. You don't have to read all of them!" she added at the incredulous looks on their faces.

"You may pick one book that you think your father and I might enjoy," said her mother, bringing over the steaming tray of chicken in tomato sauce. "One."

Xia shook her head. "God, it's so unlikely that I wound up literate." She directed this mostly toward the ceiling, but I knew it was to make me laugh.

We began to eat. More easy rhythms: compliments on their cooking and pleased demurrals from across the table. Xia's parents liked me, and I liked them, although maybe I'd always been destined to like them, because I could see Xia in them. I could chase down the zippy rhythms of her speech in her father's sentences. She and her mother had the same tendency to snap their heads back before they laughed.

As we ate, I tried not to think about what might happen at the end of summer, when Xia and I told them we were together. I tried not to conjure up images of shock and hatred. None of that existed yet, and it wasn't guaranteed. I even dared to feel hopeful sometimes. Xia's parents had taken to watching movies with her on Friday nights, and when she'd picked *Moonlight* last week, her mother had said, "Well, that was quite interesting, I think," and her father let out a neutral "Mm."

Maybe that was a normal reaction to have. The more I read online, the more I supposed that what had happened to me this year wasn't normal. Even such a small thing as my parents removing my bedroom door: that had seemed trivial beside everything else, but when I'd mentioned it to Xia, she'd gone still in that way that told me she was stifling anger for my sake.

After dinner, I got into the kitchen and managed to do exactly three dishes before Xia's parents shooed us both out of the room. We retreated into the back garden. Both of the houses flanking hers stood uninhabited, their large dark windows grayed over with dust, their patios empty of furniture. A small stone firepit was raised in the center of her patio, and Xia flicked her lighter, got a little fire going, as the summer dusk cooled around us. We sat side by side on the slippery fabric of the weather-resistant sofa, our hands moving closer until—we both glanced back through the sliding glass door—our fingers linked.

"So, you're free," I said quietly. "No more Fisherton High School."

"It actually wasn't the worst at the end," Xia said. "But maybe that was just because I knew something they didn't."

We were looking into the fire rather than at each other. I moved my fingers slowly over hers and felt my body fizz, electric.

"That was sweet of your mom," I said, "looking up the programs at UNC."

"Oh, ulterior motives 101. She's going to start pushing prelaw literally any second now. Just you wait."

"Is she wrong? You'd be a terrifying lawyer."

"What? Me? With this pushover personality?"

I smiled and let the joke fade from the air before saying, "You three seem like things are okay."

"They are pretty okay." Xia sounded pensive. "Funny thing . . . you know, they actually never knew I smoked? They caught the smell but thought it was because I hung out with burnouts or something. My mom blew up about it last night. It was kind of sweet."

"Does this mean you'll quit smoking?"

She flashed a suggestive smile at me. "What, you mean cigarette isn't your favorite taste in the world?"

I tried to keep my expression dignified, although I could feel my cheeks heating. "I can think of flavors I like better."

"Oh, yeah? Such as?"

"Wet dog. Cyanide."

Come Home to My Heart

"I'm wounded. Anyway, I'll try, now that summer's here and I don't feel like I need a controlled substance to get through every soul-sucking hour of school." She glanced back at the sliding door again, then reached up and played with a lock of my hair. "How's Mr. Avery? How's life on the gay homestead?"

I laughed. "The, um—the gay homestead is good. Lawrence and Paul are so close to understanding how the smart TV works, bless their hearts."

"They'll figure it out sometime before we finish college."

"I hope. And they've been driving me around to job interviews. I think I'm going to lifeguard at the same pool I worked at last summer."

"Gloria, that's awesome."

I didn't reply. I remembered receiving my first paycheck last summer. It had looked impossibly official with its printed routing numbers, that blue rippled background, the field for my endorsement. When I'd handed those checks to my parents, the whole transaction had felt a bit like play-acting, just an extra step to get a little allowance money at the end. This year there was nothing like a game about it.

"Hey."

I realized I'd been squeezing Xia's hand too hard. I loosened my grip, and she leaned close and kissed me, tilting my chin with her long fingers. Eyes as dark and deep as forests at night. "You all right?"

"Yeah. I'm all right."

I considered the words only after I'd said them. I knew I had been marked in ways that would not leave me. I'd never really slept the same since autumn. I jerked out of sleep contorted into strange positions, sure I'd slept through some phantom bell, no matter if it was Saturday or Sunday or a nap or the middle of spring break. I dreamed of buzzing light bulbs and woodshed windows. When I thought about the people I'd meet in the future, I worried about the ways I would need to avoid questions about my family. And I sometimes envisioned elaborate scenarios where Xia, Mr. Avery, or Paul uncovered some terrible truth about me that they'd never known, something they found repugnant and unforgivable, and they turned their backs on me, too.

But then there were the highs. Xia would touch my hand during dinner at Mr. Avery's and I'd get this giddy, childish rush, kid in a candy store. In private we held each other and whispered, and I felt the love I'd always imagined, the cold, tremendous shock. Sometimes, when we kissed, my memories of us mingled into each other and shot through my blood, compressed like a firework just before the spark. The raindrops in Xia's hair the first night she'd driven me home. How inscrutable I'd found her, how intimidating, how magnetic. Her mouth soft on mine by the river; her hands slow and cautious in the back seat; her face close against my neck at the dance. Her tears under the overpass. *This is the one right thing I've got: being able to love you.*

I had her. I had this life, the real thing. At the end of each day, I walked up to a house with a blue door and turned my key in the lock; I called the words *I'm home*. I poked through cabinets and found snacks that I liked. I texted my friends, and Xia, and I read articles online, whichever ones I wanted. In my room I looked through the catalog of math courses at Duke; I prayed to steady my internal compass, to determine what it was that God was calling me to do, and why. I thought about my future, and it wasn't a blur anymore. It was something I could see and decide.

"You sure you're okay?" Xia asked, a curious tilt to her head, her hair tumbling past her cheek.

As I looked into her eyes, I felt an irrepressible smile spread over my face, as big and uncontrollable as what I felt.

"I'm sure," I told her. "I'm awake."

Author's Note

In 2023, the Department of Housing and Urban Development found that more than 650,000 people in the United States experienced homelessness—a 12 percent increase over 2022 and the highest number since 2007. This included 111,620 children without homes.

The rate of homelessness in the United States has risen every year since 2017, and queer young people have always been particularly vulnerable to housing insecurity in its many, often hidden, forms. The Trevor Project reports that 28 percent of LGBTQ youth have reported experiencing homelessness at some point in their lives; that figure is even higher among trans youth specifically. Lesbian, gay, and bisexual youth account for only 7–9 percent of the population, but they account for 29 percent of homeless young people.

Part of the royalties from this novel will be divided among organizations in South Carolina, in my home state of North Carolina, and in my current city, Chicago, who advocate on behalf of these vulnerable and underserved populations. For details on past and current beneficiary organizations, you can visit my website, https://rileyredgate.com.

Acknowledgments

I'm so grateful to my publishing team for their support in bringing this book to life. As always, thank you first and foremost to Caryn Wiseman, my agent, and to Aashna Avachat, also at Andrea Brown Literary Agency.

I've been beyond lucky to work with the team at Union Square & Co., whose kindness and enthusiasm are rivaled only by their professionalism. To Laura Schreiber and Stefanie Chin, my champion editors, and to the keen-eyed Christine Ma, Kayla Overbey, and Grace House: I appreciate your work and your support more than I can say. Thank you to Julie Robine for your breathtaking design vision, cover and interior both, and to Tillie Walden for the exceptional jacket art.

Thank you also to my early readers—Bri, Mandy, Andrew, and Jonathan—for your invaluable insights and for your friendship, and to Angela Sanchez for your perspective, guidance, and artistry. Lastly, thank you to my friends and family, especially my parents. I love you guys.

About the Author

Riley Redgate is the author of four YA novels, including *Seven Ways We Lie* and *Alone Out Here*. Her fifth YA novel, *Look No Further*, was published under her real name, Rioghnach Robinson, and was cowritten with her sister, Siofra Robinson. Riley grew up in North Carolina and now lives in Chicago.